Rachel Lynch grew up in Cumbria and has written a million-copy bestselling crime series set in the lakes and fells of her childhood, starring Detective Kelly Porter. She previously taught History and travelled the globe with her Army Officer husband, before having children and starting a new career in personal training and sports therapy. Writing from her home in Hertfordshire is now her full-time job, and this is her first standalone psychological thriller.

Also by Rachel Lynch

The Rich

Helen Scott Royal Military Police Thrillers

The Rift
The Line

Detective Kelly Porter

SHARED REMAINS

RACHEL LYNCH

CANELOCRIME

First published in the United Kingdom in 2024 by

Canelo
Unit 9, 5th Floor
Cargo Works, 1–2 Hatfields
London SE1 9PG
United Kingdom

A CIP catalogue record for this book is available from the British Library.

Print ISBN 978 1 80032 729 0
Ebook ISBN 978 1 80032 109 0

Cover design by Tom Sanderson

Cover images © Arcangel, Shutterstock

Look for more great books at www.canelo.co

Printed and bound in Great Britain by Clays Ltd, Elcograf S.p.A.

1

Chapter 1

The road was brutally unforgiving, and the vehicle bumped and jumped about. The occupants of the truck were used to it, having lived here on the land for decades.

Farmers across the Lake District didn't need fancy bits of tarmac criss-crossing their land. They preferred to leave them to the elements. That way, nosy tourists were kept out by the potholes and muddy crossing points, where the road disappeared into slate, boulder and marsh. It didn't matter how many 'PRIVATE LAND' signs one hammered to trees and gates, some bloody adventurer from the south always thought they could wander around with an upside-down map looking for paradise.

Cracks and crevices, which filled with rocks and water from the outlying hills, froze over in winter and only the very basic maintenance jobs made them barely driveable, or at least fairly even. Come spring, everything thawed and mulched into one sloppy mush with the rain. In summer, the dirt dried to dust and great piles of rubble fell away under the wheels. Autumn was unpredictable. It could be hot or cold, muddy or dry, and one took their chances along the track. If you got stuck, no one was coming to help, that was for sure. For a start, it was miles to the nearest telephone box, if it still worked after being decommissioned by British Telecom years ago. The red ones ended up at auction or in celebrity houses, where they were showed off to hangers-on who cooed at how quirky and quaint they were, while exhibiting their own rarity and privilege by the very fact they had one. Secondly, it was private land so nobody would know you were there. And thirdly, if the farmer got to you first, well then, you'd sooner have a shotgun pellet in your backside than face him.

The vast marsh-like valley between the A66 that sliced the north fells off from the rest of them, the wilderness of Dockray to the south, the last hamlet before the glory of Ullswater, and the Helvellyn range to the west, was to those who knew, once one vast farm, owned by the Morningside family. The sheep loved the flat, spongy grassland, and the little balls of white wool dotted the landscape, making it look like a child's play farm when gazed upon from the road. Protected woodland was scattered about like bunches of Christmas trees, similar to the ones sold to decorate cakes, here and there, as if plopped down by the same kids playing with the farm. The trees hugged one another as if for safety and the outer ones stood tall and proud, daring anyone brave enough to venture in.

The fading October light was beautiful, but the driver and his companion weren't here to gaze at the view. Locals of the Lake District were overfamiliar with the hills that never went anywhere. The sunset dipped in the same place every day, and the lakes and hidden waterfalls had been forged by ancient rock long before the photographs that snapped them were discarded.

The two men concentrated on the road ahead, and the fact that it'd soon be dark. Orange and purple turned to dark grey.

The nights were drawing in and it'd soon be time to put the clocks back.

Spring forward, fall back...

The chassis was their biggest concern as they tumbled over the uneven surface. Was she strong enough to hold? The thud of boulders hitting the wheel arches clanged like metallic ghouls inside their heads and reverberated around the metal bodywork. The sharper stones pinged off the side like a percussion accompaniment. There was no radio signal, so it was the only symphony of sorts they were going to enjoy this evening.

Both men wobbled this way and that and held onto the ceiling straps for comfort and safety. At least the driver had the steering wheel to cling onto for good measure. A rough ride in a truck wasn't something that scared them, but being bashed against the doorframe was. A big enough hole in the road could send you into it at a rate of knots and break your arm. The driver kept his left hand on the wheel and his right hand on the band above his head, squinting to see in the fading light. He didn't use headlights, and he didn't change gear. There was no point, and he knew where he was going. He constantly needed the thrust of first gear to get out of yet another gaping aperture. He navigated by listening to the engine.

There was also no point in talking. They'd have their conversation back in the pub, when they'd finished, and didn't have to shout over the din. It was thirsty work, all this concentration. And a lot of effort. But they were paid handsomely for it.

Jobs were getting harder to find in Cumbria. Foreign transient workers, who were cheap, took all the catering jobs. Farming and forestry positions were declining as fast as the Titanic went down, leaving little else, apart from drug running, which was a good earner but could land you a hefty stint at His Majesty's pleasure. Something legal and well paid was what everybody desired, but didn't get, so this was good work, if you could get it. It wasn't the type of position you could simply apply for, and it didn't require GCSEs or apprenticeships, which was fortunate because the two men had dropped out of school as soon as they could. Education was for the high and mighty and those who paid attention to teachers droning on about stuff that didn't matter. It was a waste of time for anybody wanting to get a real job, in the real world.

The engine stopped screaming and the light shifted as they entered the forest. It had been raining all morning but in the late afternoon, as was not uncommon in these parts, the drizzle had stopped and the sun had come out, as if God was announcing that he was ready for his dinner. Swords of light had dropped from the clouds and, facing west, threw piercing rods of silver onto the surrounding land. Now there were only shadows as they entered the forest.

'This is the spot, lad.'

The driver pulled off, adjacent to a grass field, and the change in driving surface was akin to sleeping in silk sheets after having only a scratchy woollen blanket for ten nights. The landowner at least looked after this part of the road, because he'd once had a hare-brained idea to open a bird sanctuary. That is until they all died. Then an alpaca centre. Until they died too. Weary of what it took to keep exotic animals alive, he gave up and tried something new. Others thought Arthur Morningside was cursed by his father. Local gossip had it that Percival Morningside bequeathed the fertile half of the farm to his favourite son; Arthur's brother Samuel, and Arthur had been left with just the forest and scrubland. But whatever the reason, it was collectively accepted that Samuel was the better businessman.

The narrow lane led to a collection of abandoned outbuildings, and a watermill, where the bird sanctuary had been housed for a short while. They stopped the vehicle.

The grave had already been dug, under the trees and slightly to the left of the old dry stone sheep pen, used at one time for the Herdwick sheep that had shaped the land around these parts. The old mill which had stood unused for a hundred years or more, and the beck underneath it, made the ground softer here, and easier to dig. The smiling white faces of the Herdies, as they were otherwise known, had bent and nodded as they chewed their way over hills and dales, for a thousand years or more. But they weren't here any more. They were long gone too, over to Samuel's side, having been too much work for Arthur. The Herdies had once been the only serious living to be had here on Morningside Farm, the other animals had been for the tourists. But Arthur couldn't even make that work.

The men's heads rattled and buzzed from the rough ride, and their bones felt misplaced inside their skin, but after a shake and a stretch they were ready to begin their work. They turned off the engine and slammed the truck doors. The noise echoed into the approaching night, inviting anyone on the surrounding fells to call back, but they didn't. It was about as desolate out here as you could get, this side of the newly divided farm. Not even the sound of sheep, from over the boundary of Samuel Morningside's inheritance, pierced the evening sky – just the gentle purr of wind rustling the trees.

'Shhh, you'll wake her up,' one of the men said, bending over laughing. The other rolled his eyes.

'Don't give up your day job, pal.'

They opened the back of the truck and rolled the tarp towards them. The package had been shaken roughly during the short journey and had rolled about in the back violently. They were used to the thumps every time she hit the side but ignored it because it just melted into the background noise of all the other bangs and crashes, expected for that journey down the lane.

One man lit up a cigarette.

'Come on, we haven't got all night,' the other complained.

'It's not as if we're in a rush, beside my nerves need bloody calming down after that road. I feel like a box of frogs.'

'You're as mad as one.'

They unloaded spades, which had likely been bouncing off the corpse as they drove. It didn't matter because she was already dead. All her troubles were over, and the two men would sleep soundly tonight, after a few pints and a bath.

The smoker crushed his cigarette against a tree and threw the stub away, then signalled he was ready to help fill in the grave. They took one end of the cadaver each, which was easy because she was well wrapped up, and dragged it out of the back of the truck. They carried the load over to the grave and dumped it on the ground next to the hole with an unexpected thud.

'Oops, heavier than I thought, sorry, love.'

They both smirked.

'Shall we?'

One of them checked the grave hadn't been tampered with. You never knew if a stray cat or dog, or even a lost baby goat from another farm, or some other intruder, might have climbed down there and got stuck. It was empty, just as they'd left it. They rolled the body in and began covering it over with soil, one spadeful at a time.

'Night, night,' one of the men said, waving goodbye.

Chapter 2

Later that evening, a mile away, on adjacent land, two figures stood silhouetted by the light of the moon, peering down into the Morningside quarry.

'I never expected it to sound like that.'

'Like what?'

'Silent. No noise at all. Just a thump.'

The body had rolled clumsily off the edge and disappeared into the night, like a good-luck coin dropped by a child into a deep medieval wishing well. The delight of discovering that the shaft went on for miles, and the penny dropping forever into the cavernous crevice, instilled a belief in magic. But this was no sorcery, and they weren't children.

The body had stopped.

The light of the moon cast shadows across the quarry, but they couldn't quite see far enough. Torchlight soon confirmed that their work had been for nothing. All the effort to get him up here and dispose of him, causing them to sweat and curse, seemed wasted and they stood panting, with their hands on their knees, wondering what to do next.

'I'll get the bike.'

It took an hour to get the quad bike to the lip and another twenty minutes to drive down to the ledge. The bike only carried one – there was no room for a passenger and so one of them stayed at the top, peering down, not daring to shout out loud, lest the wind carry the grim messages to the farmhouse a mile away and tucked into the night. The torch was switched off and the wait interminable. The smell of petrol floated in the air as the quad rumbled and then stopped.

What was he doing?

The delay allowed unwelcome thoughts to creep in and halt the malice for a moment. It caused a sudden shock of fear and self-loathing. But it would do no good now. It was done. The stupid son-of-a-bitch wouldn't listen. There was no reasoning with him.

But no one should end up like this...

The quad revving up triggered a moment's further panic and the machine roaring in the night threatened to cause a collapse of the quarry wall, it seemed so vicious. Soon he was back, and thoughts of regret floated away into the darkness.

'Done.'

'Where did he land?'

'At the bottom.' He smirked, making him look like an evil apparition, only appearing to compound the sense of wrong-doing.

'It's cold. Let's go. I've been doing this all bloody day.'

–

At the bottom of the quarry face, close to the rock wall, the local undertaker lay on his side, smashed and broken, but still alive. He murmured something into the moonlight, to the two people who he knew were there at the top staring down at him. He felt no pain, even though he could feel his skull bleeding dark, oozing blood, and his body was broken from the trauma. But as he stared at the ground, and the fragmented rocks around him, a single tear escaped from his eye, and rolled across his cheek to the cold slab of slate underneath him.

And then stopped.

Chapter 3

Detective Inspector Kelly Porter wasn't familiar with Morningside slate mine, but she'd visited Honister plenty of times, climbing and walking in its vicinity, as well as buying Christmas presents for family. The report of a dead body there sent chills down her spine because nobody wanted to hear the words mine and death together in the same sentence. However, the first uniforms on the scene had said that it wasn't a working accident. The victim was not a member of the staff there. There were no reports of climbers in trouble, and she'd checked with Johnny and his colleagues at the mountain rescue. Apparently, from what the first responder told her, the bloke wasn't dressed in walking gear either. He hadn't even been wearing a coat.

She and Johnny had argued this morning before she'd left for work.

Again.

It was always the same, but different. Something as trivial as a scalding hot cup of tea, spilled by accident on an envelope discarded and seemingly unimportant on the kitchen counter could kick it off. Then, after an exchange of unnecessary words, it dawned on them that they weren't fighting about the envelope. They were quarrelling over Rob.

She sighed and tried to concentrate on the road.

With Detective Sergeant Kate Umshaw busy interviewing the family of a missing local man, Kelly had made the decision to visit the mine by herself. She mulled over what she'd been told so far by the uniformed coppers who'd been first on the scene. It looked like a suicide. People with a death wish often looked for tall features to throw themselves off, but Morningside was private land and she had to maintain an open mind. It could have been an accident, or a fight, or simply old age gripping a wanderer at the wrong time in the wrong place. But then she had to consider the possibility that it could also be their missing person. She'd read the new file, opened less than a week ago, before she left the office.

Victor Walmsley had been reported missing by his wife, Irene, five days ago. The problem was that he was a grown man of sixty-one years, and unless there was evidence to the contrary, foul play wasn't an automatic assumption, given the majority of men his age who decided to wander off turned up again after clearing their heads. However, according to his wife, their joint bank account hadn't been used and his mobile phone was switched off.

She rang Kate on Bluetooth. The traffic between Penrith and Keswick was slow. They were widening the road – which was sorely needed – but it was causing pandemonium on the A66, which was the only route into the Lakes from Penrith. It caused impatient drivers who'd travelled from the south to become aggressive and there'd been a spike in road accidents.

'No news,' Kate said. 'The wife is worried sick. It's not like him, apparently. He's got everything going for him, she says.'

'Don't they always say that?' Kelly asked. Her cynical tone was as a result of suffering her own personal dilemmas and Kate knew it was out of character.

'They seem a charming couple, and to be fair, their house is stunning, they are due to retire soon and travel the Med, you know, the usual stuff.'

'Dementia?' Kelly asked. 'Happiness isn't all about material wealth, is it?'

'Not that she's noticed.'

Kate sighed and Kelly knew she needed to snap out of her petulant depression. Things hadn't been the same since the death of their colleague, Rob Shawcross. He'd been chasing a suspect across the crags, but that wasn't the issue.

Her problem was that Johnny had been leading the group as the mountain rescue expert, and she'd never forgiven him. And he'd never asked her to.

'I'm on my way to Morningside slate mine, do you know it?' Kelly asked.

'Yes, it's off the A66 isn't it?' Kate asked.

'That's the one, have you been?'

'Years ago, to take the kids. Why?'

'We've got a dead body and it's an adult male.'

'And you're thinking it might be Victor?'

'That's why I'm going.'

'Do you want me to meet you there? I've finished here.'

'Remind me of the circumstances.'

'Victor went to work last Thursday but never arrived. She's heard nothing since.'

'No communication at all?'

'None.'

'What was his state of mind?'

'She told me there was nothing out of the ordinary and he hadn't seemed unusually distracted or worried.'

'So why report that he was depressed? I read the file.'

'She's kind of retracted that. She said she assumed he must be, not that he definitely was.'

'What was he wearing?'

'I've got a detailed description, I'll send it over to you now, then I'll meet you there.'

They hung up.

The traffic stopped and she tapped the steering wheel. The great grey shape of Blencathra loomed ahead of her to the north. Like its ancient name, Saddleback, it languished like a sleeping animal, soaking up the sunshine, ready for its next hunt. Her eyes wandered over the sloping ridge which looked like the beast's spine, and she gripped the steering wheel tighter. He'd died up there.

She felt Rob's absence keener every time she passed his desk, almost pulling at her to sit down and chat with him. The pain was still raw for her team, and she felt a tinge of irritation that tomorrow, DS Fin Maguire would be sat in his place. It wasn't his fault. Maybe it'd help; a new kid on the block.

When she'd read his file and seen his photo, she'd realised she knew him. Like her, he'd served in the Met, in murder squads for ten years. Like her, he'd left the cosy safety of a rural force, in his case Ireland, and gone off to conquer the big smoke. Like her, he'd soon had enough of it. He was younger than her by a couple of years, not yet forty. She willed herself to be charitable. The guy had been given the unenviable task of filling Rob's shoes. There was no doubt that Fin was well qualified and experienced, but her main concern was how he'd fit in.

Now, any excuse to get out of the office was welcome. A change of scenery had an enormous impact on her nervous system, like going for a run, or cruising across a lake. The crushing weight of Rob's non-existence had sullied her working space and she worried what Fin would make of it.

Chapter 4

Samuel Morningside sat in the cabin of his new Can-Am Traxter off-road buggy and surveyed his land. Penny, his young sheepdog, sat panting beside him. The Herdies were on the fell-side, munching the landscape to within an inch of its life, and his job this afternoon was to check a few of the stone walls. Skilled tradespeople were few and far between nowadays, and soon he'd be hard pushed to find anyone willing or able to do the task.

Stone walls landscaped the hills of the Lake District and Samuel's land was no different, but it took deft craftsmen to maintain it. A master stonemason could select pieces of rock and boulder that fitted perfectly together, their weight holding the structure together for centuries. It was the very end of the season when building stone walls could be attempted, down to the cold, nothing else. Spring and summer were the ideal times to get it done, but this October was relatively warm, and he thought he might as well have a go at filling some of the worst holes.

He was conducting a final check to see which walls might need some form of serious repair, come the spring. In the back of the Can-Am he had a load of Borrowdale stone. The slate quarry on his land churned out enough mass for him to build a thousand stone walls, but it was more lucrative for him to sell that on. Slate stone walls looked pretty, but his Herdies weren't fussy.

He stopped at the top of the creek, and from his vantage point he could see all the way across to the seemingly benign summits of Skiddaw and Blencathra in the north, which looked like sleeping giants. To the south, on a fine day such as this, he could trace the whole Helvellyn range in the distance, from Clough Head, across to the three Dodds and beyond. The hills sloped down to valleys and at the bottom, great lakes nestled hidden and silent. It was his favourite place on the farm and had been since he was a boy. He and Arthur, his younger brother, used to come up here with their father, on a battered old tractor, sat in the back of the trailer, rolling about with laughter as they jostled and fought for the prime spot. Sometimes, their father would go faster if he had a clear run across a field and they'd pretend they were inside a washing machine, flinging themselves to one side of the trailer and back again.

Some things had changed since then, but not all of them had.

The landscape hadn't, along with the secrets it kept. It had, of course, been cleaved in half when their father died, and the farm suddenly ripped asunder. It had been Percival Morningside's wish that the farm remained in the hands of his bloodline for centuries to come, and his two boys had done their best with the land they had, but each had dramatically different ideas about what the future should look like.

Percival was buried out here, in the grounds of their private chapel, true to his wishes, but Samuel never went there. It was on Arthur's land now; his farm having been renamed Promise Farm. The new title had made Samuel smirk with condescension over his brother's flighty ideals and those of his young wife. It hadn't lived up to its lofty epithet; there was no promise of anything over that way. Percival had known it when he split the land. So had Samuel.

His pride had prevented him from ever raising the issue of the grave with his brother. As far as he knew, the slate headstone, extracted from their own quarry, was still there, possibly lopsided by now, and overgrown, and perhaps covered in sheep shit. From here, Samuel could see the chapel roof, and could just make out the small stone cross on top. He could also see the nursing home: an eyesore on the land.

But Arthur's land was no good for farming, so it was no surprise that he eventually developed it. It was only the apparent success of the place that came as a shock. Percival knew his sons well, or he thought he had. He'd given Samuel the more lucrative of the two hemispheres, and Arthur knew it. He felt it keenly. They'd barely spoken since. But from local gossip, Samuel heard that Promise Farm, and the nursing home, made a profit somehow.

Arthur had surprised everyone with his business nose, to the extent that folk doubted it was even him behind it. It was more likely to be his wife who had a sense for money, like a shark for blood in the water. Beryl was an outsider from the start. Not only was she a wanderer and a loner who Arthur had met when he was lost in his own sorrow and self-pity, but she didn't fit into the Morningside way. She was sharp, not homely like a good farmer's wife should be, and she was loud, not demure. But her worst sin was that she was skinny, and she was in charge. Samuel was unclear if she was even English, never mind Cumbrian, unlike his own wife who he'd known since they were seven years old.

Samuel cut the engine and slid out of the cabin, bracing for the impact on his knees, which weren't getting any younger. His heavy boots didn't help, and his doctor had told him he should wear soft soles. He was told to take it easy but saying that to a farmer was like telling a mama to choose between her sons. At sixty, he should be thinking about retiring, but there was nobody to take the reins after him, and Dorian, his only son, wasn't fit.

He stood for a moment, surveying what Percival had nourished for half a century before him, and the familiar sadness at what Arthur had done welled up inside him. Predictably, he hadn't made much of the farming up there to the north, which Samuel cast a disapproving eye over now. Instead, he'd cooked up various hare-brained schemes to make money, no doubt egged on by his punchy foreign wife. Traditional arable farming was always going to be too much like hard work for his little brother. In fact, Beryl was from Cornwall, but, to Samuel, she might as well have been from the moon.

He approached the stone wall and looked behind him for Walker, his brown Labrador. But he tutted as he remembered he wasn't there with him. The animal had been by his side for fourteen years, but he hadn't come home two days ago. He missed the mutt, and he could tell that Penny did too. Walker usually trotted beside the Gator, slower of late, but always there. Each morning, since he'd last seen him, Samuel had searched the expanse of his land, believing him to be injured, or exhausted, or both. His pride prevented him from searching Arthur's land, or even telling him. At fourteen, Walker was in his swan song, and Samuel knew that his time was close, or maybe it had come already. He didn't dwell on it and concentrated on the wall. Dogs wandered off all the time, and soon came back. That's what he told himself.

He paused and scratched his head. Gloria, his wife, said he did that when he was in deep thought. He joked with her that he did it to make his hair grow back. It never did. So, he covered it with a flat cap, like Percival used to wear. It dislodged as he scratched the side of his scalp and he straightened it. The military style Shemagh had been his father's. Percival had brought it back from the deserts of Africa after his service there in the Second World War. It was gnarly and faded, like the old man himself. But even Percival Morningside hadn't lived forever.

Chapter 5

As the line of traffic snaked towards Troutbeck, Kelly realised that being trapped in the car was just as bad as being confined to the office. The same ghosts raged inside her head.

Her solo hike last night hadn't eased the gnawing agony she felt every time she was alone – that included her time spent with Johnny, because their easy companionship had changed. She supposed Josie being away at university didn't help. Johnny's daughter's absence left a gaping hole which had at one time been filled with laughter and preoccupation.

Kelly had taken herself off to Thirlmere yesterday, with one-year-old Lizzie in tow. The girl's gurgles and nonsensical chatter alleviated some of her anxiety and it had been her intention to walk away her stress. She'd parked at the reservoir and marvelled at the gold, burnt-orange leaves surrounding the man-made lake.

Everything had changed since they'd found the skeleton there in the mud in the summer. The heatwave was long gone now and farmers all over the Lake District celebrated the return of the rain. It replenished the land and she reckoned she could do with something to reinvigorate her, believing it would come from a stiff hike up towards Helvellyn.

She'd been wrong.

She'd pushed herself, forcing her body to move forward with the heavy weight of Lizzie crushing the wind out of her. She'd hoped that her lack of breath would push away the images of the dead, but instead, all she achieved was a realisation that her forty-one-year-old body was out of shape. She'd ploughed on regardless, passing three women with dogs, laughing in their shared camaraderie, and she'd envied them. She'd panted for air, taking Lizzie out of her carrier and allowing her to totter around, picking grass and pointing out sheep. Her intense need for movement could be seen, by some, as self-flagellation, but to Kelly, it was more about accessing some kind of harmony inside her body. And she didn't want to do it at the office, in front of her team. They each dealt with their grief privately.

The women had nodded good afternoon, as friendly northern folk tended to do. Her time in London had knocked the courtesy out of her. There, a curt nod when getting off the tube, or a tut when allowing somebody to pass in the street, was all the human contact one was allowed. She preferred the casual affability of the mountains.

Back in the now, the traffic eased and she finally made her way along the A66 again. As she neared the turn off for Morningside Farm, her thoughts turned to Mary, and her mouth turned up in a smile.

It had been a chance rendezvous, earlier in the year; the type that passes fleetingly and is easily ignored. But this time, she'd taken notice of the woman who'd stopped her in the street. The old lady had asked for change for a five-pound note, because she didn't have coins to give the boy collecting for a dog's home, and she didn't want to give him her last fiver. It wasn't that she wasn't generous, Mary had insisted, but — *well, you know* — *it's all I can afford… I want to give him a pound*. After the chance encounter, and changing Mary's five-pound note, Kelly had taken her for a cup of tea.

It had been in the middle of the Keswick market, and Kelly had been rushing to her father's house. She'd intended to leave the old lady to get on, but something about the woman's face, and the chill of her hands when Kelly's touched hers when handing over the change, had pulled at her. She'd taken her to Bryson's and they'd had a choux bun each.

Now she checked in on her from time to time.

She thought of her now because Mary had chosen the Morn-ingside Nursing Home as a place to live out her twilight years, as recommended by a friend of hers who passed away there last week. Mary was ninety-six, though possessed the energy of a woman twenty years younger, and Kelly had learnt that old age gave one a sense of pragmatism towards death that had helped Mary process her loss. The passing of her friend hadn't put her off. Neither, Kelly suspected, would the discovery of a body at the mine. It was the 'natural order of things', Mary told her.

Kelly turned off the main road and headed for the Morningside Farm. The estate was vast. The family had owned the land for a good century, but Kelly didn't know the history. Like most large farms in the area, they'd had to adapt to economic changes, and, by all accounts, the two brothers who inherited it, had done just that. She could see the nursing home in the distance. It interrupted the view to the Irish Sea with its flat roof and modern lines, which contradicted the ancient landscape. Like all such facilities, it looked like a hospital but not quite as ugly. Close by, on the lip of a hill, Kelly spotted a stone cross atop the gable roof of a chapel in the distance. Mary had explained that it had been used for the Morningside family for generations and was now used for the nursing home residents' funerals, which Kelly found strangely repulsive. But it was plain to see why anybody might want to choose their final resting place up there. The tiny church stood next to a lush forest, and beyond, the view to the hills as far as the eye could see. Kelly made out the silhouette of an ancient stone circle. Mist clung to the valley and rolling hills poked through the top. Without the nursing home, the landscape would have been more beautiful.

She passed a truck with two men in the front and waited for it to pass on the narrow track. Then Kelly headed for the quarry.

Chapter 6

Samuel slowed the Can-Am.

There was a commotion at the mine shop. They sold slate from the quarry. It was a small business and he employed two master stonemasons in the workshop, making placemats, gravestones and vases. It wasn't on as big a scale as Honister, which turned over up to ten million quid in a good year, but it did okay.

He doubted that the coppers had turned up to peruse his ornamental stone. Something else must be wrong. Tourists gathered outside in a crowd and Samuel sighed. He couldn't be bothered with fuss, and he hoped to high heaven that it wasn't another mining accident.

Thankfully they were rare here, but quarrying remained the most dangerous industry to work in and last year, one of their contractors had been crushed under the conveyor of a stone-pressing machine. It had been gruesome. He'd paid over a hundred grand in compensation to the lad's family, which had been covered by insurance.

He lowered himself from the vehicle and walked towards the commotion – Penny stayed back obediently. People whispered and swapped sensational stories, and he wondered if it would be good or bad for business. Probably the latter, once word got out, but first he had to find out what was going on. He excused himself and pushed through the line of people. Some of them looked at him in annoyance as he forced his way to a better vantage point, others parted willingly. In his dungarees, flat cap, heavy boots, and combat green Shemagh, most of them understood that he wasn't simply some tourist looking to take photos. His garb wasn't accidental: it kept away questions.

He found the reception desk empty and went through the back to the workshop. There he found two coppers talking to Gloria. The workshop masons stood behind her. The machines were silent.

'Samuel,' Gloria said, rushing to him. She hugged him, almost knocking off his cap and he withstood the force of her embrace, wrapping his arms around her, looking over her shoulder to the coppers, who looked on grim-faced. She was still an affectionate woman after forty years of marriage, but she didn't often show it in public.

'This is my husband,' Gloria said to them as she turned. 'This is Samuel.'

'What's up?' he asked. It was a question to all of them, not just to his wife.

'There's a body at the bottom of the quarry,' Gloria said breathlessly. Samuel sighed; it was news he could do without. He figured that somebody had fallen off a scaffold or a lift.

'Sir,' one of the uniformed coppers said. He introduced himself and his partner and began telling him about the discovery of a dead man at the bottom of a quarry face, close to the mouth of the mine.

It had been his father's decision to begin mining the slate, knowing that the yield above ground would surely run out some day. Percival had been an intelligent businessman. He'd also been a fine soldier, and no one doubted his word. Samuel wouldn't have made the leap from quarrying to mining on his own, but now it was his legacy.

'Who is it? Is he one of ours?' Samuel asked, thinking about the potential compensation he'd have to pay out if it turned out to be one of his workers, or worse, a tourist.

'No, sir, we have accounted for all the staff, kindly helped by your wife, and there are no reports of missing climbers in the area, or visitors – we've checked.'

Samuel rubbed his chin and took off his cap.

'Who is it then?'

'We're waiting on a senior detective, sir.'

'They're sealing off the area,' Gloria said.

'Detective?' Samuel asked.

'Yes, sir. It's standard for unexplained deaths.'

'Unexplained? Did he fall?'

'I've had a look myself, sir, and it looks that way, yes.'

'Well then, there's your explanation.'

'The mine's got to close,' Gloria said.

'So, if he fell, why do you need a detective to confirm it?'

'It's necessary just while we evacuate the body, sir, and we ascertain cause of death. If it was a lone walker, who fell, and hasn't been reported, then the coroner will want to know, and we'll have to identify him as a matter of urgency.'

'So, he's still there?' Samuel asked.

The copper nodded.

'They're leaving him there until the detective arrives,' Gloria chipped in.

'Who found him?' Samuel asked.

'Dorian,' Gloria said.

'Where is he?'

'He's gone back home. He's had a shock.'

'We need to speak to your son, sir. Could you accompany us back to your residence?'

'I need to have a look for myself,' Samuel said.

The faces of his audience told him he'd said an outrageous thing, but he didn't think so at all. He knew everybody round here. If somebody had died on his land, then at least he wanted a chance to see for himself to get a grasp of what had happened.

'I wouldn't advise it, sir,' one of the coppers said.

'It's my land. I know everybody who comes and goes in here for a fifty-mile radius. I'm going down there.'

He turned and walked out of the workshop, closely followed by Gloria.

'Samuel,' Gloria rasped. She touched his arm.

'You take them up to the house to see Dorian. I'm going down there,' he told her.

'I'll accompany you, sir. My instructions have been to preserve the integrity of the site.' The copper wasn't backing down, but neither was Samuel.

'Fair enough, you come with me. I'll get as close as I like.'

Chapter 7

DS Kate Umshaw leant against her car and removed her sunglasses as Kelly pulled into the carpark of the Morningside slate mine. She smiled broadly at her boss.

Kelly parked next to her and took in the size of the place. The mine was nestled between rock and marsh, and only up close was it possible to appreciate the scale of it. The news of a body in the quarry had spread and Kelly was sure that the crowd of people hanging around outside the shop wasn't usual for business this time of year. She spotted a few local journalists talking to customers and rolled her eyes. She knew them by name. She'd had her fair share of brushes with all of them.

They approached her when they spotted her car.

'Kelly, is this a suspicious death? Why are you involved?'

Kate bristled and Kelly smiled at her, expecting her to lunge for them in a swipe of frustration. The journos had no idea they trod over the lives of innocent people in their hunt for a story, most of all the victim's family. Kate was well-behaved and together they ignored them.

The problem with rumours is that stories carried more weight than fact. Fiction could jump to the front pages of the *Gazette* or *Evening News*, before the police had a chance to assess the situation. Kelly was aware that her presence made the mystery more enticing, but they got to the door without incident. The presence of two uniforms waiting there meant no one could follow them.

They were informed that the owner of the mine had gone down to the quarry to see the body.

'Who let him do that?' Kelly asked.

'It's our quarry,' a woman said.

Kelly held out her hand and introduced herself, waiting for reciprocation. Kate took off her sunglasses.

'Gloria Morningside. Samuel is my husband. He wants to see what's going on for himself.'

Kelly smiled at her.

'Well, I best get down there. Can you show me? I'm guessing you know this place best out of everybody here?' Kelly asked.

Gloria unfolded her arms and nodded, her face warming up. She looked in her sixties, the age for retiring, but Kelly knew that places like this were heirlooms, not nine-to-five jobs. Gloria's protective stance was to be expected. She glanced around and assumed that the people sitting on plastic chairs, wearing aprons and goggles on the top of their heads, were employees. They'd all have to be interviewed. She nodded at them.

Kelly and Kate followed Gloria through the workshop and out of a back entrance. They watched her get into a buggy-like vehicle, and start it like a pro. It was the way people got around huge estates nowadays.

'How big is this place?' Kelly asked as she and Kate climbed into the rear seats of the open cabin, looking for seatbelts.

'You won't find belts in here, you're on private land, you'll be okay, I'm not Stirling Moss.'

Kelly and Kate nodded and held on tightly to a pair of untouched roof straps, perhaps meant for nervous passengers. It was clear no one else travelling this way used them.

Kelly was never one for office garb and had slipped on a pair of trainers before leaving Eden House. She noticed now that Kate was dressed less appropriately, likely because she'd been on a family visit. Kelly stared at Kate's heeled shoes. Kate shrugged, acknowledging her stare, and smiling back.

They set off as the contraption belched out black fumes. It sounded like a machine gun as it jerked away from its resting place.

'The farm is seventy hectares, or thereabouts. Not including grazing pasture.' Gloria shouted over the din. 'We own a couple of mountains too.'

'That's nice,' Kate shouted back, hanging on to the side of the vehicle as it tackled a steep gradient.

Kelly knew that a hectare was almost three acres, and an acre was about the size of a football pitch. The farm was average for the area, and she'd probably hiked through land belonging to the Morningside family plenty of times, without even realising it.

They chugged up a dirt road and then turned off before the quarry appeared. It reminded Kelly of her walks up the Old Man of Coniston. The quarry there had been working since the seventeenth century and every time she saw it, she wondered at the harsh conditions. The machinery of a bygone era was still up there on the ridges making it somewhat of a living museum. They spotted another vehicle which Gloria parked beside.

'That's Samuel's. He's still here,' Gloria told them.

They got out and Kate sunk into the earth. She grinned at Kelly and opened her large bag, taking a pair of pumps out and popping them on, before putting her heels into the bag.

'I knew you wouldn't let me down,' Kelly said.

Gloria had already set off walking over the lip – she seemed a hardy woman who suffered no nonsense. She clearly wasn't worried about seeing a dead body, whatever shape it was in.

'No sightings of Victor Walmsley since last Thursday morning?' Kelly asked Kate, who shook her head.

Today was Wednesday, so that left a whole week of unanswered questions.

As they approached the lip and saw the path down that Gloria had taken, Kelly tried not to predict scenarios. It would either be Victor or not. There was no point in assumptions.

The path was like a gash in the earth and as they rounded a sharp twist in it, the magnitude of the quarry became apparent. It looked like the land had been opened by a huge machine which had ripped apart the dark grey stone beneath. Slag sat in heaps, and stone ready for the factory was piled onto vehicles. It was a tough job even with modern technology; it would have been punishing without it. Quarrying had taken place in stages consisting of shelf-like levels as work had pierced deeper and deeper. Kelly wasn't an expert, but she knew that quarries were turned into mines when they ran out of rock above ground and needed – or the owners wished for – even bigger yields. She saw the mouth of the mine and three people down there. One wore a high-vis vest and looked like a copper. The other one standing, she assumed, was Samuel Morningside. Another shape lay motionless on the quarry floor.

'You'd think they'd put in a lift,' Kate complained. 'It looks as though it hasn't been touched since before the invention of the steam engine.'

Kelly smiled.

'What happened to those carts you see in Indiana Jones films?'

Kelly strode ahead and caught up with Gloria, who was frantically waving towards the two men who had finally spotted them. Kate caught up, breathlessly.

'Mr Morningside, I'm assuming?' Kelly said, stretching out her hand.

'Sorry, ma'am,' the copper said.

She gave him a reassuring look. It wasn't his fault. Landowners were always a bit tricky round here. They saw themselves as above the law and always had done. She glanced at the body and remembered the description of the clothes Victor Walmsley was wearing when he'd last been seen.

Samuel Morningside took her hand and gripped it. He had a strong handshake, but so did she. If the presence of a dead body bothered him, he didn't show it. She found his dress curious. He looked a bit how she imagined Alfred Wainwright, flat cap and walking garb from the fifties, unconcerned what anybody might think, and undoubtedly ready for anything. Johnny owned a Shemagh just like his and she couldn't help wondering where Mr Morningside had got his from. Johnny's was issued in Iraq.

'Sorry Mr Morningside, can I take a minute to assess the area? I've got to ask you to step away, maybe over there?'

He softened. 'Call me Samuel.'

'Thanks, Samuel. Have you been close to the body?' She nodded in the direction of the corpse. The uniform hovered in front of it, as if on guard, and paying it some respect.

Kelly knew from instinct and experience that the victim didn't need an ambulance. She could confirm life extinct herself. The colour of the skin, the position of the limbs, and the sweet aroma of the effluvial, all confirmed her assessment. The season would have kept away most unwelcome visitors, but the body would have started decaying nonetheless. She turned back to Samuel.

'Close enough to know who it is,' he said.

'Really?'

'It's Vic from the funeral home.'

'Victor Walmsley?' Kate asked.

'The same, I've known him virtually all my life. But I can't for the life of me work out why he'd be here of all places.'

'Why do you say that?' Kelly asked, looking at the body. The dress description matched: navy suit, brown shoes… She also took note of the businesslike reaction of Samuel Morningside to the gruesome sight. But farmers were hardy. Gloria watched them from further away.

'Vic wasn't an outdoor guy. Look, he's dressed for a fancy board meeting.' Samuel pointed. 'Besides, I can't recall him ever coming here, so he wouldn't know his way around. The entrance to the quarry is fenced off, it's difficult to find unless you know what you're doing.'

Kelly agreed. The bone-shaking journey, courtesy of Gloria, was full of twists and turns and she'd lost her bearings quite quickly.

'Thanks Samuel, that's a huge help. When was the last time you saw Victor alive?'

'Crikey. He buried my mother five years ago. I've seen him out and about I suppose, since then. Vic's no farmer but he was a damn good undertaker.'

'I'm sorry about your mother.'

'No worries, she was poorly and old, it was her time.'

'Is this area usually busy? It's a working mine, isn't it?'

Samuel scratched his chin. 'Aye. We come up here once a week to harvest the stone. Economy.'

Kelly could see he was embarrassed. The business wasn't as profitable as she'd assumed.

'So it's fair to say that he could have gone unnoticed for a few days?'

'Aye.'

'Even out in the open like this?'

'You'd have to be coming down here for work. No one takes a stroll around here if that's what you mean.'

'So, was your son… harvesting, did you say?'

'Aye,' Samuel said.

Kelly noticed a shadow cross his face.

'Can we take it from here, Samuel? We'll need to get a forensic team down here and a crime investigation unit.'

'Crime?'

'It's procedure. Mr Walmsley clearly didn't pass away of natural causes, and so we need to work out how he ended up down here.'

'You think he was pushed?'

'Pushed or jumped, or fell. The coroner will need a report.'

'Fine. How long will you need?'

Kelly appreciated this was a working mine.

'A few days?'

Samuel released his Shemagh and wiped his brow. It wasn't good for business.

'No bother. I'll go and let the staff know. They'll be worried and I can give them some answers now we know who it is.'

'Please don't talk to the press. Was Victor known to any of your staff?'

Samuel looked at Gloria.

'Probably, he knew everyone. Future customers,' Samuel said. His attempt at light humour fell flat. 'Vic dealt with most local funerals,' Samuel added.

'Kate, why don't you accompany Samuel and Gloria back to the shop and take some statements?'

Kate nodded. Kelly saw the deflated look on her face as she left, and understood her disappointment. Kate had only today met the wife of the man who lay dead at their feet. When the missing turned to the deceased so quickly, it was tough on everyone. Kelly was happy that the lifeless man was indeed Victor Walmsley, with Kate's description and Samuel's ID, and she took her phone out of her pocket and prepared to notify the coroner, as well as forensics, and to arrange a CSI specialist to come down. As she watched Kate leave with the Morningside couple, she turned back to the body and thanked the uniformed officer. He looked relieved to be rid of the civilians from a crime scene he'd been trying to protect.

She peered at the body and looked up to the quarry face. It was a long way up and she shaded her eyes against the sun. She reckoned the poor soul had fallen sixty feet.

His body was twisted in a shape that was distinctive of the dead. The way corpses settled in their final throes was unique. It was as if he'd been thrown here by a mysterious hand and arranged in a macabre knot of flesh and hair. She walked around him, and the wind wafted the familiar scent of the expired into her nostrils. She popped on a pair of gloves from her pocket and leaned over him, checking his pockets. She found a wallet, which confirmed his ID, as well as a folded piece of paper. A quick scan of the contents, handwritten, confirmed that the deceased had written a suicide note.

> *Dear Irene,*
> *I hope you can forgive me. I'm tired. I can't do it any more. I'm sorry. It's not because of you or the children. I have let you all down. Please find peace now as I have.*
> *Victor.*

Kelly had read plenty of suicide notes in her time. They could be blunt, like this one, or rambling; there were no rules. Irene was his wife. He had two kids. They'd never get over it. Kelly had tried to understand suicide before, as part of her job, but she'd never quite managed it. To get to the stage where you believed that everybody who loves you were better off without you was, to her, inconceivable.

But finding a suicide note wasn't as straightforward as it may look. Kelly still had to prove its authenticity. She also had to investigate why he'd done it. If he had.

She sighed and folded the note back to its original shape.

What a way to go.

Chapter 8

The task of removing Victor Walmsley's body was a tricky one. Getting it out of the quarry wasn't the problem. The owners had all sorts of lifting equipment for similar tasks. It was the integrity of the body and the scene that were important, because Kelly didn't want to lose potential evidence.

An outdoor crime scene presented its own unique set of challenges. Detritus could have been left in the vicinity and the whole area needed searching. The forensic team and CSI had been at the quarry all afternoon, and they were now losing light. She'd take her instructions from Ted Wallis, the coroner, who had plenty of experience of suspected suicides. There were four options, he'd told her over the phone: Victor jumped – as his suicide note indicated – or he was pushed, or he tripped, or he was already dead and transported there to dump.

Between the CSI, forensics and the skills of Ted Wallis, Kelly expected to have an answer in a few days. She knew there were certain factors that were present – or not – on a body when one took one's own life and Ted was used to finding them.

She watched him walk down the narrow path, the same way she had. He looked concerned but warmed when he saw her, and they embraced.

'Hi Dad,' Kelly said.

He was her second chance at daughterhood, having missed much of the first due to her time in London, and her mother never revealing her true paternity until right before she died. It was an earth-shattering shock at first, but then, a delicious surprise. One which they'd both nurtured. The fact that Ted happened to be the coroner for the north-west of England was a happy coincidence and meant they worked together often, as an investigator and a pathologist. It was a merry bond, even on days like today.

'Any news?' He asked.

A blue tent had been erected over the body, to keep nature's worst effects at bay, as well as prevent nosy journos getting an angle. A body in autumn, during mild weather, would easily begin decomposing within a few hours. Outside, open to the elements, Victor Walmsley's body had lain still with catastrophic wounds; they may as well have rung the dinner bell for nature's scavengers.

By the time Kelly had got there, flies had begun to buzz excitedly around the cadaver, and they even occasionally landed on the CSI and forensic staff. They were used to it. The body was in an awkward position, but Kelly had left him in situ, not wanting to disturb the scene until Ted had seen it for himself.

It looked like Victor had fallen face first, because his legs and hips were intact. It fitted the theory that he had simply flung himself off the quarry lip and let gravity do the rest.

They walked to the tarp where Ted went in first. She followed and watched him examine the position of the body before he did anything else.

'It's Victor Walmsley all right,' he said.

Kelly thought she detected a flicker of doubt in Ted's demeanour. But it wasn't due to lack of recognition, it was something else.

'He landed on his left shoulder, then it looks like his head bounced off the stone,' Ted said.

The body lay where it had all day, amongst the scattered remnants of precious stone. Any one of them could have killed him.

'You know how rare jump suicides are here in Europe?' Ted asked her. His face had lightened, the worry gone.

She did. It was less than three per cent of all suicides. The opposite was true in Asia, where it was the favoured method for some reason. It was a nasty way to go, thinking all the way down: have I done the right thing? It was about sixty feet up to the lip. A jump from that height was survivable, just about, but statistically, the odds were stacked against you. The quarry face was about six storeys high at the highest point, under which Victor's body lay.

'Would he have died immediately from those wounds?' Kelly asked her father.

'Possibly not. His shoulder took the brunt of the impact. It might have knocked him out, but it depends on the extent of the brain injury inside the skull.'

'How long will it take you to assess whether he was alive when he hit the ground?'

'As soon as I get him on my slab, I should think. I read the suicide note you sent.'

Kelly peered at him. 'And?'

He folded his arms. 'The clarity. It's chilling.'

'I know.'

'If I were thinking of diving headfirst off a rock and smashing my body to pieces, I'd be a wreck.'

Specialised bereavement counsellors were attending the wife, and Kelly had sent Dan with them to watch for any indicators of suspicious behaviour. Only this morning, the wife had told Kate that Victor was acting normally and had no obvious worries before he disappeared, contradicting what she told them when he'd gone missing. It also begged the question, where was he for six days before he jumped? If he did. In a place where he was well known, and in a suit. How had he managed to go off grid so easily?

'Why isn't there more blood?' she asked.

'His injuries will be internal. The body doesn't always crack open when dropped from height, it breaks inside. See the blood around his ears, nose and mouth?'

Kelly nodded. The flies were having a field day there.

'It'll be a different story inside,' Ted said. 'Was anything found up on top, do you know?'

34

'Not that I know of yet,' she replied.

Several uniformed officers in high-vis vests patrolled the area at the top of the quarry, and they'd been tasked with gathering any non-organic evidence that might lead somewhere: cigarette butts, drinks, clothes, paperwork, anything that could have been left by Victor before he jumped. Or, if he was pushed, something that could have been left by his murderer. Forensic officers were searching for footprints and tyre tracks, all to be gathered procedurally, should they be needed later. They had one chance to process a scene and a strict order of method was followed.

'I knew his old man. Dale Walmsley,' Ted said.

'Ah, that explains the name. I thought Dale was their surname,' Kelly said.

Ted smiled. 'So, my priority for you is time of death and any evidence of where he might have been before that,' Ted said. 'How are we getting him out of here?'

'A quarry elevator, I was told. It's being rigged up now. So, what was your relationship with Walmsley senior?' Kelly asked.

'Are you interviewing me?'

She laughed. 'I might be. It's not easy when you know the victim.'

Ted sighed.

'Not out for a pleasant walk, was he?' Ted indicated Victor's attire. He was changing the subject.

'No, which ties in with suicide.'

'Dale and Sons handled your mother's funeral,' he said.

That was what was bothering him. She felt mean for thinking he was hiding something, and a fool for forgetting such a detail, but she hadn't booked the funeral, her sister had. She touched his hand, blue glove to blue glove and he smiled at her.

'He wasn't as good as his father,' he said.

Kelly frowned. 'What do you mean?'

'I remember him messing up a few times. He wasn't the best at keeping paperwork in shipshape, shall we say.'

Ted liaised with all funeral directors at some time or another. The paperwork had to be watertight to meet the exacting standards of the registrar. Between the registrar and the coroner, the process of birth, death and marriage are supposed to account for every person in the UK. Failure to do so could result in serious legal consequences.

'Got me in hot water a few times,' he added.

'Really?'

He nodded.

'Let's get him out of here.'

The conversation was over. If the coroner was happy for the body to be transported, then it'd be done tonight. They left the tent. Victor's remains would be wrapped carefully in plastic to preserve any evidence until he reached the mortuary. Kelly frowned again. The details of this case were bothering her already.

Outside, they spoke to the CSI.

'It would have taken quite an effort to miss that steppe.' The CSI pointed upwards.

Kelly and Ted looked to where he pointed to. He was right. Where the slate had been quarried, in massive slabs carved out of the rock, it had created an amphitheatre-like structure, which would have been romantic had it not been for the circumstances. About halfway down, a promontory about ten feet wide jutted out like a viewing platform. To clear it, Victor would have had to have jumped out with force. Kelly felt chilly. It reminded her of a jumper they had a few years back, who'd launched herself off Walla Crag, high on Fentanyl. It was as if she believed she could fly.

'We've measured up, and to land here, and to miss that steppe, he'd have had to have had a run up of about fifteen feet, at least. And at speed.'

They all knew that was an unlikely feat for a sixty-one-year-old.

'Can we prioritise toxicology?' Kelly asked Ted, who agreed.

They heard a shout from above and a signal came down that the pulley was ready. The last protective wrapping was fastened around Victor's body, and he was placed in a heavy black body bag, which should protect him on the way up. Kelly saw Samuel Morningside at the top of the lip.

'I'm going up there,' Kelly said. 'I'll see you tomorrow at the mortuary?'

'Yes, I'll get started about ten. He'll spend the night in one of my fridges.'

Ted kissed her cheek tenderly and Kelly made her way up the quarry face. The carved steps were much bigger up close, and it took her a good twenty minutes to reach the top, but it got rid of some of the tension in her body, and she didn't want to waste anybody's time by asking to hitch a ride up on the pulley with the body. She was breathless when she reached the top, about the same time as Victor did. Samuel stared at her. Kelly smiled and got her breath back.

'That's impressive but unnecessary,' Samuel said.

'Actually, I wanted to speak to you, if you don't mind. I hoped you'd still be up here, and that path over there is a long walk.' She pointed over the other side of the quarry and saw her father walking slowly up it, his head bowed. Samuel shrugged as if to agree with her.

'Does this mean we can re-open tomorrow now?' He asked her. He displayed the same dispassion as he had earlier.

'I'll have to complete the search and sign off the paperwork. It could be as early as tomorrow afternoon,' she told him. 'It was something completely unrelated actually.'

He waited.

'The Morningside Nursing Home. Is it yours?' she asked.

A cloud crossed his face, and he looked north as if looking for answers on the wind.

'No. This land was split in two when my father died. The nursing home was built by my brother, Arthur.'

'Ah, right. It's just I have a friend moving in there tomorrow.'

'Really? An older friend?'

Kelly smiled. 'Yes.'

'Well, it's his way of making the land work, I guess. Good luck to your friend.'

It was an odd thing to say. One was wished good luck before an exam or a driving test, not when moving into a nursing home. But before she could question him, he'd walked away. She watched as Victor's body was loaded into the back of a Land Rover, which had been hired by the coroner's office to take the body away. It was about the only thing that could negotiate these tracks. It sped off and she saw Samuel walk to his own vehicle, another farm contraption, and drive away. She'd hitch a ride with the CSIs.

A private ambulance would be waiting for Victor at the entrance to the shop. The death had been registered and the paperwork would make its way to Ted in good time. From there, he'd write his report and send it back to the registrar so Victor could have a decent funeral. But that could take weeks, depending on what Ted found.

Kate had waited at the shop for her.

'What's up?' Kate asked.

'Apart from Victor's last moments? Or the fact that Mary is moving into that nursing home over there tomorrow, and I can't help feeling as though it's a bad idea.'

Kate smiled at her. 'I understand you care about her, but she'll be all right.'

It was Kate's way of telling her she was being oversensitive.

'I didn't realise you had grown so close,' Kate added.

'She paid Josie some pocket money to help her pack before she went to uni,' Kelly told her.

'It's something else, though, isn't it?'

'Victor arranged my mother's funeral, and I forgot. Ted reminded me.'

'Ah. And you're beating yourself up for it. Look, work and personal life don't mix like that. When your brain is at work, it side-lines everything else. Was he concerned?'

'He indicated that Victor was sloppy. He'd made mistakes. What mistakes I have no idea.'

'He organised Rob's funeral too.'

Kelly stared at her second-in-command. Now she felt even worse, because that information had passed her by too. She felt as though she was losing her edge suddenly. The service flooded back to her in full colour and audio, and her throat constricted.

Ghosts lay in wait in the most unexpected places. She should know. She saw her mother every time she embraced Ted and watched him smile.

Dale & Sons, Kate had told her, was the largest funeral directors in the area and the first choice for most. But the fact that Victor Walmsley was more than likely to have been one of the last – if not the last – person to have seen Rob before he was laid to rest, was yet another reverberation from his grave.

Chapter 9

Mary was probably a foot smaller than Kelly reckoned she'd been thirty years ago, but she was still able to peer up to Kelly's face with a smile and hold out her arms for a hug. At first, their cups of tea had accompanied stories from their pasts. Kelly told her about her time in London and growing up in the Lakes, leaving and coming back. In return, Mary told her about moving to the Lake District during the Second World War in answer to a request for land girls. She'd never gone back home to Leicester because there was nothing left after the war. She'd settled here, married and had two children, who had long since been buried. Mary surprised Kelly with a new story from her life with each visit, but tonight, she looked anxious.

The move was a big change for her, and she'd have to say goodbye to many memories, perhaps too many. Kelly cast her mind back to her transfer from London, and the stress it caused. She couldn't imagine how packing up one's life and decamping felt at ninety-six.

'The kettle is full,' Mary told her.

It was a small sentence of four words which meant nothing, yet everything at the same time. Kelly felt lighter as soon as she closed the door and got two cups out of Mary's cupboard to make them a brew each.

'Crikey, you've done well,' Kelly said, looking at all the boxes.

'I couldn't have done it on my own,' Mary said.

'I don't believe you, I know you've done this all yourself. You're invincible, what's your secret?' Kelly joked. She knew that helpers from the home had come to help. And Josie had done a fair bit. Most of her things would go into storage, but a lot of it was to be sold under arrangements that the home organised. It was pretty standard stuff and gave Mary a bit of cash. Nursing homes – good ones – were bloody expensive and Kelly, in a way, felt thankful that neither her mother nor John Porter had needed one.

'Tea and cake,' Mary replied, winking and going to open a tub on the side. 'And Kevin Costner films on the telly.' Mary chuckled and Kelly couldn't help but join in. She reckoned the secret to enduring life was not giving a fuck.

'What is it today?'

Mary still baked most days, but it was for care staff, nurses and now Kelly. Mary's appetite was smaller than Lizzie's, who was just over one year old. Her daughter's first taste of baking was by Mary's hand.

'How is Lizzie?'

It never took long for Mary to ask after her daughter. Kelly looked at her watch and felt an instant pang of guilt, she'd be home later than expected tonight.

'I know you can't stay long, you shouldn't have come at all. An old biddy like me doesn't need you fussing. Get off home to that beautiful family of yours, after your tea and cake.'

'I swear I need locks on everything, nowhere is safe,' Kelly said, answering Mary's question. She knew that by the time she got home, Johnny would be zombified, having chased after their daughter all day. Like Kelly, he loved going to work, which was infinitely easier than looking after a firecracker on legs. They'd had to say goodbye to their nanny, Millie, this year as she went off to complete a childcare diploma. She was sorely missed. But they got regular updates from her mother: Kate Umshaw. Kelly asked after her often and told Kate the position was open for Millie when she finished, and they'd match the wages accordingly to her new qualification.

'What is there left to do?' Kelly asked.

'A good night's sleep, then we're off. I like my room. The nurses said I can have my own TV, and they have baking on Wednesdays.'

Kelly gave Mary her tea and they sat opposite each other at the small kitchen table.

'I shouldn't complain,' Mary said. 'When you get to my age, you're thankful for every day, and surprised every morning you open your eyes.'

Kelly smiled.

'So what time is the taxi coming?'

'Seven in the morning.'

Kelly knew that Mary generally awoke at five a.m. It was something to do with age, she always said. It was funny how Kelly felt as though she needed a thousand days in bed to catch up with her pre-parent levels of sleep, and yet Mary had bags to spare.

'And how's that dishy man of yours?' Mary asked. She'd met Johnny once and he'd turned on his charm, as he always did. He had bags of it. It's what had got her into his bed in the first place.

She laughed and Mary put her hand out and laid it gently on top of Kelly's. She could almost see Mary's life in her veins underneath her paper-thin skin, testimony to the use they'd had, in contrast to her own smooth hands. Mary's fingers were bent and almost blue at the tip and she squeezed them over Kelly's. Her nails were always perfectly manicured and the lady who did them had arranged to visit her at her new home. Her gold rings were loose on her fingers and touched Kelly's skin.

'It's hard on any relationship when children come along,' she said.

Kelly smiled awkwardly and stared at her friend. She seemed to be able to read minds.

'It'll be all right,' Mary said. 'When you get to your time, like me, you realise that everything happens for a reason. I'm ready to pack up and leave, I've had a good life. I'm at peace. You shouldn't worry so much.'

Mary chuckled and got up out of her chair. Kelly thought it odd that Mary was talking about the nursing home as her final destination, but she supposed that's what it was. The conversation was over. Kelly finished her tea, and they said goodbye. She thanked Mary for the cake and wished her good luck with the move and she promised to visit when she could. She didn't mention the news from the quarry.

Chapter 10

Orange and blue shadows criss-crossed the sky as Kelly drove away from Keswick and back onto the A66, home. She called Dan, who'd been with Victor's wife all afternoon.

She noted a difference in his voice – it was fresher, which she put down to him getting out of the office. She'd gotten used to Dan's strong Glasgow accent, and rather enjoyed putting him on speaker phone, just to listen to him. It had the same effect as a self-help podcast, calming her. It was familiar.

'So, she's cut up, for sure,' he began. 'He left for work last Thursday morning and never came back. He seemed normal, had no worries or stresses that he hadn't shared with his wife ordinarily. There's no indication anybody expected him to take off. He was a homely person, you know, a real provider. A big personality too. There have been people sending their condolences all afternoon. He'd managed the funeral home for forty years or more. He was very proud of his job, and irritated if anyone rubbished the profession, you know they get a bad press, boss.'

'I know.'

The old term undertaker wasn't commonly heard any more. Not because it had changed in meaning, but because it flagged up images of tall gaunt men in black suits, followed closely by the grim reaper. They appeared ghoul-like, with pale skin and questionable communication skills, Addams Family-esque. According to his wife, Victor had been a proud director of funerals, from meeting with families, to dealing with the business end: the embalmers and gravediggers.

'He sounds like a sterling bloke to be honest. I didn't realise how tough it was. Dale & Sons manages over five hundred funerals a year. Victor spoke to every single bereaved family personally. He was taught by his pa, and his pa by his grandpa, and so on.'

'So, no sign his job got to him in the end?' Kelly asked.

'No, boss.'

'What are their finances like?' Kelly asked.

'Judging by their home, I'd say I'm in the wrong business. A couple of smart cars, you know, comfortable, which is no easy deal these days. I reckon they do well enough. There are photos of exotic holidays everywhere. To be honest, boss, I struggled to put them together, you know as a married couple. He strikes me as a player.'

'A player?'

'Tanned, good looking – even for sixty-one – and a sense of adventure. She's…'

'She's what?'

'Well, the opposite, boss. Plain.'

'It takes all sorts. Did you get the impression their marriage was solid?'

'No idea, boss, who knows?'

It was a fair question coming from a man who'd recently divorced his own wife.

'Grudges? Enemies?'

'Not that I've been able to pin down so far.'

'We'll head over to the Dale & Sons office tomorrow to meet some of the staff and get a feel for Victor as a boss,' she said.

'Aye.'

She paused.

'He arranged Rob's funeral.'

Silence.

'They've got an excellent reputation,' she added. 'I get the impression that from what you've said as well, Victor wasn't just good at what he did, but the best. I've read his reviews. And I 'don't buy it that after all these years of dealing with the deceased, Victor suddenly suffered a massive trauma from it.'

She didn't mention what her father had told her earlier. That could wait.

'Aye, which leaves us with what he was doing between last Thursday and today, or whenever he died.'

'His body has been transferred to the Penrith and Lakes Hospital. Ted Wallis will have a look tomorrow.'

'So, our Victor's in the best hands then.'

'So he is.'

'Aye. I've still got some of Rob's kit at mine. I haven't touched it.'

'Oh, Dan, I didn't know.'

'Nah, it's all good.'

'Are you up for getting into the background of the people who buried him? I can do it myself.'

'No way, boss. I'm not squeamish, and Rob would have been right in there wouldn't he? Digging around the finances especially. We'll find something, you'll see. People don't wander off and end up at the bottom of a cliff because they're right, dandy and happy.'

'Yes, you're right. Good night, Dan, I'll see you tomorrow. Our new DS is starting too.'

'Aye.'

She noticed that he asked no questions about the new detective.

They ended the call and Kelly mindlessly listened to the radio as she turned off for Pooley Bridge. The village was quiet, and she drove across the bridge to her house and parked on the driveway. There were still tourists at this time of year, but they dropped off considerably after September, and the village was left to its own devices again until next summer, when they made their money for the coming year, through lets, cafes, hotels and restaurants, and of course, the steamers on Ullswater.

Kelly never ceased to notice the crystal-clear air around Ullswater, close to her house, as she walked across her driveway.

The clarity and sharpness of it, even in summer, living right next to the river Eamont, overlooked by her small terrace, was a tonic after a long day. She could hear its flow as she opened the door and poked her head around to see if Lizzie was waiting behind it to surprise her.

She wasn't.

Their daughter was fast asleep on top of Johnny on the sofa, with CBeebies on TV, and the fire made up but not yet lit for the evening. The detritus of toddlerhood prevented a straight path from the front door to the living room and she picked up toys and building blocks to avoid stepping on them. She turned off the TV and tiptoed across to the terrace doors, which were ajar, letting in a now cool breeze, closing them quietly.

The smack of normality was usually just what she needed after examining a body at the bottom of a quarry. But tonight, she felt anxiety creep under her ribcage. Homecoming was something that brought warmth and safety, but she didn't feel it.

She looked at Johnny asleep. There was a time when his floppy sun-kissed hair, and his unshaven face, cuddling their daughter was enough to soften the hard edges of her profession. He'd been distant lately. He blamed himself for Rob's death. It had hit him hard, but he kept it to himself. He shut her out. It was his way but it left a simmering resentment inside her that only caused her to agree with him that the accident had been his fault. It'd driven an unspoken wedge between them, and she was tired. Weary with the constant questioning of her own body. It didn't fit here any more, and it didn't feel right at the office either. She peered at her daughter sleeping, and the feeling went away a little. Then she walked to the kitchen and poured herself a large glass of wine.

Chapter 11

Samuel took off his heavy boots and left them in the utility room at the rear of the farmhouse, where his father had left his decades before. He could smell cooking and he remembered Gloria had said she'd put a gammon in the Aga. He was supposed to be watching his waistline, but he loved Gloria's food, and that was how she showed she loved him, it was the way it had always been. He knew it would come with a side of buttery mashed potatoes and cider gravy, and he'd have second helpings, with a few glasses of wine.

The aroma grew stronger as he neared the kitchen, which was warm from the range. It was what made the colder days in the fields worth it. Though they'd had a long punishing summer, of drought and dust, he could see in the sky's messages that the long dark nights were coming and coming quick. He went past the kitchen table and to the sitting room, where Gloria had lit a fire. It was a bit extravagant for October, but it took the chill off the late hour, especially after a thankless day. It had started out all right but had become one of those days you'd rather forget with a glass of claret and a roaring fire, and a full belly telling you everything would be okay.

They only had one indoor dog, Samuel didn't believe in all this mushy stuff about keeping pets indoors unless they were born for it, like Walker had been. He loved the outdoors too, but at fourteen – old even for a Labrador – he would much rather wait for his master in the living room, on his bed, peering up with his chestnut eyes. He'd never been a jumper, and was quite happy laying at Samuel's feet, where Gloria put his basket of the evening.

Samuel gazed at his empty bed and decided that tomorrow he'd search for him. He missed petting Walker at the end of a long day, rubbing his ears and speaking quietly to him as if he understood his stresses. Penny was different and slept outside in one of the barns.

'You didn't find him, then?' Gloria asked, as she came in and put a large glass of red wine on the table next to Samuel's chair. Gloria sat next to him and peered at the empty bed. Samuel knew it would be just for a second and then she'd be up again, going off to do something, never sitting still, but more for a distraction because she loved Walker as much as he did.

Samuel shook his head. 'I'll look again tomorrow.'

'Will you ask Arthur?' she asked.

He nodded. 'If I can't find him.'

'I'm sure Arthur would've told us if he found him,' she said hopefully.

Samuel nodded.

'It's a nice bottle, is that. Remember when we thought wine was posh?' she chuckled, trying to distract him.

'Aye, I do that. Pa used to call it dishwater.'

'Nothing but stout for him,' Gloria said.

They smiled, but shadows soon stole them away and they both stared at the fire. Gloria didn't get up, but stayed. Samuel knew there must be something on her mind other than Walker.

'Is it nice?' she asked.

'It is that,' said Samuel licking his lips after his first taste. It was like velvety smooth berries on his tongue and the warmth hugged the back of his throat and he exhaled. There was nothing like sitting in front of an orange flame, warming the glass in your hand, Walker snoring at his feet, with gammon cooking in the Aga, he thought. He took another sip.

'Tough day,' Gloria said.

He nodded and took another sip. 'Was that.'

The fire crackled. 'I never would've thought it of Victor,' she said finally.

Samuel closed his eyes after another gulp.

'None of us know what is going on, not really,' he said, with his eyes still shut, his head leaning back on the chair.

'I don't know if to call Irene,' she said.

'Of course, you should. But give it a day perhaps. She'll have a lot on her plate,' he added.

'So she will. Poor devil. I can't understand it. What'll she do now?'

Samuel opened his eyes and looked at her. He took another delicious sip and allowed it to caress him.

'Is that what's bothering you?' he asked her. 'Irene?'

Gloria nodded. 'And...'

'And...?'

'He had everything he could possibly want, didn't he? Grown up children to be proud of, Irene, a wonderful wife, a business, a fine one, the holidays they had, and the new house. Wasn't it enough?'

'It's enough for me,' Samuel said.

'Is it?' she asked.

He smiled and held out his hand to hers and squeezed. 'Yes, it is,' he said.

Gloria stood up then and smiled. 'Right, that's it then, I'll go and mash the potatoes.'

She left the room and Samuel closed his eyes again.

They could talk about how Dorian had taken it in good time. The coppers had come up here to the house and interviewed their only son about how he found Victor's body. Dorian was thirty, and used to outdoor life. He saw death almost every day of the calendar year. All right, it wasn't normally a human one, not a fully grown man, who Dorian knew fairly well, from a distance. But Samuel knew he'd be all right. Besides, if he wasn't then Gloria would've mentioned it.

'It's ready, love,' Gloria shouted, pulling Samuel reluctantly from his cocoon of comfort. He'd rather stay there all night, enjoying the fire and his wine, but his belly was grumbling, and he wouldn't miss one of Gloria's meals for the world. He stood up and went through to the kitchen and placed his glass down on the table. It was set only for two.

'Dorian not joining us?' he asked.

'No, he's already eaten. He had fish and chips. He's gone to meet some pals.'

'He's not taken it badly then?' Samuel said. 'Did you talk to him?' he asked.

'I tried to. He said he was fine. Not bothered in the slightest. He called Victor an idiot.'

'That's a bit harsh.'

'Called him a show off, swanning around town, he and Beryl acting like a couple of celebrities in their fancy cars.'

Samuel raised his eyebrows, pulled out his chair and sat down, as Gloria carved the meat and slapped mash onto his plate. Samuel was reminded just how hungry he was, and his mouth watered. Gloria had placed the wine bottle on the table, and he filled their glasses. He was about to sit down when they saw lights in the yard and heard an engine. Then a loud knocking on the door. Samuel looked at Gloria who paused mid-carve and shrugged. Samuel went to the door and opened it and found his brother's wife stood there, arms folded, face like thunder, looking expectant.

'Beryl. What brings you over here, then? Social call?'

She rolled her eyes.

He didn't invite her in. Arthur and Beryl had been over this side of their father's land possibly twice since their mother died five years ago, rest her soul. There was no love lost, they didn't talk because there was nothing to talk about. Apart from the missing jewellery, but that was all in the past now. They had no proof that Beryl took it and Arthur would hear none of it.

'Not going to invite me in, Samuel?' she asked.

'Planning to get comfortable?' he replied.

She sniffed.

Gloria appeared behind him with a carving knife and fork in her hands and Samuel had a fleeting but worrying vision of holding her back as she tried to plunge the utensils into her sister-in-law's body.

'Come in, then,' he said finally, and went inside, giving Gloria a warning look. They went back into the kitchen and Beryl came in, looking around, like she had when their Ma had died, as if seeking anything that was worth taking and selling. The wedge between the brothers had become irreversible when he brought Beryl back from his travels and announced they were engaged.

Samuel stayed standing and didn't offer Beryl a seat. Gloria went back to carving, furiously quiet.

'Say what you've come for,' Samuel said.

'We, I mean Arthur and I, want to offer our condolences for what you've all been through today,' Beryl said.

'Condolences for what?' Samuel asked.

Samuel reckoned that his slices of gammon would be thicker than normal tonight, watching Gloria with the knife. It grated on the side of the carving plate and on his nerves. Beryl stood alone and awkward. She folded her arms.

'Spit it out, Beryl. If Arthur has sent you over, it means he hasn't got the balls to come over here himself, now, what is it he wants to know? Offering sympathy isn't his style, or yours,' Samuel said.

'We can't believe what happened to poor Victor,' Beryl said.

Samuel glanced at Gloria, who stopped carving.

'News travels fast. And Victor was anything but poor,' Samuel said. He peered at her hands, expecting to see his mother's rings sparkling on her fingers. They were bare. 'You should know.' Beryl and Victor had been in business together for years, so Samuel found it curious that she had come to offer sympathy to him. Victor was her partner. Rumour said they were more, but gossip was vicious in these parts.

'It must have been an awful shock. We worked closely with him. We're as shocked as you are,' Beryl said haughtily.

'Know anything about it do you? The police will be interested.'

'Police? I thought it was suicide,' Beryl said.

'You know a lot. They're investigating. The coroner was here, with a police lady I've seen on the news.'

He watched her.

Gloria stopped scraping the knife on the porcelain dish.

'Well, I just came to offer support,' Beryl said.

'The last time you did that my mother's ruby ring disappeared,' Samuel said.

The knife clattered to the floor, making Beryl jump.

'I don't think we need to go over all that again, Prudence left me that ring.'

'So you say,' Samuel said. It wasn't an offer to discuss it. Gloria picked up the knife and turned her back, but not before Samuel saw how tightly she was squeezing the shaft.

'We were close towards the end.'

Samuel couldn't help but snort. He took a step closer to the woman who'd invaded their privacy. She stepped back.

'Look, I'm not here to make things worse between you and your brother,' Beryl said.

'You did that years ago. If you've got any condolences to pass on, why don't you speak to Irene yourself? Is there anything else?'

Beryl looked between the pair. 'I guess I should inform the police then. I saw Victor's car over by Dockray. It's been there for a few days. Just trying to be helpful.'

'Really? Turned over a new leaf?' Samuel asked.

'I'll see myself out,' Beryl said, turning to the door.

'Where did you say his car was?' Samuel asked.

'The lay-by on the Dockray Road, the one at the foot of Great Mell,' Beryl said, turning with her hand on the door.

Samuel rubbed his chin and looked at Gloria. 'They're wanting to know where he was all week, you see him?' Samuel asked.

'No. But I know he was tired.'

'Tired? You don't jump off a quarry face because you're tired.'

'I know the look. I see it all the time. I mean tired of everything, tired of life. He was exhausted.'

'There's better ways to go. I didn't have Victor down as the jumping type. Seemed to me to love life, and how money could make it better.'

'What's the jumping type?' Beryl asked, ignoring the reference to money.

Samuel stepped closer to her, and Beryl opened the door a crack, letting in the cold night air.

'You know the ones who are burning from a fire so hot they'd rather smash their heads open than watch their own skin blister.'

Beryl faced him, though he was a clear foot taller than she was. Both had faced off before, many times. Samuel used his superior height but didn't get too close for fear of being slashed by Beryl's talons, which he knew from experience were deadly.

She looked away first, banged the door, and left.

Chapter 12

Dale & Sons Funeral Directors' main office was in Keswick, in the centre of town, tucked in between holiday let offices and cafes. The industry had changed over the years becoming more user-friendly. The frontage was more like an upmarket cosmetic centre, with its white displays behind polished windows, soft lighting and flowers in vases. A dog bowl sat outside, full to the brim for passing canines, welcome almost everywhere in the walking town.

Kelly had grabbed two coffees, one for her and one for Dan, at the small deli down the street, queueing behind tourists and locals alike. The coffee was good, and Kelly was tempted to get a scoop of freshly made vanilla ice-cream in it, but she restrained herself. The last thing a bereaved relative wanted to see was ice-cream dripping off her chin. She'd gazed at the twenty or so flavours on offer, baulking at the bubble-gum and cola, drawn more to the salted caramel and chocolate.

Dan looked tired and she felt a flutter of nerves – the importance of checking in on her team's welfare haunted her daily now.

'You okay?'

'Aye. Too much red wine, boss. Don't you worry, I've my wits about me,' he reassured her.

At least he was honest.

'And Emma?'

Dan's face always lit up when the conversation turned to his new girlfriend, and Kelly's DC. Her two detectives had only gone official on their feelings once Dan had divorced his wife, but they all knew it had been carrying on for ages. She envied him his new relationship with Emma. They were an odd couple. Emma Hide was a fitness fanatic, light of step and fresh faced. Where Dan, she knew, was more of a pizza and beer type of guy. But then, who was she to judge?

She often wondered what people thought of her and Johnny's relationship. He was ten years older than her, a new dad at fifty-one. An outdoor fixture, chatty and dependable. Kelly was tough and closed by comparison. She felt distant and aloof at times, always suspicious about somebody's intentions. She'd seen enough of the dark side of human nature not to trust too quickly. Even after five years back in her native Cumbria, she still hadn't reconnected with many old friends. They'd developed different lives to hers, and she still didn't feel as though she fitted in. Her closest confidants were her father, a seventy-year-old coroner who cut up bodies; her work colleagues, who were as wary as she was; a one-year-old; and lately, a ninety-six-year-old. Those from her long-ago life all wore masks, and that was the point. She wondered now as they were welcomed into the warm and cosy front reception of Dale & Sons, what disguises they'd see come off in the coming days and weeks.

Unexplained deaths were as much about deception as they were about answers. In her experience, Kelly knew that those who were close to the deceased all had their own agendas, and as the late queen herself famously said, *recollections may vary...*

Kelly knew enough about the process of death to understand that this wasn't where the real business took place: at the funeral home. Dead bodies were stored off site, at their main facility, near the river, inside a large warehouse, where they could fit forty fridges. She and Dan planned to visit after the office.

Irene Walmsley appeared from the back of the office as the junior colleague who'd let them in locked the front door to the shop. They were closed for business today, and a note on the door told the public to direct urgent enquiries to a telephone number due to unforeseen circumstances, though the whole town knew the true reason.

Kelly and Dan were used to meeting grieving relatives, usually traumatised by nasty events. That was their job. Some of them were alone, others preferred legions of comforters. Everybody was different. Irene was alone. But their job wasn't to judge, it was to observe. No matter the outcome, if it be suicide or something else, Ted would still need to complete a report, so Victor Walmsley could be laid to rest, likely in one of his own coffins, but Kelly's mind was well and truly open. Dan looked around and she knew that he was fiddling. It wasn't that Dan was suffering the effects of his red wine, or that he was bored, it was a method of distracting a potential witness, to strip away their inhibitions and reveal what they were really thinking and feeling.

She waited.

'Mrs Walmsley, thanks for meeting us here. I'm so sorry for your loss,' Kelly said.

Kelly studied her. The woman looked more confused than in the grips of grief, and something else: perhaps bitterness. Irene Walmsley looked like an archetypal retired lady who'd worked all her life in the same place. She had a traditional short and neat hairstyle, minimal make-up, shoulders that were hunching under the duress of age, and a sad face. Kelly believed you ended up wearing your life on your face: disappointment and happiness alike. Irene was an unhappy woman, and it wasn't just because her husband had been found at the bottom of a quarry, her wrinkles and downturned mouth hadn't carved their way into her face overnight.

'It's only right I show you around.' Irene said plainly. Her eyes were red and puffy. She fiddled with her beige cardigan. She looked lost. Kelly was struck by how different she was to her husband in terms of appearance. She'd seen pictures of Victor and he looked snappily smart and almost glamorous in compar-ison, like Dan had observed too. He took care of himself. Kelly wondered if it was a sticking point between the two or if Victor liked keeping his wife in the shadows.

'Hello again, Mrs Walmsley,' Dan said, holding out his hand.

'You were at the house last night, Mr Houghton.'

'Yes, I was.'

The door knocked as somebody tried to get in, but they read the sign and walked away.

'Let's go out back,' Irene said, and they followed her through to another office, this time with examples of everything you could buy to make the send-off for your loved one as memorable as it could be. It brought back memories for Kelly of the funerals of her mother and the man she'd thought was her father for almost forty years. One thing was for sure, funerals were eye-wateringly expensive. The whole event had changed over the years, now they were more like weddings, with choices for everything from catering to coffin liners.

They sat down. Irene looked out of place in the room and Kelly reckoned she didn't have much to do with the buying public. She perched awkwardly on her chair.

'Are you active in the family business?' Kelly asked her.

'Not any more, just behind the scenes. Goodness, do you both want tea?'

She got up and walked to a kettle placed on a pretty tray, next to a fridge and a coffee machine.

'No thank you, we're good.'

'Right.' Irene sat back down.

'When you say behind the scenes, did you run the business?'

'Yes, me and Victor did it on our own, had done for over twenty years, since it passed from his father to him.'

'Well, I'm sure he did him proud. Dale & Sons has the kind of reputation you'd want in a town like Keswick.'

Dale Walmsley had been a well-known character before his own passing. Ted had worked with him for years, generating the huge amount of paperwork necessary for a dead body to be laid to rest, coming and going between funeral director and coroner. The takeover of every aspect of life, from the cradle to the grave by huge global giants of corporatism had infected almost everything, but some family businesses held on and delivered what nobody else could: the personal touch. Dale & Sons did that by all accounts. The plural "sons" was a marketing trick, giving the impression of a loving and trustworthy family dynasty. Victor was on only child.

'Thank you.'

'Mrs Walmsley, we'd like to ask you some questions, and they may seem insensitive or even irrelevant, but we'd like to get some background on Victor's movements last week.'

'I told the police already,' she nodded at Dan. 'I told them I have no idea where he went.'

'That's what we'd like to find out for you. It involves trying to establish who he might have been with. Did he have any appointments that you know of during that time?'

Irene shook her head. She didn't make eye contact.

'Did he keep an appointment diary?'

'No, Victor was old-fashioned, he carried everything in his head.'

'So, he didn't tell you where he was going last Thursday?'

Irene looked at her cardigan again and Kelly thought she saw her cheeks flush a little. She let it go.

'I'm sorry to ask this but was Victor in debt?'

Irene blushed deeper this time.

'No.'

Kelly recognised the warning daggers flashing from Irene's eyes and parked the inquiry. The woman was going to be impossible to get information out of. Her lack of transparency, given the gravity of the situation, was a red flag.

'Did Victor tell you of anyone he might have been having any bother with?'

'No.' She was adamant. 'I told Mr Houghton all this last night. If we're just going to repeat it all, there wasn't any need for me to come down here really, was there?'

'I'm sorry for running through the same things, we often seem to be doing that but it's about making sure we understand what might have happened to Victor last week. Establishing that is our priority.'

'Isn't it obvious? He wandered around in the same suit he left in, and his new shoes. He must have been confused or hurt. He didn't spend any money, and he never called anyone, and then he fell off that cliff.'

Irene's voice broke. She retrieved a screwed-up tissue from her cardigan pocket and wiped her nose. Kelly gave her some time.

'That's something I wanted to discuss with you. We found a note.'

Irene's eyes widened. Her mouth moved but no words came out.

Kelly nodded to Dan, who retrieved the file on his toughpad. He showed it to her.

'Take your time,' Kelly said.

They watched as Irene's lips moved over the words, each digging like a dagger into her heart. It was painful to watch.

'He didn't write that,' she announced unexpectedly. She gave the pad back to Dan.

'What makes you say that, Irene?' Kelly asked.

'I don't believe it.'

Kelly nodded. It was a common reaction from loved ones when they saw the finality of a suicide note. No one wanted to believe it. And in some sense, it wasn't really written by their relative. Suicide notes were penned by shadows of a former personality, a desperate and alien being who'd taken possession of the person there before.

She didn't push it. However, it told them one thing at least; that if Irene knew the real reason Victor had killed himself, *if* he killed himself, then she wasn't sharing it.

'Did he know the Morningside estate well?'

'What do you mean?'

Kelly paused. 'It's our experience that people tend to choose their location in these circumstances for a reason. Did the quarry have a special meaning to him?'

'Not that I know of. We both know the brothers obviously, who doesn't? And their wives.'

Kelly noted the acidity in Irene's voice when she said wives.

'We're good friends with Samuel and Gloria, not the other two, though.'

60

'I don't know them.'

'But you're a copper, you can't have many friends,' Irene said. 'I'm sorry, I didn't mean…'

'Don't worry, it's not a problem at all. How well do you know the brothers, and their wives? Let me get this right, Samuel and Gloria, and his brother Arthur, and his wife Beryl?'

She nodded, but not before Kelly had clocked a slight physical tick in her right eye when Beryl's name was mentioned.

Irene nodded.

'Well, Victor buried their ma and pa. We say hello and that, you know. Like I said, Samuel and Gloria are friends.'

'But not Arthur and Beryl?'

'No, it's just business with those two.'

'Business?'

'Yes, they're partners. Vic does – *did* – the funerals of the folk who died at the home, you know, he took care of things.'

'Exclusively?'

Irene nodded. 'At the private family chapel.'

'And the area? It's a big farm. Did Victor visit there much for anything other than business?'

'He bought me my table mats for Christmas, and they're made of Morningside slate from there.'

Kelly smiled at the woman's moment of nostalgia.

'And did he like walking much?'

'What?'

'Did he take himself off for walks?'

'Not in his work suit.'

'I'm sorry, I didn't mean that. It was insensitive. I mean did he walk around that particular area, for leisure?'

'Victor wasn't a walker. He was too busy. He had no hobbies really.' Irene looked away.

Kelly nodded.

'What happens to the business now?' Kelly asked, gentler than before.

Irene looked at her and shook her head. 'So, you think it's an insurance job?'

'No, that's not what I'm implying at all,' Kelly said. She waited. It was probably time to go. She'd got most of what she'd come for. Until Ted gave her his findings, she couldn't start an investigation into Victor's death with any confidence, so this visit was an information gathering exercise. She'd learnt plenty from Irene's answers and her body language already. No information was ever wasted, and Irene Walmsley was telling her more about her family and the business than she realised.

'You handled the funeral of a very well-loved colleague of ours recently, I wanted to thank you, it was a beautiful service. He's badly missed.'

Irene looked at her. 'The policeman?'

Kelly nodded. 'Rob Shawcross. I wouldn't expect you to remember.'

'I remember all our families. It's what makes us stand out. Me and Victor made sure of it. His wife blamed you, didn't she?'

'Yes, she did.'

'Victor told me it was an accident.'

'It was.'

'Anger and blame are all-consuming for the relatives,' Irene said, and they held each other's stares. Kelly wondered who Irene would blame. She got the impression, from the way Irene held her gaze, that she wanted to tell her, but the moment passed.

'Well, we won't keep you. We'll make our way over to the other site, then we'll be out of your hair. Here's my card to add to the pile you've no doubt already been given. I'm sorry if you feel overwhelmed. You know the bereavement team is excellent, you must use them as much as you need.'

'I'd rather have my house back.'

'And your children?'

'They're on their way. My son is flying in from New York, so it's taken a bit of time. My daughter has no excuse, coming from London, but she's got a toddler, so she's had to get help.'

It was a long-winded explanation, as if Irene was trying to prove that her family was solid.

Irene took Kelly's card and put it into the pocket of her cardigan. They stood up to follow her but she stopped and turned to them.

'You know I met Victor when I was fifteen years old. We've been together ever since. He was the hardest-working, life-loving and strongest person I ever knew, and that includes my own father, who is still alive at ninety-seven. Victor never would have jumped of that cliff,' she said.

Kelly instinctively put her hand out and rested it on Irene's cardigan-covered arm.

'We'll get the answers you need, Irene.'

They went out the front and walked down the street silently.

'It's amazing how well you can know somebody isn't it, but not even know them at all?' Dan said.

'You're right there, Dan,' Kelly said.

'You believe her about not knowing where he went?' he asked.

'No idea, but I did notice that there was a pile of mail on the side that had gone unopened since May. A look into the business wouldn't do any harm. We could start with Morningside Nursing Home and Victor's business partner, on our way back to the office.'

Dan side-glanced at her. 'On it, boss,' he said, smiling at Kelly. Life seemed to return to Dan's face, perhaps because she'd given him something to do, and if they didn't have Rob's nose for numbers to rely on, then Dan was just as discerning when it came to money trails. He'd worked in Glasgow's surveillance teams when they'd managed to jail the leaders of one of the biggest organised crime rackets in Lanarkshire back in 2011, after a three-year investigation.

'We need to go easy on her. Keep her on side. She's like a coiled-up spring right now, and she's keeping something from us.'

Chapter 13

Ted washed his forearms under the stream of water and meticulously followed the same routine he had since he was a twenty-one-year-old trainee pathologist in London. From there he'd transferred to Belfast and worked in trauma for five years. That was all he could stand. The wounds he witnessed remained scarred on his memory forever. The torture inflicted by both sides during the Troubles, on soldiers, children and civilians was something he couldn't understand and haunted him every time he went to work. It was worse than war. He'd volunteered for Médecins Sans Frontières for two years and witnessed the horror of conventional and unconventional weapons and the effects they have on human bodies. He'd seen about as much trauma as anybody could.

So, when he was faced with a potential suicide, having fallen around sixty feet, onto solid rock, he knew exactly what to expect.

What he was more interested in was whether the injuries sustained by the victim's fall were suffered ante- or post-mortem, and he'd be able to tell that from the way the tissues and blood behaved on impact. Simply put, if he was alive when he hit the ground then it ruled out one of their four possibilities. Then they'd have three left. But the most pressing priority was time of death so Kelly could work out how long he'd been missing.

Every new body Ted greeted on his steel slab brought a little more mortality to his ageing body. How long would it be before he'd be the one to expire? It was morbid but common at his age he guessed, even though he was only seventy-one. His father used to say three-score-years-and-ten was a good innings, and according to that he was now on borrowed time. He concentrated on the things which gave him more life: his daughter, his granddaughters and his work, though the latter was a paradox. He suddenly thought of Wendy and was thankful that there hadn't been an inquest into her death. She'd died of cancer, plain and simple. In those cases, an expensive autopsy wasn't required. Like a lot of the cases dealt with by the man soon to be on his slab.

He walked towards the main mortuary room, arms stuck up and ready to be robed by his assistant. He would put on his own goggles, sterility wasn't as important as it was inside a working operating theatre, but there were certain parameters for safety, especially with a body that had been outside in the elements for an unknown period. According to Kelly, nobody had seen or heard from Victor Walmsley since last Thursday, a week ago.

The wheels of the gurney croaked and whined as it was wheeled in, and Victor Walmsley waited for him inside a black body bag. It struck Ted that it was a less poignant moment than others inside these walls because Victor had himself been familiar with the process of death. He'd likely seen thousands of bodies in black bags over the years. Victor had been a funeral director for forty years, he'd been intimate with every stage of passing, from expiration to burial. It was a long process, and there was a strict protocol of paperwork to get through before the very end.

Ted had no idea where the final resting place of Victor Walmsley would be. Funeral directors usually had quite particular ideas about their own extinction. He'd read that the latest trend was being turned to powder via liquid nitrogen. It was cleaner for the planet than cremation, and it was quick and easy. It was also cheap and readily available. The other, more sci-fi idea he'd heard coming out of Sweden, was the act of plunging the body into alkaline to dissolve all soft tissue, leaving behind only bone, that could then be ground to dust. Efficient, impressive, but utterly macabre in his book. However, both cremation and burial chilled him to the core. Being burnt at over two thousand degrees was one thing, being slowly eaten by insects and their larvae, was quite another.

Ted unzipped the body bag once he was happy that he had all his tools to hand. They were laid out on a steel table next to him. The sluice was checked, and the suction worked just fine. An assistant helped him take the plastic wrap off Victor's head and hands, checking it scrupulously for detritus, as well as inside the bag for anything that might be missed.

Ted knew that the most important study today would be the one he would have to wait the longest for: the brain. He'd get to the head last of all, after he'd examined the external injuries and eviscerated the man. The cranial trauma would be discovered in layers as he sawed through the skull and removed the brain, preparing it to be scanned and examined under a microscope in tiny slithers of tissue. There was no doubt that there would be brain injury, however, UK red tape meant that the precise cause of death had to be logged by law. One couldn't simply write 'fall' on a death certificate. It had to be utterly precise. What he couldn't do was tell from Victor's body where he'd been all week, that was for Kelly to find out. But what he could do was establish when he died, to give her a window, and a fighting chance.

Ted examined the body visually at first, without touching it. Victor had all the hallmarks of a fall from height. It looked to Ted like Victor had landed on his left shoulder, that side of his body showed the most trauma. From a height of sixty feet, the body would have been approaching twenty metres per second in velocity, and it would have taken him under two seconds to impact the quarry floor. The simple calculation was standard, and it helped determine whether a fall was survivable. This one was on the margins. Of course, there were stories about parachutists surviving falling thousands of feet, but they were about as common as a lottery win. Ted stuck to mathematical probability. Then there was the anomaly of the steppe, maybe he jumped or was pushed off that, and not from the very top.

Victor's left shoulder had almost all but disappeared inside his body, and the left side of his head was swollen, which was a definitive indicator that Victor was alive when he hit the floor, but it didn't mean he was conscious. The body's inner mechanisms were still working when Victor suffered the fatal impact, that much was certain. Bruising was extensive, but contusions continued to develop after death. Kelly had already told him that the last known person to visit the now disused quarry edge on that side was the Morningside's son, who said he'd been walking there on Monday, and not seen a body. That gave him a window of two days, and Ted reckoned the bruising and swelling fitted with this working hypothesis.

He examined the facial orifices and the pattern of the bleeds out of Victor's nose, mouth and ears. They were consistent with the fall. He requested a pair of scissors from the trolley as he spoke into his mic, and began cutting away Victor's trousers first, then his shirt and tie. The man was dressed for work. Ted had read about suicide victims dressing up for their demise, as if it was a last hurrah on this earth. He shivered slightly.

The limbs appeared as expected after catastrophic blunt-force trauma. Ted picked up one arm, then the other and adjusted the goggles on his head to zoom in on Victor's skin. He had yet to take samples of blood, viscera and other tissue, and so the needle marks he saw came as a surprise. Ted examined the victim's liver and palpated his veins. He didn't look like a drug user, even a recreational one, however he couldn't be sure until histology and toxicology came back. He counted three puncture sites in total on his right arm. He checked his notes, and they didn't specify whether Victor was right- or left-handed: needles were usually put into the arm that was least dominant. He checked what he could see of the left arm, though it was severely broken, but he couldn't detect any injection sites. He instructed his photographer to log the findings. The three tiny holes were intravenous and not intramuscular, intradermal or subcutaneous, suggesting that Victor had something fed into his body recently, via the fastest route possible, indicating medicines or chemicals of some description. He checked his notes. Victor wasn't on any medication that would require self-administration.

Ted turned his attention to Victor's hands and feet. He scraped under his nails, hoping to determine where he'd been in the lead up to his death. Bacteria and other organic matter gathered there indicating what a person might have been up to before their death, or indeed what they might have touched, and if that could have been another human body. Ted noticed how clean and manicured Victor's nails were and admired the man's personal hygiene. He still scraped. Then he checked for signs of a struggle: defence wounds, assault (other than what the ground had done to him), binding wounds and other methods of coercion. He examined the skin carefully, starting at the feet and ending with Victor's head, trying to ascertain what had happened to Victor's body before the fall. In day-to-day life, we all pick up scrapes and bruises, but when dealing with an inquest into somebody's death, the minute details become vitally important.

Ted dictated detailed notes into his mic. His initial method was to separate his superficial findings before he got to the injuries classically associated with a fall from sixty feet. The discovery of the needle sites had piqued his inquisitive brain. This was a man who'd not been behaving as expected prior to death, and so that was Ted's first query. Victor had no medical reason to be getting IV injections, and so Ted now looked for other signs. And it wasn't long until he found one. The external bruising pattern on Victor's body followed a form to be expected from his supposed trajectory of fall. However, there were other injuries that simply didn't fit with this man's final destination at the bottom of a sixty-foot quarry face.

One of them was the bruising across the right side of Victor's face. Ted knew the difference between blunt- and sharp-force trauma and the injury fitted neither model. He expected to find on a normal fall victim a series of blunt force radiating out from the impact site, which he'd already discerned as the left shoulder joint that was smashed internally. However, the right side of Victor's face, taking in his lower jaw, right eye and cheek bone, showed signs of an inflicted wound which was not consistent with the quarry floor. He'd searched the area where Victor was found, and the ground was even and smooth. There were plenty of rocks around that could have caused the damage, but they weren't under

Victor's body, and none showed signs of coming into contact with him – in other words, covered in blood. In his experience, if a body fell onto rocks, those rocks didn't then bounce away, they became part of the end result. Besides, Ted could see that Victor's head had born the effects of the fall mostly on his left side, no doubt hitting the floor shortly after his shoulder collapsed. Victor's head was left side down when he was found, and there was no evidence that the body had bounced and turned after impact.

Ted paused to scribble diagrams and notes onto a clipboard and spoke into his mic. He measured the suspected injuries and the extent of the superficial damage they'd caused, keen to see the scale once he got underneath the epidermis, which had been broken and had begun to heal. After photographing the right side of Victor's face, Ted cleaned the right eye and realised that it was more damaged than the left, again, puzzling him. He went closer to Victor's face and studied his eye, and saw perfect indentations, parallel, as if Victor had been lying on a creased pillow. However, Ted knew from his vast experience that what he was looking at were the marks left on skin when bandages or dressings are removed.

According to his notes, Victor did not have any injuries the last time his wife saw him, last Thursday.

Chapter 14

The complex of outhouses and showrooms where Dale & Sons prepared bodies for their last farewell was positioned in a less desirable part of Keswick, tucked away behind the trees and flow of River Greta. It was quiet and secluded. Families who visited the main office were treated to the luxury of a warm, pretty environment where they could take their time choosing coffin linings and flowers. Here, the pointy end of the job took place. Kelly and Dan were pleasantly surprised as they walked in.

Three men sat at a table sipping mugs of tea or coffee, and the camaraderie took Kelly back to London when she'd worked for the Met. Long hours and late nights shrouded in red wine and cigarette smoke carried them through long cases that afforded no breaks. It jolted her and she smiled at the men who stared at her and Dan. They'd arrived unannounced, assuming Irene would inform her staff.

She introduced herself and Dan to the men whose demeanour changed straight away from casual dominance of their patch to deferential confusion when they gazed at the lanyards. They stood up.

'Who's in charge?' she asked politely.

'We don't know yet, but I'm kind of the foreman for the time being.'

The man who'd spoken looked to Kelly to be the oldest of the three – around forty – and she shook his hand, wondering briefly what might have been on it. She knew the process of death, though roughly, and understood enough to realise that they'd probably been taking a break from working on bodies that were kept refrigerated behind one of the closed doors.

'We're here to take a look around. Irene knows.'

'Who?' said a younger man.

'Victor's wife, you cretin,' said the older one who'd assumed control. His name was Bill. He didn't suit it. Bill was an old name and she wondered if he was a William, or a Will, who'd simply added a couple of years to allow him to fill Victor's shoes.

'You worked with Victor?' she asked.

They nodded.

'Right, that's a good place to start then.'

She cast her eyes around, aware that Victor had set off to work a week ago, intending to make the short journey here to tend to the dead for the day. The three men wore casual clothes. Bill looked the smartest, with corduroy trousers and an open shirt.

'Did he always where a suit to work?'

'He did. He was respectful that way,' said Bill. 'This is Eric, our embalmer, and this is Paul, a pall bearer.'

They waited for her to appreciate the pun and she winked at Bill, who nodded his approval. She shook their hands, hesitant to linger on Eric's for too long. She knew enough about embalming from Ted to know that it was a highly skilled and scientific process, and it was most unlikely that he'd have flesh adhering to his fingers, but it still put her off getting too close to him.

'Can you show me around?'

'Sure thing,' Bill said, seeming thankful for something to do. He stared at Dan, who at over six foot, looked like Kelly's body-guard. He remained quiet and played the role of her eyes and ears. She glanced at him.

'I'll wait here,' Dan said, and Kelly nodded. 'With Paul and Eric, right lads?'

They cleared a chair for him and hastily offered him a drink. Men spoke more freely in front of another alpha male. It was useful at times.

'This is our brew room, and we welcome visitors here too, that's why it's so nice,' Bill said.

Kelly and Dan looked around. From the outside, she'd expected a workshop of some sort, rugged and bare, but this was painted, crafted and decorated tastefully. Photographs of coffins, flowers and landscapes were dotted around and there were comfy sofas positioned around a pretty coffee table.

'We've been to the office in town, I wasn't aware that families came here too.'

'This is where our chapel of rest is, in town that's where they do the business of bookings and such like.'

'I see.'

Kelly followed Bill, who opened one of the many doors leading off the main reception space. They entered a simple room, which was clearly religious, as it boasted all the idolatry necessary for prayer. There was a trestle in the middle which, Kelly guessed, held the coffins for viewing. He closed the door.

'Do you cover all denominations? All religions?' she asked.

'We do, we prepare it, depending on what the family wants. We had some devout Christians in yesterday so that's the bible on the altar, and we play music if they want.'

'It's very peaceful. Was Victor religious?'

'I reckon so. He always crossed himself when we accepted a new body.'

Kelly knew that Christianity forbade suicide but that didn't mean that a believer wouldn't contemplate it. Ex-communication of the eternal soul wasn't something most modern churchgoers were afraid of any more. Faith had lost its lustre, and events like this merely reignited a sense of ceremony. They'd had a church service for her mother though, to this day, she had no idea if that's what she wanted, they just supposed. Kelly reckoned that if more families had conversations about death, it might alleviate the situation for those left behind.

'It's amazing, I feel calmer just being in here,' She said.

Bill relaxed. 'Isn't it?'

'Did Victor only come in here as part of his job?'

Bill's brow wrinkled. He crossed his arms. 'Erm, no, actually, he often came in just to sit. I hadn't thought about it before you mentioned it.'

'Well, I'm not surprised. It's comforting somehow.'

Bill stared at the altar and thrust his hands in his pockets. She hoped he was less stressed dealing with customers.

'What brought you to the trade, Bill?'

'Victor was a good man. He looked after local people, giving them jobs and the like. It's a shock. He was the soul of this place.' Bill paused and looked to the altar, as if expecting answers from it. 'When my pa passed away, Victor gave me a job. To be fair, I helped out when I was a nipper, a lot of us did. You tend to find undertakers are run by family and friends, we're close. Not like the big firms that have muscled in, like the supermarkets, they've taken the soul out of it. The original ones are still like us. Paul is my brother.'

'And Eric?'

'It's different with embalmers, they're like gold dust. Highly trained. Eric has a degree, you know.'

Kelly nodded.

'We found him through Ads, he's worked with us for about ten years.'

'Did Victor's children not want to work in the family business?'

Both of his adult children had yet to turn up to support their mother.

'Nah, they were born with good heads on their shoulders. They're clever as you like, both got good jobs.'

Bill sounded apologetic.

'What's through there?' Kelly pointed to the only other door in the room.

'That's the cold storage room.'

Bill led her through the door and inside was plainer. Trolleys and trestles lined one side, then two walls were lined with the fridges. It was similar to a mortuary set-up.

'We're fairly average sized, and Victor never wanted to go bigger, else you lose the personal touch. We can store forty bodies in here at a time.'

Kelly knew that they weren't alone, and chances were that most of the fridges were probably being used right now. They were higher spec than the ones in Ted's mortuary, but then, she supposed that was because members of the public might be invited in here under some circumstances. They looked like larders and were white rather than stainless steel like she was used to in Ted's world. It made the room more domestic somehow. The only colours in this room were the lights telling them the fridges were kept at 5 degrees. Bill took her through another door.

'This is the mortuary. Eric's on a break so it's nice and tidy.'

He meant there were no bodies on show.

The room was like a lab, and much the same as Ted's but without the machinery and weapons to invade and eviscerate. The processes in here were more dignified, though Ted was always respectful of his patients too. There were cabinets full of liquid and tubes and she knew that this was where the dead were laid out and embalmed, a process that replaced their bodily fluids with a formaldehyde solution. Several folding screens were dotted about the room, and she was told by Bill that the embalming tanks were kept there.

Kelly couldn't help feeling relief that the room was clean, fresh and well kept, and it said a lot about Victor's practices.

They walked back through the cold storage and out of the chapel, back to where Eric and Paul were chatting with Dan.

'Round the back is where we store the vehicles. We've got three hearses, five limos, two private ambulances, and of course the staff cars.'

Kelly nodded.

'Did any of you see Victor last Thursday?' she asked.

'No, he was supposed to work as normal, he always came in around eight, but he didn't show up. It was Eric who called Irene about ten in the morning. We thought he might have forgotten an appointment he was attending, or something. Irene said not to worry, but he didn't show up all day, or the next one.'

'And you worked together every day?'

They nodded.

'You knew Victor well. Did he seem out of sorts lately?'

The men looked at one another.

'Aye,' it was Eric who spoke. Bill and Paul bowed their heads.

'Ever since we buried Ethel.'

'Ethel?'

'His mother-in-law.'

Bill nodded. 'She died a couple of months back. It's not unusual for a funeral director to prepare and bury their own relatives, it's an opportunity to make sure they're treated with the utmost dignity.'

'I'm sure it is, I understand.'

'But he went quiet after that, distant like,' Bill said.

'And you all noticed?'

They nodded.

'Do you mind me asking how she passed?' Kelly asked.

'Old age,' Eric said. 'It was her time, but it hit Victor bad. He insisted on being involved in every stage of her passing. He wasn't the same.'

'Forgive me if I'm mistaken, didn't Victor handle his own parents' deaths too?'

Eric nodded. 'They were my first.'

'Ah. So, again, forgive my ignorance and rudeness if I appear blunt, but am I to understand that his mother-in-law's passing affected him in a more profound way than the deaths of his own parents?'

'That's what we said,' Paul said. Bill nudged him.

'So, they were very close?'

'Suppose so,' Bill said.

'So did Vic commit suicide?' Eric asked.

Bill batted him on the arm. The question sat awkwardly, and Kelly could tell that he asked it on behalf of Bill and Paul too. They looked to her for an answer.

'The coroner hasn't ruled a cause of death yet, and it's my job to aid him,' Kelly said.

'So, anything that you might think of that could help is most welcome, chaps.' Dan spoke up and the three men listened to him

75

intently. Kelly wished she could shut up rooms full of men like that.

'The Morningside family has been one of our best customers, especially since Prudence died and gave permission for the home to use the chapel. It doesn't make sense to me,' Paul said. Bill stared at him. Everybody waited for Paul's explanation.

'Well, you know, there are easier ways to do it.'

'Shut up, Paul,' Bill warned him.

'I was just saying, I mean we have a lab full of chemicals to do it, don't we?'

Chapter 15

Morningside Nursing Home was a short diversion south, off the
A66, on the way back to Penrith, from Keswick. Kelly tried
to hide her concern over the fact that Mary had moved into it
this morning. Secretly, popping into the home to meet Beryl
Morningside, Victor's business partner, was also a way of checking
up on her friend. What harm could it do? Besides, Dan welcomed
the delay getting back to the office.

The road was one Kelly usually took to Ullswater when she
and Johnny fancied a simple hike, behind Martindale, or a dip
somewhere along the Ullswater Way. The land either side of the
winding route was non-descript, and before yesterday, she hadn't
taken much interest in it. It was flanked with forest and gently
rolling hills, and she had previously been unaware that one family
owned it all, even less that it boasted a fully working mine, and
an ancient stone circle. Cumbria was full of surprises.

She'd pressed Ted on what he knew of the fallout between
the brothers. He told her that Percival Morningside had been
a war hero who approached his farmland like an attack on a
pacific island against the Japanese: with boundless aggression.
She considered the difference between parenting then and now.
The Victorian belief that kids needed a firm hand was outdated
now, but in Percival's era, it dominated. That generation had lost
everything, and it rendered them desperately hard.

But she reserved judgement. From what she'd seen of Samuel
so far, he'd come across as cold but nothing more. She had yet to
meet Arthur.

She missed the turn and had to perform a U-turn in the middle
of the road: a common Lake District pursuit. They found the

correct one and the car bounced as the terrain went from tarmac to layers of concrete slopped across a field. Hasty wooden signs warned them the land was private. Herdwick sheep stared at them in their uniquely ironic way. Dan held onto a roof handle. Then they came to the road for the nursing home and felt the difference in investment instantly. The sweeping drive was a beautifully tasteful compliment to the surrounding countryside. This side of the farm, to the north, was a vista of woodland and rolling hills, and the nursing home was made of local stone, only two storeys high, making the most of the scenery. Samuel's side appeared more of a working farm, which it was.

'Not a bad way to sit out your last days,' Dan said.

Kelly didn't answer. It was just what Mary had said.

'It's a gorgeous setting, that's for sure. I don't like them myself. They're so final, don't you think?'

She was aware of Dan nodding in the passenger seat. 'Aye, and they smell of old people dying.'

The honesty stung Kelly. The thought of Mary ending up in the hands of Dale & Sons was disconcerting. They parked up. There were chairs on the terrace, for gazing across the mountains on a fine day, like today. It was a place for contemplation.

The staff were welcoming and the place smelled clean, this was a good sign. She'd heard plenty of horror stories, like everyone else, of unkempt and underfunded homes, where the staff were overworked and even cruel. The rooms were light, with shafts of sun cascading across the floors thanks to the magnificent high ceilings in the atrium.

She introduced herself to the woman sat at reception and Dan nosed about, eyed closely by the receptionist, whose brow furrowed when Kelly showed her lanyard.

'I'll go and see if I can locate Mrs Morningside, I'm not sure if she's on shift today.'

The woman trotted off and Dan raised his eyebrows. Kelly tapped the countertop with her fingers. Surely everyone knew if the boss was in or not. Kelly smelled the distinct aroma of bullshit.

The woman soon reappeared, smiling.

'I'm sorry, she's not in until this afternoon.'

Kelly eyed her. 'Fine, while I'm here, can I see Mary Ellery?'

A shadow crossed the woman's face again and Kelly knew she was dealing with an employee who didn't much like work.

'I'll tell her you're here.'

The woman walked away again, and Dan told her he'd wait outside. The woman soon came back and beckoned Kelly along a corridor. She found Mary in her room chatting with a nurse, who smiled warmly when she came in.

'Kelly!' Mary said, turning to the nurse. 'I told you I'd have a visitor today.' Mary beamed. The nurse left them alone and Mary showed her around excitedly. Most of her things had been put into storage, but her most treasured possessions had a place in her new room, which was small but comfortable. Mary had been used to a whole house, full of children and noise most of her life, until they left, and tragedy struck. She'd been widowed forty years ago and never remarried, but she took a black and white photograph of her wedding with her to the home.

'And this is Alice and Cecil,' Mary told her, pointing out her children.

Kelly found it poignantly depressing that all that was left of Mary's life were a few framed photos and a warm blanket, some books and a bedspread, but it was also a reminder that everything we need is right here with us. The things we collect are but elements of passing time. The most important thing was that Mary looked happy, as if this was the right move for her. It eased Kelly's whirring mind.

'What a cracking view,' she said to Mary, peering out of the window. She could see Dan staring out to the coast, and beyond. She felt as though she was spying, suddenly, and turned away.

Mary was dressed simply in a dark purple woollen skirt and soft pink jumper, with a scarf wrapped around her body. It picked out the tones of her skirt and jumper, as did her choice of jewellery today. She looked elegant and of her time, and it warmed Kelly to

79

see that Mary appeared comfortable. She looked as though she'd been living here for years.

'Isn't it? That's all their land so I can walk out there whenever I please. You know what's funny?' Mary asked. 'I've always wanted to live in the countryside like this. I just never thought it would take ninety-six years to get here.'

Kelly placed her hand tenderly on Mary's arm and they peered out of the window together.

'I like your room,' Kelly said.

'So do I. It's big enough. I've got my reading chair, and there's seating out there. Look, let me show you the terrace.'

Kelly followed her out of the room. She knew better than to offer help. Mary was fiercely independent. She didn't even need her walker – she seemed to have gained a new lease of life from the move. They passed others in the corridor, most younger than Mary, and less mobile. To look at her, one wouldn't think that Mary could easily make it all the way out to the terrace. Her body was bent, and she shuffled lightly as if skimming the floor. She was a good foot and a half smaller than Kelly though Kelly suspected that thirty years ago, she'd taken up more space, and commanded more attention. Still, Mary exuded a life well lived.

They came to the sitting room where residents sat reading, or by the open fire – with a guard of course – or taking tea. The place possessed a certain peace that was welcome in Kelly's frenetic life. She guessed it was because the people in here had lived all of theirs.

They went through one of the bi-fold doors, and Mary beckoned Kelly to follow. Kelly waved at Dan, who swivelled around. She gestured to him to join them.

'Who's that?' Mary asked.

'He's a detective. We've been in Keswick working, Dan was with me. Let me introduce you.'

Dan walked towards them and towered over Mary.

'You're a handsome chap, you look after Kelly?'

Dan laughed. 'I do, ma'am.'

'Good. Sit down, I need to make sure she's consorting with the right types.'

Kelly smiled at Dan and allowed Mary to interrogate him. Dan had a warm manner with the older woman, and she sat listening to him defend his position as Kelly's back up, reassuring Mary that she was in safe hands should she need them. It was a habit of Mary's generation that women were in need of a man to take care of them, or at least that's what they were told. The irony was that Mary had got along just fine without one for decades.

The sun was already low in the sky, typical for the season. It was as if it had run short of fuel, and struggled to reach the dizzy heights of summer, but it was still powerful and warm. There were blankets on all the seats.

'Will you pass me a blanket?' Mary asked Dan.

He reached for one obligingly and Mary took it, wrapping it under her knees. Kelly smiled at Mary's flirting.

'That's better. That's a long walk but not too bad. You must be busy, I don't want to keep you both. You have an extraordinarily important job. Now, I've heard the gossip, and I know you're probably keeping it from me. The man in the quarry?'

Mary stared at both of them, and Kelly got an inkling of what it might have been like to have been one of her children.

News travelled fast.

'What gossip might that be?' Kelly asked. 'And, yes, we're on our way back to the office.'

'He tossed himself off a cliff, not far from here. The undertaker, Victor. You know I used to go to dances with Percival Morningside. He was a pig of a man. Threw his weight around, typical landowner, thinking he was high and mighty. I had a lucky escape there. But Victor was nice.'

'You knew him?'

'Of course, he arranged my move here, and gave me some financial advice. He's – he was – an expert.'

Kelly raised an eyebrow in Dan's direction.

'Such a shame. Life really isn't as dramatic as all that, what a waste.'

81

Dan hid a smirk. Kelly reckoned everybody could do with a bit of Mary's pragmatism; it'd make their job quieter.

'They're all a bit young in here, and a bit nutty. I think I'm the only one with all my faculties if I'm honest.'

'Well, that doesn't surprise me. Do you think you'll have anyone sane enough to keep you occupied?' Kelly asked, grinning.

'I'm not sure. The nurses are very nice. I'll make the best of it, and I've got my books. Kelly, go and ask for some tea. And the biscuit tin, it's in the sitting room,' Mary said.

Kelly left them staring at the view, and went to find refreshments. She was directed to a kitchen and poured hot water from an urn into a teapot. But there was no milk in the fridge and so she went looking, taking the opportunity to catch a glimpse of the place behind the glossy affectation. It wasn't that she had a cause to worry, more her natural questioning of things. Her mind was geared towards the underbelly of anything she saw. When faced with any veneer, she felt herself drawn to scratch off the surface to see what was underneath. She wandered blankly into an office and apologised when she saw two nurses filling out paperwork.

'Oh, I'm sorry, I'm looking for milk,' she explained.

'No worries, it happens all the time. I'll get you some milk,' one of them said, walking past her. The other went back to her work. Kelly waited awkwardly, surveying the box files on shelves above their heads.

'Dear God, somebody help me,' a voice gasped behind her. Kelly swivelled around but soon realised that it was just another member of staff, carrying boxes. The other nurse went to help her.

'I've got it Beryl,' she said.

Kelly turned to her. 'Beryl Morningside?' she asked.

'The same,' the woman snapped, tossing the boxes onto the floor.

The nurse manager took up all the space in the room, making Kelly feel like a common lay person, like medical employees sometimes liked to do. It was one of those rhetorical encounters with a member of a professional body that was designed to make the uneducated contrite in the face of superior authority. Kelly forced a smile and reached out her hand.

'Detective Inspector Kelly Porter. I was told you weren't on shift until this afternoon.'

Beryl Morningside stood up and placed her hands on her hips, examining Kelly as if she were a prospective employee. Fat chance. She shook her hand limply.

'Well, I'm definitely here, as you can see, but I'm not officially working. Can I help you?'

'Can we speak in private?'

Beryl slapped her hands together, getting rid of invisible dust and nodded, taking her out into the corridor and to another room. She beckoned her inside and closed the door. Kelly found her extraordinarily haughty, and entirely disinterested in why a detective might want to speak to her. The woman's hands still rested on her hips. Her hair was scrunched up on top of her head and she wore jeans and a dark T-shirt, which had smears of dirt on it. But she looked fit for her age, which Kelly guessed around fifty-odd. Kelly had clearly interrupted some sort of clear up.

'It's about Victor Walmsley, your business partner.'

'Ah. Yes, God rest his poor tormented soul. I'm trying to go through our papers to see where this leaves me.'

Kelly had met people like her before. The woman had no time for emotion and got down to business before taking a breath. She must have been a formidable partner.

'We're gathering information at the moment, about Victor's movements last week.'

'No idea, he left me high and dry.'

'Was he concerned about the business?'

'Victor wasn't a talker. He had no reason to worry, but obviously he did.'

'How long were you partners?'

'Five years or there abouts.'

'And he dealt with all the nursing home funerals, is that correct?'

'Correct.'

'Any debts?'

'Not with me.'

Beryl wiped her brow with the back of her hand.

'When was the last time you saw him?'

'Just before he took off.'

'And how would you describe his mood?'

'Not suicidal, but who knows? I'd suggest being married to Irene wasn't a walk in the park.'

'What do you mean?'

Beryl sniffed and shrugged. 'I mean she's draining. She's one of life's moaners. Complains about everything. I imagine Vic was under a lot of pressure to keep her happy, but never quite did. Sorry, that's none of my business, just an observation.'

'Any other observations?'

'He looked ill.'

'Really? You mean seriously ill? Was he seeing a doctor?'

Beryl shook her head. 'No, Vic was very private. But he was slowing down, and he looked – how shall I put this – yellow, you know? Like liver disease or something. I asked him and he wouldn't tell me. Like I said, he was very private.'

'I might need access to your shared business files in the near future, depending on our inquiries,' Kelly told her. 'It'd be much easier, and quicker if you gave us permission to access them voluntarily.'

'Why is there an inquiry? I thought it was suicide. Open and shut.'

'We're keeping an open mind until the coroner completes his report.'

'Of course, anything to help. Are you the Kelly Porter who is Mary's friend?' Beryl asked.

'I am. I'm supposed to be fetching milk for her tea. She's out on the terrace talking to my colleague.'

'Lovely lady,' Beryl said. 'I'll get your milk,' she said.

They left the room and Kelly watched Beryl Morningside disappear into another room, reappearing with milk. Kelly took it.

'We'll look after her. She knows what she wants,' Beryl said, walking away.

Kelly took the milk and went outside, where a nurse had delivered the tea. As she walked towards Dan and Mary, she could hear them laughing. If she was looking for an excuse to be worried about Mary's welfare at her new home, she hadn't found one.

Chapter 16

The glorious sunshine across the mountains couldn't shift the feeling inside Kelly's guts. It was a short ten-minute drive across the M6 to Penrith and she dropped Dan at Eden House before heading to the hospital mortuary to see her father.

As she parked, a notification from Kate told her that Victor Walmsley's car had been found, abandoned in a lay-by that was a popular walking start for the hike up Great Mell Fell. A member of the public had called it in this morning. Kelly did a quick reckoning in her head and roughly estimated that it was about three miles away from the Morningside Farm quarry. In other words, it was walkable. And it was also a breath away from where she'd turned in the road with Dan this morning. She pictured the land around it. It was about as isolated as anywhere in the national park. She called Kate.

'DS Maguire is here,' Kate whispered. 'What do I do with him?'

Kelly pretended she'd forgotten about his arrival, but the truth was that she was glad to be out of the office when he turned up. She wanted to see how he fitted in, rather than have to babysit him.

'He's a DS, fill him in and get his ideas, if you have time.'

'Poor bloke is a bit lost, but I've taken a shine to him,' Kate said, softening Kelly's manner. It wasn't his fault he'd been sent there.

'Put him in charge of handling the car,' Kelly said. 'And apologise for me,' she added guiltily. At least she'd be able to see his limits, walking into the middle of this mess. Besides, she'd be there soon enough.

'That's quite a hike for Victor from the quarry,' she said, going back to the news of the car.

The area around Great Mell was muddy and boggy farmland. But then she remembered Victor's shoes, which were immaculate, like his general attire. His suit, apart from the obvious tears due to the trauma suffered by his body, had looked clean and in good shape. Not the kind of appearance one might expect from somebody hiking three miles over hills and across streams, and through sheep shit after abandoning a car, just to throw yourself off a quarry face. She knew a few closer and more accessible crags in the area, especially around Aira Force further down the road, that would do just the same job.

And Victor wasn't a walker. He was too busy, Irene told them. Too busy with the dead to have a life himself.

'We're tracing the car's movements to see if we can work out how it got there. Though we'll be lucky to get any CCTV footage round there. I'll arrange statements from all staff at the mine, as well as house calls along the Dockray Road, not that there are many.'

Of the few farmhouses nestled in among the scrub, they both doubted one might have CCTV but they had to check.

'I know the lay-by,' Kelly said. 'There's space for about four cars. It's tiny, he must have been seen. And why go in a suit? It would have taken him hours to reach the quarry from there, I don't buy it.'

'Yep, that's exactly what Emma said. She and Dan are discussing it now. In fact, Dan has told me to tell you that if you say it's beautiful up there…'

'It's not as beautiful as the Highlands,' Kelly finished her sentence. Dan liked to remind them of Scotland's beauty whenever he could.

Kate lowered her voice to a whisper. 'He seems to be getting on with Fin ok. They're talking about football. I think they've bonded over Scotland and Ireland having both been invaded by the English.'

Kelly chuckled and Kate returned to her usual volume. Fin descended from the Republic of Ireland and the fact that he'd found something in common with Dan, even if it was their common animosity towards English heritage, comforted her. She didn't give a damn about politics or history, and so the happy union was welcome.

'There is some good news. There's a blind spot on the A5091 which can be lethal, the National Trust installed a camera last year so if he drove in from the north, he'll be on it,' Kate told her. 'I remember there used to be a guesthouse down there too, near Troutbeck, where the road turns off. I can't remember the name,' Kate added. 'I'll look into it. And the press department wants a statement. "Unexplained death" isn't holding water and apparently Irene is being harassed at home. It's caught some local interest, Victor was well known, and liked to court attention, so his sudden death has caused a few ripples. He's a bit of a local celebrity.'

Kelly found the image of an A-list undertaker curious.

'I'm at the hospital now, so I'm hoping the coroner has some preliminary answers for me. Can we hold them off by saying this is procedure, and not to jump to conclusions, and respect privacy of family etc... Damn, and maybe not use the word jump.'

'Yeah, I'll cobble something together. And I'll find something for Fin to do.'

'See you later, then.'

They ended their call. Kelly locked her car and headed to the main entrance of the hospital. She'd been inside the massive memorial to the sick and dying more times than she cared to remember. She'd said goodbye to her mother here. If there was one saving grace when somebody loses their battle with cancer, it's that the coroner isn't involved. A GP can sign a death certificate with carcinomatosis... and that's that. Wendy didn't end up on Ted's slab and Kelly was forever thankful for that. As she imagined Ted was too. There was no way that Ted would ever be expected to examine a loved one, but at that time it wasn't well known that they'd once been lovers. Rekindled after forty years of secrecy.

She walked through the foyer and grabbed a coffee from the shop close to the lifts. As she turned around, a young man caught her off guard and she almost dropped her coffee cup.

'Kelly Porter, can you comment on the Victor Walmsley case? Did he commit suicide? I believe there was a note?'

Kelly stopped in front of him, not that she could get around him anyway because he blocked her track. She stared at him. He must have been about twenty years old, straight out of college, no doubt sent down here to track her down because the paper knew she'd be overseeing the autopsy.

'Which paper are you from?' she asked.

The kid seemed encouraged and smiled.

'*The Gazette*,' he said.

It made sense, they all knew her there. He'd obviously been given her photograph and told to wait here until she turned up. He smiled at her, and she felt pity for him. She almost told him that he was in the wrong profession, that his interference could often put more lives in danger than they saved, if they ever did that. She wanted to tell him to go home to his mother, have a good meal and find another job.

'There really is no point you hanging around here. I have no comment, you can contact the press office at Eden House.'

His face fell and she realised that she'd just given him his first setback. He didn't yet understand how these things worked. She walked away, irritated, and took the lift down to the basement. She put down her bag and coffee and washed her hands, before placing a mask over her face. She saw that Ted had left a small pot of Vicks out for her and she took it, smearing some under her nostrils. She drained her coffee, knowing she wouldn't fancy any of it inside the mortuary room. She went through the steel doors and felt the chill. She was glad she'd worn a walking jacket, which she zipped up.

Ted turned towards her, and she could see his eyes soften above his mask. She waved and took a steel stool close to him.

The timing of her visit couldn't have been worse, as Ted reached for his saw. Kelly saw that Victor Walmsley's head was already elevated by a special headrest designed for one purpose only, and that was so the physician could better access the chest and neck when cutting it open. Ted had already done this. She'd seen the Y incision plenty of times before, but it always caught her by surprise. It was the reason she preferred not to open tins of food. Johnny did it for her.

Ted removed his mask.

'I've got plenty to tell you,' he said.

She raised her eyebrows. She struggled to move her eyes from the exposed cadaver but forced herself to look at her father.

'The most important information I guess you want is that he was alive when he hit the ground. However, he has a few ante-mortem scars and wounds that are unexplained.'

Thankfully, Ted put down the saw and spent some time showing her what he meant. He showed her the IV punctures and the imprints across his face and Kelly asked him for a possible hypothesis. She tried not to stare at Victor's wounds around his shoulder and head area too closely. Ted was a scientist, and so he didn't theorise, however he knew that Kelly had to start with factual probability, and work backwards, ruling theories out one by one. They worked in quite opposite ways, but both desired the same outcome.

'I can't tell you what it all means but I can tell you that shortly before he died he had several injections, possibly even via cannula – I can see indentations around one of the sites that would support this. The imprints around his face I would suggest are dressings for the bruises underneath that have begun to heal. It's my opinion that the key to how they came about will be found in his movements over the last week of his life.'

'In other words, when he was missing. But no one has any clue where he was,' she said.

'Quite. That's your job.'

'I still wouldn't swap,' she said. 'His car has been found about three miles away from the quarry. Have the clothes been bagged and tagged already?'

'Three miles away by road?' he asked.

'No, over hills and bogs.'

'Yes, they've been processed, but I can tell you right now that they show no signs of having been worn by somebody who was out for a hike over boggy terrain.'

Chapter 17

Instead of heading to Eden House, Kelly drove back to Keswick, directly to Irene Walmsley's house. It was easily justifiable, but in the back of her head, she also knew that she was avoiding meeting Fin Maguire.

The press outside Irene's house had been placated with cups of tea from the family liaison. They milled about like vultures waiting for a titbit of news. Victor Walmsley's standing in the local community, Kelly was quickly learning, made good copy and it seemed that everybody wanted to know what had happened to him.

She parked a street away and walked up the hill to the Walmsley house situated at the end of an exclusive cul-de-sac. The house was large and handsome: a reminder of the profit of his trade. Everybody died.

There were around seven reporters sitting on the opposite side of the road, talking into phones and generally keeping themselves busy during long spells of barren news. It was a reporter's life: boredom punctuated with potentially career-changing moments in time. The young chap she'd seen at the hospital was there and she turned away from him just as he recognised her. She knew her presence would cause a fuss, but she couldn't help that.

She approached the double-fronted façade. The gap between the haves and have-nots was most obvious in the north of England. The house must be worth a few quid, Kelly reckoned as she rang the doorbell, ignoring the shouting journalists.

'Kelly, did Victor jump?'

'Kelly, have you anything to say to the press?'

'Kelly, why did it take a week to find him?'

'Kelly, was it true Victor was having an affair?'

She was prepared to ignore them, but the last question caught her off guard. She didn't show it. Instead, she turned her back and swung the iron knocker on the wooden door. It was answered quickly because Kelly had rung ahead to notify the liaison team. She was ushered in and told that Irene was in the dining room. Kelly knocked lightly on the door.

'Irene? It's detective Porter, may I come in?'

The reply was whispered, but it was affirmative, and Kelly went in, closing the door behind her.

'Why are they asking all these questions? I can't stand it,' Irene said.

She looked haggard and harassed. She was sat on a dining chair staring at the master armchair at the head of the table. Kelly assumed it was Victor's. She remembered her father taking the same spot at their much smaller table and the memory irritated her. Just because a man was given the lord's chair didn't make him a master.

'I don't know, Irene. They've been asked to be respectful, but they always want a story. Try and ignore them.'

'But I don't even know what to tell them because I don't know.'

It was accusatory and Kelly felt it.

'We're going as fast as we can. Unfortunately, the press wants answers before they're there to give.'

'It should be illegal.'

'I agree, but we have free press for a reason. Your husband was a popular figure whose death has created great interest, it's a testimony to how he was regarded around here.' Kelly tried to soothe the widow.

She pulled out a chair and sat down opposite Irene.

The press interest hadn't been expected. Not on this scale at least. Local gossip was an element of her work she'd always struggled with, and it made her job more complex. Interference could skew anybody's processes and she was determined not to let it. But shutting out the noise was easier said than done, especially for a grieving relative.

'I want to ask you a few more questions, Irene, if that's all right. The coroner's exam has raised some issues...'

'Issues?'

Kelly nodded. Irene's already puffy face looked haunted.

'We've also found Victor's car.'

'Oh my, where?' Irene asked.

'It's parked over near Great Mell Fell, do you know it?'

'I've heard of it, it's down by Morningside Farm, isn't it?'

Kelly nodded. 'About three miles away from the quarry.'

'What was he doing out there?' Irene asked.

'That's what we're going to find out. Can I ask if Victor was on any medication?' Kelly tried to make the question routine.

'Heart pills. Blood thinners. Statins. And...'

'And?'

Irene looked down at her skirt and picked at it. Kelly waited.

'He was prescribed anti-depressants.'

Irene blushed.

Kelly acknowledged that the stigma attached to mental battles was real and affected the older generation more than the younger one, simply because they weren't supposed to admit weakness back in their day. It was drilled into their DNA as sure as their hair colour or number of toes. But it matched what the lads at the funeral home had told her this morning. The embarrassment could explain Irene's reticence and contradictory statements.

'It's not something to be ashamed of. Did he struggle with particular worries?'

'I don't know. It got worse as he got older. I put it down to stress.'

'What about money worries?' Kelly asked gently. 'Is that why you told us he was his usual self? It's understandable you wanting to paint a favourable picture of him.'

By way of an answer, Irene swept her gaze around the expensively decorated room, as if to say, really? But that was just as big a red flag for Kelly as anything. Often the wife was kept in the dark if a man controlled the purse strings. She moved on.

'Was he ever administered intravenous medication?' Kelly asked.

'Like in hospital?'

'Yes. Through a vein in his arm.'

'Not that I know of, but he did become quite secretive, he could have had an appointment that I didn't know about. Was he ill?' Irene was giving her more snippets of information each time she was questioned, but Kelly didn't see it as particularly odd at this stage. Family often opened up to them slowly.

Ted had already confirmed with Kelly that Victor's medical notes showed no recent hospital treatment on record.

'Not that his GP told us. Did he use recreational drugs?' Kelly asked, bracing for the inevitable fallout.

'What?'

No relative likes to think of their loved one as a junkie, but that's not what she was asking. Drug use among those who were deemed respectable inside communities was on the rise and had been for decades. High functioning addicts were in every walk of life, they just hid it well. It was plausible that Victor administered something to take the edge off, in secret. He was in the right business to have access to such things.

'Why are you asking me that? Are you accusing him of taking drugs?'

Irene was suitably horrified but over the years Kelly had seen plenty of family members in the grips of denial.

'I'm not accusing him of anything, Irene. The coroner found puncture wounds in his arms, from needles.'

Kelly held Irene's glare, trying to work out if she knew. It wasn't difficult. Most people were bad liars.

'No. I never ever saw that, or knew about it. My God, what did he inject?'

'We don't know until the results of his tests come back.'

Irene stood up and paced the room. The woman was suffering intensely from shock after shock and Kelly felt sincerely for her.

'I'd like your consent to investigate Victor's financial arrangements. I'd like your blessing,' Kelly said.

Irene stopped pacing and looked at her.

'My blessing? In other words, if you don't get it, you'll look anyway?'

Kelly didn't reply, but she didn't look away either.

Irene tutted. 'Do what you need to.'

The frostiness took Kelly by surprise.

'I'm sorry, Irene. All I can do is try to find out what Victor was doing in the week leading up to his death. It's not personal. I don't want to hurt you, and I wish I didn't have to nose around.'

Irene softened a little and nodded. Kelly glanced around the room. The decor matched the splendour of the outside of the grand house. They weren't short of cash, that much was obvious, which was why she wanted to delve deeper into the state of Dale & Son's finances. This place would take some upkeep. She knew that some people were capable of hiding fantastic amounts of debt to the point of collapse, and she had to consider if that's what they were witnessing here. There was a sense of general wealth in the house, and it wasn't showy, it was subtle, but Kelly saw it everywhere. She knew enough about interior design, from when she'd bought her first house in Pooley Bridge, to spot hidden investment. The table was highly polished and laid with silver, the carpet was a deep shag, the curtains were made from heavy, thick fabric, the mirrors and clocks on every wall were heavy and tasteful, indicating age and quality. And she'd noticed two cars in the drive – both expensive models of Mercedes – as well as further vehicles at the funeral home. Irene wore rings that weren't fashionable or available forty years ago when Victor proposed to her, and certainly wouldn't be worn by most housewives in Keswick.

'Have you eaten?' Kelly asked. Irene shook her head.

'Are you happy to stay in here? Is there anyone I can call for you?'

Another shake of the head.

'When you said that he might have had an appointment that you didn't know about, did he routinely take himself off for what could have been meetings?'

Irene gazed at her, and the hazy aspect to her manner disappeared. Her eyes cleared and Kelly knew she'd hit a nerve.

'What I mean to ask is if he regularly had periods away? I know you told my colleague Dan that he didn't go off for long periods, but were there times when you wondered where he was?'

'I'm not his mother.'

Kelly sensed somebody else's voice asserting itself, as if Irene had been told this by another person, perhaps close to Victor, as a warning.

'Of course, you're not. I must ask, Irene, it's routine with cases like this. Was Victor involved in any other relationships?'

Irene's cheeks blushed again. Kelly felt intense sympathy for the older woman. Their generation didn't discuss things like this.

'No. Never.'

'I'll leave you alone,' Kelly said and stood up and gently opened the door. She turned, and Irene looked up at her.

'Just one more thing, Irene, had Victor hurt himself in the last week before he went missing?'

'Hurt himself?'

'Did he have any injuries you can remember? Did he have a fall, or I mean…' she instantly regretted her words. 'Did he trip, or tell you he'd had an accident?'

'Why?'

'The coroner has identified some bruise patterns on his face sustained before he died.'

'No. The last time I saw him, he didn't have any injuries. I told you he didn't jump.'

'When are your children arriving?'

Irene sniffed. 'Sometime this afternoon.'

'Is there any other information about Victor's life that you want to share with me?' Kelly asked. She gave her another chance.

Irene's face jutted upwards in defiance. Kelly saw in it the signs of a woman in pain, and the agony of loss. But she also picked up on a weariness, as if Irene had been losing Victor for years. The sentiment was in the hesitation, as well as the glance away to a photo on the sideboard, a highly polished piece of mahogany furniture. In it, Victor beamed back to the photographer. He was flanked by several people. Irene got up and stood in between Kelly and her view of the image, so she couldn't see the other people in it. A second passed between them, but she let it go and left the room.

She took the opportunity to peer into the kitchen, to take in the opulent fixtures and fittings, as well as the sitting room, which smacked of the same kind of comfort that only an impressive amount of money could buy. She reserved judgement, because people come across money in many ways. It could be inheritance from Irene's family – perhaps Ethel – or it could simply be that the senior Mr Walmsley had left a hugely successful business for his son to run. Many things could explain wealth and few of them might be pertinent to her investigation. However as Kelly left the house, she held in her mind the fact that Victor Walmsley still worked when he clearly didn't have to, unless there was another reason for it, and statistically, men were far more likely to commit suicide because of financial worries than any other.

Chapter 18

Samuel drove his John Deere Gator across a field. He noticed some of the leaves on the great oak trees were slowly turning orange at the tips. He felt each passing year keenly, and didn't care to count how many he'd spent up here with his father, fixing walls, herding sheep, checking the land and surveying crops. The weight of Percival Morningside's legacy sat heavier than normal today, and he frowned as he approached the perimeter of his farm. He hadn't visited the graves in five years, not since his mother died and he and Arthur had exchanged their final words.

He'd sworn he'd never come back.

Percival and Prudence Morningside lay side by side in matching plots, overlooking the prettiest edges of the farm, which was now divided. The chapel, and small graveyard containing several ancestors, were on Arthur's side. Both brothers had sworn to their mother they'd tend to it after she was gone. Samuel hadn't kept his promise. Guilt tore away at him but he didn't trust himself to wander on to Arthur's land and not lay a hand on his brother if he saw him. But Beryl's visit last night had perturbed him.

The plot was more a giant mausoleum underground and had cost Percival Morningside ten thousand pounds to arrange, even though it was on his own land. The digging, the state-of-the-art zinc liner, ground-breaking – literally – for its time, the consecration – an obscene waste of money in Samuel's opinion – and the ornamental stone over the top, had all mounted up. People said that Prudence died of a broken heart, but Samuel knew different.

His body jerked as the Gator hit uneven ground, but Samuel gained refuge in the assault because it took his body elsewhere, anywhere but where he was going. He still didn't really understand why he was going there, just that he was drawn to it. He told himself it probably needed a tidy up. He knew Arthur could never be bothered, just as he wasn't fussed about much in his life, apart from the visceral loathing of his parents. Samuel realised that he missed the pretty church, which hadn't been functional for decades. Suddenly he felt a need to make sure it hadn't been left to rack and ruin, and he sped up the Gator.

The sun was about as high as it was going to get at this time of year and Samuel wondered at the stone circle on his land, which he drove past in the Gator most days. It had never been excavated or moved, the whole time he'd been alive at least, and before that, his father wouldn't hear of it, nor his father before him. He imagined people from long ago, perhaps in sheep skins, or even the fur of now extinct bears that frequented the woods in legend, or the odd jaguar pelt – who knew what roamed in the ancient woods before people ruined them. He could see their silhouettes dancing and wondered if they were as cruel as people nowadays. He'd heard that primitive tribes were fairer, but their lives more brutal. Their rituals and paganism, littered with connections to the land, appeared simpler and more beautiful than what he witnessed nowadays on the news and before his very eyes. He'd reached the age when all humans questioned their very existence.

One thing was for sure, his life was less lethal with Percival gone. But the same wasn't true of his mother's passing. She'd left a gaping hole in his heart – or where he thought his heart was – and he missed her softness every day.

His only arguments with Gloria were about Prudence. And Arthur. It was always the same. She never let it go. There'd been no money left, just what she had in a box under her bed to bury her with and they gave that to Victor Walmsley for the privilege, despite already having the hole, the venue and the words. All Victor had to do was provide a hearse, a coffin and a few pall bearers and he still charged more than what Prudence had stashed. All the Morningside money was in the land. Resentment bubbled under Gloria's skin, and she couldn't wash it out of her system. Samuel believed that harbouring such feelings made you sick.

'Why did you let him get away with it?' She asked every time.

She knew the answer, but she still had to ask, never getting a reply, just because the sound of her saying it gave her the reassurance she was after, that she hadn't been walked all over like they knew they had. But sometimes, the print of a boot over your face was better than the alternative. Better that than Arthur carrying out his threats. But Gloria didn't see it that way and Beryl visiting last night had brought it all back. Samuel knew that he could go on for the rest of his life ignoring his brother, but women weren't like that: they carried resentment in their DNA. Beryl's visit had rocked their peace, and he didn't know why.

From a distance he could see the stone testimony to his parent's perfection. The permanent monument to their lives, under which their bodies were being mummified, starved of oxygen, inside coffins that would never decay. Samuel couldn't decide what was worse: rotting, being cremated, or – as his parents had decided – being desiccated and immortalised forever in repose. They all equally horrified him. He'd had plenty of morbid conversations with Victor on exactly that topic and he knew that Victor wanted to be rapidly frozen like a harvested pea, then smashed in a machine, and what was left ground to dust. It was clinical, but Samuel couldn't see how it was less painful. Mind you, the dead don't feel anything, or so we're told.

He stopped the Gator and held back, about fifty metres from the perimeter of his land. Beyond it was Arthur's. The church was in touching distance, or that's how it felt at least. He'd expected to face an overgrown chaotic mass of bushes and hedge, planted organically around the resting place, in fact he hoped that his view would be blocked by nature, and then he could use it as an excuse not to go further. But the church looked the same and even the trees were in the same place as when he and Arthur were kids. It was pristine.

He got off the Gator and walked the rest of the way, peering around pensively, expecting Arthur to jump from behind a tree and challenge him. He didn't. He reached the wooden gate and absorbed the peace on the wind. The trees blew gently and majestically, as if beckoning him inside. He could see the words carved into the stone clearly inside his mind.

Dearest father and brother, Grandfather and son...

Cherished mother and Grandmother, always missed and loved...

The irony had choked him up back then and it still did. The words, which were after all just words, were hastily jotted down on the back of a cigarette packet in the pub by Victor, when he'd asked him what other families wrote. They meant nothing and certainly didn't come from Samuel. He pushed the gate and went in, aware that he was technically trespassing. The graves of his family were to the north side of the chapel, where Percival had requested. He'd been adamant about it. He argued that the sun faded the stone over time and to the north face, they'd be protected. It was a silly fancy but when faced with one's own mortality, no one could explain the final wishes of the dying. No one argued with him. Prudence told Samuel years later that she preferred the west side, because it faced the mountains and the sea beyond. There was something about the mysterious vastness that suggested the afterlife to her. It was only when she was buried on the north side, next to her husband, that Samuel remembered her words and felt sorrow for not standing up for her.

He approached the graves.

Flowers hugged the ground either side of the stone. They were perennials, lovingly planted by a stranger to him, unless Gloria did it... No, she wouldn't, surely. Dorian perhaps? Surely not Arthur or Beryl. The bushes on each side were pruned into shapes that complimented the curves of the graves and drew the eye down the hill to the west, between the slopes of Blencathra to the north, and Clough Head to the south. Cradled like two children coming home to their loving maker. The whole scene was nothing short of ceremonial and he cast his eye back to the stone circle behind him, which had watched over the grave – and a great deal more – for dozens of years. Suddenly Samuel wondered who else was buried under the watchful eye of the primeval stones. There must be scores of them, maybe hundreds, this place could have been a village at one time, and the circle where they met to trade, pray, get married and sacrifice goats, or whatever they did.

The tiny hairs on his forearms stood up and he felt as though he wasn't alone, but he pushed the thought aside. He wasn't superstitious. He'd seen too much of the pain caused by real humans to believe that ghosts were even close to the evil wrought by those still alive. He wasn't scared, just curious, and a little spooked. This place had secrets and that's why Percival had chosen it as his resting place. He felt the power of it and fancied himself immortalised, like the arrogant old bastard he was.

Samuel kicked a stone.

He felt like a ten-year-old again, kneeling on the grass, head bowed, rubbing sheep shit into his skin as punishment from his father for not oiling the tractor engine like he was asked.

He faced west and the meeting of the rock, where he knew the A66 cut through – just a valley thousands of years ago. It drew him, and beckoned his soul far out to the Irish Sea. There were no answers out there, but maybe there was redemption.

'Dad?'

Samuel sprung around and spotted his son.

'Dorian?'

Samuel wiped a tear from his eye.

'Gosh the wind gets my eyes up here, what a view!'

'I've never seen you up here, Dad,' Dorian said.

'Aye, I come here now and again, you've looked after the place?'

Dorian shrugged. 'Mam said it was okay.'

'Of course it is pal, you've done a sterling job, just look at this place.'

'You've never been here, have you Dad?'

Samuel bent his head down. 'No, son.'

'I look after it for Grandma,' Dorian said. 'You should come here more often, you don't have to talk to him, just her,' Dorian said.

Samuel looked at his son and back to the grave, nodding.

'Does your uncle Arthur know?' Samuel asked.

Dorian nodded.

'Have you been in the chapel?' Samuel asked.

Dorian shook his head. 'No, it's for Beryl to use for her ceremonies. It's always locked, I tried it.'

'Her ceremonies? What do you mean?'

'You didn't know?' Dorian asked. He gave his father the look which Samuel had come to recognise as the apathetic acceptance that his family didn't talk to each other. He rolled his eyes and pointed around the corner of the chapel.

'It's used by the nursing home, it's their graveyard too, now.'

'What?' Samuel's hands began to shake, and he felt suddenly lightheaded.

'Dad, don't kick off, it's pointless. What do you care anyway? You said yourself you never come here.'

Samuel marched around the chapel, to where his son pointed and stopped dead when he reached the other side, the section which caught the sunshine. The location he would have chosen for his own final resting place, had Arthur let him.

Before him, in ground that he only ever remembered as Morningside earth, a handsome garden had been planted, and memorials were dotted about. One fresh grave was dug, with a plaque above it, which looked at first to be a makeshift headstone, but on further inspection turned out to be an advert.

'Good God!' Samuel swore when he read the details. It boasted of plots for sale right here, in the 'glorious surroundings of God's hand...'

'What the?'

'Dad,' Dorian said.

Samuel felt his son's hand on his arm and turned to him.

'Dad, let it go. It's Arthur's land, you said you didn't want it. You told me you got the mine and quarry instead.'

'But this is where my parents are buried! How could he?' His rage bubbled under his skin and his neck and face turned red, then purple.

'It's not Arthur, it's Beryl who brings them here, and her boyfriend. They're ex-residents, Dad. The land has been legalised for private burial. I suppose Victor is her ex-boyfriend now, too.'

'I can see that! For how much? How much does that blood-sucking bitch charge? Did you say Victor was her boyfriend?'

Dorian didn't reply.

'How do you know all this, son?' Samuel asked.

'You know I see Uncle Arthur when I'm out on the land. Your argument isn't mine, you know that.'

Samuel stared at his son, but he didn't see his face, instead, tears filled his eyes and broke loose, trickling down his cheeks. Suddenly, he felt a well of paternal pride towards him. The lad had handled the last few days admirably. Now, it seems, he was talking to his uncle too, and Samuel felt a pang of jealousy. But he wasn't a lad, he was a man of thirty years old. Here Dorian was, the most mature of them all, with his floppy hair and dirty overalls. Samuel turned to the graves of his parents once again and back to the new plots which were filling up fast with old codgers from Beryl's nursing home who paid God knows what for the privilege, legitimised by Victor for a fee, of course.

'Beryl and Victor?'

'Come on, Dad, everybody knows about them.'

Samuel often underestimated his son. It was to do with the fact that he still lived at home, ate his food and had his mother tend to him. But here, in the sunshine, stood man to man, he realised that Dorian was very much separate from them, with his own life and his own eyes. Samuel nodded.

'Aye, everybody knew, except Arthur,' Dorian said quietly.

Samuel walked closer to the grave of his mother. If he faced the graves, he could avoid looking at the disturbed earth and all the imposters in the ground around the corner, facing the sun. It was too late. Dorian was right. Arthur had been given an impossible task. The lion's share of the profit-making farm had been given to Samuel by a vengeful and brutal man, and Samuel's eternal shame reminded him that he'd been happy about it, cruelly smug, even.

But Percival's plan hadn't worked. Arthur was not only surviving but thriving. Or at least Beryl was.

'I have to speak to him,' Samuel said.

'No, Dad, don't. Leave it. This isn't your property.'

'But the chapel,' Samuel said weakly, knowing that his arguments were in vain. The chapel, the graves, the plot and the consecrated land were Arthur's to do with as he pleased, even if that involved his wife running a small business out of it. He looked at the chapel and saw it in a different light. Next, she'd be doing weddings there. Christ, it had potential. He swallowed what he accepted plainly to be jealousy, and reflected on the toil it took to keep his farm running.

He walked away, back to the Gator, knowing that finally, Percival Morningside had been put firmly in his place. He had successfully driven a wedge between his sons, and one of them had triumphed over the other, but it wasn't the one who Percival had bet on.

Chapter 19

Kelly returned to Eden House and took the stairs. She inhaled deeply, pausing at the door, and entered the open plan office, searching for a familiar face, finding an unfamiliar one. A man with a warm smile and broad shoulders sat comfortably perched on a desk behind Dan, who was working at Rob's desk. He stood up and Kelly walked towards him. Inside, her heart thumped. She stole a glance at Rob's computer, which by rights shouldn't be switched on, but a pang of joy fluttered through her chest, and she knew that Dan was right to sit there. He stopped working when he heard her.

'Detective Porter, it's an honour,' said the new arrival in a soft southern Irish lilt. He held out his hand, which was large and warm, and his touch felt like safety. He was as tall as Rob and possessed the same still assurance. He wore smart trousers and an open shirt too, and smelled of freshness. Suddenly she was torn between liking him and betraying Rob, but she saw that Dan felt it too. He smiled up at her as if to say it was all right.

'DS Maguire, likewise, I believe we met once, in London?'

'It's Fin, ma'am.'

'And it's Kelly.'

'I was a rookie, you cracked the Denton case,' Fin said.

'Wow, that was years ago.'

Memories flooded back from her time in the Met, some good, some not so good.

'I'm learning from the best,' Fin said, nodding at Dan.

'Rob's new software,' Dan said.

She stood behind him and looked over his shoulder and saw that he was studying an excel sheet, designed by Rob, dated four months ago. Rob had written it just before he died. She read the title, and saw that it applied dynamic reasoning, along the lines of the IT system HOLMES, to financial inquiries. One had to input figures and sources from a company or individual, and the software did the rest.

'It's genius,' Fin said.

'He was,' Kelly said. She felt Fin's presence very close to her, and wondered at his brazen confidence.

'So I hear. I want you to know that I have no intention of trying to take his place. I want to fit in.'

Kelly held his gaze and nodded, turning back to Dan. She got the impression from the gritty Scot's demeanour that he'd already had this ice-breaking conversation with the newbie. The initiation process was over. Fin was, for now, welcome in the team.

'Is this widely available?' Kelly asked, referring to the software, and pushing away the feeling that the air had been sucked out of her chest.

'Not that I know of. Rob designed it but never had a chance to share it.'

She stared at the screen and imagined Rob spending hours over it, no doubt relishing the submersion in figures and facts.

'I'm inputting what we have from Dale & Sons,' Dan said.

'We've got their files already?'

Dan nodded. 'They arrived about half an hour ago. Whatever you said to Irene worked like magic.'

'Afternoon,' Kate said as she walked out of Kelly's office carrying a box of cakes. 'How was the autopsy?'

Kelly smiled. Kate's bearing had perked up too and she soon realised why. Fin took a cake and Kate smiled at him.

'Delicious,' he announced.

'I like a man who appreciates sugar and fat,' Kate said.

Kelly watched the interaction and then skewed her team back to the matter at hand, a little too impatiently.

'The autopsy was fascinating. He was alive when he left the cliff face, but Ted's unsure if he was conscious. Looks like he'd been treated recently for something, he had IV marks and bandage indents, which is interesting because Beryl Morningside suspected he was ill.'

'Terminal illness? Keeping it from his wife?' Kate asked, munching on a treat.

'That's one theory,' Kelly replied. 'Dan's using Rob's new software to delve into Dale & Sons, so we might get more answers.'

Kate looked at Rob's screen much the same as Kelly had: wistfully and longingly, as if Rob might appear with a mug of coffee the longer she lingered. But then her brow furrowed.

'That's a lot of funerals, I had no idea so many people popped off around here of old age,' Kate said, peering at the screen. 'It's not Eastbourne.'

They gathered around Dan.

'Have you seen the prices?' Dan said. A Scot with a dislike of parting with cash, he pointed out the costs of the various privileges and add-ons of death. 'Give me one of those,' he said to Kate, who passed him the box.

'Bloody hell, what was that coffin made of?' Kelly asked, pointing to one figure.

'Willow,' Dan said.

'The eco-choice,' Kate said.

'That's what everyone thinks. They're made in China and add six hundred quid to fuel costs and God knows how much carbon to the atmosphere,' Fin said. He'd been paying attention.

'What about that one?' Kelly asked.

'I looked it up,' Dan said. 'This is your Rolls Royce of coffins, American, airtight, thanks to a rubber seal, and made of teak, which lasts eighty years, lined with stainless steel. They call it the mummy-maker.'

'What's that for?' Kate asked, alluding to a ten-thousand-pound fee.

'Grave plot,' Dan said.

'And that? Did they have two?'

'Good question,' said Dan, double checking the information. 'That's the second one I've found.'

'Second what?' Kelly asked.

'Charge of ten grand that I can't explain.'

'Ten exactly?' Kelly asked.

Dan nodded.

'And it went through Dale & Sons from the bereaved family of the deceased?'

'Not quite. The ones I've flagged up are all probate transactions from estates with no beneficiary. I've ordered copies of the wills to cross-reference.'

'So where did the funds go?'

'I'm still working on that,' Dan said. 'I can only see what's coming in and out of Dale & Sons accounts.'

'Was it for the church, or perhaps a wake?' Kelly asked.

'Nope, they're accounted for. I'll keep looking.'

'Whose funerals are they?' Kelly asked.

'Let's have a look. The first is Constance Thorngill, and the other is… Philippa Biden. Mean anything?' Dan asked.

'Nope,' Kelly said. 'Do you have a funeral for Ethel Farrow? She was Victor's mother-in-law, Farrow is Irene's maiden name.'

'Let me see. Rob incorporated a search bar so you can input and search anything, and it'll cross-reference it.'

He clicked the keys. 'Here she is.'

Kelly read the screen, noting the items on the left-hand column, which were paid for, presumably by Victor and his wife Irene. 'Burial plot, ten grand, coffin, fifteen grand, what?'

'Was she royalty?' Kate asked. 'My mother's funeral cost five grand in total.'

'Same, give or take,' Kelly said. 'Search up Prudence Morningside, Samuel told me Victor buried his mother too.'

'Here she is, but her costs are significantly less. Probably because she owned the land.'

'Can you find the accounts where the funds originated from?'

'I think so, with time. It should all be here. Smell a rat, boss?' Dan asked.

'Possibly a very small rodent,' Kelly said. 'It's probably nothing, I'm way behind fashion, these things clearly cost a fortune, which would explain why Victor was so personally wealthy.'

'So why jump off a cliff?'

'What was the date of Ethel's funeral?'

'Fifth of August,' Dan read.

'Victor's colleagues at the funeral home said he began to withdraw after that.'

'I hated my mother-in-law,' Fin said. 'I celebrated my divorce like a graduation,' he smiled. Kate gazed at him and Kelly stared at her, confounded by her friend's descent back to teenagerhood.

'Exactly,' she said. 'Everybody hates their mother-in-law.'

But that wasn't the only thing bothering her about the huge sums of money made by Dale & Sons profiting from the regular funerals of old ladies. Apart from the investigation staring her in the face, her main worry was Mary. How much money she had, and what she planned to do with it.

Chapter 20

'Sign here for me, dear,' Beryl told Mary.

'I haven't got my glasses,' Mary said.

'No bother, the line is here, my love, there we go.'

'So shocking about Victor,' Mary said.

'It is. But it doesn't change a thing here, my dear. We'll take care of you.'

'He was a lovely man. Very handsome. He reminded me of my husband's best friend. We were in love, and Oswald knew it. That's why he married me, to keep me from him.'

'That's nice, Mary.'

'You're in love, aren't you? I can tell.'

Beryl guffawed slightly but recovered her cool and pushed Mary's hand to sign.

Mary took Beryl's lead and held the pen over where she said, signing her name along what she assumed was the correct line.

'Marvellous,' Beryl said. 'Now, let's get you back to your room so you can get ready for afternoon tea.'

Mary took Beryl's arm and the nurse looked away.

'Everything will be all right, you'll see,' Mary told her.

Beryl's body relaxed a little.

'It's why I chose you to send me off. It's a curious situation when one must choose between this or the company of strangers to do the final business, to make sure you're seen on your way, as it were.'

They shuffled towards Mary's room.

Suddenly Mary stopped. 'What if I'm not ready?'

Beryl held her.

'I've got somebody to miss me now,' Mary said.

'The policewoman?' Beryl asked.

Mary nodded.

'Is your friend planning to visit often?' Beryl asked her. They arrived at Mary's room and Beryl escorted her in.

'Oh yes, until it's my time,' Mary said.

'Oh, come on, now, let's not talk like that.'

'She reminds me of my daughter, Alice.'

'This is Alice, isn't it?' Beryl asked.

She picked up a photo and Mary nodded.

'She was travelling the world and seeing things I only dreamt of. She was so brave. She was in Australia, all on her own. Kelly is brave too, I can see these things.'

'I know you can, Mary. We're your family now,' she said.

'Alice had the wanderlust,' she said to Beryl, who allowed her to tell her stories, listening patiently. She patted her hand as Mary hung on to her arm. 'She shouldn't have got in the car,' Mary said wistfully.

'Do you need a blanket and your handbag to take to the sitting room? It's all about comfort here at Morningside.'

Beryl distracted her.

'I've heard that. How about a whisky?'

'Of course, coming right up. How do you like it?'

'A splash of water.'

'Done. I'll get it brought out to you, are you going to sit with Winnie again?'

Mary nodded and smiled. Winnie was her first friend in the home, though it was a somewhat one-sided relationship. The woman hadn't spoken once, but she could nod her head and smile, and she'd developed her own sign language for the staff, who understood her. Winnie was seventy-eight years old, but looked older than Mary, though when Mary thought in terms of comparisons, she realised that anyone older than her would be approaching three digits. Age meant little after half a century. She remembered her sixties and seventies like dreams as if they were chapters of a book, tossed aside and picked up occasionally by accident. Those decades seemed a lifetime ago.

'And that's Cecil,' Mary said, pointing to her son in another photo.

'I know, what a handsome chap,' Beryl said.

Beryl gathered her things then took her to the sitting room, where she settled her into a seat, at a table next to Winnie, and brought a blanket.

'I'll go and get that whisky,' she said.

'I like afternoon tea already,' Mary said.

Winnie's eyes were bright and engaged and Mary wondered if she knew where she was. Most of the residents in here milled about and chatted quietly as if they were repeating the same reels of life over and over, not really anchored in the moment. She was the only sane one in here. Her conversations so far had been snippets of names, dates, and memories of long ago, and her most lucid transactions came from the staff, who she told jokes to and entertained with what wit she had left, surprising herself with how much she remembered. Most of it was about the war. Funny how her generation remembered the 1940s as 'the war' but there had been so many since. Still, everybody knew what she was talking about.

She liked Winnie, even if she was a little vacant. Winnie had been a mere babe in arms during the war, but still, she was a good listener.

Mary looked out at the well-tended grounds, and towards the mountains, and reminded herself that this was her first day here in her new home. She considered how she felt. Mary accepted that her main emotion was resignation rather than excitement. She'd lived through too many house moves to remember in her long life. Now, as she gazed out over the fields and the forest at the bottom of the valley, she recalled her first, the one she'd shared with her husband. It was amazing how she remembered him as he was when they first met, a lot more than she did when he passed. The black and white – now more sepia – photo on her bedside cabinet showed a stiff, smart man in uniform. But she remembered her life in colour, the way he carried her over the threshold of their house when they were married, to their bed for the first time.

Winnie broke her reverie by pointing to the forest. Mary followed her gaze and saw a truck travelling down the track towards the woods. Mary smiled and to her surprise, so did Winnie. Perhaps this was Winnie's favourite view, she certainly hadn't moved from the spot much since Mary had arrived.

A nurse brought tea and placed a plate of biscuits on the table. It wasn't afternoon tea at Fortnum & Mason but she guessed it would do. Soon, another nurse placed a whisky in front of her and winked – that was better. She took a biscuit and nibbled it. Dentures were a bother, plus her tolerance for butter and sugar had waned over the years and now her dreams were filled with clotted cream and toffee. A sip of whisky helped her forget how old she was, for now.

Life could be a lot worse, Mary told herself. Every morning she was given another sunrise, she thanked the stars. There was a time – long ago – when she'd thanked God, but that had stopped when her son Cecil died. He'd been nine years old, playing on the train tracks. It was a lifetime ago. Alice never got over the loss of her brother, and travelled to the other side of the world when she was old enough – as a way of running away, physically and emotionally. Mary was too old to run now. Besides, she knew that the world was still the same at the end of the race. It didn't matter how far you travelled, the memories had a way of hitching a ride, so what was the point? The secret was to be content where you were.

She looked at the forest and saw that the truck had disappeared. Winnie was frowning, but still pointing. Mary sipped some more whisky. She had to remind herself that this was a working farm. Beryl had explained it all to her. Vehicles bobbing up and down going about their business was normal, in fact, it kept residents like Winnie occupied.

She sighed. If this was where she'd end her days, then so be it. The view was perfect, and there was plenty to watch. It was her intention to occupy her time by making up stories about those around her, to keep herself entertained. She didn't follow soaps on TV because life was infinitely more interesting.

'Are you all right, Winnie?' she asked.

Winnie looked at her and Mary noticed some spittle at the side of her mouth. She got up, taking a napkin with her, and shuffled to the other side of the table to wipe Winnie's mouth. When she did so, Winnie stared at her and raised her hand to hold Mary's. Her skin was ice cold, but her intentions as warm as a summer's day. And Winnie was crying.

Chapter 21

It had been a long day and Kelly looked forward to getting home, flopping on the sofa, being jumped upon by Lizzie, and enjoying a large glass of red. The trees were on the turn, and all over the Lake District, the summer was dying and giving way to autumn. It was as if liquefied gold, bronze and copper were being poured over the land, covering the lush green and blue that had swathed the hills for months. Soon, burgundy, purple and tan would take over and the leaves would fall, which was pretty much how Kelly felt after a draining day like today.

But her mood was more buoyant than it had been of late, and she admitted to herself this was because of Fin. He'd thrown himself into the team, without ego or reserve, and she liked that. He'd respected their grief but eased it too, by honouring Rob's talent and skill. It had settled the team and she was thankful. After spending most of the week worrying, now she felt relief as she smiled to herself.

It had also lightened the tone around the office, especially Kate's swooning, which had brought them together secretly in the coffee room, whispering and giggling like schoolgirls.

She parked her car and got out, noticing that the sky was turning dark earlier every day. She opened the door and noticed straight away the absence of warmth from the fire, or noise from Lizzie, or the smell of cooking. Johnny must have been called out, she thought. He knew plenty of people to call to take care of Lizzie, should he need, so she wasn't worried. Until she walked into the lounge and saw a woman sat on her sofa, in her favourite place, holding a glass of wine, and reading to Lizzie from one of her favourite books, as Lizzie nodded off next to her.

'Kelly,' Johnny said, and she spun around to see him walking from the kitchen, with his own glass of wine, looking distinctly uncomfortable. He coughed, which was Johnny's way of introducing something awkward. Suddenly she felt funny in her skin, and she braced herself for bad news. She let her bag fall and went to pick up Lizzie from the stranger, cradling her child's nodding head as she did so, and kissing her soft plump cheek. The one-year-old stirred but not enough to fully wake up, and Kelly was bereft because she could have done with familiarity right now, she didn't like surprises.

'I should have put her down for a nap, but she was comfortable,' Johnny said.

The woman smiled and took a sip of her drink. She was around the same age as Johnny – so older than her. Kelly wondered briefly if Johnny had a sister he hadn't told her about. Whoever she was, Kelly knew she was going to learn something new.

'Kelly, this is Carrie, my erm...'

'Ex-wife,' Kelly finished for him. She stood where she was, holding Lizzie, who stirred finally, and nuzzled into her mother's neck.

Carrie stood up and Kelly assessed her as if they were about to run a race. Carrie was petite and soft with age. Her body appeared tired, as if she'd run a marathon. She was barefoot and stood about the same height as Kelly. But her eyes sparkled with warmth and Kelly felt drawn towards her.

'Your daughter is beautiful. I was just telling Johnno how adorable she is.'

Johnno. He'd never revealed his ex-wife's name for him. Kelly kept a straight face. The woman wanted something, and it wasn't her own daughter because Josie was at university. Her mind drifted to her stepdaughter as if readying herself for a battle over Josie.

'Josie isn't due back until December,' Kelly said, as if reminding her mother of her daughter's schedule. 'I'll go and put Lizzie down.'

Kelly tried to be pleasant, but Johnny had told her some unkind things about his ex-wife. She frankly had no time for the woman. Josie had left Carrie to live with her dad when she was only fourteen, which Kelly thought told her everything she needed to know. But this woman before her seemed to challenge that assessment.

'Of course, sorry, I won't keep you. I didn't come to see Josie.'

'Why don't I take Lizzie up?' Johnny said.

Kelly glared at him. *You're not getting out of this one*, she thought. 'No, that's fine, I'll be back down in a minute.'

She took Lizzie upstairs and laid her gently in her cot and tucked her in. Lizzie would likely sleep until around eleven, when she'd need a bottle of milk to get her off for the whole night. Kelly watched her daughter scrunch up her backside and tuck her legs under her body. The night had turned fully dark now.

She closed the curtains softly and sighed.

Johnny had some explaining to do. Her first reaction on realising this stranger was Carrie had been of a fierce mother bear given what she'd been told. Kelly had known hundreds of kids like Josie, estranged from parents. When you got to the bottom of it, it usually was because the child was scared. Josie was a woman now, starting her life at university, and to Kelly's knowledge hadn't spoken to her mother in months. The last instance had been forced by Johnny, when Josie told Carrie about being accepted into university.

Kelly had watched Josie's body language closely during that conversation, when Josie had been on the phone, and it was clear that she found it a distinctly painful ordeal. Kelly had questioned then, the benefit of forcing someone to communicate with somebody simply because of blood ties. Kelly was reminded of her own sister, Nikki, how she'd tried to pretend that the bonds of biology were enough to smooth things over for their mother. But Wendy had seen it, clear as day. It had taken Kelly a while longer.

She also remembered the countless conversations they had about Carrie's behaviour during Carrie and Johnny's marriage.

He wasn't perfect, she knew that, and when he was in the army, he'd been selfish, immature, and not ready to commit to both home and duty, but all that was years ago. She backed away and closed Lizzie's door quietly. She closed her eyes, and her shoulders sank. There was only one question she wanted answered. What did Carrie want?

Vanity and a silly childlike ego made her tiptoe to her bathroom and check her face. What was she looking for? Armour? Something to show that Johnny wasn't the same man he'd been then? A shred of evidence to show that Kelly had created a new life for Carrie's ex-husband and daughter? Her own arrogance overwhelmed her, and she accepted that whatever had passed between Johnny and Carrie twenty years ago was still in a bubble of time she had no knowledge of, and could never change. It was there, like an old bandage over a wound that may or may not be healed.

She went downstairs, after putting on some lip gloss and running a brush through her hair. She also changed into a soft grey tracksuit, which she hoped gave her a youthful edge.

Carrie and Johnny stopped talking when she reached the bottom step and Kelly noticed he didn't look at her.

'So, Carrie, shall we start again?' Kelly said. She reached out her hand and Carrie extended hers, warily, a bit like a suspect.

Kelly sat in the one-seated sofa chair they'd bought to place next to the fire, but there was none tonight.

'No fire?' she asked Johnny.

'I'll start one,' he said.

She observed his relief at having something to do and she realised with a jolt, that it wasn't the first time since Rob died, that he had avoided direct conversation and instead sought distraction. She had interpreted his distance as grief, like her own. They all needed space, but now she questioned if Johnny hid something else as well. Her heart pounded as she remembered only last year, their split over the Ian Burton case.

Betrayal: can it ever heal? Her body screamed at her like it did when she knew a witness was lying. Her discomfort sat on her shoulders like a giant weight, and she wanted to go back to work.

She watched Carrie, who finished her wine, and placed the glass on the coffee table. Johnny had told her that Carrie had a drinking problem and Kelly wondered if that had been a lie. Somebody with an alcohol problem didn't sip pretty glasses of expensive red wine and leave it at that. Was she reformed? Had she sought help?

'I'll dive right in, Carrie, why are you here?' Kelly asked.

'Josie said you had bigger balls than her dad,' Carrie said.

'What?' Johnny swivelled around from his kneeling position in front of the fire. Kelly smiled.

'If it's a welfare check, Josie's fine, but she's eighteen now. An adult.'

'I know,' Carrie said.

Kelly watched Johnny curiously. He'd gone back to lighting the fire and it roared as the firelighters caught. He wasn't in charge. He was rattled. She'd seen glimpses of it before, when his grip on those around him slipped, like Ian Burton, like his daughter, and when Rob literally tumbled from his grasp.

'I'm in a bit of a scrape, actually, we both are,' Carrie said.

Kelly noticed that when she said 'we' she looked at Johnny.

'How so?' Kelly asked. Her skin felt hot under her sweatshirt.

'I'll go and get more wood,' Johnny said, standing up.

'You do that, *Johnno*,' Kelly couldn't resist the dig. She watched him as he left and wanted to shout to ask him what the hell he was doing leaving her with a woman he'd hated for years. He was walking away. Deserting. It was something alien to Kelly. And when she turned back to Carrie, she knew the woman had read her exact thoughts. The look on her face said, *See, this is what I put up with, now do you get it?*

Kelly checked herself. Panic did weird things to people. It was a one-off.

The doorbell rang and both women jumped.

'Excuse me,' Kelly said.

She went to the door cursing whoever was behind it. But when she opened it, her father stood on the step, beaming, with a bottle of wine in one hand and a bunch of exquisite pink roses in the other. His face fell and she realised that she was scowling.

'Everything okay?' he asked.

'Yes, sorry Dad, come in. They're gorgeous, are they for me?'

He smiled and handed them to her, reaching for a kiss. She took them and opened the door wide.

She leant over to him and whispered in his ear. 'Johnny's ex-wife is here.'

He stared at her and she shrugged. 'I've just walked in, and she was sat here with him.'

He took off his coat and hung it in the usual place behind the door and went into the sitting room. Kelly followed behind with the flowers in her hand.

'Carrie, this is my dad, Ted. Dad this is Carrie, Johnny's ex-wife, and Josie's mum.'

Carrie stood up and Kelly struggled to picture her and Johnny together, ever. But then the same might be true on Carrie's part, she had no idea what Johnny had told her. Suddenly fact merged with fiction, and she was cast adrift for the time being. Unanchored.

'Josie is like a granddaughter to me, she's an incredible young woman, I hoped we'd meet someday,' Ted said to Carrie, taking her hand warmly.

Kelly turned away, heading for the kitchen to find a vase for the flowers, smiling to herself and shaking her head at how smoothly her father patched things over. He was a saint, and she couldn't have planned his visit more perfectly herself.

Whatever it was Carrie wanted would have to wait.

She heard Johnny come in from his terribly important log mission and greet Ted with what Kelly heard as absolute relief. She went back into the sitting room and found her father happily chatting away to Carrie about Josie. The look on Johnny's face told her that he'd been saved from the edge of a chasm, for now.

Chapter 22

The small talk in front of the fire was excruciating, and if it wasn't for Ted, Kelly would have gone to bed hours ago, without dinner or pleasantries. They'd all drunk too much wine. She'd found out that Carrie liked walking her dog, though Kelly had no idea where the animal was. She'd also learnt that Carrie had met Johnny at a military ball, hosted by her father, a general. This was news. And she'd learnt that Carrie couldn't swim. Snippets of the woman's life rained down on Kelly and into her wine as she stared gloomily into it, desperate to get the hell out of the situation.

'Where are you staying?' Ted asked.

Carrie looked at Johnny, and Johnny looked at Kelly.

'There's a tenant in the flat,' Johnny said. Johnny referred to his holiday let, which was more or less permanently full.

Kelly kept her lips closed in case thoughts charged out of her mouth like a steam roller and caused irreversible damage.

'Dad has the spare room when he stays,' Kelly said finally.

'I don't want to be a bother,' Carrie said.

'I can get a room at the Crown,' Ted said.

'No,' Kelly said.

'Do you mind the sofa?' Johnny asked his ex.

Kelly glared at him. She knew she was being rude because Ted reached out his hand and placed it on her arm.

'I don't want to impose. It's been a lovely evening. What's the Crown? Is it local?' Carrie asked.

'It's a pub five minutes into the village, I can walk you there,' Ted said.

Kelly felt anger boiling up inside her at the curious human trait of making the very person feel comfortable who was the cause of everybody else's unease.

'Johnny, can I talk to you for a minute?' Kelly asked.

He froze and she realised that she hadn't seen him do that in a long time, if ever. She looked at him. His body was awkward and his face difficult to read. It had been a rocky road to reconciliation. Then she looked at Carrie, who gathered her things up. She wasn't how Kelly imagined a general's daughter.

Kelly went outside to the terrace and Johnny followed.

'What is going on?' she demanded.

'Nothing, she just turned up.'

Johnny spread his hands but even with that innocent pose, Kelly didn't believe him. The realisation was unsettling.

'Did you really expect that I'd want her staying here?'

He shrugged.

'Johnny?'

'Yeah?'

'Look at me.'

He did.

'What does she want? I thought you hated the woman. Why is she here and why are you being so pleasant to her?'

'It'd be rude to have somebody turn up on your doorstep and be offensive.'

'That's not what I mean, and you know it.'

He looked away.

'I owe her money,' he said finally.

'What? Why?'

He sat down on a lounger and exhaled.

'We had investments together. They didn't work out. One of them was high risk.'

Kelly noted his voice change and her tummy flipped over.

'Wasn't everything split during the divorce? Assets and debts?'

He looked at her. Her stomach gurgled and suddenly the red wine sloshed around and made her desperate for the toilet.

'We're not divorced.'

Chapter 23

The next morning, Kelly didn't wait for Johnny to come downstairs. And she didn't prepare him breakfast. She'd spent the night in Josie's room. They'd knocked through the spare room last year, and made it into two, one for Lizzie and one free for Ted to use. His door remained shut and she found it unsurprising that he'd overslept, given the late hour they'd all retired to bed, after too many glasses of wine. He told her that when you reached his age, sleep was overrated, and lie-ins pointless. She'd found it impossible to comprehend at the time, when she was suffering the worst period of sleep deprivation she'd ever known, shortly after Lizzie was born and waking every four hours for milk. It just seemed inconceivable that she could ever not want to sleep.

Now she didn't even want to eat and skipped breakfast. She made sure Lizzie had her cereal and a pot of pureed pear, before she took a deep breath and went upstairs to gently knock on their bedroom door to tell Johnny she was leaving.

When Kelly and Johnny had gone back inside from the terrace last night, Carrie and Ted were gone. Kelly hadn't waited for her father to return, instead, she'd taken a duvet from the spare room, and a pillow from Josie's bed, and hid underneath it in the dark until sleep had come sometime after. It was still dark when she woke, and she knew she'd had a restless night because her head felt foggy. Or it could have been the red wine. She didn't wait for Johnny to answer, she just made sure he was awake and that he knew she was leaving.

'Kelly...' he asked as she turned from the door. But her foot was already on the second step.

Finally, now, during daylight hours, when life buzzed inside her head, she had something to focus on and couldn't wait to get to work. She gathered her things quickly and left the house, hearing Johnny's footsteps on the stairs.

'Kelly,' she heard again, as he came down, but she slammed the door behind her.

As she walked to her car, clarity engulfed her. Closing the front door had severed the bond between her home and work life and she now considered the busy day ahead. She pulled away. The feel of the wheel in her grasp solidified the distance between them.

Penrith was shrouded in drizzle and the mountains behind were hidden under a veil of grey.

Technically, the death of Victor Walmsley was in the hands of the coroner, but Kelly still had to produce a report and interview all those of interest in his life. Today, she'd track down Dorian, who'd found the body, but from first impressions, was either incapable or unwilling to string more than a few words together. It wasn't necessarily a red flag, it could indicate nervousness. From what she'd learnt from Samuel, his only child was somewhat of a recluse on the farm and showed no signs of moving out and getting his own life, despite being thirty years old.

'Morning, boss.'

Kate greeted her as she entered the incident room, covered in a sticky layer of downpour that had worsened as she'd left the carpark. She shook her coat and smiled at Kate. Fin turned around from his place at Dan's desk and smiled.

'Morning. Nice and warm in here,' she said. *In more ways than one...*

'I've managed to pin down Dorian Morningside, he's expecting us at ten,' Kate said.

'Good.'

'Dan and Emma are grabbing pastries, I've been working on the spreadsheet,' Fin told her.

'That's great work. I'd like to take you out to show you around, but we've got a busy morning,' Kelly said.

'I understand, in your own time. Maybe after this is over,' he said. His eyes lingered on her more than a few seconds and Kelly was aware of Kate's stare as she went to her office. Negotiating her friend's sensory powers whenever she was in a delicate mood was tricky, and she wasn't inclined to share her feelings. As expected, Kate followed her.

'Everything okay?' Kate asked.

'Shut the door.'

Kate did so and sat down in front of her boss.

'What's up?'

It was impossible to keep anything from Kate, and she needed to get it off her chest, so Kelly took a deep breath and told her what she'd found when she got home last night. Or, technically, who.

'They're not divorced.'

'What?'

Kelly said nothing because she had no idea what to say. She was still working out her own reaction to the news in her head, it was like wading through mud.

'They have investments together apparently, and I get the impression one has gone tits-up, and the wife is here to collect.'

'How much?'

'I didn't get that far. Johnny's lucky to still have his balls intact at this stage.'

Kate laughed. 'Sorry, it's not funny.'

'How could he deceive me like this?'

'You don't know all the facts.'

'What is there to know? He lied to me. I should never have taken him back after the last time. I'm such a fool.'

'Wait a minute. Take a breath. Let me get this straight. She was there last night, and you haven't had time to talk properly about why?'

Kelly nodded.

'Then you have to at least give him a chance to explain.'

Kelly sat back in her chair, wishing life was simpler.

'Fancy getting breakfast in a shallow attempt to distract you?' Kate asked, standing up.

Kelly smiled and nodded. 'How's Fin getting on?'

'Sterling. And he's not bad to look at,' Kate said.

Kelly smiled at her friend. It was a playful distraction.

'A healthy dose of reverse misogyny first thing in the morning hurt nobody,' Kelly said ironically.

'He's compiled a list of funerals undertaken by Dale & Sons and he's cross-referencing them with the charges and deposits into their business account, as well as the transfers to the Walmsley personal account. He's trying to find any anomalies that might indicate they were struggling, or if they had any significant debts owed. What he has found already is that several of the deceased transferred their entire estates to the nursing home.'

Kelly paused what she was doing and looked at Kate.

'Entirely legal, of course,' Kate added.

'I haven't had Victor's autopsy report yet, Ted is still working on it.'

Kelly thought about her father and how gracious he was to Carrie last night. A flash of jealousy gripped her.

'I'm looking forward to putting this one to bed,' she added.

Kate still loitered at the door. 'It's perked everyone up, hasn't it? Having Fin here,' Kate tapped her fingers on the door frame.

'It has. I think I'll come and work in the incident room for a bit,' Kelly said.

She knew she'd been avoiding it; hiding away from her colleagues, as if that might divert her guilt. She gathered her things and Kate watched her like a hawk.

'Cosy,' Kate said as she walked past.

Chapter 24

Kelly drove along the A66 towards the turnoff to Morningside Farm. The windscreen wipers worked overtime as they strained against the worsening weather. Kate sat in the passenger seat and read out updates from the public appeal for witnesses along the Dockray Road.

The visibility deteriorated further once they turned off at Troutbeck.

'Is Victor's car still in situ?' Kelly asked.

'Fin arranged for it to be towed to the compound this morning, once the area has been searched.'

'We've got time to take a look,' Kelly said.

The land either side of the road was bleaker in the rain. It made everything grey and depressing. Apart from a few guesthouses and pubs in Troutbeck itself, there was nothing apart from Forestry Commission signs all the way down to the turning for Morningside Farm. Looking west, one could be forgiven for thinking that it was neglected marshland all the way to the mountains. Kelly had driven down the A5091 a dozen times in the last few months, and she'd never once stopped to take in the scenery because it was so dull and monotonous. Now it intrigued her.

'What's that?' Kelly asked, peering through the deluge on her windscreen.

'It looks like the guesthouse I was telling you about.'

Kelly had never noticed it before. It was a double-fronted house with a simple sign outside advertising overnight stays and a fantastic cooked breakfast. It had a small carpark.

'Let's go and see if they've got CCTV.'

She pulled in and they ran to the entrance, with their coats over their heads. The simple foyer consisted of a hallway with a desk and a bell sat on the counter with a note attached telling visitors to ring. Kelly did. A woman came out of a door behind the desk and smiled at them. They both showed their lanyards and the woman's face fell, disappointed they weren't punters. The good news was that she confirmed there was CCTV in the carpark, and it was in full working order. The woman was happy to send over the whole file for last week to Eden House and even asked if they wanted a cuppa before they braved the rain again. What she couldn't tell them was if any of her guests had witnessed a lone man walking across the road in the direction of Morningside Farm earlier in the week. For that, they'd have to take all the details of people staying there and contact them individually.

Kate took a screenshot of all the guests for the last week and the week before too, seeing as Victor had been missing since last Thursday. In Kelly's experience, people who were planning on taking their own lives often drove around for days before, and parked up in strange, isolated places to think. They thanked the woman and ran back to the car. It was going to be one of those days when the Lake District punished its visitors mercilessly, with gallons of water sucked up from the great lakes by dark grey clouds, just to dump it back down in a never-ending cycle.

Kate sent the names and contact details through to Fin who said he'd work on them right away.

'He's trying to impress you,' she said.

Kelly glanced sideways. 'He's trying to impress us all.'

They set off again and it wasn't far down the road until the lay-by came into view and they saw a couple of vehicles and police tape through the gloom. They saw that a forensic team was still working around Victor's car. It hadn't been towed yet. Kelly knew they were tackling an impossible job because the rain was their enemy in cases like this. Inside, the car would be preserved, but outside, any detritus or prints would be compromised. A police board had been set up on the side of the road appealing for witnesses to an incident, with a number to call.

'You stay in here, I'll go and see how far they've got,' Kate said.

Kelly watched as her second-in-command ran to the forensic van, where two officers were talking. Kate spoke to them for a few minutes and ran back, spraying Kelly with drops of rain from her jacket.

'They're finishing up. Nothing of note inside the car, they've collected the usual samples.'

Kelly's car was pointed towards the west where the quarry lay across the sloping hills.

'What was the weather like on Tuesday night?' Kelly asked.

'It was gorgeous on Wednesday, wasn't it?'

'Because there was a storm on Tuesday night, I remember the windows rattling.'

'Not a great time to be walking across there,' Kate said.

'Nope.'

Kelly pulled out and they went back the way they came, turning off for Morningside Farm. The tarmac road split and Kelly pointed at the fancy sign for the nursing home, and a smaller one directed them in the opposite direction to Samuel's land. His half was still called Morningside Farm. Arthur's, they noted, had been renamed Promise Farm.

'Nice name.'

Kelly turned her wipers to full speed and strained to see the road ahead. She slowed down and they watched sheep huddling for shelter in groups on the grassland. Finally, the turning to the home of Samuel and Gloria came into view. Hopefully, Dorian would be good to his word and was waiting for them.

He wasn't.

They stood in a pretty farmhouse kitchen, dripping, watched by Gloria as she pulled freshly baked bread out of her Aga. It smelled divine.

'A slice of cake while you wait?' Gloria offered.

'That would be lovely,' Kelly said, thanking her.

'And a nice cup of tea,' Gloria added.

'He's out checking the boundary, he won't be long,' Gloria told them, offering them towels to help them dry and a seat by an open fire in the lounge while they waited.

'He knew we were coming at ten,' Kelly said to Gloria.

The whole house smelled of home cooking and it disarmed them, wooing them with the familiar warmth of maternal love poured into baking tins.

'Dorian's timings aren't the best, and he doesn't wear a watch. I've called him but he ignores his phone when he's out walking.'

'I thought you said he was checking the boundary?'

'Yes, and he's walking. He prefers to walk, though the Gator is so much quicker. He might be in the forest, where there's no signal.'

'Forgive me, am I wrong in thinking that the forest is part of your brother-in-law's land?'

'Yes, it is, but Dorian checks it for his uncle.'

'I don't mean to pry, it might be a sensitive matter, but do the two families have a good relationship?'

Gloria's decolletage reddened.

'Not really, it's difficult to forgive betrayal. But the lad talks to his uncle, if that's what you mean.'

'Thank you, it's always good to have background. That can't be easy, with your farms being so close. I didn't mean to pry.'

Gloria checked her watch and toyed with her collar. Kelly moved on.

'He'll be absolutely soaking in this.'

'He's used to it. Better that than sat at a desk growing old.'

Kelly had to agree with the logic. There was something rustic and historic about the way of life presented by Gloria, and it was the same in all the farmhouses Kelly had been in.

'Where's Samuel?'

'At the mine,' Gloria said. She took a seat opposite them after pouring tea and handing out cake.

'How are the staff holding up?' Kelly asked.

'They're made of strong stuff. There used to be accidents all the time before we made it a commercial venture. Cumbrian folk are hardy, you're not from around here?'

'I am but my accent is a little tame, I lived in London for fifteen years.'

'Hell on earth, I imagine,' Gloria said, smirking. 'What about you? Cat got your tongue or are you the watcher?' Gloria poked fun at Kate.

'You got us there, that's how we work. You know, like the movies, to catch you out and trick you into revealing all your secrets. I'm local too, though the country accent is different to Keswick,' Kate responded.

'City folk.'

Kelly and Kate exchanged a look. Keswick town people being called city folk amused them, but they let it go. Gloria had no doubt lived most of her life out here on farmland surrounded by zero ambient light, and only livestock for noise. Kelly reckoned she could probably kill a pig with her bare hands. She had that wild homestead look about her.

They tucked in and made small talk.

'So, Arthur didn't fancy the farming life? He chose to diversify?' Kelly asked.

Gloria stood up and reached for a slice of cake.

'He believes he was given the unprofitable half of the farm, and he never forgave his father for it.'

Kelly noted her resentment.

'Was it true?' Kelly asked.

'No. A good farmer would have made the best of it. There's plenty of watercress down by the forest, which could have been harvested. Then there's the Herdies, but he got rid of them. He doesn't like hard work, that's all. Neither does his wife.'

'I met his wife Beryl. Nursing seems like hard work to me,' Kelly said.

Gloria raised her eyebrows.

'She's not a nurse. She's got a few certificates in caring for the elderly, though fat lot of good that did my mother-in-law.'

There was acid in her voice.

'Was it her idea to open a home? I wasn't aware untrained staff could do that.'

'Oh, she'll have beat the system somehow. She likes to think she's important, you know the sort.'

Kelly felt Kate bristle beside her. Beryl Morningside just became more interesting.

'It's an eyesore, and all those old folk decaying away in there, it's inhumane. I want to be put to pasture when I'm useless and be no bother to anyone.'

'Rather a stark difference of opinion to a medical professional, then?'

'You're right, they keep 'em going for as long as possible, for no reason.'

'I think the home is an attractive addition, myself,' Kate said.

'She speaks,' Gloria jibed.

Kate took it well.

They heard a noise, and it sounded like the slam of a door.

'Here he is,' Gloria said, getting up. 'You dry?'

'Pretty much, thank you for looking after us,' Kelly said.

'Does she push you around? Is that why you're quiet?' Gloria said to Kate, who smiled and nodded. So did Gloria.

'Wait here, I'll tell him he's to get cleaned up and come in here in a good state, not dripping like a wrung-out alley cat.'

'She'd make a good detective,' Kate said after Gloria had disappeared. 'Eyes like a hawk.'

It was ten minutes before Gloria came back into the sitting room with Dorian, who followed her like a twelve-year-old, belying the man he was. He was well built and strong but looked pampered. He also looked nervous. Kelly and Kate were used to it, they expected any interviewee to be reticent at the very least. It was the loud ones they most suspected. He sat down where Gloria told him, and his mother sat beside him.

'Hi Dorian, has your mother told you why we're here?' Kelly asked.

He nodded but didn't look at them. He'd made an attempt to clean himself up, but his hands remained covered in farm mud and his socks were worn through. There was no mistaking he belonged outside.

Kelly's phone buzzed, she apologised and turned it to silent, noticing that it was her father. She could do without a precis of last night. It could wait.

'You're a difficult man to track down,' Kelly began.

Dorian said nothing, simply staring at them both, like his mother told him to.

'We need to go over the events of Wednesday with you. It must have been a very unsettling experience, finding Victor like that.'

Gloria reached her hand over to Dorian's lap and petted it. The gesture made Kelly feel awkward.

'I was walking out,' he said.

Kelly nodded, waiting for more.

'I check the farm every morning.'

'What for?' Kelly asked.

He looked at his mother, who smiled at him.

'It's my job. I check things like the walls, and the trees, and the weather. Oh, and the machinery too.'

Kelly glanced at Gloria, who returned an apologetic frown.

'Right. So what were you checking at the mine on Wednesday morning?'

'Quarry.'

'Excuse me?'

'I was at the quarry, the mine is underground.'

'Ah, yes, excuse my ignorance. The quarry then, what were you checking?'

'I drive past the lip every day and make sure that it hasn't collapsed.'

'I thought you said you were walking.'

'I drive to the remote parts and get off the Gator and walk.'

Kelly recalled what the CSI had said about the track beneath the lip. 'Right. So, the lip, it was intact?'

Dorian nodded. 'Like Uncle Arthur said it would be.'

Kelly glanced at Gloria, who looked embarrassed suddenly.

'So, when did you speak to Uncle Arthur about it?' Kelly asked.

'I saw him out checking.'

'He was checking too? There's a lot to be checked on the farm, isn't there?'

Dorian nodded.

'So, he checks his land, and you check yours, and you often meet?'

'No.'

'So, sometimes or occasionally?'

A nod.

'Ok, so on Wednesday, what time did you see him?'

'It was just a chat. He'd been to see Grandma and Grandpa's graves.'

Kelly noticed Gloria stare at her son in shock.

'And where are they?' Kelly asked.

'They're buried in the chapel cemetery, on Arthur's land,' Gloria said.

'I see.' Kelly sensed the same resentment again. 'The chapel the nursing home uses for their burials?'

If Kelly could have touched Gloria's skin, she swore it'd be burning up with disgust. Beryl and Victor's use of the chapel obviously wasn't approved of.

'So, Dorian, you had a chat, and Arthur told you what?'

'That everything was in order, not to worry.'

'But you carried on your checking?'

'Yes, and that's when I saw something at the bottom of the quarry face.'

'It looked unusual?'

'Yes. I went down and found Victor.'

'And did Uncle Arthur come with you?'

'No, he'd left already.'

'What did you do when you realised it was a body?'

'I called Mum.'

'And it was you who called the police?' Kelly asked Gloria, who nodded.

'Samuel was out repairing walls.'

'When you check the land, Dorian, you must notice anything out of place, you check so thoroughly every day. Can you remember anything out of the ordinary?'

He nodded and looked at his mother.

'Go on, tell them,' she said to him.

'Somebody had been down to the steppe, and it wasn't me.'

Chapter 25

'Jesus, it's like getting blood out of a stone,' Kate said as they drove away from the farmhouse, soaked again from another downpour. The tea and cake though had been a welcome diversion. 'I can't decide if it's hesitance or shyness at the intrusion because they're so private, or whether he's just bloody obstinate.'

'Or he's terrified of his mother and does everything she says,' Kelly said.

'Except see his uncle,' Kate retorted.

'Quite. She was desperate to appear like business as usual,' Kelly said.

Her phone buzzed again, and it was her father. She sighed.

'Something up?' Kate asked her.

'No, Dad's been trying to call me, and I reckon it's about last night. I'll see what he wants, he's tried to call me a couple of times. Do you think this weather will break today? I'd like to get a feel for the layout of the farm. Victor came from somewhere, and I doubt it was his car.'

Kate stared out of the window after checking her weather app, which told her that the rain wasn't going anywhere today. Kelly started the car and set her phone to loudspeaker, and called her father.

'Dad, you're on speaker,' she warned, hoping that would be enough to prevent it from being a personal call.

'That's okay, it's not about last night. I've had some test results back from Victor Walmsley.'

'Already?'

'Yes, I'm very persuasive when I'm curious.'

'Go on,' Kelly said.

'No narcotics or alcohol. However, he had advanced sepsis.'

'What?'

'I ordered some microbiological samples because I didn't like the look of his heart. It's damned difficult, but not impossible, to diagnose sepsis post-mortem, but I thought it would be important to rule out. I saw significant petechiae and purpura of the pericardium, myocardium, as well as discolouration of the atria, congestion in the lungs, lymphoid depletion, and haemorrhagic necrosis in his liver.'

'Dad, I love you, it's just me and Kate in the car, and she loves you too, but I don't speak fluent autopsish, you know that, do me a favour.'

'Sorry, I'm getting carried away. In plain English, he was riddled with sepsis and if he hadn't died from the fall, then he'd have died within hours of that. I can say with authority that his body was already in septic shock so he must have been suffering for quite some time before he fell.'

'How much time?'

'Up to ten hours is my guess.'

'Guess?'

'Informed assessment.'

'What I really need to know is what sort of shape he'd be in at the top of that quarry face.'

'He wouldn't have been able to stand on his own, let alone jump off.'

'Fuck.'

'I was wondering how long it would take you to scrape up an expletive once I told you. Good morning to you too.'

'Sorry, Dad. Can I just clarify. What if he'd been suffering the effects of sepsis for ten hours preceding his fall, but he'd been at the quarry face for all that time, could he have fallen off?'

'In theory. However, it's my opinion that given the prevalence of staphylococcus aureus in his tissues was so severe, he would have been likely unconscious when he went over the edge. This

139

explains the lack of trauma to his arms, as most people, when they're falling at a rate of knots towards the ground, whether they meant to or not, instinctively put their arms out to save them.'

'I'm thinking about what the CSI said about that steppe. I've had a witness tell me that there are tracks up there that shouldn't be there.'

'Me too. If he'd have simply rolled off the lip, he'd have ended up on that.'

'Thanks, Dad.'

'Sorry for making your day harder.'

'Not at all, that's your job, now I need to open a murder inquiry, because he was taken to the site by somebody, yes?'

'Yes, that's what my findings suggest.'

'You're a scientist, can't you just give me a finite rather than a suggestion?'

'You know I would if I could. What I will say is that − all things considered − I think he was pushed or rolled off that steppe. Nobody could have heaved him off the top and missed it, unless they had superhuman strength.'

'My witness says you can get a farm vehicle down there but not a full-sized car or truck.'

'So that's where you start, good luck.'

They hung up.

'Let's go and see Arthur Morningside,' Kelly said.

They turned into the entrance for Morningside Nursing Home but drove past the house and carried on to Promise Farm. Arthur and Beryl lived in an old barn conversation that was modernised after the land was split. Samuel and Gloria got the main house in the arrangement. Gloria had told them a steady stream of family titbits over tea and cake. She had a loose tongue and they both agreed it might come in handy. Before they left the car, they contacted Eden House to update the case to a murder inquiry.

They went through the routine of hanging coats over their heads and got out of the car, sprinting to the front door and shaking their coats. Kate knocked. They waited then knocked a few more times, but there was no answer. They shrugged and Kelly put her coat back over her head and indicated she'd go around the back. Kate remained at the front of the property. The rain had formed puddles in between the gravel and Kelly fully stepped into one that was hidden, and swore loudly.

'Oi!'

A loud voice boomed, and Kelly bumped into a hard wall, in surprise. Everything was grey in the rain including stone walls. She bounced off it and hit her head on a gate. A man marched towards her, and she held up a hand, keeping the other on her coat. The brotherly resemblance was uncanny and she guessed he was Arthur Morningside.

'Sorry to barge in, I'm with the police,' Kelly shouted. He'd gained on her quickly and was up close before she could repeat herself.

'Who?'

'The police. I'm Detective Inspector Kelly Porter. I met your wife at the nursing home, she didn't mention it?'

The man looked menacing. He was large, broad, with worker's hands and unforgiving eyes.

'No, she hasn't, why?'

'Look, here's my ID,' she said, showing her lanyard. 'Can I come under there?' Kelly asked, nodding in the direction of the barn behind him. He wore a full-length wax jacket with a hood, and large heavy boots – he looked warm and dry underneath. He finally nodded after checking her ID and they went under cover. She shook her hands dry, or as much as she could, and got the impression that she'd never get dry today at all.

'I take it you're Arthur Morningside? I've met your brother and sister-in-law. In fact, I've just seen Dorian.' She smiled in an attempt to start afresh. He softened a little and she saw warmth in his eyes that hadn't been there before.

'I'm just asking questions about Victor Walmsley because I'm sure you've heard his body was found on your brother's land. Dorian mentioned you just now. He said he saw you on Wednesday morning, near the quarry.'

'Who knows why a man does that.'

'Does what?'

He stared at her, and she studied his weathered face. He was younger than Samuel, but his face looked as though it shrouded an old soul, who'd been around a lot longer, and lived a life outside these lands, bequeathed to the brothers by their father.

'Kills himself,' he said.

She let it pass. There was no point in alarming potential witnesses before the news broke that Victor Walmsley did not kill himself. He had help.

'Dorian said you were out there by the quarry on Wednesday morning,' she said.

'Aye. Always am, but I didn't see Victor. Are you sure he killed himself?' Arthur asked.

'Why do you ask?'

'It's out of character for a man to do that, a man like Victor with everything going for him. It doesn't make sense. What Victor wanted, Victor got.'

Kelly sensed him stiffen when he talked about the deceased.

'The coroner is investigating the details.'

Arthur examined her face.

'Well, it'd be better for Irene to hear. You know, if he was pushed because of some grudge or argument, rather than doing it himself. It makes him more of a man.'

Kelly looked around. The shed was filled with farming paraphernalia, but she'd been given the impression that Arthur's half of the farm didn't function as one, and hadn't since Percival split the land.

'You knew Victor well?'

'Well enough. Our families go back decades, centuries even. His always had the undertakers, and mine had the farm. Generations of them. He was the last of them, like me. I have no kids, that's why I always stayed in touch with my nephew, when I was allowed to, because he's all I've got. I stop and talk to him when I see him out and about. It sometimes means trespassing on my brother's land.'

Kelly thought she saw a twinkle in his eye when he said this.

'So, Wednesday, you saw him close to the quarry and you had a chat?'

'Sure did. He's not considered a great talker, but he is to me. He was out checking like he does, when he's not at the gym, and I waved him over and told him everything was as it should be.'

'When you say that, do you mean you'd checked the quarry?'

'Nice try. I wasn't close enough to the quarry to see over the edge, if that's what you're getting at. I had no idea Victor was down there until I heard it on the radio. Samuel didn't bother telling me but that was no surprise.'

'When was the last time you saw Victor?'

Arthur sucked his breath in. 'Perhaps a week before he went missing. Irene came and told us in a panic.'

'Why would she tell you in person? You were quite close then? I mean as couples?'

The information didn't fit with what Irene had told her.

'We got closer when her mother was ill.'

'Ethel Farrow?'

Arthur nodded. 'She was in the home for a few days before she died, it was tragic. The doctors missed it at every opportunity. They're a bunch of worthless amateurs if you ask me. Ethel and her husband paid National Insurance all their lives and never took a penny, then when she gets sick, they treat her like garbage. She died in pain. Victor felt responsible.'

'Why?'

'Mainly because he had private health insurance and Ethel was too proud to ask for help. Irene felt helpless and so, when a man can't help his wife, he loses hope. But it was quick in the end.'

Kelly tried to work out what Arthur meant.

'I didn't know Ethel had been in your nursing home.'

'It's my wife's business. I provided the bricks and mortar. She makes it work.'

'So you don't get involved in it at all?'

'No. I don't much care for old people, they're selfish and burdensome. When I get like that, Beryl is under strict instructions to shoot me with my shotgun, quietly, out in a field, or the forest, and bury me.'

'And what if Beryl isn't around?'

Arthur stared at her, and Kelly realised that he wasn't used to being trumped when it came to fatalistic humour. Kelly's cynicism wasn't something that was welcome in every conversation, but Arthur had tried to shock her, and it hadn't worked. It would take a lot more than somebody professing their support for assisted suicide to make an impression on her. However, it did tell her the measure of Arthur Morningside.

'Then I'll do it myself.'

'So it is possible for a real man to kill himself.'

He ignored her.

'Did Victor ever mention he was seriously ill?'

Arthur looked genuinely thoughtful, as though it were a possibility, though Kelly knew that it wasn't.

'No, was he?'

'Are you aware of any enemies that Victor might have had? Did he owe money? That sort of thing.'

'No, he was doing well, business was booming, and old people save tons for their funerals now, they're as lucrative as weddings. He was conceited, high and mighty, arrogant and fairly obnoxious, though, so, enemies? Yes, to be sure.' Arthur grinned.

'I see. Want to expand on any of that assessment?'

'Not really, that's your job, isn't it?'

'What about your wife's business arrangement with Victor, was that going well?'

'You mean the funerals? Yes, I guess they looked after one another.'

She scanned Arthur's face for signs that he might be included in the list of people who might dislike Victor Walmsley.

'How would you describe the relationship between your wife and Victor?' Kelly asked.

Arthur didn't answer straight away. It was the first time she'd seen the man falter. She'd hit a nerve.

'Kelly, there you are.'

Kate stood behind her.

The moment was lost and Kelly thanked Arthur for his time and gave him a card with her details on it. She said goodbye and walked away with Kate. The rain had eased a little, but it was steady and constant, and they were both soaked again. The warmth of the car made steam bellow around in clouds and mist the windows.

'That was interesting,' Kelly said.

'Families.' Kate stared out of the window. 'They say blood is thicker than water, but if it all falls apart, it's the nastiest thing.'

'It appears that the two Morningside brothers are estranged. It's bitter, they don't even go onto each other's land. But Arthur is fond of his nephew. It's sad.'

'I never told you, but I had a similar experience with my mother when she died. I have two sisters.'

Kelly concentrated on the difficult navigation of the track and slowed down, straining to see through the rain pelting on the screen. Her wipers were on full.

'You've got two sisters?'

Kate nodded. 'When Mum died, they crawled out of the woodwork, where they'd been hiding for a decade, and demanded a share of Mum's money. Inheritance does weird things to people. That's all I'm saying.'

'What happened?'

'I fought it. Mum was fully with it when she died. Her body was broken from years of Lupus, but her mind was sharp. I couldn't let it go, I had to fight.'

'I understand that,' Kelly said.

'They could have pulled out at any moment, and respected Mum's wishes. They could have saved so much pain. But it went to county court, and they sued me under probate litigation. I think it's the most stressful thing I've ever done, and that's saying something when I've raised three girls pretty much on my own.'

Kelly smiled. 'Jesus, Kate, I'm sorry.'

'I won.'

Kelly slapped the steering wheel. 'Of course you did. So that made it all worth it.'

'No. By the time I'd paid my costs, there was nothing left, and now I look back and think that's what they wanted all along, just to hurt me. It wasn't about Mum.'

'That's outrageous, if you won, you should have been awarded costs.'

'Nope. My sisters pled poverty and the judge sympathised with them. Having upheld the will, he said we should each pay our own legal costs because the case could have been avoided.'

'But it was their fault,' Kelly said.

'I know, but in court no one cares.'

Kelly fell silent.

They turned on to the A66, the rain still slowing everything down. The odd nutter sped past, in the outside lane, spewing up all sorts of sludge behind them, making Kelly curse.

They drove the rest of the way back to Eden House in silence, apart from the rain battering on the windows and roof. Their minds were each focused on families and how they often tore themselves apart.

Chapter 26

'That's Victor's car,' Dan said. Fin sat beside him at Rob's desk.

Kelly and Kate stood behind them watching the computer screen. No one had asked why Dan simply didn't transfer the software onto his own computer, so he could work at his own desk. But gathering around Rob's space was comforting. And now Dan's desk was Fin's. Emma carried a tray of coffee and a box of cakes that Dan had bought in town. A new cupcake van had opened, and they liked to support local business, at least that's what Dan said. Even Emma took one.

CCTV from the Keswick area had been collated and Dan and Emma had been working on narrowing it down to sightings of Victor's car.

They watched the footage as they chomped, and Kelly and Kate wheeled chairs across the room to get comfortable. Emma sat close to Dan.

'This is the A66, going east,' Dan said. 'It's eight fifteen in the morning, on Thursday the third of October.'

'The day he was last seen by his wife, leaving for work. But he's not going to work,' Kelly said.

'Correct, he's driving away from Keswick.'

'Do we know it's him driving?' Kelly asked.

'Yep, at this point, it's him. Look, if I forward to eight fifty-two, you can make out the driver – this is the camera at the junction of the B5322, at Threlkeld.'

'Since when was there a camera at Threlkeld?' Kelly asked.

'Since that horrific crash last year,' Emma said.

'You attended,' Kate said to her.

Emma nodded.

Road traffic accidents were unforgettable, especially fatal ones.

'We know he never showed at work that morning,' Kelly said. 'So, where's he going?'

'This is the speed camera at Scales, look he's indicating right, to come off the A66.'

'Isn't that the first exit to the campsite, opposite the carpark for Blencathra?' Kate asked.

They nodded in unison.

'And the quickest way to get to the Morningside and Promise farms.'

'He handled the funerals at the Morningside Nursing Home so he could have had business there,' Dan said.

'We should check the nursing home CCTV in their carpark to see if that's where he was going,' Dan said.

'Let's request it,' Kelly said.

'Dan, how far have you gone through this? Did he leave?'

'I've been to the end of the day, and into the early hours of Friday the fourth, he doesn't leave this way, but there is another road out of the Morningside estate further up the A66, at Trout-beck, it's the one most visitors know to use for the slate mine shop.'

'Samuel Morningside has CCTV at the shop, have you got it?'

Dan nodded. 'I've been through it, there's no sign of Victor Walmsley from Thursday the third. So he didn't go shopping.'

'There's nothing else down there apart from the private home of Promise Farm and the nursing home, it narrows our options, at least,' Kelly said.

'But that means that somebody from the home must have met with him, and the appeal for his whereabouts last week procured no sightings after his wife said he left for work at seven fifty-five,' Kate said.

'Any sightings at the weekend?' Kelly asked.

Kate shook her head.

'What about the A5091?' Kelly asked.

'So, this is the footage from that road,' Dan said. 'And I found this.'

He tapped a few keys and the screen changed.

'This is from the camera at the crossroads that takes you over Kitto Beck if you turn east to the lay-by where his car was found yesterday, where you'd park to hike Great Mell Fell,' Dan said. 'I started with Thursday the third and there were seventeen cars that turned off here, east, all week, then on Tuesday morning, the eighth of October, at three fourteen in the morning, I found this.'

They watched as a car approached from the north. The headlights filled the screen, and it was impossible to make out the model, colour or make of the car at that point. However, after it indicated to turn left, travelling east, they were able to make a positive identification. It was Victor Walmsley's Silver Audi. Kelly read the number plate out when Dan paused the footage.

'Who's driving? Is it him?' Kelly asked.

'We'll need enhancement to be sure, but Victor was a tall guy, and well built, I've estimated that he'd be a bit further back in the seat. Also, this person has light hair.'

'Victor was bald,' Kate said.

'Look. We'll have to get confirmation from the forensic photography assessment, but I swear that's a ring on the driver's right hand,' Dan said.

Kelly squinted and they moved closer to the screen. Dan magnified it as much as he could.

'As far as I can remember, Victor wasn't wearing jewellery,' Kelly said.

The frame was paused on the car a second before it turned, and the right hand was on the steering wheel, and the head of the driver was slightly left looking.

Kelly stood back and sighed.

'In the middle of the night, that could be glare, or reflection, but you're right about the hair, it's full and light,' she said.

'So it wasn't Victor,' Kate said.

'Dan, forward a couple of hours will you?' Kelly asked.

'Okay,' Dan said, shrugging.

'Slowly,' Kelly asked.

'I can do frame by frame.'

A couple of minutes later Kelly asked him to stop.

'There,' she said. 'What's that? Something is crossing the road.'

'I think that's a hare, boss,' Dan said.

'For God's sake,' Kate said.

They waited for Dan to resume his search. Kate took another cupcake from the box.

'Wait, go back,' Kelly said.

'Awayyego,' Dan said. Kelly knew this to be Scottish for an expression of disbelief. It meant even Dan was impressed.

'That's somebody crossing the road,' Fin said.

'What time is it?' Kelly asked.

Dan read the time from the top of the screen.

'It's five past five in the morning,' he said.

'They're carrying a bag.'

'Great work, what about the footage from the guesthouse?'

'Fin?' Dan asked.

'Nothing, he didn't go south, before his car ended up here.'

'He must have been in the area all week. Why didn't anybody know?' Fin asked.

'This person did,' Kelly said, nodding to the image on the screen.

Chapter 27

Arthur took the card the policewoman had given him and threw it into a fruit bowl, obsessively filled by his wife. He preferred meat. Beryl was fixated with the stuff you put in your body because she didn't want to end up like her patients: desperately decrepit and worn out. She believed that if you ate right (her way) and didn't smoke or drink, you had a better chance of longevity. Arthur thought it was all a load of sheep shit, but he didn't tell her that.

There were other ways for a human to be toxic.

He retrieved his stash of Marlboro cigarettes from the cupboard in the boot room and went out to the rear porch, where he lit one up and took a deep drag, watching as the rain pounded the land. It burnt quickly and he lit another, sucking hard and blowing out vapour which stuck to his clothes. Beryl would smell it, but she would also ignore it.

He stubbed out his second cigarette and left the porch. Within seconds his clothes were soaking. He'd left his jacket in the boot room and now he felt his clothes get heavier as they were pounded from above. He walked to the back of the property where there was a generous terrace, looking west, across his land. In the greyness he could still make out the nursing home because its lights burnt brightly, but he couldn't see the forest from here, because the land, trees and sky all merged into one that far away. The water fell in torrents of horizontal waves.

Beryl said that cigarette stubs took decades to decompose, but what did he care? By then he'd be long gone, but he wouldn't be buried with his father, trapped in eternity on this land, in the cold earth, never escaping his grasp. He'd be laid to rest far away, where no one could find him.

As if in response to his mood, the rain fell harder. He thrust his hands in to his pockets and began walking away from the stone terrace, through the gap in the low wall, across the field, towards the home. The ground was spongy underfoot and his clothes felt heavy. He missed having a companion by his side. The family had always had dogs. He imagined a four-legged chum trotting loyally next to him and panting as he trudged through a dip in the field, which was full of water. Beryl didn't like dogs. He was soaked through to his skin now and he didn't care. The rain was soothing, as if it washed away the thoughts whirring around his mind. But he knew that no matter how hard it hit him and rinsed out his anger, it couldn't clean his insides. It didn't matter how far he walked, he still carried the same head on his shoulders, and memories, like stains on a white jersey, never came out. He didn't feel cold, just numb, and as the home drew closer, he decided to walk around it and into the forest.

He wished he had a gun with him so he could at least let off some tension by pulling a trigger, but there was nothing to shoot this time of year. The government protected all the vermin on the land anyhow, with their laws and conservation. Even when livestock was killed, as it strayed from Samuel's land, and they found evidence of predators bothering the flocks, they still couldn't do anything about it. It was one of the reasons he'd sold his sheep to Samuel as part of the deal to split the land. It hadn't been so much an agreement as an imposition though. Both brothers knew that the chances of surviving solely on the income this side of the farm were remote. The forest wasn't large enough to harvest timber, and the land wasn't arable. His father knew what he was doing when he had his lawyers divide the farm north and south of the road that ran straight through it. But as he gazed at it now, through drips of water running freely from his eyebrows, he knew he should be proud of what he and Beryl had achieved. But part of him was thankful that Percival Morningside wasn't here to remind Arthur that it had all worked out because of Victor. The thought unsexed him and he felt worthless, as if his father were standing beside him.

The orange lights from the nursing home looked warm and inviting, but he didn't attempt to go in there and dry off. He walked straight past the walled gardens and carried on down to the forest, which was his only sanctuary. A shiver made his body jump and he realised that he was being foolish, but stubbornness prevented him from turning back. As he left the field and crossed the shallow stream, he came to the outskirts of the wood and, under the trees, the rain struggled to penetrate fully, instead dripping in great globules as it fell off branches and leaves.

They'd planned to build a bird of prey centre here, to attract money from tourists, but the birds hadn't fared well. At first, birds from the UK and abroad had taken to their new home. A specialist had even been employed and aviaries built. But it didn't take long for the first birds to fall ill, and the authorities to deny their licence. One by one, they'd lost every animal to disease. Then the llamas. It was as if the wood was cursed, like the rest of the land.

Arthur approached a series of buildings that were overgrown with bushes and vines. They'd planned a tea shop, but now it stood rotten; empty and desolate. The signs could still be read, and they swung rhythmically in the wind, making a cacophony of empty sounds, like a symphony for the dead, as he walked.

Deeper into the wood, he was almost fully protected by the rain. He came to a small brook that had run through the land for centuries. Arthur sat on a log and recalled his father showing him and Samuel how to fish. Tiny brown trout used to swim quite happily with the flow of the water, until the birds began to die, and the fish then seemed to give up in sympathy. It was as if Arthur's very presence on the land sapped it of its vitality. Beryl reminded him whenever she got a chance, just like his father had.

The first time he'd tried to thread a wriggling worm onto the hook held steady by Percival's enormous hand, he'd messed up and pierced his thumb instead. Percival had tutted and grabbed it from him, doing it himself. Samuel succeeded first time. He remembered the drops of blood falling into the brook and being washed away with the current. Samuel had been given a shotgun at the age of twelve, Arthur had to wait until he was fourteen.

On Samuel's land, his Herdies grew fat and thrived. Here, close to where Percival had died, nothing lived. Not even the residents of Beryl's nursing home lasted that long. But at least their deaths made money.

The rain eased a little. Or it may have felt like that because he was under a heavy canopy of overgrown and neglected trees. They'd been left to their own devices for years, the only thing the forest was good for was dumping rubbish so Beryl didn't have to pay the full tariffs for getting rid of medical waste. It cost a fortune and she argued that the land would take care of it if they buried it. As if on cue, he smelled the aroma of refuse close by and looked up at his surroundings, taking them in fully. Rotting leaves, and wet mud have their own peculiar smell and he quite liked the scent of raw dirt. He always had. His boots were always muddier than Samuel's, and his face never as clean when they used to bathe at night.

This was something else.

He got up and realised that the cold had seeped into his bones, and he ached. He stretched and walked towards the bushes where the reek seemed to originate. Under the canopy there was a mound, where he presumed rubbish had been buried. Then he remembered that this was where they buried the birds. They were supposed to dispose of them legally, filling in countless pieces of paper, to conform to EU standards. They wanted to charge him ludicrous amounts of money to take the carcasses away. Victor had helped him navigate through the lot. Victor knew how to bypass the red tape making sure the paperwork was filled in correctly, and the documents signed off. But the birds never made it out of here, and no money ever changed hands, although it did on paper.

Victor knew how to look after his friends. A pang of guilt coursed through his body as a vision of Victor's crumpled body invaded his thoughts. And Beryl's horror at losing her loyal cash cow. It was all she cared about. Even in death Victor was more important than anything else. At one time, he'd wished he'd killed the man himself, but not now; those feelings had gone.

The stench brought him back to the present: the mound shouldn't smell like it did. The birds were long gone; about three years now, there would be nothing left but bones. This scent was fresh. He walked past the mound and carried on up the brook, wading in his boots, following the smell. The feeling of not wearing protective clothing in such horrendous weather was liberating. It was a non-conformist act comparable to failing his O Levels, or disappearing off the farm to travel across Asia, instead of staying behind like Samuel.

He covered his mouth when the stench grew stronger, and he knew from experience that it was carrion of some sort. Also, that it had been dead for a few days. He lifted a canopy of branches and peered underneath and saw the carcass of an animal. At first, he thought that the deer had come back, but he knew that wasn't the case. Mismanagement and over-hunting had meant that reproduction had fallen off, and the single herd left on his land had been reduced to one stag, who had nothing to impregnate. His hopes were dashed as he realised exactly what it was. The poor thing had been reduced to a bundle of fur and maggots. He recognised it as Walker, Samuel's brown Labrador. Walker must have strayed over here, poor thing, and either become disoriented or passed out exhausted. The mutt must have been due his time anyway. But that wasn't his worry. He had no problem dealing with the mess, it was how he was going to tell Samuel that perturbed him.

Chapter 28

Kelly unlocked the front door with her key and opened it quietly. She peered around and walked inside, taking off her soaking coat and untying her trainers. Her socks were wet, and the house cold. She tiptoed through to the lounge, thinking that Lizzie and Johnny had taken a nap, and cursed when the fire wasn't lit. She shivered and rubbed her body.

'Hi,' Johnny said out of the dark.

Kelly jumped and swore, scared out of her wits.

'Jesus! What are you doing in the dark? It's freezing in here.'

'I only just got in myself. I went to take Lizzie for ice-cream, but we got caught in the rain. I think we should talk.'

'Where is she?'

'She fell asleep in the car. I put her to bed. Her room is warm.'

'You should have kept her awake,' Kelly said.

He stood up and spread his hands. It was a cheap shot, she knew. Their routine with their daughter was fluid and always had been. Now she was dictating that he impose terms that were neither agreed nor reasonable, as if they were in court.

She dropped her bag and went to the kitchen to put the kettle on. He followed her. The feeling of being uncomfortable in her skin which had begun last night, took hold of her again.

'I'm sorry,' he said.

'Sorry for what? Lying to me? Making a fool out of me? Allowing Carrie into our home without informing me? You choose.'

Tension made her body stiff, and she knew she was being unhelpful, but she couldn't help it. She was tired. Drained from being shut out and lied to. Coming home was supposed to be a relief.

Now, stood in her own house, she was unsure what to do first; check on her daughter, or make a hot drink.

'I need to change,' she said.

He reached out for her arm. 'Kelly,' he said.

She stopped and looked at him. His face was the same. The house was the same. Pooley Bridge ticked along as it had done yesterday, but she felt different.

'Look, why don't you make me a cuppa and I'll get out of these wet clothes, I've been out all day and I'm freezing.'

It was a concession. One she wasn't truly willing to give, but it bought her time. She left and went upstairs. She closed their bedroom door and peeled off her trousers and socks. She sat in the dark, contemplating how to get warm. She took off her sweater and placed the wet lump of items into the washing basket. She dressed quickly into a dry pair of running leggings and a T-shirt and slung a jersey over the top. She dried her hair quickly with the dryer and her hands began to warm up.

She peeked into her daughter's room and saw Lizzie curled up on her front, legs tucked underneath her, snoozing happily. Kelly walked to her bed and stroked a strand of hair away from her face. The soft light from the lamp next to Lizzie's bed softened her mood and she sighed. When she went back downstairs, Johnny had started a fire – the crackles popped and darted inside the grate. A gentle warmth had begun spreading throughout the room. She sat down on the sofa opposite the fire and Johnny sat next to her. He'd made her a cup of tea; it sat on a table. She picked it up and cradled it.

'Tell me everything,' she finally said.

'There was never a right time,' he began.

Kelly closed her eyes. Allowing him to talk without interrupting was arduous. She realised he'd begun with an excuse. She bit her lip and forced herself to keep her mouth closed.

'I guess we never really talked about it.'

For a man who was a certified counsellor, he now struggled with his words, but Kelly tried to be patient. She had to give him a chance to explain.

'I didn't think it mattered. It's just a piece of paper. When Carrie walked out, I wanted to start again. I gave her the house. She kept the car and the dog. And Josie at first. We both wanted to avoid the courts, which would have been financial suicide. The last thing we wanted was to give a bunch of cash to lawyers to line their pockets, so I suggested we keep our investments and I'd pay her dividends every month. We worked it all out and it seemed fair. My earning potential was larger than hers, and I guess I bought my freedom.'

'You gave me the impression she was unreasonable, unhinged even. Yesterday she struck me as somebody who is not like that at all. You could have warned me.'

'She turned up here without warning, it was a shock for me too. I knew that three of our investments were going south, and haemorrhaging money, but I thought they'd pick up.'

'Why didn't she just call you?'

'The bank has foreclosed on the mortgage. I had no idea. She was scared and put off telling me until it was too late.'

'But if you turned the house over to her then it's not your problem.'

'It's not as easy as that. She's homeless. Because we're still technically married, it's my financial burden as well.'

'*Technically* married? You are married. Don't dress this up, Johnny. You're insulting my intelligence.'

'Sorry.'

'That's the thing, isn't it? You're saying sorry. Anyone can say sorry. Sorry is just a word. What I need to decide is if it's enough. Sorry as a get out of jail free card. You have it in your back pocket, and it means you can do what you like with no consequence, and then just produce the card, and we go back to square one. I don't think I can do that anymore.'

Her own words shocked her. The weeks and months when he took himself off for hikes, pretended he was all right, had private telephone conversations with ex-army mates and all that time he ignored his family, now came rushing back in a tsunami and Kelly realised she was at breaking point. She'd thought that when this time eventually came, when they sat down together and addressed what had happened, she'd lose her shit and be unreasonable. There'd be screaming and tears, but now she felt none of that. It was as if she didn't have it in her. Maybe the tears she'd cried for Rob had exhausted her store, and there were none left.

Another, more worrying, realisation dawned on her too. It was what she'd said to Kate in the car. Had she even forgiven him for last time? Truly? It wasn't the same but then perhaps it was.

Their fall out over the Ian Burton case had trashed their trust. She questioned whether she'd ever found it again, or she'd just smoothed things over because her heart was bruised, and Lizzie needed a father. He'd lied to her then, and he was lying now.

She felt a fool.

'Where is she? And what does she want?' she asked.

'She's at The Crown.'

'And we're paying, I presume?'

He nodded.

'We just need to talk things through and come up with a plan.'

'A plan? A financial plan?'

'Yes.'

'How much?'

'How much what?'

'You know exactly what I'm talking about. How much will it take to get you two out of this?'

Johnny stood up. He faced the fire, and she knew it was bad. Her chest hurt. She was a mature woman, a mother and a detective. She had physical responsibilities, but she also had a part of her that was intangible. It was the element of her that no one saw except for him. It was something that couldn't be saved in a bank account and couldn't be wrung out like a child's bib if it got dirty. It wasn't something that could easily be fixed because you couldn't see it. She felt the same sensations in her body as she had when she found out that he was counselling Ian Burton. A brutal murderer who he had sympathy for.

They'd faced each other in court, on opposite sides of the law. She'd told herself afterwards that he had only been doing his job, and she hers. But it triggered her deep distaste for injustice. Her perception of what justice should be. She'd seen, first-hand, what Ian Burton did to his victims, and those he controlled. Johnny either had an enormous capacity for forgiveness and compassion, or else... that was her dilemma. She wasn't sure she knew him. Not really, not enough.

Old familiar sensations bubbled up in her body and she identified them as old foes. She felt unsafe. Not in the sense that Johnny would hurt her physically. She knew he'd never do that. But he made choices that left her feeling vulnerable. The Ian Burton case challenged her professional capability. Now his decisions and duplicity may threaten their financial stability.

'How much?' she asked again.

He turned around. 'A hundred and seventy grand.'

Kelly felt her stomach stiffen and her guts hit the floor. Scenarios flew around her head... losing the house... debt... a different future for Lizzie. It was too much.

Suddenly Mary popped into her head, and she saw her old, wrinkled face, wise beyond what any social media star could ever aspire to, saying, *Well dear, take what life throws at you and get on with it.*

Kelly's body calmed a little and the chemicals of shock subsided.

'The flat?'

'I can sell it.'

'Army pension?'

His mountain rescue work was voluntary.

'A grand a month,' he said.

'Other investments? You said three had gone tits-up.'

'I can sell them, but I'll be penalised because they've got early release clauses.'

'I need time to process all of this,' Kelly said. She took a sip of tea. The one person she wanted to talk to right now was her father. Even if he didn't have a magic wand, he'd still know what to say. But she'd have to face someone else first. She got up, finished her tea and put the cup in the kitchen.

'I'm going to see Carrie,' she said.

'I'll come with you,' he said.

'No, you won't.'

Chapter 29

The Crown was busy, Kelly reckoned the dreary weather brought more people in to drink and warm up by the fire. There was something about crap weather that made people want to talk about it, especially in England, and even more so in the Lake District. It could make or break a day. It could decide a future. It could destroy a farmer.

And it was Friday night.

Johnny had given her Carrie's mobile number. She'd made a childish quip about them paying for that too, and his lack of response told her that it was more than likely. She'd put on a bit of make-up, still needing to somehow face Johnny's wife with an exterior of armour, just in case.

She worried that Carrie would pin all the debt on Johnny as legally, their assets were equally shared under marriage laws. Kelly also knew legally, that this was none of her business.

Thank God Josie was at university.

She shook her umbrella and put it into the stand, nodding a hello to the bar staff, who she knew by name. She saw Carrie by the fire, who waved at her with a broad smile. Kelly felt slightly sick. She went over and asked if she wanted a drink. Carrie stood up.

'Thanks for coming,' she said.

'Thanks for meeting me,' Kelly said.

'I'll have another wine if that's okay,' Carrie said.

'Sure, white?' Kelly asked, looking at Carrie's glass that still had some straw-coloured liquid at the bottom of it. Kelly remembered once again Johnny saying his ex-wife had an alcohol problem, but the woman here looked in control. Kelly questioned if she should have believed anything Johnny told her. When Kelly had returned from London all those years ago, she had really been looking for somebody to hold onto. And Johnny had made it all feel so easy.

She went to the bar. The woman behind the counter waved at her and nodded she'd be next. She ordered two glasses of wine but then changed her mind and ordered a bottle and took it to where Carrie was sat.

'Busy day? Johnno says you work hard,' Carrie said.

Kelly smiled and took off her coat. 'I've had better weeks.' She poured the wine and took a sip. Carrie's pet name for her husband was becoming more palatable as Kelly got used to the betrayal.

'Thank you. And thank you for sorting this out. Your father is lovely,' Carrie said.

'He is.'

'I saw the release of the photo this afternoon on the local news. Is that your department? Who are you looking for?'

Carrie's inquiry was benign. The reference to her work was an icebreaker but Kelly wasn't in the mood. The frame from the CCTV footage was one of a set they'd released via the press department in an attempt to identify who'd been driving Victor Walmsley's car.

'Yes. I'm always trying to find nutters.'

'So who are they?'

'If we knew that we wouldn't be requesting help from the public.'

'I heard that releasing photos sometimes made the criminal go to ground.'

The last thing Kelly needed was an armchair chat about criminal profiling.

'It's not Netflix.'

'Sure. I understand your hostility. I'm just making conversation.'

'I know. It's unnecessary. I thought you were divorced.'

'Ah. That makes sense now. Johnno can be selective with the truth.'

Kelly felt like she was wandering into a trap and put her glass down. She was drinking too quickly and didn't want to become emotional.

'Why are you here?' she asked.

'It's the only way I can get Johnno to face his responsibilities. I've called him, and I warned him, but he buries his head in the sand.'

'I think we're beyond that. You both owe a shit ton of money and I want to know if your stories match up.'

'What did he tell you?'

'You go first,' Kelly said.

She studied the woman sat opposite. Carrie was ordinary looking, older than her, she guessed the same age as Johnny. To be evicted from one's home in midlife must be terrifying. But then she remembered that she only had herself to look after. Josie had chosen to live with her dad, and his girlfriend.

'Thank you for looking after Josie, she worships you,' Carrie said.

'You didn't come all the way from Manchester to tell me that.'

'Manchester? No, I moved to Kendal four years ago.'

Kelly stared at the woman's eyes and took her glass, draining it.

'It's cheaper. I needed to downsize. I really didn't need a four-bedroom house after Josie left for good.'

'Why Kendal?'

'It's pretty up here. I needed a fresh start, and I met a guy.'

'Congratulations.'

Carrie smiled. 'So, what do you want to know?'

'Everything. Why you two are still legally bound. What the figures are exactly, and how this involves me.'

'It doesn't involve you.'

'So why were you sat in my house when I came home last night?'

'Josie said you'd know what to do.'

'Josie? She knows about your financial woes? That's irresponsible, isn't it? As well as unfair.'

'Yes, she's had to grow up much faster than she should.'

Kelly's foot tapped. Regardless of the dark and the rain, she wanted to run away, up a hill, down a valley. Anything but this.

Carrie took a deep breath and began talking. 'We agreed to split our assets fairly. I have to give it to him, Johnno was always on the lookout for ways to make money when he was in the army. He did well. But he took risks.'

'Isn't that what investment is all about?'

'Yes, but not when you're gambling with others' livelihoods. Look, I didn't come here to argue with you about Johnno's financial sense. That ship has sailed. It really doesn't matter that we never got divorced, he loves you, I can tell. I was with Johnno for twenty years.'

Kelly felt her body stiffen. She knew enough about people to be wary of their definitions of love. 'What happened?'

'Iraq, Afghanistan, you know, the usual stuff.'

Kelly let the sarcasm pass. 'Couldn't you work through it?'

'I tried. We tried. But when you're left alone with a baby, and you're listening out for the knock on the door from the chaplain every night, you slowly fall out of love. It leaves you numb. It was hostile in the beginning, but we worked it out financially. Avoiding lawyers was important to both of us. If it's any consolation...'

'No, it isn't.'

'Right. So the fact is that some of the investment plans used to be legal, and now they're not, and the penalties are back-dated. It's all come at once, and we've got a huge tax bill.'

'Tax evasion?'

'No, that's not what it's called.'

'I don't care what it's called, if that's what it is.'

'I couldn't pay the mortgage, and the bank is ruthless. They've foreclosed and I had to be out last week.'

'How long have you known?'

'About what?'

'Banks don't foreclose overnight, and they don't kick you out onto the street the next day. How long has this been going on?'

'Best part of a year.'

'And Johnny knew?'

Carrie nodded.

Kelly recalled the conversations about the holiday let business Johnny wanted to set up, his urgency, and her not paying attention. The fact he never wanted a joint bank account. Letters disappearing from the pile of post and him saying they were junk mail. Her mind whirred, the wine was having its effect. She hadn't eaten.

'I'm starving, want to eat?' Kelly asked. 'I'll get some menus.'

Kelly walked away and the act of moving relieved her tension. The familiar desire to be somewhere else enveloped her. This morning, she'd been desperate to escape to work, and then she'd been looking forward to the safety of home. Now she didn't want to go home. She came back with two menus.

'The burgers are fantastic,' Kelly said. 'Do you have a plan?'

'For a burger?'

Kelly allowed herself to smile.

'Sorry, yes, I do. I brought divorce papers with me so we can draw a line under this once and for all. We must clear the debt, I want Johnno to commit to that, and then I'm going to Spain.'

'Spain?'

'Yes. The man I've met is Spanish. Josie knows.'

Kelly swallowed and looked at the fire. Even Josie had secrets it seemed.

'So why couldn't all of this have been sorted out over the phone?'

Carrie smiled. 'Johnny doesn't pull himself together until everything has fallen apart. He kept telling me he'd sort it. He didn't. I knew he wouldn't face it until I was stood in front of him.'

'In front of me, you mean?'

'Yes. Sorry.'

'So that was the final bargaining tool? Get me on board and you'd get what you want.'

'This isn't what I want. I wanted the investment schemes to work. We would have both been sorted for life. But it's never that easy, is it? We've lost everything and we both need to start again. There's no reason to be married any more.'

Kelly poured more wine. The last comment hurt. Johnny's need to remain married for financial reasons outweighed his desire to divorce for her.

'I'm sorry, I didn't mean it how that came out.'

'No, I understand. It was a financial arrangement, just one that he didn't tell me about.'

'I would have told you, but women don't tend to listen to the exes of their fellas, I wouldn't have either. You believe anything when you're in love.'

'Ready to order?' Kelly asked, ignoring the last comment. Carrie nodded, and Kelly took their order to the bar. When she came back, Carrie had laid out some paperwork on the table.

'That's everything. You'll see, if you go through it in your own time. I want you to see for yourself, that it comes to about a hundred and seventy grand.'

At least Johnny hadn't lied about that.

Kelly placed the papers into her handbag.

'Well, a couple of burgers aren't going to blow the budget, not tonight at least. Another bottle?'

Chapter 30

'Still not found him?' Gloria asked Samuel.

He shook his head.

'I know I should've kept him home the last few months. He's likely given up somewhere and laid down to sleep, poor fella. I just want to find him to bury,' he said.

Gloria put her hand on Samuel's shoulder and patted it.

'Walker'll make it home, he always does.'

The door knocker made them jump.

'That'll be Irene,' she said. She left Samuel by the fire. They'd invited the widow over for dinner.

He stared into the orange flames and cradled his glass of wine. Fridays for the rest of humanity was a time of relaxation and release from the week. For farmers, it was just another evening. But having Irene over was the least they could do. Their families had supported one another for decades, if not centuries. He remembered Percival saying that you looked after your own. Older and wiser, Samuel now knew that he hadn't meant that to be family or friends, but those who kept your darkest secrets.

The Morningsides and Walmsleys; one took from the land, and the other gave back to it, in a never-ending cycle of life. They had to stick together to make sure they made it through the next generation. But with Vic, the last of the Walmsleys, now gone, and Percival's land split asunder, the empire of the two old men was coming to an end. He knew it. Arthur knew it.

He enjoyed a moment's peace in knowing that Walker had laid down to give up his last breath just like his legacy was doing now. It was fading – had faded – to nothing.

Gloria came back into the room looking pale. For a second, Samuel thought it was the police, and he started, almost spilling the contents of his glass. He sat up straight, questioning her with his frown.

'Samuel, it's Arthur, he's here to see you,' she said.

Samuel placed his glass softly down on the table beside him and readied himself to get up from the seat. He recalled the last time he'd seen his brother in the flesh. He'd been driving the Gator across his land and spotted the large bulky shape of his brother in the distance. It was a moment of recognition that only siblings understand.

He'd played with Arthur a thousand times in the grass, with toy soldiers and guns made of sticks. He knew the way his body moved and the way he turned his head when he heard a bird: invaders to the little boys, how they'd pitched their rifles aloft and taken aim. Their minds were full of other worlds. In them, they were free of a general to bark commands. They were their own law. Independent of tyranny, in the fields, down by the stream, hidden away from adults that ruined their imaginations with orders and punishments.

'Shall I invite him in?' Gloria asked him.

Samuel looked at her without answer. She softened and came to him, holding her hand out to pet his arm.

'I'll bring him in,' she said softly and left.

Samuel stood in the middle of the room, waiting.

He heard footsteps in the hall and then a shadow crossed the light from the lamp. He fought with the turmoil inside his chest and couldn't find a comfortable position to stand. He put his hands in his pockets then took them out again. He shuffled from foot to foot.

The large dark shape of his brother filled the doorway and blocked the radiance from the hall. Arthur stopped at the lip of the threshold and stood staring at him, full in the face. It was always Arthur's way. You either looked him in the eyes or not at all. A habit that infuriated their father because it searched his soul and stripped him bare of his deceit.

Samuel coughed awkwardly. He could barely form his lips around his brother's name.

'Arthur, what brings you out at this hour?'

'Samuel,' Arthur said.

Samuel could hear the clink and clatter of Gloria in the kitchen.

'I'm not staying, don't be worried, it's not a social call,' Arthur said.

'What's up?' Samuel asked. Suddenly he wondered where Dorian was. He wasn't sure if the panic he felt was more about Dorian's welfare or whether Arthur knew before he did what had happened to his son.

'It's Walker,' Arthur said.

Samuel almost breathed a sigh of relief but then realised what his brother was telling him.

'You found him?' Samuel asked simply.

Arthur nodded.

'I'm sorry. He was down by the beck, in the woods, next to the old shed.'

They called it a shed, but Samuel knew full well that Arthur was talking about the ancient stone ruin in the forest that had lain forgotten for centuries, where they played as boys. It stirred memories inside Samuel that he'd thought he'd buried forever.

'Was he...'

'Aye. Gone. For a day I reckon. I wrapped him up warm and proper.'

'Thank you,' Samuel said. 'I appreciate that. It was his time.'

'Aye but he should have been with you. That was your spot,' Arthur said.

Samuel stared at him and nodded. 'Aye, it was. Where is he? Can I see him?'

'Aye, he's in my barn. He's not too pretty, mind. He should be buried soon.'

Samuel nodded again.

They stood face to face, neither moving nor talking. Samuel squeezed his eyes together with his thumb and fingers and said a silent goodbye to his companion.

'Thank you for dropping by,' he said finally when he opened his eyes. 'I'll get my coat.'

When they went through to the kitchen together, Gloria was on edge. She searched signs in both men's faces for evidence they'd had a fight, or similar, but found none.

'Arthur found Walker, he's gone,' Samuel said, bowing his head.

Gloria stopped fiddling with dinner and looked at the two men she'd known most of her life.

'I'm going to bury him,' Samuel said.

'But dinner...'

'Don't wait up,' Samuel said and grabbed his coat and keys. His boots were by the back door on the rack, and he turned away from her, stooping down to pull them on, behind the door. Arthur waited for him, and Gloria glared at him. He held her scowl and she looked away first.

They left the house and Samuel peered up to the sky and saw that the rain had paused. There was a break in two dark clouds and the night sky peered through as if telling him he was doing the right thing by putting Walker to peace straight away. Samuel looked around for a vehicle but there was none.

'Did you walk?' he asked his brother.

'Aye. Needed the air.'

Samuel smirked. He knew the feeling.

'Get in.' He nodded to his truck. They got in side by side and for a second Samuel had a vision of them driving around the estate together, checking their land, jointly owned, no falling out, no strife, and no wives. It stilled his heart and they set off.

'Remember the birds?' Arthur asked.

Samuel turned to him. 'Birds?'

'The Bird of Prey Centre I was planning.'

'Ah, yep, I remember. Didn't work.'

Samuel regretted the tone of satisfaction he let slip. He knew Arthur felt it.

'They all died,' Arthur said.

'Sorry,' Samuel said. He wondered if this was an attempt at small talk or if something else was coming.

'Walker got me thinking,' Arthur said.

'Aye,' Samuel replied, indicating he was listening. They bumped along the road and Samuel turned off for Arthur's land, as if he'd been doing it for the last twenty years. A cutting stab of grief gripped him as he mourned all the lost time. They could have been sharing pints, dinners and plans for the future. It was too late now. Too many words said in anger and haste. And two wives stirring things up. But now here, inside the cabin of his truck, it was as if Samuel wanted to make everything right. Away from all that had poisoned their blood, this was his opportunity.

'You missed some sheep over the years,' Arthur said.

'Thanks to the foxes, disease and hawks – the big ones get the lamb's eyes – we always lose some, why?'

'I didn't mean that. You had a couple that wandered off?'

'I suppose. Their carcasses rot into the land, it's natural,' Samuel said.

'Well, I've had three or four wander into the forest – I guessed they were lost – and anyway, they either ate something or fell, I don't know what. I should have said. I knew they were yours, but, well, you know...'

Samuel tried to process what his brother was telling him. Maybe it was his way of doing exactly what Samuel himself desired, which was to try to communicate. Sheep was a safe and familiar topic, but there was something else.

'You got rid of them for me? Well, thank you, I had no idea.'

'I know, I should have said.'

'No worries,' Samuel said.

'Sure.'

They bobbed along the road and Samuel saw the lights of the nursing home. If he squinted, he could make out the shape of the chapel on the dark horizon. He glared at it.

'I didn't know you were using the graveyard – or rather Beryl is.' He nodded to the silhouette of the chapel.

'I didn't know how to…'

'It's your land,' Samuel said. He suddenly didn't want to ruin the moment.

'But the sheep,' Arthur persisted.

Samuel scrunched his brow. 'The sheep? The ones you found?'

'Yes.'

'Something you want to tell me?'

'Did Dad ever have any problems with the stream? I mean the water table? Stuff dying and getting poisoned, and the like?'

'You've had problems over there?' Samuel asked. Then the penny dropped. He gripped the steering wheel. 'Arthur, if you think I…'

'No, I don't. That's not what I mean. It's not why I'm asking. I'm telling you that I think something has killed all those animals, the Herdies, the birds, and now Walker. I was thinking of running some tests.'

Samuel breathed. He wasn't being accused of anything. Arthur was asking his advice. As the younger brother, Arthur was looking to his bigger sibling for guidance. Samuel's grip on the wheel softened and they neared Arthur's stone house.

'Go round the back, he's in the shed. I put him in an old lambing box.'

Samuel parked in front of a large barn. They got out and Arthur took him inside. Arthur flicked on a small electric light and Samuel saw a lump laid on fresh straw, covered in a blanket. He knew that Arthur hadn't had lambs in here for years, making the gesture all the more touching. Then the stench hit him but it wasn't enough to put him off. Farmers' noses were different to everyone else's. They both went to Walker and Arthur knelt down next to his brother as Samuel lifted the blanket and peered into his old friend's face.

'Poor lad. There you go. Rest easy,' Samuel murmured as he stroked his ears. The body was cold but his fur still soft.

'Sorry I wasn't there for you, pal,' Samuel said. He turned to his brother. 'Will you help me?' he asked. Arthur nodded and reached his hand to pat his brother's arm, then pulled away. They stood and Samuel lifted Walker up while Arthur made sure the blanket was tucked in.

They walked back to the truck where Samuel placed Walker down gently. He turned to his brother.

'What sort of tests?' he asked.

'I'm not sure.'

Arthur turned to the dead dog and Samuel followed his gaze, understanding finally what Arthur meant.

'A fresh specimen,' Samuel said quietly.

Arthur nodded.

Chapter 31

Kelly decided to get a cab to Keswick to see her father. She required a resetting of her overloaded brain. The half an hour inside a taxi would go some way to dealing with the wine she'd drunk. She needed a familiar face that wasn't hiding anything from her. She'd texted Johnny and told him not to wait up. She'd ignored his replies. The cab stopped outside Ted's house, and she paid with her card and got out.

He was waiting for her. He looked tired but his eyes always twinkled brightly when he greeted her.

'Hi Dad,' she said, falling into his embrace. He kissed the top of her head.

'Come in, long day?'

He closed the door behind her and went to the kitchen to get a bottle of red wine and two glasses. She looked at the claret liquid; she shouldn't perhaps have more but she knew she would. The fire was going and she plopped herself down on a sofa in front of it. He sat next to her, handing her a glass of wine, and waited. He had that poise of an older, wiser person and she instantly felt comforted.

'I really don't need this,' she said, nodding at the glass in her hand.

'None of us ever does, but we do it anyway,' he smiled and took a sip.

She could tell it was expensive and she smiled at the irony that the more sophisticated the drink, the more palatable the excuse to imbibe it. She sighed deeply and leant her head back.

'Oh, Dad. I just don't know what to think. Johnny owes his wife a ton of money. They've got shared investments that have gone wrong. I think they were in some evasion scheme and HMRC has caught up with them.'

It felt good to get it off her chest.

'Oh dear. And this has come as a shock?'

She nodded. 'They're still married and I'm not sure what my ego is more offended by, the money or the fact that he's not divorced.'

'How much are you talking?'

'One hundred and seventy grand.'

He whistled and shuffled in his seat.

'Exactly. How could I have not seen this coming? Why didn't I know? I trusted him completely. I'm such an idiot.'

'You're not an idiot, sometimes it's easier to let things slide a little. I'm sure he is suitably ashamed. I think I know him as well as anybody and he loves you.'

He was the second person to tell her that tonight and she questioned what it meant. Love. The enigmatic elixir to everything. She wasn't so sure. Besides, Ted was from a different generation; one which stayed together despite ups and downs, as if it were some kind of competition. They were a stubborn old lot.

'Can you get your hands on that kind of money?' he asked.

'He can sell the holiday let, and I've got some savings, but, Dad, it changes our whole future together. That's the kind of money pensions are made of.'

'I can help,' he said.

She put her hand over his and smiled at him. 'No. I'm not letting you do that. I'm not here for you to give me a solution. This is my problem. I just needed to sound off.'

'Look, I know how proud and independent you are. All I'm saying is that you don't have to face this alone. I have money.'

'Take me to Vegas,' she said.

'What?'

Kelly laughed out loud, and it felt good. Ted joined in and they clinked their glasses.

'Actually, I was thinking,' he said. 'I want to take the family on holiday somewhere. Maybe it should just be me and you,' he said.

She turned to him. Tears threatened to cloud her vision and betray her, but she kept them back and hoped Ted hadn't noticed.

'I'd love that.'

'Where should we go?' he asked. 'I've never been to Vegas. I think it might be fun.'

They clinked glasses again.

They stared at the fire and sipped their wine.

'On a completely different note, I wanted to ask you if you knew anything about the Morningside family on a more personal basis. They've been around for centuries.'

'Are you suggesting I'm that old?' Ted joked. 'I've heard plenty about them. I knew Percival and Prudence through meeting them at dances back in the day, in fact, I'm sure I had the pleasure of introducing your mother to Prudence. They were part of the elite back in the day. I also knew Victor Walmsley's father. It's a small world around here, like you know. I didn't think it was important at the time. I've been thinking about them. What do you want to know?'

'Victor shared business with Beryl Morningside, she's Percival's daughter-in-law, she married Arthur. She runs the nursing home that was built on Morningside land. She's the head nurse, but I found out she's not trained, is that legal?'

'You don't have to be medically trained to run a home, but you do have to have clinical staff. Do you think his death has something to do with the home?'

'I've no idea, but he wasn't thrown off that quarry face in the later stages of sepsis for nothing and you know it's usually about money.'

'The thing I can tell you about Percival Morningside is that he fought in the war, and he was a hard man. The gossip was that he ruled with an iron rod at home. But then they were the times. The family was very wealthy, and I imagine that was split between the two boys when Percival died.'

'I can't help thinking that something went wrong.'

'What do you mean?' he asked.

'It's an ideal arrangement, isn't it? Wealthy landowners scratching the back of local business, something goes wrong, and one ends up dead. But I haven't worked out the brothers yet. Victor died on Samuel's land but the nursing home, where Victor conducted his business affairs, is on Arthur's land.'

'Morningside Nursing Home?' Ted asked.

Kelly nodded.

'I do remember signing off some of their death certificates. I have to say I did question one of them.'

'Really? Recently?'

'No, a couple of years ago. I didn't know the GP personally, and I queried the cause of death. The woman had only been in the home for a month, and she hadn't been treated in a hospice or hospital. It's unusual, let's say. You'd expect "old age" on the death certificate of lots of people after seventy years old, but this one stuck in my mind because it was the second in as many months from the same GP, and the registrar came to me about it to double check a few details. I called the GP.'

'Two deaths at the nursing home in two months? What happened?'

'Oh, it's not the frequency that bothered me. People die in nursing homes all the time. It was the GP. I couldn't find him.'

'What do you mean?'

'When anybody dies the death certificate gets signed by the GP, then it goes to the funeral home, of course, then the church, or whoever is in charge of the body, etc. etc., and finally it makes its way back to the registrar. The process takes a couple of weeks unless it's rushed through. If it involves me of course, it can take longer.'

Kelly knew that suspicious deaths had to be double, and triple checked by the coroner.

'So the registrar called me because he wanted to make sure he was doing everything correctly. People get nervous when there's a spate of deaths, it's natural. The buck stops with me and I'm a safety net for anyone who's unsure.' Ted chuckled.

'I'm happy to take the flack, if you like. Anyway, I said I'd oblige and I called the GP like I said. I couldn't find him. I remember because with all the to-ing and fro-ing, it took about six weeks to get the damn paperwork done. Anyway, the home apologised profusely, said there'd been a mix up and the wrong GP had been entered on their system, and I finally got an explanation from the right one. I signed it off in the end and everyone was happy.'

Kelly looked at her father staring into the fire, and she knew that he was reliving the paperwork. It was in his nature to question everything, and she could tell that he was going over what he remembered in case he'd missed something.

'Maybe look into the GP they use?' he said.

'Who? The home?' she asked.

'Yes. And look at the register of deaths for the home.'

Kelly could tell that his mind was whirring. She'd planted a seed and she hadn't intended to. She hadn't really been barking up that particular tree, but she'd jolted something inside his memory and now she was curious. The lads at the funeral home had mentioned Victor's mother-in-law, then there were the other two names that had appeared, Constance Thorngill and Philippa Biden. And Ethel, then finding out that Prudence spent her last days in the home too. All the women were privately wealthy.

'Do you remember the name of the deceased?' she asked him.

He shook his head. 'Afraid not, but I can find out.'

They sat quietly in contemplation, together on the sofa, staring into the fire, each grappling with something they couldn't quite put their finger on. Maybe it was the wine. Maybe it was the excitement of a holiday. Or perhaps it was that Ted had flagged something up that warranted a check. She'd already made up her mind to pop into work tomorrow. They had a murder inquiry on their hands, and she felt no guilt being absent from Johnny over the weekend. A tinge of contrition grabbed at her over her daughter, but she knew that was her maternal conditioning making her feel ashamed for abandoning her responsibilities. It made her blood boil that women were programmed to feel this way and she asked Ted if she could stay over tonight. Johnny was a good dad. He could cope.

'Of course, darling, is it that bad?'

'I just need a breather, Dad.'

Chapter 32

'I'm so sorry, Samuel had to go out last minute,' Gloria said to Irene.

'Well, I get you all to myself, then,' Irene said. 'To be honest, I'm overwhelmed with so many people coming to the house. I was dreading having to go over it all again with Samuel.'

'Oh no, don't think that, Irene. He wouldn't bring up the past.'

The two women busied themselves with niceties.

'I know, I just mean it's nice to escape and simply sit with you for the evening. Can we do that? I feel as though the house has been a circus all week.'

'Come on, let's take our dinner on our knees in front of the fire. I'll open a bottle of wine.'

Gloria filled two deep bowls with casserole and potatoes and put them on a tray. Irene followed her into the lounge, and they sat by the fire. Gloria poured some wine into their glasses and apart from the crackle of the fire, and their spoons on the edges of their bowls, a peaceful silence descended on the room.

'It's delicious,' Irene said.

'It's nice this, isn't it?' Gloria said. 'Sitting here, without the men droning on about farming.'

Irene looked wistfully into the fire. 'Or funerals.'

'I'm sorry, I didn't mean…'

'Don't worry, Gloria, I know what you meant.'

Irene put down her bowl and took a sip of wine. 'I think that's the first proper meal I've had since they found him.'

'Is there anything I can do?' Gloria asked, finishing her food and putting down her own bowl.

'Make sense of it all?' Irene said. It was a plea that Gloria felt keenly. Irene's eyes revealed a deep sadness that reminded her of Prudence in her final days. They were the same as the eyes of a fattened calf on his last day before the truck came to take him to slaughter.

'The police are camping in my house. They mean well. And now they won't go away.'

'Why's that? Do you want them to? You can tell them.'

'No. It's not that I don't want them there. It's just that they told me tonight, before I came here, that Victor's death is now a murder investigation.'

'Murder?' Gloria grasped her glass hard, trying not to spill it. It was a word that was unwelcome in such a domestic setting. The blaze of the flames, the casserole, and the dim lighting all conspired against the phrase. It wasn't right. It couldn't be true.

'What did they say?' Gloria asked. Her breathing had quickened, and she felt her cheeks go pink.

Irene took a deep breath. 'They explained to me that the coroner found that Victor was unconscious when he fell off the quarry. I've thought about it. It's a comfort in a way. He didn't kill himself. I told them he didn't. I knew he wouldn't. Even when they showed me the note, I knew it wasn't real.'

'He left a note?'

'That's the thing, they found one, but he can't have written it can he? Not if he was murdered. It means somebody wanted everybody to think he killed himself, it was done on purpose, it was no accident.'

Gloria felt her skin go clammy.

'Who?' Gloria instantly regretted the question, but she couldn't help herself. She was thinking aloud, and it was a genuine puzzle. Not only did the crime not fit their little lives, but also she couldn't think of anyone who might want to hurt Victor.

Irene snorted gently. 'They have no idea.'

'Do you think they might be wrong?' Again, Gloria kicked herself at her insensitivity.

Irene shrugged. 'Who knows? They're not perfect, are they? It's not like our day when you trusted the police to get it right. They're always making mistakes. I just don't know, Gloria. He was secretive. I've been thinking. A lot. It was his eyes. They'd stopped living, if you know what I mean.'

Gloria knew very well what Irene described. She'd seen it in everyone she loved. It was as if the soul of a person disappeared before their body ever did. Disappointment, betrayal or apathy at impending nothingness... Whatever it was, she'd seen it. She nodded.

'When did he lose his spark?' Gloria asked.

'When he buried my mother.'

Gloria stared into the fire and pondered. 'Were they close?'

'No, they hated each other. Well, that's probably a little strong, but you know how it is with in-laws. She told him he wasn't looking after me, she accused him of carrying on.'

'Carrying on? With whom?' Gloria was horrified but salaciously fascinated too.

Irene ignored the direct question which told Gloria that she knew who.

'But towards the end of her life, he was tender towards her, and then when she went, he started to go out for long drives on his own.'

'Did you tell the police?'

'No, it's a private family matter.'

Gloria could tell that Irene's sense of propriety was ruffled by the very thought of involving the police in her personal affairs. She wanted to tell Irene that wherever Victor might have gone on his drives might hold the key to who he became involved with, and possibly to who killed him. But she didn't want to push Irene too much. The woman had suffered enough. She stared at the fire.

'Dessert?'

'I'm full.'

'Apple and cinnamon pie?' Gloria tempted.

'Oh, go on then.'

Gloria got up and went to the kitchen, thankful for something to do. She felt helpless. Samuel was out with his brother for the first time in a decade, and now Irene had shocked the life out of her. The door opening made her jump, and she spun around. It was Dorian.

'Oh, love, it's you. There's dinner left,' she said and smiled at him.

'Thanks, Mum. I'll get some now.' He took off his boots and jacket and threw his keys in the bowl on the side. Gloria felt a little more grounded with him in the house. He represented a little piece of her; returned to prop her up as she struggled to keep herself together. She sighed and sliced apple pie. The custard was already warming on the Aga.

'Where've you been?'

'I went for a pint.'

'Oh? Where?'

He was always vague.

'Why, does it matter?' he asked.

'No reason, just asking.' Her earlier feeling of succour dissipated, and she felt shut out once more.

'Everybody's talking about Victor Walmsley. What a scumbag, he deserved what he got,' Dorian said.

'Shh, Irene is here,' she whispered.

He nodded.

'They say he was murdered because he was greedy, and he charged too much.' Dorian lowered his voice.

'There's talk of murder?' Gloria asked, shocked it had got around so fast. The violence and the need for people to gossip about tragedy caught Gloria by surprise. 'People are jealous of success,' she said. 'It makes them nasty.'

She took two bowls of pie and custard into the lounge and left Dorian in the kitchen.

'I heard what he said,' Irene said, taking a bowl from her.

'I'm so sorry, he repeats everything word for word,' Gloria sighed. 'He didn't mean anything by it.'

'I know, Gloria, but I'm starting to think the gossip might be right. The police are looking through all our accounts. I'm scared they'll find something.'

'Like what?'

'Something illegal.'

'Oh, no, not Victor. He was straight as a dye. Don't worry. They have to look into everything don't they? What could Victor have possibly done that could be dishonest?'

Irene didn't answer.

'Irene? Do you know something you're not telling me?'

'I questioned him once about a bill that he presented for an estate.'

Gloria felt her pulse quicken. 'You used to do all of the accounts, I remember that, you're so clever. I could never do it. I recall telling Samuel, you had a head for business.' She was aware she was waffling.

'It was Prudence's bill.'

Irene's words stopped her dead and she stared at her, open mouthed.

'I stopped doing the accounts after that, but I still checked. Behind his back. I felt awful. I just couldn't help myself because I knew I was the best person for the job. I knew they wouldn't be done correctly. I worried all the time about getting fined by HMRC. They pick up on the smallest things.'

Gloria waited.

'He asked me to step away.'

Irene picked her hands.

Gloria realised she was holding her breath.

'He was overcharging.'

Irene stared at her lap and Gloria saw tears well up in her eyes. She put down her bowl, got a tissue from her cardigan pocket and passed it to Irene.

'Two weeks ago, I threatened to report him.'

Irene wiped her eyes and Gloria put down her own bowl. She gulped some wine.

'I killed him, Gloria.'

'No, you didn't.'

'I did. Whatever he was hiding, the thought of getting caught for it and paying the thousands in fines he would have got because of me, it killed him.'

'Do you know where he went for that week before he died?' Gloria's voice was a whisper.

'Yes, because I followed him.'

Gloria paused mid-mouthful, her spoon hovering above the custard.

'He was carrying on.'

'No?'

'Yes, he was.'

'Who?'

A bang in the corridor startled the two women and they peered towards the door. Gloria went to it and put her head around the door, just as Dorian disappeared upstairs to his room.

Chapter 33

The next morning, a hot shower didn't wash away the grime Kelly felt inside her brain. She changed into sports kit she kept at Ted's for walking, and used the make-up she carried in her work bag. She nursed a sore head. Ted cooked her eggs and bacon, which helped a bit. And she'd had thirteen missed calls from Johnny.

By the time Ted dropped her off at Eden House, the incident room had received dozens of calls in response to the photos released by the press department. On the one hand, a man in a suit and shiny leather shoes walking around the lakes was an anomaly easy to spot, but on the other, the general public always became dramatic when an appeal was launched. She knew she had to handle sightings with care. And they were dealing with a potential window of a whole week, when Victor could have been spotted at any time, and in any location, across the national park.

Johnny had called twice more when she'd been in the car with Ted, but despite Ted's raised eyebrows, she'd ignored him. She knew avoiding him was worse, but she couldn't face him. Not now. Not in the middle of a murder investigation.

She replied once, by text, from her office, asking after Lizzie. 'She misses you,' came the reply, and Kelly felt anger at the blatant emotional blackmail. She also felt a pang of pure guilt, and that, she guessed, was the point. What mother wouldn't feel rubbish for putting her work before her baby? And Johnny was using it to distract her from what he'd done. She rolled her eyes and made her third coffee. He'd also reminded her that it was Saturday and this infuriated her even more.

'Brief at eleven?' She asked Kate, who'd joined her in the staff kitchen.

'Sure. I'll get the team together. You okay?'

'I slept at Dad's last night.'

'Still angry at Johnny?'

Kelly ripped open a new box of coffee pods and the cardboard tore in her hands. A couple dropped onto the floor.

'I'll take that as a yes,' Kate said.

Kelly sighed and leant against the worktop.

'Why is everything so much more complicated with a child? If it was just me, Kate, I'd walk.'

'Really?'

'Yes, really. The pressure to be a certain way and keep things together like some kind of model family is crushing my head.'

'It took me twenty-three years of marriage to find that out. Until I got up enough courage to give the finger to expectation.'

Kelly smiled and Kate put an arm around her shoulder.

'Do you wish you'd have left Derek earlier?' Kelly asked.

'Definitely. Our generation are programmed to be independent lionesses, but at the same time adhere to the gender stereotypes of the age. It's exhausting. We're Amazonians and Mother Marys all at the same time.'

Kelly laughed at the analogy but appreciated the seriousness of the comparison. Kate was right. She felt obliged to hold everything together, not because it was right but because they were brainwashed as women into thinking that the alternative was wrong.

'You should know in this job that the ideal family doesn't exist. If you decide to split up for good, Lizzie will survive. It's ok to do what you must, to keep sane. Don't go mad for two decades like me. I'm still getting over the guilt. The girls ask me why it took so long to leave. Millie told me last week she knew we were never going to last. It's humbling, and a bloody sodding waste of time. By the way, I'm not trying to sway you, but Millie is fed up with college, she's thinking of leaving to nanny full time.'

Kelly took the information on board.

'You'd think the number of lives I poke around in I'd have learnt something by now,' Kelly said.

'Not the case at all, it's called hope, most of us suffer from the affliction. There are no obvious symptoms, just a never-ending self-flagellation of lingering around situations that have already turned to rat shit.'

'On that note,' Kelly said. 'Did you see the report on Victor's car?'

'Yes, I did. Clean as a whistle, not even a bottle of water or a sweet wrapper in there.'

'I've never met a man like that.'

'Me neither.'

They picked up the spilt coffee pods and walked to the incident room together with their mugs.

Fin sat at a table, ready with a writing pad, looking as fresh as green grass.

'Morning, Fin,' Kelly said.

'Morning Ladies. I did some extra work on the nursing home residents buried by Victor last night,' he said.

'And?' Kelly asked.

'Each one, apart from Prudence and Ethel, had lived in the nursing home less than a year, and each had no next of kin. They bequeathed the nursing home their entire estates.'

Kelly stopped in her tracks, as did Kate. They stared at him.

'I won't even ask how you found that out. Is it possible Victor and Beryl were on the take, and there was a third party involved?' Kelly asked the question to herself as much as to her two colleagues.

The others joined them, and Kelly prepared for the brief.

Ted had agreed to send over the death certificates and registrar's notes on the deaths she'd queried, and she had to go over them before eleven. Today, she fancied staying in the incident room with everyone else, as if that would keep her safe from any further stress. The large TV screen on the wall, which had local news on loop most of the day, loomed over them and the footage was filled with images of Victor's abandoned car, and library videos of Dale & Sons' funerals. It was morbid stuff, but even Kelly had to admit that it was fascinating to watch. The media was continuing to promote Victor as a local celeb, and that might aid their investigation.

Fin ran his hand through his dark hair and gathered papers into a pile. 'I have to say, this case reminds me of one we had in Manchester a couple of years back.'

'Really, how?' Kelly turned her attention back to him as the others settled in their seats.

'It's got all the hallmarks of embezzlement of the elderly residents of the nursing home, and if Victor was in as deep as we suspect, then he could have made enemies out of a relative we don't know about.'

Kelly nodded. 'Makes sense. We just need to prove it. The murder was planned. The note, the hasty treatment for sepsis, or that's what we suspect.'

'I'm thinking a male. It would have taken a fair amount of strength to lob him off that quarry lip.'

'And knowledge of the area, and that it's quiet most of the time,' Kelly added.

'If Victor was up to his eyeballs in fraud, then it's likely that his business partner knew too,' Fin added.

Kelly nodded. They were disturbed by her phone. She answered it and excused herself, first checking that it wasn't Johnny. It was her father. She went into the foyer.

'Hi Dad. Thanks for breakfast, I feel more alive now,' she said.

'Anytime, it was nice having someone to look after. I've just got off the phone from the registrar, and we discussed a few interesting things together.'

'Go on,' she said. He had her full attention.

'He recalled the case I was telling you about last night.'

'I'm all ears, I've got a few minutes before I have to brief my team, fire away.'

'These things stand out because the paperwork has got to be so tight, there are a thousand tick boxes that need approving for each death. Nursing homes are a little different in that they normally come through their on-call GP, who they rely on when they have a resident pass away. It happens more frequently in that setting as you can imagine,' he said.

'Of course.' She couldn't help feeling that Ted felt responsible for any errors Victor might have made.

'Her name was Constance Thorngill. She was seventy-five years old. The registrar was more than a little concerned when I phoned her. These are official documents. Well, we discussed it and agreed that we'd done everything as per protocol. However, I retrieved the paperwork, and I pulled the certificates for all the deaths at the home in the last five years for you. They're all signed by the same GP, until I queried it two years ago over Ms Thorngill's death. Then it was changed and that is the GP they've used ever since.'

'Right, I think I'm following. Have you spoken to the GP?'

Kelly glanced over to Fin, who she could see was watching her through the glass. He held her stare. He'd picked up on the same scent as her father and it stirred in her familiar rousing sentiments of the battle during a serious investigation. He thought like she did.

'That's my problem. I'm sending over the files for you. I've checked. I tried to get contact details for both GPs and I hit a wall. They're not on the medical register. Well, they were, but one died in 1976 and the other in 1977.'

'How can that be possible?'

'Well, I blame modern computers taking over everything, it was different when everything had to be logged by hand. The names are almost identical, and so apparently that was the problem, they were entered wrongly on the register. But, and this is my worry, how did they get through the system in the first place. There are four deaths signed off by Doctor A Gentle, and five by Doctor A Gentel, after I queried the first. There is an A Genter registered, but the other two, like I said, have been dead for forty-five years.'

'Wait a minute, are you telling me that there have been nine deaths at the home all signed off by doctors who died forty-five years ago?'

'Yes.'

Kelly could tell by his tone that he was embarrassed, but also puzzled. She knew this meant he could get into a lot of trouble for his oversight, if indeed it wasn't a mere mix up, but it didn't sound like it. His usually controlled demeanour had deserted him, she could tell by his voice.

'How is that possible?'

'I honestly have no idea but as coroner I must open an investigation into it and get some answers. I'm hoping there is a straightforward explanation. I've been on the phone all morning since you left. I don't want to worry you. This is my oversight. It's serious, Kelly.'

'What sort of straightforward explanation?'

'That it was a paperwork error, and the GP who signed off on all nine deaths is in fact Doctor A Genter, who is indeed registered. But I can't get hold of her. I've left messages.'

'Is she local?'

'Her details record her as practising in Kendal. But that's not what worries me.'

'There's more?'

'If it was the same GP, you'd expect the signatures to be the same. They're not. Take a look at the files I've sent over for you. Meanwhile, I'm reporting Dale & Sons to the national association of funeral directors, however, the governing body is voluntary so If they've done anything against their code of practice, they may receive a fine, at most.'

'Dale & Sons?' Kelly's stomach felt heavy. 'They handled all of these deaths?'

'Yes.'

'Thanks, Dad, speak soon.'

Kelly ended the call and walked back into the incident room, and approached Fin.

'That was the coroner. He's questioning some of the death certs from fatalities at the nursing home. How many did you look up?'

Fin searched his notes and counted them.

'I've got eight.'

'He's got nine.'

'Dan, did you manage to trace the wills of those deceased at Morningside Nursing Home?'

'Working on it. A few of the solicitors were willing to comply with a simple request from us but three of them require a court order.'

'Fair enough. I think I have enough to get that done.'

He peered up at her. 'Really?'

She walked to the white board and wrote several bullet points, then explained what her father had told her over the phone, asking Fin to embellish it with his own research. He was a pro, and everybody listened. Dan whistled. It was a sobering possibility.

She linked her toughpad to the white board and opened the email from Ted. Nine names stared back at them, in separate files.

'Let's have a look, then, shall we?'

She opened the first and read the details of the death certificate out loud.

'Cause of death, old age, further explained as CVD, coverall for a dicky heart. Look at the signature. Doctor A Gentle died in 1976. So, we're potentially looking at identity fraud to commit clinical and financial fraud.'

She let it sink in and opened the other links. The next certificate was for Constance Thorngill. The next was for Philippa Biden. The one after that was Prudence Morningside.

'If I was a betting man, I wouldn't be taking a punt on surviving Morningside Nursing Home,' Dan quipped.

Kelly felt sick.

She found the file on Ethel Farrow, who was Victor's mother-in-law, then a lady called Brenda Shaw.

'None of the certificates are signed by A Genter, the only local GP registered officially on the medical register with a name close to that of the signatures, according to the coroner.'

Silence.

'I've got another banger for you all, I got sidetracked by this new information. We've now got a murder inquiry on our hands,' Kelly announced. 'The coroner has confirmed that Victor would not have been physically able to jump off anything due to advanced sepsis. So, he was pushed. It's highly likely that wherever he was in the week prior to his death holds the key to finding his killer. A few motives are emerging, but they're complicated and unclear so far.

'The likelihood of this being a stranger murder is fading by the minute. I want to know where Victor Walmsley was all week. Whoever wrote his suicide note likely killed him. That's our key. He vanished for seven days straight without a trace, but there will be one and we need to find it. We've been given nine extra officers on this so I'm tasking them with interviewing the quarry staff, setting up road checks to and from Great Mell Fell, as well as finding out what went on in the area in the past few weeks. Climbers, walkers, holidaymakers, events, fairs and labourers at the two farms all need to be interviewed and checked out. His car was clean, and you know that's a red flag, forensics are processing it because whoever drove it to Great Mell Fell, it wasn't Victor. They must have left something behind.'

'The fact is that Dale & Sons buried at least nine nursing home residents from the Morningside home, in the last five years, and it appears that the official paperwork registering their deaths is questionable. My first query is who signed these documents, because the presiding GP didn't exist at the time of death. And my second question is who was covering for who? Morningside Nursing Home or Dale & Sons? I want everybody on this today, until we get answers. Dan, you said we have a couple of the wills to hand?'

Dan nodded. 'Three, boss.'

'Right, my priority is to secure court orders for the others. By the end of play today, I want to know who benefitted from these residents' deaths. Fin has already started work on this, Dan, work together. The coroner has emphasised the seriousness of this. Submitting incorrect information onto a death certificate is a serious criminal offence. Heads will roll. I want to know if Victor knew about this and, if he did, if it relates to his death.'

'I've already started a spreadsheet, boss,' Fin said.

She noticed that he'd stopped writing and was looking at her, with his hands in his pockets. She could only describe his gaze as one of trust mixed with admiration, and it made her feel as though she was blushing, but, damn, it felt good.

'Gloria Morningside told me that Beryl isn't a registered nurse. Kate, I want you on that. A medical professional staging a suicide would know that it'd be picked up at autopsy.'

'If an autopsy was necessary.'

'A qualified nurse would know that. Right, let's get to work. I think it's time we formally interviewed both Irene Walmsley and Beryl Morningside.'

Chapter 34

'Kelly, there's only one thing to do in this scenario. By law, those folk were buried illegally. I'm applying to exhume their remains,' Ted told her over the phone.

'What?'

'I have no choice. The anomalies on the paperwork need explaining. Each one of them was buried on Morningside land, at the Promise Farm chapel.'

'How do you go about that?'

Kelly had never been involved in the exhumation of a body. She'd heard about it. A case in London had required it once but it wasn't one of hers. All she remembered was that the officers present told her it was a grim job. No one knew what the state of the bodies would be after years in the ground.

'It's reassuring that they weren't cremated, that would make my life more difficult. This way, I order the exhumation, and the remains are examined.'

'For what?'

Kelly was missing something. She didn't know how shoddy paperwork could result in such a dramatic outcome. In police work, such an expensive and serious decision would have to go through a handful of senior cops to be signed off, and paid for. But Ted was His Majesty's senior coroner for the north-west, and apart from the King himself, he could do what he damn well liked. It was a tradition going back centuries. Despite that she heard trepidation in his voice.

'When there are unanswered questions, like in this case, the whole process needs to go back to the very beginning, to check every aspect of the person's death, including the cause.'

'How long will it take?' she asked.

'It depends. Once I get the court order, which should be this afternoon, it's a case of employing local contractors to dig up the site. You need to inform the landowner.'

'Nobody wants their land digging up, not least close to a lucrative business. I should imagine the owners won't be best pleased.'

'Especially if it turns out that the mistakes were wilful and with their collusion,' Ted said.

'I need help on this, I've never come across it before. Do I have grounds to close the nursing home?'

'You'll have to check that one, I'm afraid I can't help you. I would imagine you have to be in possession of evidence of suspected collusion first.'

'Which I haven't got. And, thinking ahead, that won't become clear until you have the bodies in front of you.'

'Correct. There's nothing finite about this, and I can't give you the answers until I trace the paperwork from beginning to end, and the one person who might be able to throw some light on this is…'

'Victor Walmsley,' Kelly finished for him.

'Exactly. And he's dead.'

'So, this should form part of my inquiry into his murder. How expensive is it and whose budget is it?'

'Don't worry, it's my budget, it's in the public interest because our registration of births, deaths and marriages is protected by law.'

'That's a relief. At the very least I can interview the owners of Promise Farm, because whatever happened was on their watch. I don't have anything to charge them with, but one of them might know something. I need to get Mary out of there,' she said.

'Your friend?'

'Yes, she moved in on Thursday.'

'Old people don't like change. She probably won't thank you.'

'Do I lie to her?'

'Why don't you interview the landowners first? It is possible that the home isn't involved.'

'I know. I've considered that. Right, we'll speak later, let me know how you get on. Good luck with getting anywhere at the weekend.'

'This is the sort of thing that gets people moving no matter what day it is,' Ted said. 'I've only ever done it twice before. It gives people a renewed sense of vigour, shall we say. Anybody caught messing with the system faces stern consequences, which is why the laws are there in the first place. It won't take me long, I guarantee it.'

'Dad, are you ok? Are you in trouble?'

He hesitated.

'I'm keeping an open mind, somebody has to take responsibility for these errors.'

'But, your reputation...'

'Kelly, don't you worry about me, just find out who killed Victor and why. Let me take care of the paperwork. I've made mistakes in my life, God knows. Sometimes, they turn out to be big ones. But I honestly can't remember.'

They hung up.

Kelly shook off her concern. Her father was right. He was always stoic, and would face whatever came of their inquiries, but she was determined that he wouldn't be held responsible for somebody else's deviousness. If Victor Walmsley was forging paperwork for personal gain, then she'd make sure the case against him was watertight.

She felt her phone vibrate and looked at the incoming call. It was Johnny. She ignored it and walked back into the incident room to update the team on the coroner's intentions.

The news stopped the noise of typing, chattering and shuffling.

'At least it's not our budget,' she said. 'Can I have a volunteer please, to accompany me to Promise Farm to deliver the good news?'

Fin flung up his hand and Kelly smiled. 'Get your coat.'

Chapter 35

'Arthur, good afternoon.'

Kelly held out her hand. Arthur shook it, acknowledging her.

'This is Detective Sergeant Maguire, we're here to ask you a few more questions, sorry to bother you on a Saturday, may we come in?'

Arthur opened the door wider, and they went into the large entrance hall. The decor was smart, grand even, and it gave Kelly a taste of the man's lifestyle. It was well decked out, and surprisingly stylish and refined for a man of Arthur's appearance. He looked awkward.

'Is your wife at home?' Kelly asked.

Arthur turned his head over his shoulder and shouted for Beryl, who came downstairs. She was dressed in casual clothes, and slippers, but she wore a veiled cloak of stress across her face. She sauntered over the bottom step and peered up to Fin, giving Kelly the impression that she was a woman who'd made it her life's work to use her demure profile to further her interests.

'To what do we owe this pleasure?' she purred, smiling from under her eyelashes at Fin. Kelly imagined the ploy working when Beryl was thirty years younger. She was a completely different woman to the one she'd met lugging boxes at the nursing home.

They remained in the hallway, uninvited further.

'I'm sure you'll be aware of the current investigation into the death of Victor Walmsley that occurred on your brother's land on Wednesday,' Kelly said.

The couple glanced at each other. Fin remained silent and solid by her side.

'Our enquiries have spread to include Promise Farm,' she added.

'Why?' Beryl asked. Her face was open, but Kelly detected a change in the frequency of her voice. Neither expressed regret at Victor's passing.

'Because he was your business partner, Beryl.'

'Shall we go into the kitchen, and I'll make us some tea? Arthur, don't just stand there, get the cake out of the pantry,' Beryl ordered.

They followed her like a posse of children on a school trip. Arthur disappeared, reappearing with a plate holding a cake. Kelly and Fin sat down, and Beryl placed a kettle on the range cooker. The kitchen, like the hall, was opulent and impressive. Kelly would have loved a space like it but didn't have the room or the funds. It was old farmhouse chic combined with modern comfort.

'The coroner has flagged up concerns over Victor's business,' Kelly told them. Fin watched Arthur, who cut slices of Victoria sponge. Kelly and Fin pulled out chairs and sat down.

'*His* business?' Beryl asked.

'Yes. We've been tracing some of the funerals that Victor dealt with, and it led us to the chapel on your land, where we know the funerals were held. There is paperwork for everything these days,' Kelly smiled. Beryl turned her back and busied herself with the teapot.

'Victor buried some of my residents. We opened the chapel to ceremonies seven years ago. It's intimate. The residents like it,' Beryl said.

It was a curious statement given they would be dead by the time they benefitted from the arrangement.

'How close was your partnership with the deceased?' Kelly asked.

Arthur vanished back into the pantry.

'It was a business arrangement. I met Victor through Arthur when Prudence was ill. Prudence was my mother-in-law.'

'We're aware. I believe she spent a brief time at your nursing home.'

'That's correct.'

'For end of life care?' Kelly asked.

Beryl glanced at her husband, who had finally sat down. 'We didn't know that at the time, but yes, she didn't have long. The cancer was terminal. We made her comfortable.'

'And, forgive me, you are the chief medical professional at the facility. Are you?'

At this, Arthur looked uncomfortable.

'Yes,' Beryl replied.

Fin was her witness, Beryl had just admitted clinical liability for the residents in her care.

'I have some news that might come as a shock, perhaps you'd like to sit down?' Kelly said to her.

Beryl remained standing. 'I'm good. You get used to shocking news in my job.'

'As part of our inquiry into the death of Victor Walmsley, the coroner has concluded that the case must now be investigated as a murder inquiry.' She let the news sink in.

'Murder?' Arthur said.

Beryl's face turned pale, and she pulled out a chair, sitting down.

'There's more. Some of Victor's paperwork registered to Dale & Sons has flagged up anomalies that the coroner isn't happy with. He's taken steps to investigate further.'

She waited. Fin watched. Beryl picked her hands; Arthur folded his arms angrily.

'Victor buried my mother,' Arthur said. His voice was laced with hostility.

Kelly nodded. 'As well as other residents of the Morningside Nursing Home. The paperwork on some of the death certificates has been found to be incomplete or unsatisfactory.'

'What?' Arthur whispered. Kelly sensed an incendiary rage building up inside the man and Fin sat up straight.

'The coroner has personally instructed an exhumation of the ground at the chapel.'

There was no sweet way to put it, and Kelly waited for the fallout, watching Arthur closely. But she didn't expect Beryl to be quite so belligerent.

'He can't do that,' she said. Her cool exterior deserted her. Her voice screeched annoyingly.

'It's private land,' Arthur said, over his wife.

'Can we stick to the facts here. I'm merely informing you of his decision. Whether it's private land or not, the graves themselves become the jurisdiction of the coroner if the burials were themselves improper.'

'Improper?' Beryl snorted. 'What the hell are you insinuating?'

Arthur flashed his wife a warning gaze.

Fin pushed his chair back.

'Did you bring him here as your minder? What sort of people do you think we are?' Beryl said. 'You can't just come in here and make demands on private property, even if you are the police.'

'It's a court matter now. The bodies of the deceased will be exhumed on their authority. I'm afraid if you refuse to comply, then the order will be enforced and that's something I'm sure everybody wants to avoid.'

'Are you threatening us? You want to dig up bodies and we're just supposed to allow it to happen?' Beryl's body shook.

Kelly noted the pair's dynamic crumbling as panic set in.

'She's telling us that we have no say in it,' Arthur said to his wife calmly, then turned to Kelly. 'When will this happen?'

'As soon as the court order comes through. We'll have to close the chapel and seal it off, however, the nursing home can remain open for now. But I would request that you comply with our inquiries. We'll need to see all your paperwork on these past residents who were buried in the chapel grounds. There are nine in total, so far.'

Kelly passed Arthur a piece of paper. It detailed the names and dates of death and burials of the graves Ted wanted to exhume.

Arthur's expression was steely still and he passed the piece of paper to his wife. Her face was thunderous, turning pink in patches. She looked as though she might combust. The woman had lost control.

'The court is obliged to make the ground good again after the work. It is a major inconvenience, I know, but there is no point fighting it. I can see you're upset. It's not personal.'

'You'll note your mother's name is on the list, Arthur. I'm sorry.'

Arthur pushed back his chair and it scraped along the tiled floor.

'You can't do this,' Beryl repeated.

'Do you recall any of the anomalies on the death certificates?' Kelly asked her.

Beryl glared at her.

'I remember Victor rushing his work, telling me he was over-stretched. I regret using him, I remember that much. Who will pay for this?'

'The state,' Kelly said, noticing Arthur staring at her wildly.

'And what after? Who'll put those poor souls back? Who'll rebury them?'

'The coroner's office will be in touch about those particulars. My job is only to inform you and allow you this opportunity to share any discrepancies regarding these residents' deaths with us.'

'Why? What is all this for?' Arthur asked calmly.

'I'm sorry, I can only tell you what I know which is if paper-work is filled in incorrectly, then the whole process is rendered illegal, and it's a serious offence. The coroner wants to re-examine the deceased.'

'Re-examine? This is outrageous. Victor took care of all the paperwork. What if you find *anomalies* as you put it? Whose responsibility is it if the man who put them there is dead?'

'Beryl,' Arthur hissed. 'Show some respect.'

Kelly allowed them to squabble. It was useful.

'The families... this is impossible. We can't allow it.'

'You're not listening, Beryl,' Arthur turned to his wife. 'We have no choice.'

'On the note of the families, we're having some trouble tracing the relatives of the deceased and that's where you can help us,' Kelly said. 'We'd like access to your files on these residents, like I said, it shouldn't take us long. If you can prepare the paperwork for us then we can be on or way.'

'Now?' Arthur asked.

'Yes please,' Kelly replied. 'We'll wait.'

There was a moment's impasse as Kelly stood her ground, not making any sign to leave. Arthur got up and left the room. Beryl glared at them, as if they were idiots. Kelly recognised the stench of arrogance that followed the woman around and had yet to decide if it was because she was involved somehow, or if she spoke the truth and suspected Victor of something.

'When you said Victor rushed his work, could you give us examples?' Kelly asked her.

Beryl didn't reply. Instead, she marched to the door and took a coat off the hook. Rats deserting the sinking ship perhaps.

'I'll meet you over there, I presume you drove here?' Beryl asked.

'Yes, sure. We'll see you there,' Kelly said, nodding to Fin. It was their cue to leave. They got up and thanked Beryl for the tea and cake, which they hadn't touched, and Kelly glanced towards the hallway, where Arthur had disappeared. They saw themselves out. As they approached the car, Kelly turned around and strained an ear.

'Can you hear that?' she asked Fin.

'Full blown shitstorm?' he asked.

Arthur and Beryl were having words.

'I had a boss like you in Manchester,' he said.

'Like me?'

'Unafraid, straight, fearless.'

Kelly pulled on her seatbelt. 'That's fine praise, I'm not as bold as I seem.'

'Yes, you are. I've heard the rumours, and now I've seen it for myself.'

'What else did you hear?' she asked. She started the car and pulled away for the short drive to the home.

'You don't like praise.'

She laughed.

'So, what did you make of them?' she asked.

'Both liars. Extortion at the very least. Defrauding the NHS.'

'You're a company man, aren't you?'

Kelly referenced some coppers' penchants for fact ticking, and Fin showed all the signs. He had an encyclopaedic knowledge of UK criminal sentencing, which by global standards, was some of the most complicated in the world. She'd read his CV in full.

'And you're all justice and retribution,' he shot back.

She started the car and Fin put on his seatbelt, proving her point.

'I bet folk follow you anywhere,' he said.

She pulled away. He'd said it as a compliment, and he was still looking at her when they left the Promise farmhouse. Fin was getting too close too soon, though a secret part of her wanted it. Wanted him.

He lingered long enough for her to remain lost for words, then he got back to business.

'As for the murder, that's where this case will drag you into the weeds. It's the crimes of passion that get bogged down in lies. At least with money and numbers, I'm on safe ground.'

'No feelings involved, then?' She asked.

'I didn't say that. The force needs both.'

'Do you see either of them as murderers?'

'People never surprise me. It's why profiling is a load of old bollocks if you ask me. Of course they could have done it. So could the lad, Dorian. So could his dad, Samuel. You're talking about a family here who for whatever reason, and we need to find that out, hate each other, and hate is stronger than love. Victor's death was just the final act, because he was the one who held the purse strings. Has his will been read yet?'

'I assume his wife is the sole heir.'

'I wouldn't bank on it.'

Chapter 36

It wasn't Beryl who met Kelly and Fin at Morningside Nursing Home, but her husband Arthur.

'I thought your wife was coming to meet us?' Kelly asked, as she got out of the car to greet him. Fin slammed his door and nodded to Arthur.

'She had some last-minute business to attend to. She's told me where I can find all the files you need. Besides, the girls inside can help, it's not a great task, is it?'

The collection of sentences was impressive for the man who'd barely said much to Kelly before. He'd been coached, that much was clear. She had little choice but to accept Arthur's help, in the absence of his wife. Neither he nor his wife were suspected of a crime, but Beryl certainly raised eyebrows with her absence. They walked towards the entrance to the home and went in. A couple of nurses greeted Arthur and he nodded curtly to them. He went to Beryl's office and announced what he wanted to a woman working behind the desk. She looked rather flustered. Kelly took the opportunity to ask after Mary. It was also a way to get the nurses to relax and help them in their task: the familiar touch.

'How is she settling in?'

'Oh, she's a model resident, she keeps everybody entertained,' the nurse said. 'Do you need her file too?'

'Yes please,' Kelly said, before she had time to think. It seemed an opportunity to make sure that Mary was safe. Though how she was to do that from a file she didn't know.

'Can you see if she wants a visitor?' Kelly asked.

The nurse nodded and left, showing Arthur where he could find the files they needed.

'Fin, can you?'

'You have a pal in here?' he asked.

'I do.'

He grimaced, which did nothing for her anxiety.

She followed the nurse into the dining area, where she smelled the remnants of lunch. It was a mixture of roast meat and gravy, it hung in the air and clung to the furniture too. She hoped that for what Mary was likely paying, it was better than most of the hospital food she'd seen served at the Penrith and Lakes.

'Let's see if she's sat in the conservatory. Would you mind waiting here?'

'Of course.' Kelly looked around and absorbed the sounds of the pleasant living area. She'd spoken at length with Ted and the hospital. The average rate of deaths in a care home with a capacity of twenty, would be just less than two per year. So the figures themselves didn't point to anything sinister. It wasn't as if residents of the Morningside were dropping like flies, however, Ted still wanted to see the paperwork.

'She's on the terrace, and she'd love to see you,' The nurse said.

Kelly smiled and followed her outside. There was a nip in the air, but the sun was shining. She spotted Mary straight away and was struck by how frail she looked in these surroundings, compared to inside her own home. Independence counted for a lot, she pondered. Mary had a blanket over her knees and was sat quite alone. It made Kelly's heart ache a little.

'Hello Mary, I was passing through...'

'Kelly, what a lovely surprise. Sit down next to me, are you cold? Would you like a blanket?'

'I'm fine actually. This is quite warm for me, I've been out and about. How are you?' She sat down, feeling foolish for worrying. The home seemed to be functioning just fine. Again, she doubted the extent of what Beryl knew of Victor's dealings.

'Oh, I'm all right.'

Mary peered across the land towards the sea and Kelly noticed a sweep of melancholy cross her face. She followed her gaze and sat in silence.

'Oh, there it is,' Mary pointed suddenly, raising her hand out of her blanket. Kelly looked to where she gestured and spotted a truck bumping along a track close to the forest.

'Do you know them?' Kelly asked.

'Oh no, it's just our entertainment for the day. I guess it's workmen or the like, going about their business. My friend Winnie looks out for them. We make up stories about what they might be doing as they puff on their cigarettes,' Mary said. She chuckled and Kelly couldn't help but smile. It was a moment of pure simplicity that allowed her to escape her daily grind. She toyed with telling her about Johnny and Carrie. In her experience, old people had infinite wisdom when it came to life's problems.

'So, what are your theories?' Kelly asked.

'Winnie doesn't talk, I think she went a bit gaga years ago, mind, she always knows when the truck is here.'

A wistful shadow crossed her friend's face once more.

'I think I made a mistake coming here,' Mary said.

'Really? Have you not settled in?' Kelly asked.

'I have. It's comfortable, and the view is spectacular. But I miss my home. Don't you think that when you long for something and you finally get it, it always disappoints?'

Kelly watched the truck disappear into the forest.

'Perhaps. Has something happened?'

Mary tucked her hands back inside the blanket and smiled.

'I made a friend I didn't expect to.'

'That's nice.'

Mary nodded. 'It is, but it's ruined my plans.'

'Oh. Is it Winnie?'

'No. I thought I was ready, but I find I'm not, and now you're here, I realise I want to leave.'

Kelly placed her hand on Mary's blanket across her lap and felt for her hand.

'If that's what you want then stop the sale of the house and move back.'

Mary took a long time to respond.

'At my age, sometimes it's best just to accept things as they are. Otherwise by the time you've changed them, you're right back where you started, with the same problem.'

'Maybe it's teething problems?'

Kelly felt a sinking in her gut because if the investigation escalated then the home would have to close.

Mary patted her hand from under the blanket. 'That's exactly what it is, my dear. Teething. Not that I can remember what teeth felt like, but I'm sure you're right. Now, tell me your news.'

Kelly looked away. 'Where does the van go?' She asked.

'They come and go and never seem to do anything.'

'Who is it?'

'Always the same two men. They're middle aged and look like labourers, their tools rattle around in the back of the truck and cause a din. I fancy they go down there to smoke and to eat their packed lunches.'

Kelly gazed towards the forest.

'Have you ever lied Mary?' She asked.

Kelly instantly regretted her forwardness. But Mary began to smile.

'Of course I have. Everybody lies. They say they don't but it's part of survival. A little untruth here and a massaging of the facts there. We humans will do anything to get what we want. Well, almost anything. Have you lied, or have you been lied to? I think I can tell by your face that it's the latter, isn't it? It hurt, didn't it? What you need to ask yourself is what the lie covered up. Does it matter? What caused the lie?'

'Johnny's still married.'

'Ah. A lie between lovers. That's the toughest one of all. Is he still married to her because he loves her? Have they been carrying on?'

The old-fashioned phrase for illicit bonking made Kelly chuckle.

'No, it was – they both say – for financial reasons.'

'But you feel left out and disrespected. That's your ego.'

'My what?'

'The part of you that imagines – foolishly – that the world revolves around you. Believe me, we oldies don't have one. It's like a second skin and the only skin you have at my age is saggy and forgettable, besides I haven't the time. That's the part of you that's wounded. Does it really matter?'

'They're in debt and she's turned up looking for payment.'

'Ah, so that's why you're miffed. You've lost control over something. Money. You know money isn't real. Love is real. Money doesn't last. It can be burnt just like paper, but love is indestructible.'

Kelly watched Mary and she felt a moment of calm pass throughout her tight shoulders. The weight she seemed to be carrying was gone, even just for this moment.

'You have so many choices nowadays. It was simpler in my day. Brutal but straightforward at least. I don't know which I prefer. Do you love him?'

'Boss.'

Kelly spun around. It was Fin.

'Can I have a word?'

'Are you working?' Mary asked her. 'You work with very handsome chaps, Kelly. Are you going to introduce us?'

'We are, sadly. It's the investigation into Victor's death, and we're here to ask a few questions of the owners, that's all. Fin, this is my friend, Mary. Mary, this is DS Fin Maguire.'

'Pleasure, ma'am,' Fin said, going over to Mary and bending to kiss her cheek.

'If I was fifty years younger I'd get up,' Mary said to Fin, who laughed. 'You're investigating Beryl?'

Something in the way she said it made Kelly pause. 'Erm, not directly.'

'Ah, maybe I was right, then. Fate has intervened. I think I want to go home.'

'What do you mean?'

'You know your gut is your biggest brain?' Mary said.

'Is there something I should know about Beryl?' Kelly asked Mary.

'Probably. I think there's something about everyone that needs telling isn't there?'

'Do you want to go back inside?' Kelly asked Mary.

'No, I'll stay here. I'll miss the view, and the gravediggers.'

Kelly had stood up to follow Fin. Now she stopped.

'The what?'

'Oh, it's just a story. The men. It keeps me entertained. They're hiding something and Winnie laughed when I said it was bodies.' Mary laughed to herself, and Kelly stared at the treeline. Then she followed Fin inside.

'There are files missing,' Fin told her as they walked away. 'And your friend's is one of them.'

Chapter 37

As Kelly and Fin pulled away from the home, with the files they'd collected loaded into the back of Kelly's car, a van arrived and passed them and parked in the nursing home carpark. Kelly looked through her rear-view mirror and saw Arthur Morningside appear to greet them, and he and the driver shook hands.

'Environmental health?' Fin said, reading the side of the van.

Kelly stopped the car and reversed. Arthur spotted her and Kelly saw a shadow cross his face. They got out, just as the driver of the van began talking to Arthur.

'Everything all right, Arthur?' she asked as she approached them. 'Anything I should know about? Morning,' she greeted the driver, who was dressed officially in a crisp white shirt with a gold winged insignia, black tie and epaulettes, and he reminded Kelly of an officer in the Royal Navy. He held a clipboard onto which several papers were attached.

'A separate issue, another headache. It really isn't to do with the home,' Arthur said, sighing.

He looked stressed. The bloke had suffered a few shocks this morning.

'Please, go ahead,' she said to the man from environmental health. Fin walked around the van, inspecting it.

'Like I said, Arthur, it's a positive result for sodium pentobarbital.'

'What is?' Kelly asked.

'We have a water issue, that's all. Do you mind?' Arthur said.

'What is it exactly?' Arthur asked the visitor.

'It's a sedative used to tranquilise or anaesthetise,' Kelly interrupted before the man could answer Arthur's question. He
nodded. 'She's bang on, who are you?'

'The police. Where's the source?'

Arthur tried to interrupt again but this was now a conversation
between Kelly and the man with the paperwork. Kelly reached
out her hand.

'May I?' She read the report. Arthur tutted and looked at his
boots.

'A dog?' Kelly asked.

Arthur nodded. 'He strayed onto my land, bless him, he was on
his way out, but I think he somehow ingested something rotten
down by the stream. Could it be the groundwater?'

'You don't often get medical grade barbiturates popping out
of nowhere in nature, in my humble opinion,' Kelly said. 'Not
enough to kill an animal.' She looked towards the home. 'Where
does the waste travel?'

The man from environmental health nodded, grasping her
thread. Arthur panicked and grabbed the paperwork.

'We got the same results from the other samples too,' the man
said.

'Other samples?' Kelly turned to Arthur. The man looked at
Arthur, and Kelly examined the two men, one startled, the other
confused. Neither spoke.

'Arthur, can you tell me what is going on?' Kelly asked.

He sighed and took a deep breath. 'We've lost a few of Samuel's
sheep and a whole aviary of exotic birds down there too. It was
years ago, but now Walker, that's Samuel's dog.'

'How many years ago?'

Arthur glared at her. 'The birds died six years ago, the sheep
since then. Walker yesterday.'

He looked away. The man from environmental health was
talking.

'We're going to have to find the source, until then, Arthur,
if the home is connected by waste or supply to the pools down
there, then it may have to close,' he said.

'Oh Christ.' Arthur rubbed his eyes.

'Wait, if you suspect the waste of the home is to blame, can anyone explain to me what a nursing home would be doing with enough sodium pentobarbital to contaminate the ground water and to kill local wildlife?' Kelly asked.

The man sought permission from Arthur and Kelly could see that he was torn, but it was too late for that.

'I'm aware that it may be used to treat severe seizures or even insomnia, but what sort of quantities are we talking?' Kelly pushed them for an answer.

Arthur had turned pale. He ran his fingers through his hair and wandered blindly back to the home, without answering her.

'Arthur, where are you going?' Kelly asked.

'To find Beryl,' he replied.

Kelly turned back to the man, to listen to what else he had to say.

'Research is limited, and mainly coming from euthanised animals in the USA, but my initial assessment is that if it's killing animals in the surrounding area, they're eating something from the forest floor.'

'Which forest?'

The man looked around to get his bearings and he rubbed his chin. 'The samples were taken from down there,' he said, pointing. Kelly followed his gaze and peered at the forest away in the distance. It was where Mary had been staring earlier.

'How soon can you find out where the contamination is coming from?' she asked.

He rubbed his chin again. 'Depends. Once we've completed a thorough assessment, then we'll start digging,' he said.

'If you close the home, where will the residents go?'

The man shrugged nonchalantly; it wasn't his problem.

Chapter 38

Arthur walked across the field back to Promise Farm. He couldn't think straight. A desperate need welled up inside his gut. It was the desire to run. All his life, he'd dealt with problems by fleeing the scene. He did it when he and Samuel were little boys.

He recalled one time when Samuel broke the choke lever in his father's tractor. It wasn't even a good tractor. It was an old and battered 1948 Farmall, which their father had kept going for decades with love and oil. But it wasn't the intrinsic value of the contraption that meant anything to him, it was the passion and sweat he'd put into maintaining it, as well as the significance he attached to it. It had been a product of the war, which Percival had participated in, and letting anything from that era go was like losing a limb to their father. Their sheds had been full of apparatus, gadgets and appliances from the forties and fifties onwards, and they were sacrosanct items, as if placed on a sacred altar: worshipped for being idols of a bygone age, where his father had always belonged. The choke lever had come clean off, and he and Samuel had fallen about laughing, if only for a second, until it dawned on them that they might be in trouble. It had been a sunny day, as summers from memory tended to be, and they'd run the old engine into a hay bale for laughs. Percival had been at a local farmer's meeting, no doubt chatting about cuts after the war, taking his opportunity to spew vitriol at the government. Arthur could still smell the fuel, and the weight of the lever in his hand, when Samuel threw it at him to catch.

He could also recall the sting of his backside after his father had beaten him. It didn't matter how many times Samuel pleaded with him to stop, insisting it was he who broke the choke. Percival beat Arthur so bad that he couldn't sit down on a tractor for a week. His father's face, full of rage, no doubt aimed at the war, and the politicians who started it, screwed up in front of his, terrified him even more than the ten lashes with his father's belt. The shame burnt more than the violence.

He'd run over five fields, only stopping when his head felt light, and he was desperate for water. He hadn't gone home for two days, living off the land, drinking from streams and becks, with animals as his only companions. It had been Samuel who'd found him. He'd brought a bag of food and some TCP for his wounds. He'd fallen asleep beside him, under a bush, on a rug Samuel brought with him.

The memories burned in his head and by the time Arthur made it back to Promise Farm, he was crying, though he couldn't say when the tears had started. It was the salt in his mouth and the watery blurriness of his vision that jolted him back to the present, and he stared blankly at his surroundings, and marched straight past the house.

Run, Run…

Without being conscious of the effort, or the movement in his legs, or the boots on his feet trudging over the marshy grassland, he'd walked all the way to the forest. Now he stopped and looked around, just as he had over forty-five years ago, with the pain of a beating etched on his face. His heart raced. He was a child again and he looked around for shelter, as if waiting for Samuel to come and bring him food.

But it wasn't Samuel he found down by the old sheep shed, its stone walls crumbling and bleak, it was only the echoes of the past and his own panic hammering through his chest. The early afternoon sun twinkled in shafts through the gaps in the tree canopy. In the shady parts it was cool, but in the sunlight, the heat welled up inside his body and threatened to combust. He stepped into the dark and calmed his breathing.

He heard a vehicle and spied a truck chugging away back to the farm. No doubt it was Brian and Tommy going about their business – burning rubbish or fixing equipment – but he saw no smoke. Beryl insisted on keeping them on, though Arthur said they weren't needed. He could handle the land himself, with Dorian's help occasionally. Beryl's loyalty to the two men was a puzzle, because she'd never fostered any interest in the farm and spent most of her time at the nursing home, and less time with him.

Beryl had been a deserter too.

That's how they'd met. Travellers seeking enigmatic balls of golden light to evict the shadows. The circuit across the world, set up for lost souls like them, was a well-trodden path for life's sprinters, scuttling from hostel to hostel, from Bondi to Venice beach, safe in their collective brokenness.

They'd met in Cape Town.

Their combined hatred for their parents, and other figures of authority, bonded them, and the rest didn't matter. Until they ran out of money and his father fell ill. Samuel had begged him to come home, which he did, with Beryl in tow, but everything had changed. Nothing could ever be the same.

He sat down on a rock and pulled at blades of grass. He sniffed one as if searching for proof of the poison that was infecting his land and killing his animals. It was odourless, except for the sweet dampness of lush shoots. He threw it away and bent down, scraping the earth with his fingers.

What was under there? Had his father known? Had he planted something before he died, knowing that it would sully Arthur's chances for the future?

The rot had ruined any venture he and Beryl had tried. With each new idea, disaster lay ahead. Until the nursing home. They threw everything into it, despite Beryl having no formal qual-ifications, even gaining Prudence's support, which is why she'd agreed to be their first resident. She was determined to make it a success and even though she was dying, and the cancer spread quicker than anyone imagined, she slept there for five nights, hooked up to tubes and monitors, until her last breath, with the family around her.

Now she was to be dug up.

He looked at his hands, which were smeared with grime and dirt, and asked how it could have all come to this. But then a breeze rattled through the trees and shook him out of his self-absorption. Prudence would have had stern words with him. He tried to think what she might have said. She would have put everything into perspective and concentrated on the facts. But a nagging doubt crept up to his ribcage.

He was questioning everything lately. And he realised that this is what Prudence taught him to do. Stick to the facts. Even after a beating, his mother pointed out his fortune.

'You're lucky he didn't kill you,' she'd say.

'You need to learn to be a man.'

Through his tears, he'd nod and agree with her. But there was one thing she couldn't find the silver lining for. And he'd only ever seen it the one time.

She'd never feared her husband, never shirked hard work, didn't blink when they couldn't afford to slaughter a lamb for themselves, and didn't budge when Percival slammed around, smashing things and chuntering to himself, as was his way. Always the pragmatist.

Until that one time.

He'd not seen fear like it. She'd grabbed his hand, which was hooked up to machinery, as wine coloured liquid pumped into her. Then she'd pulled him close. As she was about to say something to him privately, urgently, away from anybody else's hearing, she'd fallen back onto her pillow, exhausted and unable to put her words together. He'd put it down to her being finally terrified of something: death. Wouldn't anybody be?

Beryl had interrupted the moment and it passed. But now, as he sat staring at the stream, and listening to it whoosh across the stones, he remembered her face. Prudence never ran. She always stood firm. It was a sign, he told himself. He had to stay and face whatever was coming. Rational thought was the only way to stay sane. Everything could be explained. *Be a man.* Even when your wife ran to the arms of another…

But in that moment, on her death bed, Prudence had looked as though she'd wanted to run too.

Kelly got back into the car and Fin watched her. She sighed deeply and sat in front of the wheel.

'What was all that about?' he asked.

Kelly explained.

'He said they might have to shut the home because of the contamination.'

'Hold on a minute, I think he's jumping the gun there,' Fin said. 'Shutting a home takes weeks, you can't just kick residents out in the street, the council have a duty of care.'

'But Mary is self-funding.'

'It doesn't matter, most of the people in there will be reliant upon social care, believe me, and the Care Quality Commission will have to put it on special measures if, and only if, they find the source of the contamination is a result of their own negligence. Besides, didn't you say that the samples were taken in the forest?'

Kelly nodded.

'So, it might have nothing to do with the home. They must investigate first. I'll call the CQC.'

Fin reached for his phone and found the correct number. Kelly started the engine. She desperately wanted to go back inside and warn Mary, but she also didn't want to panic her for no reason. She tried to think what she would do if she didn't know anyone personally in the home. That helped. She started the engine and pulled away slowly, listening to Fin's conversation with the Care Quality Commission. When he'd finished he told her what they'd said.

'They've confirmed that the report has been filed. Environmental health have the power to shut a home, but only once it's been investigated. She said the investigation was primarily to ascertain if the water supply to the home is affected, because this would be the first obvious hazard. They can do that without closing, for the time being. It's been formally put on special measures while they investigate. She said that a team has been sent to take samples from the water supply inside the home, and she'll send me an update once they have it.'

'I suppose we would know if anybody had been taken ill inside the home. Maybe I'm overreacting?'

'No, the jobsworth from environmental health spooked you, understandably, but he's acting over his pay grade. He shouldn't have said that.'

'You think it's safe?' Kelly asked.

'If sodium pentobarbital was floating around in the tap water, we'd know about it because we'd have twenty deaths on our hands,' Fin said.

'Good point. They do their work, we do ours. While we're here, the coroner wanted me to check something at the quarry.'

Fin stared out of the window as Kelly drove back onto Morningside land and across to the slate mine shop.

'Where in Ireland did you grow up?' she asked him.

'County Kerry. I miss the ocean.'

Kelly glanced over to the passenger seat. Fin could see the Irish Sea from his side, and she could tell he was nostalgic.

'Do you go back?'

'Not enough, but then when I do, it's never the same.'

Kelly smiled. 'That's what I thought, until I came back here.'

'Why did you leave London?' he asked.

She sighed. 'It's a long story.'

'You've got me trapped.'

'An error of judgement.'

'In a case?'

'No, I trusted my boss.'

'So, it's true.'

Kelly turned to him. 'What?'

222

'Matt Carter threw you under the bus.'

She hadn't heard his name for so long. It jolted her. People knew. Gossip hadn't just travelled; it had endured.

'I like to remember him as Matt the twat. Oh, look, we're here.'

They parked and got out of the car, and Fin smiled at her.

'I worked for him too,' Fin said.

'Drop it.' Her heart raced.

'I'm happier now.'

That was the end of it.

Inside the shop, they found somebody who was able to take them to the quarry. Thankfully, Gloria Morningside wasn't around to complicate matters. The journey was quick and less bumpy this time. When they arrived, Kelly walked over to the lip and peered over.

'Can you get down there?' she asked the woman who'd driven them in a Can–Am which seated six.

'Not in this, but it's easy in a small Gator,' she said.

Kelly and Fin looked at the path which led down. The tracks which she and Ted had spotted on Wednesday weren't there now, the rain had likely washed them away. She'd have to double check to see if forensics had taken moulds.

'Who drives the Gators up here?' Kelly asked.

'Dorian,' the woman replied.

Chapter 40

'Digging will commence on Monday,' Ted said to Kelly over the hands free in the car as she and Fin drove back to Eden House.

'The owners aren't pleased,' she told him.

'I'm not surprised, it's unfortunate, but the ball is in motion now. I'm sure it's a shock to them but it'll be better for their business in the long run that the paperwork is sorted.'

'On that note, I've just been in the nursing home, and the filing system was patchy at best. We retrieved some but not all the files we need to look at. Apart from that, we were leaving when an environmental health van pulled up. Seems like the land at the edge of Promise Farm is contaminated, they're having a rough week.'

'Contaminated how?'

'Historic deaths of livestock animals, and a recent dog.'

'From what?'

'Poison, I guess. They found traces of barbiturates in the recently deceased domestic canine.'

'Interesting.'

Kelly appreciated that her father was thinking. She could almost hear his brain whirring.

'Environmental health and the CQC are dealing with it, but thanks, Dad. I'll let you know what comes from it. We also checked the steppe, you can drive a Gator down there. Do you recall if forensics took moulds?'

'Yes, they did, I'll hurry them along.'

'Thanks, Dad.'

They hung up and Fin called Dan on Bluetooth to check in. It seemed that Dan had hit a brick wall when searching for the wills of the nursing home residents who'd died there since its inception seven years ago.

'They don't exist. Each of the solicitors was instructed to pass their files on to the nursing home, but get this, it was done in each case, only a few months before the deceased passed away,' Dan said.

'Do we have contact details for who they were taken over by?' Kelly asked, concentrating on the road ahead.

'Yes. In each case it was Beryl Morningside. The solicitors were instructed to sign them over and by law they must. They keep records, but it could take a day or two to retrieve them, I'm expecting them on Monday morning,' Dan told them.

'But the wills kept by the solicitors would have been the current versions?' Fin asked.

'Exactly.'

'Even when you change the custodian of your will, don't you have to have a solicitor to oversee?' Kelly asked.

'Yes, and for each one, it was a solicitor who worked out of Barrow-in-Furness, but I can't find any record of them operating beyond 2010.'

'Over ten years ago,' Kelly said. 'Any mention of Victor Walmsley?'

'One of them told me that it's quite common when end of life care is in place, for a person to transfer their will to a nursing home, and be facilitated by a funeral home, when that funeral home is the nominated company to handle the arrangements. He spoke to Victor Walmsley himself before he transferred the documents. He also told me that he offered to act as legal representation throughout the whole process, but Victor insisted it would be handled by their own solicitors in Barrow-in-Furness.'

'Which doesn't exist,' Kelly said.

'Yep.'

'But I assume that the paperwork was signed off, and correct?'

'Yes, which is why he was surprised to receive a phone call from me.'

'Any updates on sightings of Victor?'

'Actually, we've got somebody here waiting to be interviewed. I haven't had time to arrange it, he walked in off the street. He's a bird enthusiast, I'm just reading the note. Yep, that's all it says.'

'Anything else?' Kelly asked.

'The CCTV from Morningside came up blank, nothing at all. No sightings of Victor or his car, so he didn't have a meeting there.'

'So that means we have proof that Victor didn't drive this way when he was missing, after the camera caught him turning off the A66, and the camera from the guesthouse in Dockray proves he didn't go out the other way either,' Kelly said.

'So he must have remained within that area the whole week,' said Dan, echoing what they all thought.

Chapter 41

Beryl stared through the grimy window at Arthur's back as he walked away from the decrepit barn by the beck. His arrival had knocked her off guard, and she'd watched him as he sat pitying himself by the water, staring into space, like he used to when he was stoned. She'd always tidied up for him and made sure he held on through whichever crisis was unfolding inside their marriage.

She was exhausted.

The small stone shed had been there for decades, maybe even centuries. It was cool inside, and she shivered. She didn't normally spend this much time looking around at its interior but having been silent and unmoving for the past twenty minutes or so, in order to remain undetected by Arthur, she'd distracted herself with the stone, the floor and the dust-covered boxes she stored there. It was the only place on the farm which she knew was safe. It was the one space where she could switch off, take a minute, sort through the thousand jobs she had to do and protect the things that were private to her. Arthur had never been interested in it, after the aviary closed. It had been a great idea at first – or so Arthur thought – and their business plan, and the quality of the birds they imported, were expensive and guaranteed to make them money. Until they didn't. One by one, the birds succumbed to mysterious illnesses, the eagles first, which flew away for days on end, exploring their new domain. Then the hawks and vultures had been affected, until all of them were gone.

It had caused a spiral of despair in her husband that she was used to. Or, at least, she'd grown used to over the years. Arthur, she'd accepted, had to feel rewarded, otherwise, he headed straight down into a pit of self-pity, exactly where his father had put him. She was well aware that family traumas could take over a person's life until there was nothing left of them, but she too had suffered. Her childhood hadn't been perfect either, but her attitude was made of resilience and determination, rather than self-reflection and destruction. She'd fought hard for everything she had and wasn't about to give up because of a setback. She and Arthur were opposite creatures. That's why she had to mollycoddle him like a little brother.

Life wasn't fair.

The animals died. That didn't mean that the farm was forever unviable. You moved on; found something else. It was exasperating. And each time she did just that, coming up with solutions to their problems, he slid further into himself and disappeared right before her eyes. His descent into total loss – of himself, of hope, of joy – was almost complete. But she didn't blame herself. That was firmly parked at the door of his family: his father, mother and brother. There was no way she was ever going to carry that particular burden. It never once occurred to her that she added to his despair.

She sighed and got up from the plastic chair on which she'd been perched. She opened the door and it creaked with unfamiliarity. It let in tiny gusts of fresh breeze, and she took deep breaths. Her most pressing problem was how to throw the police officer off the scent she'd picked up, thanks to her questioning of how Victor ended up at the bottom of Samuel's quarry. If it wasn't for that, none of this would be happening.

Confident that Arthur had gone, she took her telephone out of her pocket and called Brian. He and Tommy would have to return here and work all afternoon now, if they were to get everything done before nightfall. She cast her eyes over the boxes, mostly ones which had been in here for years, but several she'd brought here just this morning, and calculated in her head how long it would take to burn the lot. If the police thought they had a right to trespass on private land, and dig up bodies, then she planned to make their job as hard as it could possibly be.

Tommy answered the phone.

'I've got another job for you two,' she said.

She explained what she wanted doing, as well as where and when, and they agreed a price.

She slammed the door shut behind her and used the key to lock it. Arthur had no idea it even worked. She slipped it into her pocket and walked back towards the home. No doubt, DI Porter would have done her digging by now. If only Vic was here, he'd know what to do. Their relationship had begun innocently enough: through Beryl's research into building a nursing home ten years ago.

A good woman should never be ignored, Vic had told her.

Arthur had taken his eye off her for too long, and by the time Beryl had officially signed with her new business partner, it had been too late. Her heart, as well as her bank account, were firmly taken care of.

But now, once again, like a returning stench, she was alone again. Every problem that was generated by the men in her life followed her around like a whingeing child.

She strode ahead with purpose. Vic had left a mess, it was true, but it was nothing she couldn't handle. She just had to get Arthur on board again, if she could shake him out of his self-pity.

Chapter 42

Kelly read the notes on the gentleman who was waiting for her in an interview suite. He'd called in because he'd set up an animal hide at the location where he thought he had a pest problem. The Forestry Commission tended the woodland all over the Lake District, and the trees which straddled the A5091 were no exception. She had no idea until now that trees were so vulnerable to attack from disease, rodents and insects. She saw the mighty structures as invincible. The news that they perhaps weren't was a shock.

Dean Strawbridge was what a Cumbrian might call a twitcher, or a curtain botherer. In other words, he sat in secluded camouflage hides and spied. But not on people, on animals. And a special type of animal: the aggressive and dangerous ones which might cause harm to his trees.

One such hideout was set up opposite the lay-by used by hikers to park their cars before they went for a leisurely walk up to Great Mell Fell.

Kelly entered the room and greeted him warmly. He looked like the outdoor type; he wore heavy boots, which were covered in mud, a long wax jacket, an old green jumper which looked like it had seen better days, and a flat cap. His cheeks were burnt ruddy from outdoor weathering, and he smiled broadly at her, like those attuned with nature were accustomed to.

'Good afternoon, Mr Strawbridge, thank you so much for waiting, I was out of the office.'

'No worries, it's nice and warm in here. I'm not used to it. They gave me coffee.'

She noticed his hands hugging a mug from upstairs. Kelly smiled and pulled out a chair, sitting down opposite him.

'It's Dean, please,' he said.

'Ok, Dean, let's have a look at your camera footage, shall we?'

He rummaged around in his pockets and pulled out a USB.

'It looked like deer damage to me at first, but I know the Morningsides don't have deer on their land, so I was stumped to be honest.'

Kelly hadn't come down here to listen to a lesson on herbivore habits, but she listened patiently. One often learnt something from the most random witnesses. Besides, he had a smooth intonation to his voice. It reminded her of her father's.

'It's not my business why you set up a hide there, Dean,' she said.

She wanted to put him at ease. Poachers operated in the Lake District like everywhere else. It wasn't her concern. She opened the laptop that was on the desk and inserted the USB. He carried on talking.

'Deer activity decimates populations of trees. They like to mark their territory and they have a good scratch to remove their antler skin too. It's my job to monitor the health of the trees on the Morningside land.'

'I understand that's the Forestry Commission's job?' Kelly asked.

'Aye, I work for them. Some folks just take the money and plant and fence. I look after them.'

Kelly smiled. 'That explains all the guards around the trees?'

He nodded.

'Then I thought it might be grey squirrels. People think they're soft and cuddly, but they're a pain in the royal backside, excuse my French. They gnaw the stems to reach the sweet sap, they love it. But if they drink too much of the sugar the tree dies. It's my job to stop that.'

'Quite.' She opened the file from the USB and turned the computer to face him, so they could both see.

'Can you talk me through this?'

He put down his mug. 'Aye.'

'So, the Forestry Commission has responsibility for trees even on private land?' she asked.

'Aye, it's an arrangement going back decades. We regulate private forestry and give advice.'

'So, you had Samuel Morningside's blessing?'

'Aye. I've known Samuel for years, though I went to school with his son.'

'Dorian?'

'Aye, same. Nice lad.'

Kelly found it curious that a man the same age would refer to his peer as such. It was as if he saw Dorian as younger and certainly not of his era. But then Dean was one of those men who looked and acted older than his years.

'Does Dorian help you out? I know he likes to check the property too.'

'Ah, he does. He enjoys it. He sometimes comes to the hides and tells me if he's spotted bark beetles and the like.'

'Dorian seems to know every inch of the Morningside land.'

'Aye, he does that.'

They returned to the footage. It was dark, and difficult to discern what they were looking at, but Dean's commentary was exemplary.

'Night vision has come a long way in the last ten years. The software we have picks up electrical current as well as heat. Look, there's a badger.'

Kelly wouldn't have had a clue what she was looking at had it not been for Dean's help. It occurred to her that they could ask him to take a look at the footage of the person who dumped Victor's car. She followed his finger and made out the shape of a large rodent-looking animal, and then saw its eyes. The shape was white, indicating a heat source.

'They're flies,' he added, pointing at a misty swarm buzzing around the camera.

She concentrated on his explanation and forced herself to be patient.

'Here we go,' he said. 'I saw the appeal for witnesses and when I next checked the hide footage, I found this. It's dated Tuesday the eighth, this week.' He said proudly.

She looked at the time. It was three twenty-five a.m. Kelly recalled the footage of what they thought was a woman driving Victor's car, from the camera at Kitto Beck. Here they were pulling into the lay-by. The figure got out and Kelly knew it was the same person caught on the other camera by the way they moved and their general shape and posture, though they appeared as a white source of heat rather than a fully formed human.

She sensed Dean's excitement. 'I read his car registration in the appeal. This is it isn't it?'

'It is,' she said.

'But that's a woman,' he added.

She stared at him. 'How do you know that?'

Dean paused. 'Erm.' He looked at his feet.

'Dean? Is something wrong? You told me you think it's a woman, how do you know?'

'I, erm. Crikey.'

She waited. She was more than a little curious, and he wasn't going anywhere. 'I'll wait until you recall,' she told him.

He sighed. 'You catch all sorts on these cameras.'

'Really?'

'I don't watch. I just check them for animals, but, well, you know, I see all sorts. People use the lay-by to meet at night. Men and women.'

The penny dropped.

'Oh, I see,' she said. 'You mean they meet to…' she raised her eyebrows, searching for the correct terminology. 'Have sex in the lay-by?'

'Yes,' he said with a sigh of relief at not having to say it out loud himself.

'I don't watch.'

'That's all right, Dean, it's none of my business. All I'm inter-ested in is you saying this is definitely a woman.'

'It is. Look,' he said.

She looked at the screen, hoping she wouldn't have to witness an illicit hook-up in Victor's car, though it would give her another angle to work, that was for sure. He forwarded the footage to three forty-eight a.m.

'What's she doing?' she asked.

'Waiting.'

At three-fifty-two a.m. a second car – a truck – pulled into the lay-by and parked next to Victor's car. Kelly sat up straight and a tingle went down her spine.

'Have you magnified this?'

'Here,' he said. 'You want the number plate?'

He flicked some buttons and the picture focused on the vehicle's number plate. It was readable. Kelly's heart soared. Then he reverted to the footage. The driver of the truck got out.

'Look, that's a man, see the difference in his bulk and gait?'

Kelly did. The figure driving the truck was bigger in stature and frame, and having something to compare their suspect to, it was obvious.

'I'm no detective,' Dean said. 'But something struck me as odd.'

Kelly listened. Dean Strawbridge would be an excellent detective to have on any investigation.

'That is an electronic device.' He pointed to the head of the male driver.

She squinted but saw nothing unusual.

He tapped some keys once more and the area around the male's head magnified. 'Look.'

All she could see was a tiny squiggle, which to be fair could be a hair languishing on the computer screen for all she knew.

Dean beamed at her.

'It's a hearing aid,' he said.

Kelly watched in amazement as Dean showed her the couple getting in and out of Victor's car, as if tidying it, and then at five-o-one a.m. the man got back into his vehicle and drove off, and the female disappeared out of sight, to walk across the road. All of it was caught on the Kitto Beck camera.

She turned to Dean and could have kissed him. He might look like a giant oaf, grimy and nocturnal, but he may have just cracked one of the mysteries of this case.

Chapter 43

Samuel answered the door. He held it wide – so welcoming he'd become after one small but significant visit from his brother yesterday. Arthur stood in his doorway.

Arthur came in and he closed the door.

'Gloria is out,' he told his brother.

'So is Beryl,' Arthur replied.

'Drink?' Samuel offered.

They sat down in the kitchen, pulling out wooden chairs that scraped along the tiled floor. They appreciated one another's weariness and didn't say much as Samuel got back up to grab a couple of beers out of the fridge.

'Thank you for telling me about Walker,' Samuel said.

'No bother. You'd have done the same,' Arthur said, taking the beer offered.

They popped the rings and took a deep gulp, in unison, then placed the cans on the table, still holding them. The simple movement in synchronicity jogged an unfamiliar sense of déjà vu in both of them and they locked eyes for a brief second, each wondering where the last decade had gone.

'How's things up at Promise?' Samuel spoke first.

He always did, as the older brother. Arthur was often too scared of his father to offer any new information, unsolicited.

'Going to rat shit, like always,' Arthur said, offering a cynical grin.

'Really? I thought the home was doing well, people pay through the nose to stay in those things, and if they don't, the government picks up the tab,' Samuel was genuinely surprised.

'We're being investigated by environmental health.'

'What for?'

'Whatever killed Walker. I brought the report.'

Arthur reached into his pocket and slid out the folded piece of paper, which looked as though it had been read a few times already. He passed it to his brother. Samuel took his reading glasses from a bowl on the table and popped them on his face to study the report. After a few minutes he looked up.

'Sodium pentobarbital? That's a horse tranquiliser Dad used to use.'

Arthur stared at him. 'That's why he gave me that land.'

Samuel could see where this was going. 'Wait, before you jump to conclusions...'

'Dad had horses, and I know he ran up some sizeable veterinary bills when they were sick,' Arthur said. *Like Walker. Like the birds.* 'God, it was Dad. He dumped their carcasses in the forest on purpose, to avoid the vet bills.'

'What are you talking about?' Samuel asked. 'Sick with what?'

'Walker was poisoned. He ingested something in the forest, like the birds and the sheep.'

'But anything left by Dad wouldn't be toxic now, surely?'

'He buried it on purpose to stop me making anything of the land.'

'Arthur, calm down. Just go back a step. What are they going to do?'

'They're coming first thing Monday to excavate around the beck to do some tests.'

Samuel raised his eyebrows. 'And what did the copper want?'

'She's here every day with some question or another. Beryl doesn't like her.'

'Beryl doesn't like anyone. Sorry.'

'She wasn't always like this,' Arthur said. He looked melancholy.

'They never were,' Samuel replied.

They smiled knowingly, as if it was a universal fact that all women change over time.

'There's something else,' Arthur said.

Samuel waited. He took his glasses off his nose and folded them.

'There was an issue with some of the paperwork at the home and the residents that were buried up at the chapel are being exhumed.' Arthur looked down at his hands and then took another swig of beer.

'What?'

Arthur let the shock settle.

'There's nothing we can do about it. Apparently, it's part of the investigation into Vic's business. They don't think he was filling in death certificates properly.'

'That's pretty serious. You know Beryl came here on Wednesday night asking us about Vic?'

'No, I didn't know that. What did she want?'

'She said you knew. I was as shocked as you are now, so was Gloria. We said we didn't know anything. The police will do their job, and that'll be that. Is she hiding something?'

For a second Samuel thought that Arthur might get up and leave. After all he had no right asking such questions.

'She's jumpy.'

'What about?'

Arthur took a final tug on the beer can and closed his eyes.

'They're digging up Mum's grave too,' Arthur said.

Samuel's face turned grey.

'I'm sorry. Beryl and Vic sorted the paperwork, remember? The police are investigating every death at the home, including Mum's.'

'Christ,' Samuel said. He stood up and paced the kitchen. He kicked the dog basket, trying to rid himself of the bad news but also the grief that Walker wasn't in it. Arthur watched and didn't speak, like he had done all his life. He watched his older brother for signs for what to do next.

'What were Beryl and Vic up to?' Samuel demanded, turning on his brother, his face red.

'Nothing, I swear to you. But...'

'But what?' Samuel sat down and looked into his brother's eyes. 'I could always tell when you were scared. You kept yourself small and out of the way, and you stopped rushing about, as if any drama would come back on you. It was like you shut down. Made yourself invisible.'

'That's how it felt,' Arthur replied.

'You're doing it now,' Samuel said.

Finally, Arthur spoke. 'Vic came to our house to see Beryl. He wasn't missing that week, he was with her.'

Chapter 44

From the lip over the quarry, Dorian surveyed the land. He sighed with contentment as he noted that the police tape had now gone. They had no right to be here in the first place. The land belonged to the Morningside family and nobody else. It was his job to survey and make sure no one trespassed, or worse, poached. The penalty for stealing slate was a minimum of six months in prison but Dorian reckoned they deserved more. If that's what Victor was there to do and he'd paid with his life, then so be it.

The rolling hills, dales and fields looked back to normal now, and it soothed him. He'd got used to the horizon being changed by the nursing home. At first, his dad had said it was a bloody eye sore, and it was true. But he no longer listened to much of what his dad said. He'd rather spend long hours in the gym sculpting his body, than at home with his father moaning about how hard life had got and what a traitor Uncle Arthur was. He sounded like a broken record.

The problem with his father was that he was busy but not useful. He didn't utilise his time well and ended up frustrated and lost. He'd forgotten how to simply be at one with the land. Building muscle and listening to his body enabled Dorian to attune his keen empathy with the nature around him. He had little time for the modern way. In Uncle Arthur, he recognised a kindred spirit, which is why he kept an eye on his land.

On the edge of the farm, close to the forest, he spotted something out of place and Dorian furrowed his brow. He realised that it was the forest itself that was different, and he felt his hand twitch. It was a familiar reaction to anything being not quite right. He'd had it all week, ever since he'd found the undertaker at the bottom of the quarry. He looked to the trees on Uncle Arthur's land, where the sheds crumbled, and the beck ran serenely through it.

It was unmistakeable.

A steady stream of dark grey smoke lifted to the sky and Dorian didn't know whether to raise an alarm or ignore it. Arthur's labourers burnt rubbish all the time, and he was used to seeing farm fires, but they were normally next to the outbuildings and gave off a lighter smoke. This was dense and enough of a concern to make Dorian want to go and investigate.

He'd brought the Gator and he looked at his watch. It was late afternoon and the time of day, on a Saturday, when the farm was quiet. Auntie Beryl often gave people extra work on the farm but still, if they didn't know that a fire was raging down there and they discovered that he did, then he'd never forgive himself for not raising the alarm. He made his mind up to investigate and jumped on the Gator, starting her up and speeding off in the direction of Arthur's land.

It didn't take him long, and as he got nearer to the forest, the wind blew the acrid smoke his way and he recognised the familiar aroma of burning material. It wasn't manure, and he didn't think it was fuel. He parked the Gator at the edge of the forest, in the shade of some trees, and walked through the dense undergrowth. He knew all the trails and had played in the bushes and trees when he was a child, building camps with his uncle, until he'd gone away, and by the time he came back, he was a man. He knew his way around with his eyes closed.

But he slowed when he heard voices, thinking the fire was legitimate after all. He continued to walk through the trees, but he paused and held back when he saw two men laughing and throwing piles of rubbish into a fire pit. There were boxes of the stuff and Dorian hung back in the shadows, wondering what to do. He recognised the men as Brian and Tommy who worked for Beryl and Arthur, but something told him not to disturb them. Instead, he made his way silently round the back of one of the sheds, which was where they were getting the boxes from before opening them and burning the contents. He flicked his eyes around but saw no sign of his auntie or uncle and contemplated his dilemma. He didn't want to appear a busybody or a spy even, and risk damaging his relationship with his uncle, who'd clearly told the men to do the job. But he also considered if what the men were doing was deceitful and unknown to their employers. His auntie and uncle would at least want to be informed what was going on, or that he was concerned. It would show that he cared and that he took his job of checking very seriously.

He slipped behind the shed and noticed that the men were drinking.

Maybe this was some kind of campfire, and they were going to invite friends, or perhaps they had been sacked and were burying evidence. Whichever it was, he knew that he had to tell Arthur. He checked his pocket but realised he'd left his phone in the Gator, on silent, so as not to disturb him when he received a text from his mother, which he did twenty times a day. He heard her voice in his head warning him that, one day, he'd regret not having it and it would be the end of him.

Smoke bellowed his way as the wind changed and he covered his mouth, so he didn't cough.

Then he heard a woman's voice and recognised it as Auntie Beryl's. Just as he went to step from behind his cover, she spoke, and the tone of her voice made him stay put. She wasn't in a good mood.

He held back. He could see the three figures through the trees and watched the two men stop what they were doing. Auntie Beryl put her hands on her hips.

'How long?' she asked.

'We're going as fast as we can.'

'All this smoke is going to attract attention. If anybody comes down here, make sure they don't leave,' Beryl said.

Dorian held back and crept along the wall of the shed, where he forced his back up against the wall as much as he could. Then he heard Beryl leave.

'She's one hell of an uptight bitch. What do you reckon we're burning anyway?' one of the men asked the other.

'Who cares? As long as she pays us. It's likely something illegal, knowing Beryl.'

They laughed.

'Cigarette break? We don't need a light.' They laughed at their joke and wandered off to smoke, leaving the fire to rage.

Dorian crept around the shed and slipped into it, noticing that there were still some boxes inside. He approached them and peered around. As quietly as he could he slid out a file from one of the boxes and began to read, but it was medical information on a patient at the home and he had no idea what it meant, apart from that it was Beryl's private business. Now he felt foolish for sneaking around and decided that the best thing to do was to make himself scarce and creep away like he'd come.

But the men had finished their cigarettes and were returning, laughing about something else. He quickly sank low behind an old rusty plough, discarded long ago by the look of it, and waited. His plan, if he needed one, was to wait it out until the men had finished, and then leave.

One of them came in and pulled out another box. He dragged it with both hands and the noise of it scraping along the earth grated on Dorian's nerves.

'Let's call it a day,' he said.

'We could always keep it,' the other said.

'Insurance.'

Then the door was slammed and locked.

Dorian sat still, listening hard for signs they were leaving so he could get back to his vehicle and forget he'd even been here. He peered at the grimy window and wondered if he could smash his way out. Nobody would notice. The decrepit structures in the forest were falling down. He waited for the men to leave.

He stared at the grimy window and gazed at the sky, which was turning shadowy with the sinking sunlight. Soon it would be dark, and they'd give up, then he'd work out how to get out.

Chapter 45

Kelly stared at the screen on the police national computer. The truck she'd seen on the hide footage provided by Dean Strawbridge had been traced to an address in Keswick. It was registered to a man named Brian Wells and according to the stats, he'd owned it for ten years. There was no business name attached to the file so that told them it was a personal use vehicle. A squad car had been sent to the address.

She looked at her Garmin watch, purchased so she could track her walks and keep an eye on her heart rate, which was now over a hundred. Weekends for most people were supposed to be a release from the tough week preceding them, but for police officers in the middle of a serious investigation, they were just another working day. However, the same couldn't be said for forensic services. The police could chase around the Lake District all they liked, getting choked behind tourists, caravans and postal deliveries but the fact was that the labs, specialist services, offices and call numbers they relied on for chasing evidence all closed. Even hotels were sluggish in replying to their calls at the weekend, busy with their own spikes in bookings.

Kelly sat in a swivel chair in the incident room going over what they had. Dan had been working non-stop on the technical details of the murder case. But following the money trail in any case was the most time-consuming activity, which is why she held little hope of getting any solid results today.

At the end of the day, most crime came down to sex or money, or both. She scribbled on a pad in front of her and tried to link the information she had to date, her brow knitted in concentration.

They'd had no promising reports of sightings of Victor from last week and this told her one thing: he was stationary. His wounds indicated the same thing. The CCTV footage confirmed it: he'd been in the area of Morningside Farm and hadn't left.

Kate getting up from her chair broke her train of thought.

'You can go home,' Kelly said to her. 'I'm planning to, after I hear from the uniforms I sent to check out the truck.'

'It's about something else, but, yes, I would like to go home, even if it's just to watch TV on my own.'

'Andrew busy?'

Kelly referred to their superintendent who Kate had been seeing for a year now. No one in the office had really expected it to last. The pressure of gossip around the force, and the tension associated with serious cases often worked against romances between ranks. But, against the odds, they were still an item. Kate assured her that they never talked shop, and knowing both well, she believed her.

'It's his weekend with his kids,' Kate said. 'But it's not about going home, Dan just gave me this.'

She read the printout which consisted of five pages. It was information found on Victor Walmsley's computer, which had been taken from the offices of Dale & Sons on Thursday.

'What is it?' Kelly asked. She scanned the document. All she could see was a list of searches on the web. Domain names, weird titles and references, and lots of numbers. She'd seen enough printouts of people's search histories to know that what she was looking at had been hidden on Victor's computer and some bright spark in the tech department had discovered it, but the exact nature of the sites wasn't obvious.

'What am I looking at? These dates are regular and repetitive.'

It was true, whatever Victor had been searching for, he did it a lot.

'Tech says it's the dark web. Plenty of illegal stuff,' Kate said.

'Interesting, any idea what specifically?'

'They don't know yet, these sites are almost impossible to crack. It takes Interpol years to research this stuff. It was sent to us as standard because Victor's computer equipment was seized. What would Victor be doing on the dark web?' Kate asked.

Kelly was distracted by thoughts of returning home to her daughter and snuggling into her neck, to get that reassuring comfort from the innocent. The other part of her dreaded confronting Johnny. But now those whims melted away.

'Kelly?' Kate nudged her.

'Bulk buying something?' Kelly said. Kate furrowed her brow in confusion.

The dark web was a murky world of illicit trading, which hid IP addresses behind a network of anonymous traders who handled the deadliest contraband across the globe. It was a bit like the black market used to be in the good old days, but online.

Pirates.R.US.

It was not only illegal but fast-moving and almost impossible to trace. Interpol spent years putting together cases worth billions of euros to catch career criminals.

'If Victor was cutting corners and massaging paperwork, then he could get what he needed from here. People sell their mothers for the right price.'

'Or their mothers-in-law,' Kate quipped.

'And I bet you can buy dodgy ID too, like certified GPs and probate lawyers from Barrow-in-Furness. Has anybody had time to access any of the sites?' Kelly asked.

'No, he's only just received this notification. We need specialists.'

'Fin?' Kelly shouted across the incident room. Fin sat back in his chair and wheeled himself across the room.

'Didn't you do drugs squad in the Met?'

'For a bit.'

'Did you have anything to do with the dark web?'

'Occasionally, we dabbled.'

Kelly gave him the printout, and he scanned it quickly, rocking on his chair.

'Interpol and Europol collect data on domain names and store them. We could start there, but they become obsolete very quickly, most of these might be renamed by now, it's how they stay ahead of the law. The dark web is a monster, like an ocean, it's constantly moving with tides and sewage. It's virtually impossible to get live tracing on a domain because they morph and flow. But if they have evidence of the products linked to these sites, even if they are no longer running, we might get an idea of what Victor was doing.'

The only department Kelly knew of to access the dark web in any kind of sophisticated manner was the child abuse team. It's how they operated to catch career criminals who'd moved the selling of their vile images from magazines and postal delivery to the world wide web. Kelly, like most detectives in any UK police force, was behind the power curve when it came to the illicit dealings of the dark web – generally accepted as about fifty per cent of it. Every time they cracked a way into the servers offering anything from a lifetime of hacked Netflix accounts to buying arms from Afghanistan, those intent on circumnavigating legal trade hopped one step beyond. When she'd worked in the Met, hundreds of officers trawled through dark web content every day, searching for evidence of crime, but it was maddeningly slow and as slippery as a rain forest frog. It was like an onion, but one that kept growing more and more layers, each to hide the last one peeled off. Cybercrime was the largest growing sector in the world, and there were plenty of rogue states willing to take a cut to host servers offering contraband goods and services.

Their best hope of accessing such information was the Cybercrime unit in the Met, and Kelly knew an old colleague of hers who she could ask.

Dan joined their conversation.

'Boss, Dale & Sons were struggling financially until about five years ago,' he said.

'And what changed five years ago?' Kelly asked out loud.

'Victor began his business relationship with Beryl Morningside,' all three officers said in unison.

'Do you think Victor and Beryl were in business other than as caring nurse manager and undertaker? There's got to be more to it,' Dan asked.

'You're the one whose been looking at his accounts. What do you think?' she asked him.

'Ripping off residents and taking their money when they die? It's not exactly the crime of the century, is it? It could even be legal if we find the paperwork is kosher.'

'Is it?'

'It's looking that way boss. If the residents signed over their estates before they died and they were of sound mind. I checked with legal, then there's no crime.'

'But then there's the fake GPs and the coroner's investigation. And why did Victor end up dead?' Kelly knew Dan was being cautious but the idea that they wouldn't be able to nail Victor for his past crimes deflated her.

'An argument over money, who shares what?' Dan suggested.

'An argument that lasted a whole week?' Fin asked.

'Beryl is hiding something, that much is clear, else we would have found all the files on the nine deaths at the home. I think it's enough for a warrant for the nursing home and Promise Farm,' Kelly said. 'But not an arrest, yet.'

Kelly's mobile phone buzzed, and she answered. She smiled as she ended the call.

'We've got Brian Wells. He's on his way in. He should be here in half an hour.'

They stared at her.

'What else, boss?' Fin asked.

She grinned. 'He wears a hearing aid.'

Chapter 46

Kelly and Kate entered the interview suite and sat down opposite Brian Wells. He was a large man with calloused hands and weathered features typical of the outdoors life.

'Afternoon, Mr Wells, thank you for coming in,' Kelly said.

'Nah bother. What's this all about my truck? You know it's doddery these days, ancient in fact, it's been in the garage more times than I've had hot dinners.'

Kelly appreciated the blathering; it was a sign he had something to hide. They'd get to his alibi in good time, after they'd shown him the footage of the figure caught on Dean Strawbridge's hide camera.

'Right, well maybe this will be a very short meeting then,' Kelly said, smiling.

It worked. Brian relaxed and allowed his hands to fall onto his lap, taking them out of his pockets. The fact that his truck was the same model Mary and Winnie watched with interest on the farm proved nothing; there were thousands of them. But Kelly had exemplary facial recognition skills and she'd seen Brian's before, driving a truck past her at Morningside farm on her first visit when Victor's body had been discovered.

'What is your job, Brian?'

'Labouring. All my life.'

He showed them his hands.

'Never had a day off.'

Kelly saw tiny beads of sweat forming on his forehead.

'And who is your current employer?'

'I go here and there, you know?'

'Can you be a bit more specific?'

'I've done work for Samuel Morningside.'

'On the Morningside estate? Of course, that's where I've seen you.' She smiled.

Brian looked nervous.

'When was your last job?'

Brian scratched his chin and pretended to think.

'Burning rubbish, this morning.'

Kelly understood now why she smelled the faint aroma of acrid smoke, as if he'd been camping with the boy scouts all week.

'Where?'

'At the farm.'

'What about Promise Farm? Do you carry out work for them too?'

'Not for years.'

Kelly and Kate glanced at one another; the information didn't make sense.

'Were you working Tuesday just gone? The eighth of October?'

The chin scratch again.

'Early morning, more specifically,' she added.

Scratch.

'How long have you had your hearing aid, Brian? May I call you Brian?'

'Everybody does. It was my pa's name. What was the question? I'm hard of hearing.'

'Yes, I see. I was asking about your hearing aid.'

He fiddled with it on cue, buying time.

Kelly opened the laptop in front of her and turned it around.

'Can you watch this and tell us if you recognise anybody?'

Kelly and Kate sat patiently, knowing the video intimately second by second, frame by frame. Brian's demeanour changed just at the bit where the truck pulled up and the man with the hearing aid got out of it. He began to fidget and twist in his seat. Kelly silently thanked the gods for Dean Strawbridge and his odd obsession with nocturnal animals.

'Is that you, Brian?'

He didn't answer.

'Hearing aids show up on the latest night vision technology because of their tiny electrical signals. It's amazing, really.'

Brian couldn't speak.

'Before I arrest you for handling stolen property belonging to a murder victim, Brian, can you tell me who the woman in the video is?'

Chapter 47

Dorian swallowed hard. He'd never experienced thirst. True thirst. He'd told his mother he wanted a drink a thousand times or more. When they were out in the fields or rounding up Herdies with Penny. Samuel always carried a couple of bottles of local spring water on his vehicle. He never bought it. The springs all over his land produced the sweetest tasting and purest water.

But now, after what he guessed was only a couple of hours, all he could think about was water. The air inside the shed was stifling. He didn't know for sure what time it was because he didn't wear a watch. Nobody who worked the land and lived by its clock did. The sky was darkening and so he reckoned it was almost time for sunset.

He'd exhausted himself. Sure the men weren't coming back, or his auntie Beryl, he'd tried to break off a piece off the old plough to crack the window because he'd found it locked tight shut. It was as ancient as the fields, or at least it looked that way. Rust and grime had welded it into position, and it didn't budge. Anything he found to hand merely bounced off the tough old glass. He was stuck. His only hope was that the men came back and unlocked the shed. But that might not be until tomorrow. Thinking himself a hardy type, he thought it would be a fairly straightforward wait, if uncomfortable. But he had underestimated his thirst. The last of the sun dipped away from the forest but the temperature inside the stone relic didn't abate much. He was desperate for a drink.

He'd taken off his T-shirt, having left his sweater in the Gator. If only he'd left it where somebody could see it, then they'd have realised that somebody else was around. But he'd hidden it out of sight, by instinct, something telling him he wasn't supposed to be there. He figured that if it got cold at night then he'd at least have an extra layer to put on.

His eyes had grown accustomed to the dim light, and he'd counted the stones making up the walls. He had tried his hand at stone walling himself and knew how impenetrable they were. He'd already looked for weaknesses but found none. The shed must be hundreds of years old and at first, he'd admired the workmanship, thinking how beautifully it had been constructed but now he hated every boulder and crack. He'd pushed where he thought he'd spotted loose stones, but he knew that on the other side of the interior layer there were more. It was useless and he resigned himself to a long night without water.

The floor was earthy and damp, having been abandoned and unloved for years. It was also covered in cigarette butts, no doubt from Brian and Tommy. He tried to distract his mind and imagine the Herdies sleeping in here centuries ago, sheltering from the cold nights in winter. He fancied he could smell them.

There were a few discarded boxes, and he tore them up to make a bed for himself. The labour made him hotter, and he fought for air, wishing there was a gap in the stones to let him breathe. Resting, he lay down and tried to make his mind wander to happier times, but each time, his brain took him back to water. Lakes of it. Streams, becks, waterfalls, hidden pools and taps gushing with the stuff. It tormented him.

That's when he heard the drip.

In the ever-darkening shadows, his senses became honed to noise, and he focused on where he heard the tapping of water hitting rock. He went to one corner and removed all the discarded equipment from it, exposing the wall, checking every inch to find the source of the rhythm that was driving him mad.

But he couldn't find it.

Then he realised with abject disappointment that the noise was outside. He pressed his head up against the stone and listened to water dripping beyond his grasp. Then his ears attuned to the beck. The swishing of the water made him swallow and he realised that his lips were dry.

He chuckled to himself at how stupid he was. He knew that the beck was there all along and couldn't believe his idiocy. His mother would be laughing herself if she were here. The beck ran through the forest and emerged right next to the clearing where the men had been burning rubbish. He knew also that becks and streams ran underground, and the chances were that it went under this very shed. He went back to the plough and ripped off an arm from one of the old levers, then fell to the floor and began digging. It might take him an hour or so, but eventually, if there was water under the shed, he'd find it.

Chapter 48

Kelly dropped her bags at the door. Her shoulders hurt from carrying stress all day, in fact every day since Victor's body had been found.

All the way home she'd been thinking about Mary and how to approach the subject of money. If Mary had signed over hers to the nursing home, then there was no way any judge would find her unsound of mind and rule the transaction illegal. Mary had no family, just like most of the nine women who'd been buried at the chapel on Promise Farm. But that's all she knew because her file was missing along with others.

But now she was home, the nagging truth emerged more clearly. What she was really avoiding was the conversation she needed to have with Johnny.

Mary's comment to her about changing her mind about something niggled away at her, but she was tired, and her brain felt numb, which was why she'd come home for a break. Brian Wells wasn't talking. They'd arrested him and he'd been shown the inside of a cell, where he'd remain until he was assigned a lawyer in the morning.

It was unlikely that the warrants would come in tonight, and they'd be lucky to get them tomorrow, though she'd asked her father to pull a few strings. Ted knew the two magistrates who signed off her court orders personally, and she often asked for his help. Monday seemed an age away and she had to make sure she did this by the book.

Leaving the office had been hard for all of them, in fact, Dan and Emma had stayed. But then she understood that pull. She'd worked on the murder squad in London with Matt the twat, and they'd never wanted to leave the office either, only to make love and drink.

On Monday they'd also start to exhume the bodies from the chapel land. At least she knew that the most recent burials would yield complete bodies for Ted to work with. The older ones, depending on the quality of the coffins, might be just bones. Yet Dan had told her that all the women had opted for the most expensive funerals, so there was hope. Ted even assured her that there might be viable tissue to examine.

They knew Victor didn't go to work last Thursday, and that he went instead to an area close to the farms, and so far, they'd had no sightings of him publicly until his body turned up. There were several plausible theories: he visited somebody, riddled with guilt over something, wanting out. They argued and he was murdered for it. Or, Victor didn't know what was going on, found out, and sought revenge, it backfired and he was murdered for it. Or, Victor was terminally ill, sought illegal end of life care, it went wrong, he got sepsis and it was covered up. She could cobble together circumstantial evidence for each scenario, but nothing solid had emerged so far, except the video given to them by Dean Strawbridge, but that only proved somebody else was driving Victor's car, it didn't mean they killed him.

The house was quiet, and she wasn't used to it. Her balance was off, and she craved domestic noise and chaos to soothe her nerves. She'd told Kate earlier about her meeting with Carrie in the pub last night. Kate had asked about Josie's relationship with her mother.

'Josie can be fiery. I'm not taking sides, at all, I just think that Josie had a place to run to when things got tough between them. If all fourteen-year-old girls had that option, don't you think the majority of them would take it?' she'd asked her friend.

'Good point. Yes, I would have lost my girls years ago if they had somewhere to run to every time they thought I was Satan for telling them off.'

'I think the point here is that whatever happened was in the past and not on my watch. Staying married for financial reasons makes sense, but he still lied and I'm frankly sick of questioning his moral integrity.'

It was true, Kelly was growing weary of being caught out by Johnny's mistakes.

'That's a big ask on a relationship, that anyone has enough moral integrity to impress their partner. Isn't that wishful thinking and something that only Instagram influencers get to pretend they have?' Kate had asked.

'I'm sure you're right, but it still doesn't help me figure out whether I can actually be arsed with it at the moment. I'm surrounded by liars all day long, I really don't want to go home to them too. Besides, why are you making excuses for him? You said yourself, you wish you'd left Derek years ago instead of giving him the benefit of the doubt each time he let you down. I don't want to waste my life forgiving somebody who never learns. A mistake is a one-off, when they do it again it's a pattern, and I'm sick of being disappointed.'

Kate had stared wide-eyed at her, but it felt good to get it off her chest.

'It sounds to me like you've already made up your mind. Let me know if you need Millie sooner rather than later.'

Kate's words sat with her now as she threw her keys on the side and kicked off her shoes. Her body felt tired, but she knew it was the weight of her heart. It wasn't broken. It had never healed.

Faced with an empty house, a flash of guilt seized her as she realised that she was wishing away her future. Mary always told her to be careful what she yearned for. Then another, completely new spectre caused her stomach to tighten. Johnny spent more time caring for their daughter, on balance, because her job was more demanding. What if they split up and he demanded custody of Lizzie?

She walked through to the kitchen and a shaft of autumn light sliced the floor in two, as it usually did in the late afternoon.

The soft sounds of seventies music wafted from the radio, which was turned low. She went to the fridge and peered forlornly at the offerings inside. Everything required effort and she had little energy left. But that was the point: she needed to replenish her fuel levels but couldn't be bothered to do so. She reached for a yogurt pot and a spoon and leant against the counter shovelling it into her mouth, wishing she could come up with something more inventive.

Johnny's silent appearance at the doorway almost made her drop it and she took a sharp intake of breath.

'God, you scared me! I didn't know you were in. Is Lizzie asleep?'

Johnny nodded. His shoulders were sunken, and he looked tired.

'Work busy?' he asked.

'Yeah,' she said, stopping eating, casting aside the yogurt pot and closing it.

'I came home for a break, my brain is fried.'

'Is that what home is to you now?' he asked.

It was a good question, but unfair.

'Isn't that what a home should be?'

'But you don't rest here, you just come and go.'

'Jesus, that's brutal. Wasn't that our arrangement? You're the one who fucked up.'

'I did.'

'You did.'

He looked at her and she realised in the small second it took for him to look away, that she didn't love him any more. It wasn't the Ian Burton case; it wasn't the money; it was everything. The distance, the silence, the shutting out, and the secrecy.

'I can't trust you,' she said.

'What can I do to make it right?'

'Make what right? Go back in time and not lie to me?'

'I told you this place is safe, I'm not going to touch any of your money. The house is in your name. My debts are just that. I'll sort

Carrie. I've been on the phone to a financial advisor. I can sort it. It'll be a squeeze but it's my problem. I've filed for divorce this morning, Carrie will sign the papers as soon as she gets them, and we'll split the whole liability. It'll be in my name.'

He was waffling and his sentences all merged into one, like a machine gun dump of guilt.

'When's the money due?'

'Next March. The work I've done on the flat should cover it.'

'Carrie is nothing like I imagined her to be.'

'We weren't right together. It doesn't mean we're bad people.'

'I guess raising a child together tends to hold a mirror up to who you really are doesn't it?'

'And do you think I'm a good dad?'

His eyes were glassy. She'd witnessed the way he cared for Lizzie in the middle of the night, the way he tended to her when she was sick, or feverish, how he got up early at the weekend to play with her, to give Kelly a lie in.

'Yes, you're an amazing dad. To both your daughters.'

'I've got you to thank for that,' he said. 'Josie wouldn't have moved in here if it hadn't had been for you.'

'Well, you can flatter me all you want but I'm nowhere near a perfect mother, or stepmother.'

'If you believe I lied to you on purpose than you must decide what to do. It's your choice. I want to stay here. I want us to be a family.'

'No. Not this time. It's too much. I can't rely on you to tell me the truth if I forgive you and we go on as normal. You didn't tell me for a reason, and I think it's because you knew how I'd react. You chose to mislead me.'

'I didn't, Kelly, it all became overwhelming so suddenly.'

'That's bullshit, and you standing here defending it just shows how right I am to put an end to it. You've crossed a line. It's a limit I didn't know I had until you broke it. But it's done and now it can't be undone. To ask me to carry on is like asking me to change who I am, and I can't do that, not even for you. Or Lizzie.'

259

The effect of her words on him was visible. She had to close her eyes because the gut-wrenching pain threatened to smash her resolve.

She felt him come close, and she stepped back.

'What happened?' he asked.

'Don't do that. You caused this. You did a thing, and I can't stand it. Don't dare try to treat me as unreasonable. Respect my decision, please, Johnny. Don't make this harder than it is.'

Five years ago, she'd been tired of being messed around by men who loved themselves more than anybody else. Then Johnny had shown her for a while what it was like to be loved for being yourself. Now, though, she realised she didn't need anyone to do that for her. She wasn't angry or resentful. She only felt peace that she was doing the right thing. The constant pull between home and work shouldn't be painful, she realised. She loved her job, and she remembered all the times Johnny had tried to get her to quit. He'd used Lizzie to convince her. Thank God she hadn't listened. Few of the people around her were what they seemed.

People, it seemed, always let you down.

It wasn't just Johnny who'd done it. The man she'd thought was her father had too. The news that an inquiry had found him posthumously guilty of abuse of process and misconduct was still raw. Good old John Porter, legend, and bona fide force of nature had been hailed as a hero. But at home, he'd been distant and aloof, forcing his daughters to look to themselves for flaws. Then she'd found out the true extent of his influence at work, surrounded by other misogynists and corrupt coppers. Shame on the family was only made bearable by the fact that Wendy wasn't alive to see it.

Then there was Wendy herself. Matriarch on the outside and doormat on the inside, rather like an armadillo, but infinitely more dangerous to growing women who looked to their mother for a role model.

Maybe she was sick and tired of people not being who they said they were.

'Millie is coming back to work for me,' she said.

'No,' he said.

'What? Don't make this a battle. Don't do to Lizzie what you did to Josie.'

She saw the pain that she'd inflicted but it was a necessary cut.

She was finally letting go of other people's baggage. She forgave Wendy for abandoning her to her father's dominance. She forgave her sister for hating herself so much that she took it out on the person closest to her. They should have been partners, but Nikki was now a distant memory in her past.

Kelly turned to the sink and held onto its rim, as if hoping it would support her through the rough times ahead. Some of the tension in her shoulders had disappeared, and her gut told her she'd done the right thing. Now she just had to stick to it.

Chapter 49

Arthur watched his wife come in. No lights shone in the grand cottage that was more like a mansion. The pretension that had gone into the fine furnishings and modern provisions remained in the dark. He didn't want them illuminating.

'Where have you been?'

He made her jump.

'Jesus, Arthur, what the hell are you doing sitting in the dark?'

'It's where you put me. I think it's me who needs an explanation,' he said.

'Don't be childish, Arthur.'

He half-smiled that she treated him like a toddler then blamed him for behaving like one. He didn't care any more.

'We have to tell the police why Victor was here,' he said simply.

'Don't be ridiculous. Do you want to go to jail for his murder?'

'No, but I won't because I didn't murder him.'

'Well, neither did I. Grow up, Arthur, the police won't see it like we do. We need to give them an alternative.'

'There's no "we" here, Beryl, Victor came to see you. The game is up, I told Samuel why he was here.'

'What? So you've made up? How touching. After everything I've done for you. And what do you think your brother is going to do to save you? You know as well as I do that the police are looking at both of us. If I go down, then so do you.'

Her words stung. He stared at her in the dark and remembered when they'd met. He'd fallen for her risk-taking, identifying it as something that resonated with his will to self-destruct. Now, she'd dragged his whole family down with her. And yet here she was, still threatening him, whereas Samuel, his estranged brother for a decade had done just the opposite. After telling him the position he was in, Samuel had offered to take the blame, as if that might make up for having never protected him like a brother should. Samuel had told him that it was his fault he'd never made anything out of Promise Farm, gloating that their father had given him the rotten half. But Arthur didn't need protecting then, and he wasn't about to start asking for it now.

'You never told me what Victor wanted,' he said.

'You never asked. Why start now? I've provided for you, haven't I?'

The slur on his ability to do anything right seared into his skin like hot needles.

'Always the little worrier,' she added for good measure. His reduction to foetus was almost complete.

'I helped Victor, you saw that with your own eyes.'

'Yes, you did. Just like you helped my mother.'

She stood in the doorway and threw her keys into the bowl, missing. They clattered to the floor. Even in the dark he could see her grin.

'You said you'd called an ambulance,' he said.

She ignored him.

'All I ever do is protect us,' she said.

Her voice had soured, and her statuesque stillness made the tiny hairs on his arms stand up. It was as though he was in the presence of something malevolent.

'You only ever help people,' he said quietly, through gritted teeth.

'Exactly. Now, I've got work to do.'

'Here? You're going to tidy up your mess?' he asked.

She glared at him, and he saw her eyes narrow. His own had become accustomed to the lack of light.

'Our mess. Your brother's mess.'

He could have complained and told her that she was wrong. He could have stopped her and corrected every word, but he didn't. He was tired. Sick of striving for something better. Something that never came because after all, what is success without honesty? Her blaming Samuel for everything was laughable but he let it go, just like he let everything go.

'I've hidden the keys,' He told her.

'What?'

'The police will get a warrant for this place soon enough, and when they do, everything will be just as it was. You can't get in.'

'Arthur,' she said. It was a warning growl and one that he'd become so used to that it bounced off him. He didn't move.

'You're joking?'

He didn't reply.

'Give me the keys,' she demanded.

'No.'

'Arthur, don't be a childish idiot.'

Here we go again, he thought. The words no longer meant anything. He realised that all these years he'd been trying to find something that meant more to him than his own self-loathing for what his father had done to him. But he'd been looking in all the wrong places and found something even more hateful.

She approached him carefully, slowly at first, but as she neared him, she made a grab for his pocket, and they tussled. He pushed her off him and she fell to the floor. She sprung back up and tried again. She'd always been strong and agile, like an alley cat which has to defend itself whether it wants to or not.

'I'm not giving them to you. I don't have them.'

She tore at his shirt, and he held her flailing hands. Her hair fell out of its ponytail, and she hissed at him – some obscenity or other – and he pushed her away again. This time she fell harder.

She got up and grabbed something from behind the door and he realised as she neared him that she was holding the boot rack, which was made of iron. He dodged her as she swung it down and it crashed onto a chair. He heard the creaking of wood and a splinter as the chair cracked.

He hadn't expected this.

He dashed for the door, slamming it behind him, then running to the spare room. He'd lied about the key; it was in his pocket. He used it to unlock the door and went in, closing it behind him and locking it quickly. Just quick enough, before she grabbed the handle and started to swear at him at the top of her lungs.

But Arthur remained unfazed. He could take it. It's all he'd listened to for years. She kicked the wood, and he pushed a cupboard in front of it and sat down. His mind went to somewhere peaceful, and he forgot about the thuds and the words, which were heavier and more damaging. He could keep this up all night, if he wanted. If she didn't leave him alone.

The door was made of oak, and the window was too high for her to reach unless she got a ladder, and then she'd be unstable. He was cocooned in here. He smiled at the irony that there was more of Beryl inside the small room than there was out there beyond it. The moonlight coming through the window illuminated her belongings. He cast his eyes about them, knowing that whatever he'd seen with his own eyes was just the surface of the cesspit that was hidden in here. But he made no attempt to look through it or even put the light on.

The bangs and crashes grew quieter, and he steeled himself for a very long night.

Chapter 50

In the dawn light, Arthur sat with his legs wide in front of him, bent over a box, asleep. He woke with a start and swore. His neck had seized up and he rubbed it. He ached. Remembering where he was, he checked the room for signs that Beryl had come in during the night, and realised that she hadn't. The door was still locked, the cupboard remained in front of it, and the window looked intact. So much so that it made the air inside the room stale and stuffy. His skin was covered in a layer of unwelcome sweat, and he rubbed his eyes, which felt as though grit stuck them together. Moving was painful and he felt all his fifty-eight years.

He gazed around the room and the orange shadows from the rising sun made it look like a museum storage facility. The hospital bed remained in the middle of the room. The IV drip was discarded and useless as it hung to the floor, without a patient to bring it to life. Saline bags were scattered on the floor and bottles of pills, bandages and bowls remained where he'd last seen them. The sheets were stained with fluid and the pillow still indented where a human head had lain, in agony and confusion.

Arthur sat for long minutes until he realised that he needed to go to the toilet. His bladder was aching, and he got up slowly, looking around for something to urinate in. It didn't take him long to locate something to piss into. He relieved himself into a funnel placed into a glass jar, found amongst the detritus of Beryl's medical stores. Satisfied, he went to the sink in the corner and took a long drink of water, then, gripped with panic he turned off the tap and stared at it. The water was killing animals, but he reassured himself that it didn't affect the house, it was somewhere outside, in the ground, by the beck. The environmental health would find the source tomorrow. He was becoming paranoid. He wasn't even sure if he could last in here until the police came, and he didn't have his phone. He hadn't thought things through too well.

He went to the window and peered out. Beryl's car was gone. He walked to the door, dragged the cupboard away, and put the key in the lock, turning it gingerly. He opened it and poked his head out, straining his neck for sounds of another human in the house. There were none.

He came out timidly and went along the hall, checking all the rooms along the corridor, finding no signs of Beryl. He'd left his phone in the kitchen, by the cooker, he remembered, and went in there to look. It was still there. He went to it and picked it up. It was almost out of charge, so he found a charger and went back to the spare room, locking the door behind him again, kicking himself for not bringing some food with him from the kitchen.

He went back to the sink, after plugging in his phone, and doused his face and hair with water, waking him up somewhat. Then he pushed the hospital bed to the wall and began dragging boxes off shelves and opening drawers and cupboards. If it took him all day, he was happy to sit here and read every single piece of paper he found, and that was his plan. It wasn't the best one, but it would have to do for now.

Tomorrow his mother's body would be exhumed, and he wanted to know why. Somewhere in all these files, hidden in here, even as Victor lapsed into unconsciousness on the bed, were the answers he sought. He wasn't leaving until he found them. Whatever Beryl was up to – and he truly wished that he was wrong – no judge in the land would believe that her spouse didn't know about it. His defence couldn't simply consist of ignorance. What would he tell them? That he feared her? The reality of that hit him and the only thing he could do to take his mind off the consequences of his behaviour was to keep searching.

He didn't know what for until he saw it.

It was in a drawer inside a file.

He sat down amongst the mess he'd created, surrounded by the evidence of other people's lives and how they'd wasted away, and read it. The contract was dated a couple of months ago and it made Morningside Nursing Home the sole beneficiary of Victor's will.

Chapter 51

When two squad cars and a forensic van drove up to Promise Farm on Monday morning, they found Arthur Morningside sat with his head in his hands, on a hay bale, outside a barn. Their brief was to search the cottage and outlying buildings for any signs of illegal contraband, as well as paperwork pertaining to the nursing home, or medical facilities.

The vehicles slowed and parked, and a woman got out of the van. Arthur allowed his hands to fall from his face and he stared at her. She indicated to her partner in the passenger seat that she'd handle it. Meanwhile, he prepared the equipment they'd need, as well as the evidence boxes, bags, labels, and envelopes.

'Arthur Morningside?' she asked, slamming the vehicle door.

'Who wants me now?' he asked. He looked shattered and devoid of any more interest in what the day might bring.

'Clarissa James. We have a warrant from the Cumbria Constabulary, sir, to search these premises. Do you have anywhere else you can stay, sir? We may be some time.' She cast her eyes over the place and took in the scale of it, popping gloves over her hands. 'We'll be as quick as we can,' she lied. It was merely a ruse to get the owner to piss off. She walked across to him and gave him a sealed envelope. Inside contained the letter that would usually send the receiver to the pub, or to the edge of sanity, whichever was the nearest, usually it was the pub. Unless they were a criminal, in which case, they'd already be in the slammer.

This man didn't look like a typical perpetrator of crime. He came across as simply a bloke who owned a nice house and could perhaps have been a farmer once. She knew of the nursing home and of the rift between the Morningside brothers, from her mother, who was her source of gossip around the area. But one thing she'd learnt from her time as a forensic specialist, and a crime scene officer, was that you never knew what lurked beneath the outer appearance of the people you met. She was hardened to the secrets people kept. She'd known old grannies caught hiding dead cats, and schoolteachers keeping secrets, as well as nice men in their late fifties, like this one, capable of obscenities she'd rather not talk about.

Arthur swallowed hard and took the letter, ripping open the seal and reading it, while his hands shook. Clarissa watched him closely. She was used to members of the public receiving such long and complicated notices, which obfuscated around issues to confuse and distract. Some were uncooperative and made them wait for lawyers and family to come and argue against the order. But most accepted it. But this man simply popped it back into its envelope and walked away, disappearing behind a barn.

'Mr Morningside?' Clarissa shouted after him. But it was no use, she watched as he wandered across the field behind the barn. Where he was going was anyone's guess, but it wasn't their job to stop him.

They'd noticed as they pulled up that the house was wide open. The front door beckoned them, and Clarissa shrugged and begun to help her partner set up. The job of the uniformed officers in the squad cars was to help fetch and carry, and of course deal with any obstruction from the owners. On this occasion, it looked as though they weren't going to encounter any, unless Arthur Morningside had disappeared behind the barn to retrieve a shotgun. It had happened. Once.

Clarissa informed one of the uniforms that they were now dealing with an empty property and asked him to let Eden House know. Oftentimes in these situations, the police wanted to interview the owner of the house shortly after they began unearthing their buried treasure.

She helped carry box after box into the house, which she saw was beautifully decorated. Meanwhile, two uniformed officers erected a barrier of plastic tape across the gate and around the back entrance to the house. No one could enter apart from the officers on duty and DI Kelly Porter, who should be on site shortly. She overheard one of them speaking to the detective on a mobile phone and he came back to her with news. She hadn't yet put on her forensic costume of plastic blue and white overalls, which made her sweat profusely and her body heat up to unmanageable levels in summertime. Even before she pulled on the full garb, having already covered her shoes so they could cart everything inside, she was hot and bothered by the exertion, and wished she used the gym membership she paid for every month. She put her hands on her hips for a breather and listened to the officer.

'DI Porter is ten minutes away, she'll be here soon,' he told her.

She nodded. She was always thorough when preparing for a search. Sometimes a fine fingertip forage, looking for fibres, hairs and miniscule personal items was required. Not so here today, though, of course anything that stood out as meriting further inquiry, for example, stains, evidence of criminal activity and the like, would be bagged and tagged. However, the main brief for this one was distinct. Technically, those dealing with the forensic search, like her, rarely had the whole picture to hand. However, Clarissa had enough experience to piece together the strands of the search. Everybody knew the case of the murder of the funeral director, Victor Walmsley, and the gossip was he'd been in the pockets of the Morningside family. She'd bet a year's salary on this search being connected to that, but the inclusion of the nursing home was a fascinating addition.

Contraband, paperwork, medical supplies.

She repeated the brief in her head. It sounded like they were about to bust a covert operation on major fraud. Contraband meant anything from goods acquired without the knowledge of His Majesty's Revenue and Customs department, to hardcore drugs and evidence of people smuggling. This, Clarissa James felt in her gut, was a big one.

Chapter 52

Trucks and vans had rumbled in a constant stream along the tiny road past Morningside Nursing Home all morning, and Mary could tell that the nurses were nervous. She knew the signs from long experience; now all she had to do to sense it was be in the same room as somebody carrying the burden of an elevated heart rate and some bad news. Mary wished she'd had the gift when she was younger. But then any skill that was worth anything at all, eluded most until it was too late, and life was all but over. That was the true tragedy of life and why she hadn't believed in God for many years. At best, the earth, and all life in it, was an organic anomaly of the universe: an accidental ecological mass; at worst, it was a blood sport for a lustful and cruel supreme being who enjoyed witnessing suffering. Either way, there was nothing to inspire awe or wonder, and certainly not servitude or worship.

She'd learnt in her many years that only logic and science could explain most things. And that's why she possessed the ability to remain emotionally calm in scenarios that most humans found sources of acute distress and misery, like the nurses. Something had spooked them and instead of applying logic and switching off their easily offended sensibilities, the nurses were displaying all the signs of fear and danger. But what were they scared of?

She knew that Kelly's visits over the weekend had something to do with it, and she also knew that it was related to Beryl's absence. Beryl was in trouble and Mary sighed. Nothing good in life was ever guaranteed to last. And certainly nothing illegal. Kelly was a clever girl and Mary knew the moment she'd met her that she'd eventually figure it out. Someone with her nose for right and wrong couldn't possibly ignore the signs. It almost made her want to hang around to see the outcome. Mary sighed again. Things hadn't worked out the way she'd expected.

The vehicles spewed up dust and grass as they passed on verges and stopped and started, or reversed when they'd taken a wrong turn. The place was crawling with them. Mary had read the signs on the vehicles and reported back to the nurses, for something to say. Winnie, her only friend in here, was confined to her bed, poorly, or that's what she'd been told anyhow, and the rest of them were veritably geriatric. Her only sensible conversation was with the men and women in white and blue coats, with name tags and jobs to do, which she constantly interrupted.

'That's one from the water board,' she said to no one in particular. No one heard her.

'And that one is a forensic van.'

She walked to the window, leaning on the back of a chair. She found that in the short amount of time she'd been in the home, her mobility had deteriorated. The less she moved her body, the more it let her down and closed off to itself. She tutted and walked across to another chair, then to another and another. Satisfied with her exercise for the day, she sat heavily in a chair facing the window so she could continue watching the stream of vehicles.

A lone figure marched towards the woods, and she memorised every detail in case Kelly asked her later and it turned out to be important. She also had some news for her regarding the picture she'd seen in the evening news too, released by the police regarding Victor Walmsley's car.

She decided too that it was probably time she told Kelly about her conversations with Victor and Beryl, when they'd met to discuss her own funeral arrangements, and the paperwork she'd signed. As well as the ones with only Beryl present. The ones that made her tremble.

Inside, the large conservatory was warm and cosy. Outside, it looked windy and bleak. Winter was on its way. It was her least favourite season, which is why she'd chosen to move into the home in October, so it would all be over by the time the season that had taken her children arrived. Bad news always travelled on inclement weather.

From her viewpoint, she couldn't see Promise farmhouse, but it looked like that's where all the vehicles were heading, then one turned towards the home and she got up slowly, holding onto her metal frame. She sighed; her knees were weak and her back ached. She marvelled at the power of the human mind. Two weeks ago, she'd been shopping with Kelly, zipping around looking at dresses and make-up the youngsters all hankered for. They'd watched two teenagers trying lipstick and giggling to themselves. Now, after a few days in here, accepting her decision and what was to come of it, she'd already begun to die.

But now she didn't want to.

She cursed her legs. They'd been hijacked by her brain. The brain she'd tricked into thinking that the end was inevitable. But no longer was. She shuffled to the hallway and seeing nobody about, took a rest, leaning on the frame and breathing hard. She carried on and made it to the front door, where security alarms prevented anyone coming in who might wish harm on the residents. Mary couldn't help but chuckle at the concept. Everybody in here had gone beyond the point of worrying about death. The home was a holding station between their past life and the next one. They kept their bodies alive through eating and sleeping, but really, they were passengers on a journeying locomotive that wouldn't return.

Two vans pulled up outside and Mary read the slogans on the side of them; they were from environmental health. Men got out and opened the back doors of the vehicles, pulling out lots of modern equipment. She felt an arm through hers and turned to see a nurse pulling her away from the door.

'Come on, Mary, let's get you back to the warm.'

It was a silly statement; firstly, because she was already warm, and the doors hadn't been opened to let in the cold, and secondly; the nurse looked far more scared than she did. Mary smiled.

'What's going on?' she asked.

'We don't know. I think they're here to do some tests.'

'Getting shut down, are we?'

'Of course not!'

'Is it the food?' Mary quipped.

The nurse went to answer but realised that Mary was toying with her.

'I want to stay here, I'm doing my exercise,' she said.

A man buzzed the intercom and waved to the nurse who stiffened next to Mary's body.

She was scared of something.

'Where's Beryl?' Mary asked her.

The nurse ignored her and buzzed the man in, opening the doors wide on their electrical arms, letting in gusts of icy wind. Mary shivered.

'Good morning!' she greeted the men, who walked past her with boxes of equipment.

'Are you bringing us some five-star meals?' she asked.

'Aye, love, steak and caviar,' one man joked.

Mary laughed at his good humour, glad to witness signs that not everyone in this place had given up.

She followed him but couldn't keep up, but it didn't matter. As more boxes were brought in, a steady stream of men walked past her, and she was able to find where they were taking all the items. It was to the boiler room at the back of the home. It was where all the electric and gas boxes were housed, as well as the water mains. She knew this because it said so on the door.

She rested against the wall and watched the stream of equipment being taken into the room.

'What's going on?' she asked.

'Checking the water, just doing our job,' a nice young fellow told her.

'The water?'

'Aye.' He rested having delivered his last load and put his hands on his hips. He breathed heavily.

'What for?'

'Quality. We're making sure it's safe for you, love,' he added.

'Bit late for that isn't it? Some of the people in here have lived here for years.'

'Just following orders, love.'

'Quite. I've heard that before, in 1939.'

He frowned at her, probably because he had no idea what went on in the world before his birth, which she estimated at about 1980.

'I'm curious. I live here,' she said, smiling.

'You've got nothing to worry about, love. There's a problem further down the valley, in the forest, or so I'm told. We're just making sure it's not coming from here, then you can stay open.'

Mary raised her brow. 'Thank you, will you be long?'

'Just the morning and we'll be out of here,' he reassured her.

She shuffled back to the main entrance and out of the front door, unnoticed.

Chapter 53

Gloria peered out of the window. From the house she could see dust rising from the road, and a steady line of vehicles going to Arthur's. Samuel had left early, to search for Dorian again. He'd not come home for a second night and he still wasn't answering his phone. She'd paced the floor of her kitchen all night long, in between chastising herself for fretting over a thirty-year-old. But then Samuel told her that Beryl was missing too.

It was too much, and Samuel didn't appreciate how much she had on her plate, what with Irene swearing her to secrecy over the fact that she knew where Victor had been last week. She'd told her she must report it to the police, but Irene had refused. She'd said she wanted a fresh start, away from here, possibly near one of her children. Gloria could only assume she wanted to forget, but Gloria couldn't forget, and she was torn. But there was no time for that this morning and her priority was finding Dorian, who'd never liked mobile phones. The lad had never got on with the iPhone they'd bought him, and she knew he threw it either in a pocket of a discarded jacket, or the cabin of the vehicle he was driving. She'd already checked; the Gator was missing, and she knew he'd taken it because Samuel hadn't.

Despite her son's mature years, she still worried like she had when he was fifteen. A mother never stops fretting over her child. She knew he'd turn up at some point, like he always did, maybe having drank too much and left the Gator at the pub and slept over at a mate's house. But she couldn't shift the uncomfortable knot under her ribcage.

A loud bang at the door startled her and she rushed to it thinking Dorian had forgotten his key.

It was Irene.

She looked flustered and red faced. Gloria invited her in, but she was irritated by the intrusion. She didn't like uninvited guests, it put her off her stride.

'Is Samuel home?' Irene asked breathlessly.

Gloria shook her head, closing the door as she watched Irene check the windows in the kitchen.

'Are you all right?' Gloria asked finally.

'No.'

Gloria watched her nervous energy spill over into the room like a pan of boiling milk bubbling over on the Aga.

'Where is he?'

Gloria took a deep breath. 'He's gone to see Arthur.' She didn't tell her Dorian was missing. Gloria waited for Irene's response. The woman stopped shaking and calmed somewhat. 'Really?'

'Really, looks like they're rekindling some kind of bond lately,' Gloria said.

'You don't seem best pleased about it,' Irene said.

'You'd be right there, Irene, I'm not. But what do I know?'

'Has it anything to do with Beryl?'

'No, why would it have?' Gloria snapped at her guest.

'She has a habit of stealing other people's men.'

Gloria glared at her, and her mind whirred with disgusting images of Beryl seducing her son, not her husband.

'I didn't know where to turn, Gloria. I've lost everything.'

'Oh, pet, I'm sorry. Of course, you have,' Gloria said softening, realising the woman's ongoing pain. She chided herself for being impatient. 'Are the kids with you now?'

Irene nodded. 'They arrived late on Friday, just after I saw you. You haven't told anyone?'

'Not a soul. Not even Samuel. But I still think you need to tell the police.'

Irene nodded. 'Victor's lawyer brought this for me to read this morning,' Irene said, handing Gloria an A4 sized envelope. 'Read it.'

Gloria took it.

'Go to the part where it mentions beneficiaries, the rest is all irrelevant,' Irene said.

Gloria opened the envelope and pulled out the paperclipped pieces of paper, flicking through them. She realised that it was Victor's last will and testament, and it was stamped as confidential. She peered up at Irene who urged her to go on. She scanned the document until she came to the clause which, to any relative, was the most important: where was all the money going? She expected to see the names of Irene and her children, but she didn't.

The sole beneficiary of Victor Walmsley's estate, including Dale & Sons, wasn't his family, but Morningside Nursing Home.

'Dear Lord, Irene, you must tell the police. This is enough of a reason for Victor to come to harm. Money is the root of all evil, or so they say, and look, this is your proof.'

'I can't do it, Gloria. The children...' she said.

'What's worse? The children knowing Victor was having an affair, or them losing every penny that should have been theirs?'

Chapter 54

Kelly arrived at Promise Farm with a sore head once again. Johnny had packed some things yesterday and gone to his holiday let in the village, which she thought had been occupied but wasn't. Another lie. She'd spent the small hours on the phone to Kate, drinking wine, which she regretted but she stood by her decision. Millie had arrived early this morning to look after Lizzie and it had been a heart-warming reunion. She'd left them giggling and mumbling to one another.

She spotted Clarissa and waved at her.

'The bloke was here when we arrived, but he wandered off. It makes our life easier,' Clarissa told her. They'd worked together many times before. 'I think I know why he did,' Clarissa added. 'Follow me.'

Kelly snapped on some shoe covers, a mask and some gloves and walked through the kitchen, down a hallway and up the stairs. The house was alive with the sounds of a forensic investigation: tape being unrolled, boxes being packed, and the shuffling of plastic covered feet, other than that, one might assume it was a normal home.

'This door was wide open,' Clarissa said.

They'd walked along the corridor past bedrooms but this one had caught the forensic officer's attention.

'No effort to tidy up. Looking at the owner trudging his way across the field, with his sunken shoulders, I reckon he did it on purpose.'

Kelly looked around. She walked across to the hospital bed and wondered how long Beryl had kept it here. She picked up the lifeless tubes coming from the IV stands and checked the saline bags. She took in the empty boxes and bottles strewn over the dressing tabletops and noticed the drag marks across the floor. Her mind raced with visions of Victor's right arm, and the puncture holes discovered by Ted. Her eye wandered to the writing desk in the corner, where an open pad of paper was abandoned, along with a pen. She walked across to it and retrieved Victor's suicide note from a file in her phone. The paper matched.

'Have you found any clinical waste?' Kelly asked Clarissa. Victor's blood would still be present on needles and drip equipment if this was indeed where he spent his final week. But no matter how much she scanned the scene, she still couldn't work out why he'd ended up in here.

Clarissa nodded. 'Bagged and tagged.'

'Is all this enough to hold someone here who is very sick? Perhaps suffering from sepsis?'

Clarissa nodded. 'Absolutely, it's like a hospital ward. Whoever set this kit up knows a thing or two about medicine.'

Kelly agreed, but her mood was depressed. She wasn't elated like she ought to be at such a discovery. It was the horror of it. The idea of Victor being kept here, terrified and very poorly, deteriorating with every passing hour. Their case could very well be solidified in this room.

The pair had begun the business by skimming the cream off the top of old people's life savings, overcharging for glamorous funerals. But now there was compelling evidence that when Victor entered this area on Thursday, he'd never left. It was somewhat of an anticlimax.

'Are you ok?' Clarissa asked her.

Kelly smiled weakly. She nodded, but inside her chest she felt an overwhelming constriction. It was one thing taking advantage of the aged, and tricking them out of a few thousand pounds, but when greed turned to murder, Kelly knew they had more than a happy opportunist on their hands. And looking around the room, she also knew that Beryl Morningside was a sophisticated criminal and must have been doing this for years.

Her mind turned to the exhumation due to take place first thing tomorrow morning and her stomach turned over, making her feel queasy. She left the room, with Clarissa's last question left hanging on the stale air of the makeshift torture chamber, though it had the veneer of a kindly treatment room, like one might set up for an ageing relative who'd chosen to spend their final days at home.

She stepped outside and ripped off her mask, gloves and shoe covers, and breathed the fresh air deeply. She was thankful that the day was overcast, welcoming the dreary weather to match her mood.

She was not ok.

She called Dan first and explained to him exactly what they needed to focus on to bring the case together. They'd been prioritising the wrong information. Thinking this was a case of fraud and coercion, she'd got Dan to work on the money. It was important, but now she knew that they had to build a case around the fact that in all likelihood, Victor Walmsley had spent his final days being treated in a macabre Frankenstein-like theatre, here on Promise Farm. Their chief murder suspects were Beryl and Arthur. Kelly found it difficult to extrapolate one from the other, and she thought of the strength it would take to launch Victor's body off the quarry steppe, and recalled Arthur's large hands with a chill. But Beryl had other accomplices too. Brian Wells had refused to cooperate, but armed with this new information, Kelly realised the answer had literally been staring her in the face on screen, caught on CCTV. The woman in the video, alongside Brian, was more than likely Beryl.

So, she had three accomplices, but why? They still didn't have a motive.

She didn't want to believe it. She never did. But evil came in all sorts of guises. It played behind the faces of the innocent, and she'd locked eyes with monsters who'd had pretty smiles and who'd cherished loved ones with soft hands.

It didn't make sense, but no murder ever did. There were reasons, for sure: money, greed, narcissism, obsession and power;

all the usual suspects, but at no point in her career had any of them ever provided a satisfactory explanation for her.

She instructed Dan to run a background check on Beryl Morningside, release her photo to the press department, put out a land border alert, and get a warrant for Morningside Nursing Home financial records. They still had a case to prove, even if they didn't have all the answers yet. And it would take them months. Beryl might have been destroying files but everything these days left a digital footprint too.

'Get a message to Brian Wells' lawyer, I know the woman with him on the CCTV is Beryl Morningside.' She didn't give Dan time to respond.

Next, she called Ted and told him what forensics had found.

'What I don't understand,' she told him, 'is how did he go from turning up here on the Thursday, to suffering from sepsis and being treated for it by the Tuesday?'

Ted took a deep breath in and sighed. She imagined him scratching his head.

'My guess is that he injured himself somehow, after he arrived at the farm, or he was assaulted. Then they tried to cover it up by treating him, but that didn't work, so they got rid of him.'

Kelly chewed the scenario over. It fitted together. They'd have to prove it and argue it in court, unless they caught Beryl Morningside and she confessed. It was abundantly clear that both had run off, Arthur only this morning, which gave her an idea. She thanked her father and went to find Clarissa again, treading carefully.

'Which direction did the owner go when you last saw him?' she asked.

Clarissa pointed through a window towards the woods.

Kelly knew that environmental health was on site today, trying to work out where the source of the sodium pentobarbital was coming from.

She set off towards the forest.

Chapter 55

Kelly found Arthur sat on a log, next to the beck, staring at the water.

For a potential fugitive, he'd stayed remarkably close to home, making Kelly believe perhaps he didn't have something to run from.

The noise of the digger was deafening but Arthur didn't seem to notice. She approached him quietly and sat next to him. No wonder the bloke needed some space, his mother was about to be dug up at the chapel. The equipment had arrived and Ted was on his way to liaise with the anthropologist who was to oversee the exhumations. It was no surprise that Arthur wanted to be out of the way.

He turned gently and acknowledged her presence. Instead of talking, he handed her an envelope. It was A4 sized, and it looked as though Arthur had been rolling it up between his hands.

'You saw the room?' he asked.

'Yes.'

'This was in it.'

Kelly unrolled the envelope and emptied its contents. It didn't take long to work out she was looking at a will. The will of Victor Walmsley. After reading for a few minutes, she understood. What she held in her hand was a workable motive. She cast her eyes over the assets listed on Victor's estate and knew that his benefactor stood to gain an impressive amount of money. Everything had been signed over to Beryl and the home, and Kelly felt a glimmer of hope that Arthur wasn't involved. His face belonged to that of the bereaved and wounded. She had no idea how long they'd been married but it must have been a few decades. But then she also felt wary because she'd met people like this before, who at the final moment of being caught, turned on the charm and tried to play innocent, while the partner got away.

'Were you there?' she asked him.

He shook his head. 'I suspected. They were carrying on for years. We had separate lives for the most part and I never went in that room.'

'I find it difficult to believe that you lived in the same house and didn't at least hear Victor. You'll have to convince a jury of it Arthur, not just me.'

Suddenly the digger stopped, and she looked up at the trees hoping for inspiration. The sound of birdsong returned, and she cleared her mind.

'How long have you known about the will?' she asked.

'I found it last night.'

'Did you see your wife? Do you know where she is?'

He hung his head and shook it, and Kelly was reminded of a deflated children's balloon at the fair, causing the child to cry. His pain was real.

'Jesus! You all right, love?' somebody shouted behind her. At first, she thought the question was directed at her, and she jumped, sensing danger, but the man was looking at somebody else.

It was Mary.

'Mary! What on earth are you doing?' Kelly jumped up and went to the old lady, who looked as though she might collapse at any moment. Arthur was close behind her and they took an arm each. Arthur grabbed a plastic chair, which had been discarded by the treeline. He placed it behind her, and they helped her into it. She was out of breath and her face was grey. Just then another man emerged from the bushes carrying an old oil drum.

'Looks like somebody's been burning stuff in this. Sometimes fire residue, depending on what's been burnt, can leech into the soil, so we always look for evidence of it, but this is just somebody's rubbish.'

Kelly checked that Mary was getting her breath back and went to inspect the drum. Inside, she saw scorched papers. It was lazy work and she reckoned if there was anything in there worth salvaging, they'd be able to save some of it. The bottom was full of ash, and it was soaking wet, though the items on the top hadn't quite been destroyed.

'Leave it there, I'll have a look through it.'

'Can't let you do that, madam, I'm under strict orders. You three shouldn't be here as it is, are you residents of the home?'

Kelly swapped ironic glances with Arthur, and Kelly introduced herself, flashing her lanyard.

'Oh, sorry, love, I had no idea.'

Kelly made two phone calls in quick succession. One to the forensic team at Promise Farm, to send somebody to collect the oil drum, and the other to the nursing home, to send somebody to help Mary back.

'I don't want to go back, Kelly,' Mary said.

'You know each other?' Arthur asked.

'This is my friend Mary, she moved into your nursing home on Thursday.'

'I want to go home,' Mary said.

'This is Beryl's husband, Arthur,' Kelly said. Mary stared at him but didn't smile.

'Where is she?' Mary asked.

'We don't know,' Kelly answered.

'Anyone know what's in there?' one of the workers shouted, interrupting them. He nodded to the stone barn. 'It's locked,' he added.

'It's empty,' Arthur said.

'Why is it locked if it's empty?' Kelly asked. 'Have you got a key?'

'I can find one.'

Arthur seemed happy to have something to do. A nurse arrived, breathless from her sprint across the field.

'Mary! There you are! I've got your chair, but I couldn't get it through the trees.' The nurse put the blanket across Mary's knee.

Kelly said she'd help her to the chair. Arthur left and strode out of the woods.

'Arthur! Don't wander off again, now I've found you,' she shouted.

Arthur stopped and looked back to her. He threw her something and she caught it, it was his car keys.

'I'm not going anywhere,' he said.

'Dorian!' The holler made them all jump.

'This is the place to be,' the worker quipped. 'Who's this now?'

Samuel emerged from the undergrowth and stopped when he saw the gathering.

'What's going on here?' Samuel asked, taking in the sight.

'It's a long story,' Mary told him.

'Who are you?'

'I'm Mary. Who are you?'

'I'm Samuel.' He turned to them, puzzled. 'Detective, Arthur, sorry to barge in, I can't find Dorian and the Gator he was driving is under a bush back there, I've been looking for him. His phone is in the Gator too. It's not like him.'

'When did you last see him?' Kelly asked.

'Day before yesterday. He hasn't been home. I know he took the Gator out because I saw him on it. I don't know why he'd be down here, and he wouldn't leave his phone.'

Kelly looked at Samuel's face and the pain etched into it. The kind that haunts an ageing man when his thirty-year-old son is a stranger. She recalled Beryl's lewd appreciation for Fin; it wasn't too fanciful to think she could also seduce a thirty-year-old. A sinking feeling passed through her stomach.

'I'm going to help get Mary back to the home,' Kelly said. 'Samuel if you're worried, then call the police and report him missing, though I must warn you, because of his age, he won't be a priority until he's been missing for forty-eight hours. Is there anywhere else he could have gone?'

Her motive for escorting Mary back to the home wasn't entirely altruistic. She intended to send somebody down here from Clarissa's forensic team to take moulds of the tyres on Dorian's Gator.

'I'm sure he's fine, Samuel, lad,' Arthur said.

Kelly thought it both curious and heart-warming that the brothers called each other the term of affection. It was a Cumbrian habit. They didn't look like two men estranged from one another.

'He doesn't like his phone anyway, you know that. Where have you looked? I'll come with you,' Arthur suggested.

'Right, that's a plan, come on, Mary,' Kelly said. She left them to ponder as she and the nurse helped Mary to the edge of the woods, to her chair.

As they neared the home and the nurse wheeled Mary to safety, Kelly's phone rang. It was Dan.

'Brian Wells has made a statement via his lawyer, implicating an acquaintance of his called Tommy Harrison. He's saying they were both with Beryl Tuesday night. She paid them to help empty Victor's car and clean it after she'd driven it to the lay-by at Great Mell Fell.'

'Did she pay them to get rid of Victor's body?'

'He's denying all knowledge of that, but he did say that she pays them for other jobs too.'

'Like what?'

'Like grave digging.'

Chapter 56

Kelly's nerves threatened to beat out of her chest as she stood alongside Kate Umshaw and her father, the coroner, at the edge of the first grave to be exhumed, in the grounds of the beautiful chapel overlooking ancient Morningside land.

They'd chosen the most recent grave site of Brenda Shaw to start with. Ted explained that due to her recent burial, he'd have a better chance at determining cause of death, and they'd work backwards after that to the oldest burial site: that of Prudence Morningside.

It was a glorious day.

The sun shone over the valley and illuminated the chapel graveyard in its glorious isolation and splendour. It was a stunning place to be finally put to rest. However, they weren't here to survey the wonder of the national park, as they stood underneath a white forensic tent that fluttered gently on the breeze. Inside it, the light seeping through the polyethene cast shadows over an already grim task. A forensic anthropologist stood by, overseeing the whole exercise, to make sure it was done properly. The last thing they needed was any mistakes coming back on them and a relative crawling out of the woodwork asking questions and challenging process. Which is why Ted was here, to ensure protocol was followed to the letter this time around.

Kelly's palms were sweaty. She stole pensive glances towards her father. Kate folded her arms and sighed.

'How deep are these things?' Kate asked.

'They don't say six feet under for nothing,' Ted said.

'Is it really necessary?'

They communicated over the noise of the digger, and when it stopped, they peered at the driver, expecting him to say he'd finally hit a coffin. The anthropologist explained that the digger was only a tool they could use so deep, then they had to do the rest by hand, which is why they'd employed grave diggers from Kendal, who had nothing to do with the nursing home set-up.

Beryl Morningside was still nowhere to be found. Her photo had gone to the national press and all ports. In Kelly's experience, criminals like her, with years of experience and layers of deceit to cover them up, were often arrogant and made mistakes when caught out. She was confident that it was only a matter of time before she was picked up, and Kelly wouldn't be surprised if she was still inside the boundaries of the national park. It also wouldn't come as a total shock should Dorian be found with her.

'There's nothing in there,' the digger driver shouted.

Kelly thought she'd misheard. The anthropologist stepped forward and Ted joined her in peering over the lip of the huge hole.

'The integrity of the ground is sound,' she said. 'It's never been dug before. There's nothing in there.'

Ted turned to Kelly who asked for an explanation.

'The soil disturbance consistent with a grave site is different to the surrounding earth, it's softer, there's no sign of it,' he told her.

Kelly couldn't speak.

'I suggest we excavate another site,' Ted said.

Kelly could tell by his solemn tone that he feared the worst. If Brenda Shaw wasn't in the ground like she was supposed to be then where the hell was she?

The digger driver stretched and drove to the next plot. They'd erected a tent large enough to cover four graves they'd chosen to excavate this morning. It served a dual purpose: it protected the site from the elements because old coffins tended to fair badly when exposed to fresh oxygen, and it kept the press away. Because this was private land, they hadn't had too much bother from the general public, though some had tried to trespass on Morningside land to get a macabre view, no doubt to film and post on social media.

The fumes of the digger made Kelly cough and she stepped outside for some fresh air while the next site was prepared. The headstones had been carefully removed and placed outside next to the chapel wall, though three out of the four had cracked and broken.

'Cheap composite,' the gravedigger announced. At this, Kelly and Kate had exchanged glances.

Constance Thorngill was next.

Kelly couldn't help thinking about how much the damn things cost – she'd seen the invoices from Dale & Sons. And wherever the coffins ended up – certainly not in the ground where they were supposed to be – she hoped they were worth it for the unfortunate stooges of Beryl and Victor's scheme. Taking life savings from the elderly was shocking enough but robbing them of a proper burial cast the business partners to another level of organised crime altogether, not counting the abject lack of respect given to human remains.

It didn't take long for the digger to start working again and Kelly headed back inside the tent. The earth up here next to the chapel on Promise Farm was thankfully soft and the digger made light work of it. Again, she wondered at how deep they had to go. Earth piled up and was swiftly taken away by the hired labourers. The anthropologist held up her hand and the digger driver paused once more. She peered into the hole and touched the surrounding soil. She turned to them and shook her head.

Kelly stared at the grave. Ted folded his arms and rubbed his forehead with one hand. Kate left the tent.

Chapter 57

Arthur and Samuel made their way back to the woods. Arthur had located the shed key under a pile of other keys in the boot room, and he strode towards the forest, keen to show the detective that he was true to his word. It was good to get away from the house, where the radio blathered on about his wife who was wanted by the police nationwide. But his thoughts weren't of Beryl, they were of his brother's anguish at not having heard from his son, and he surprised himself with how much he cared.

There was still no sign of Dorian, and Gloria was going stir crazy back at the house. To make matters worse, Irene was there, and Samuel was avoiding going home to comfort his wife. Neither brother wanted to look Irene in the eye knowing what they did about her husband's relationship with Beryl.

They strode with purpose and pace and ignored the distant sounds of digging coming from the chapel grounds. Arthur sensed a renewed vigour in his stride, beside his brother, and the realisation was enough to keep him believing he'd made the right decision to go to the police. The sound of the diggers grew quieter as they entered the forest which was silent and cool.

'He'll be off with some woman, in her bed, and if I were him, I'd stay there all week until this bloody mess has blown over.' Arthur tried to reassure his brother.

'Aye,' Samuel smiled. They chuckled as they reached the clearing by the beck.

Five men were huddled around a hole. Their hands on their hips indicated that they were discussing something important only men wearing high visibility vests can do.

But their faces told a different story.

'Everything all right, chaps?' Arthur asked.

'Can you stand back, pal?'

'I've brought the key for you,' he said, holding it up.

'We're going to have to tape off the area until we get further instructions.'

The man took the offered key but was distracted and scowled at Arthur, who seemed to be in his way.

'What's going on?' Arthur asked again.

'Is the detective up by the chapel?' another worker asked a colleague.

'She is,' Arthur replied, trying to join the conversation. 'This is my land, and anything you have to share should come through me first.'

This seemed to offer some clarity and the worker nodded. 'Right, sir. Yes. Can we take a moment?'

The man led him to the edge of the clearing, away from the others.

'We've made a discovery, sir. I really need to inform the detective, and my boss. We need to keep the area free of contamination.'

'Contamination? Isn't that what you're here to find?' Arthur asked.

'I think we might have found it.'

'That's good news, what is it?'

The man looked away and sighed, as if toying with letting Arthur in on a big secret.

'Has this area ever been used as a burial ground?'

The question made Arthur snort, but he caught himself when he saw the seriousness on the man's face. Samuel had joined them and listened intently.

'Birds. And llamas, and perhaps horses and sheep,' Arthur confessed.

'He's telling the truth,' Samuel added.

The man stared awkwardly at them.

'We've discovered human remains.'

Arthur's head whirled. 'No, you're mistaken. They're animals, I lost dozens of sheep, and an aviary full of birds, maybe the odd fox, but that's no shame.' He was babbling.

'They're not sheep, sir.'

'You're an expert now?' Samuel shouted.

'Follow me,' the man said to both of them.

They did so and approached the hole. They peered over the lip and saw blue tarp. The man took a stick and moved it to one side and Arthur jumped backwards, tripping on a tree root and tumbling to the ground with a thud.

'Jesus,' Samuel said.

'Like I said, I need to get a message to the detective straight away. Bob, take a look inside that shed will you, lad. I'm going up to the chapel to inform the police.'

The man called Bob caught the key that was tossed to him and went to the shed. Arthur stayed on the ground, as Samuel came to his aid and helped him up.

The man called Bob unlocked the shed and went inside.

'Fucking hell,' Bob said, rushing into the stone building. The other men followed, and Arthur heard them shout. The man who he assumed was their supervisor hadn't got far and returned when he heard the commotion.

'What now?' he asked, as if today was turning into his least favourite of the year so far.

'There's a man in here!'

Before he could think, Arthur saw his brother rush to the shed. Then the desperate cry of a wounded animal which came from the man who'd never shown even the slightest emotion before. Arthur stared at the open doorway and saw a man's boots sticking out. The repetition, over, and over again, of his brother saying Dorian's name rang in his ears.

Chapter 58

'What do we do now?' Kelly asked her father.

Ted gazed across the valley and then down to his feet.

The anthropologist emerged from the tent shaking her head. 'The grave of Philippa Biden is empty too.'

The arrival of a man in a high visibility vest was unexpected, especially because he was sweating and could hardly catch his breath. He pointed towards the forest and bent over, holding onto his knees.

Kate helped him to a bench overlooking the valley and he recovered somewhat.

'There are bodies down there by the beck. We found them.'

He was speaking in hyperventilated staccato bursts and Kelly could feel his panic.

She looked at her father, and they locked eyes for a few seconds. She saw that they realised the same thing in the second it took to absorb what the environmental health worker was telling them.

'Bodies or remains?' Ted asked scientifically, keeping calm.

'Both.'

'Human?'

The man nodded. His skin was grey.

'There's an unconscious man in the barn too.' He breathed deeply with his eyes closed and Kate stroked his back.

Kelly strode off, followed by her father, and they headed to the treeline. It was a decent walk away and she waited for her father to catch up.

'Go ahead without me,' he said.

'No, I'll wait.'

It was as if she wanted to delay the inevitable.

He gathered his breath and caught up with her, and they made their way to the woods, where they soon heard crying.

Inside the canopy of the trees, they found several workmen stood around looking shocked and bewildered. They looked over the lip of the hole they'd dug and saw for themselves. But Kelly's immediate attention was drawn to the wailing from inside the open stone building. It was the same one she'd asked Arthur to find the key for. She went to the door and saw Arthur with his head in his hands, next to Samuel, who cradled his unconscious son, Dorian.

'Ted!' she shouted. He joined her and knelt down over the unconscious man.

'We called an ambulance,' a man said from the door. 'He's got a faint pulse,' he added. 'I'm still on the line.'

Ted rolled up his sleeves and knelt down, checking Dorian for vital signs.

'Look,' Kelly said.

Next to the scene, where Samuel cradled his son, rocking back and forth, was a hole, and next to that a discarded tool. She peered inside it and saw that the groundwater was accessible from it. A vision in her head formed of Dorian inside the shed, perhaps locked inside it, desperate for water – God only knew how long he'd been in here – digging for liquid and finding it. Whatever was down here contaminating the water was still here and Dorian had drunk it.

As their eyes accustomed, they spotted several pools of vomit scattered about the floor.

Kelly left the shed and took the phone from the man who'd called emergency services, she barked instructions.

'We need a stretcher party, or a helicopter, for a suspected poisoning, and the forest is inaccessible from the road. I'll meet you out of the woods, on the road,' she said. She ran with the phone out of the trees, to the small track which went as far as the gate at the edge of the woods. She calculated the amount of time it might take for an ambulance to negotiate the gravel and potholes. It didn't look good. She had no idea how long Dorian had been in the shed, or how much of the groundwater he'd ingested.

She heard no sirens.

'Has it been dispatched?' she panted into the phone.

'Yes, madam, is the patient breathing?'

'I'm not with him, I'm at the road now,' she gasped for breath. She'd sprinted all the way.

'Can you stay with the patient madam,' the woman droned on.

'Tell the crew he's ingested sodium pentobarbital from groundwater, we have no idea at what level.'

Kelly looked up towards the nursing home and a raincloud hovered over to the east. She'd thought they caught a criminal in the act of fraud, skimming off wealthy individuals and even faking funerals to save even more cash. Now, it dawned on her that Beryl and Victor had planned something so sinister even she couldn't quite grasp the magnitude of it.

She understood now.

The bodies must have been buried in the forest for one reason only, to save money. The horror of it overwhelmed her and she sat down on the soft grass. She peered over to the nursing home and saw it in the distance. It appeared grey through the darkening weather, and sinister, like some factory used to process old people to exhort their money.

Then it hit her.

The dark web. The sodium pentobarbital.

The drugs used for assisted suicide. How else would Beryl have been able to get the victims to sign over their entire estates?

She found her personal phone, hooking the other one under her chin, keeping the emergency services on the line.

'Is he breathing, ma'am?'

'Yes!' she screeched.

She pressed the number for Kate, who'd stayed with the anthropologist up at the chapel. She answered.

'The bodies are in the forest.' She spoke in bursts of fire, like a machine gun.

'Ma'am?' The 999 operator asked.

'Kate, it could explain the contamination.'

'What could?' Kate asked her.

'Ma'am?' the 999 operator asked again.

'They got it from the dark web, the sodium pentobarbital, and they killed them and dumped their bodies to cover up what they did, but also to save fucking money on funerals. Dumping them like trash in the forest was cheaper than digging real graves. Kate, I feel sick.'

'Ma'am?' the 999 operator insisted.

'Where is it!' she demanded down the other phone.

'They should be with you now,' the woman said calmly. Kelly knew enough about the emergency services to know that's what they said to everyone, and there had been more strikes this week.

But in the distance, she heard sirens, and she ended the call to Kate. She sprinted to the top of the track, a phone in each hand, and saw an ambulance turning off the main road onto Morningside land. She waved her arms and jumped up and down like a madwoman and they spotted her. They negotiated the bumpy road and slowed to where she was.

'Stretcher, you need a stretcher, come on I'll show you.'

Two paramedics got their packs out of the van, and they took off behind Kelly at pace. They arrived on scene and took over from Ted who communicated vitals to them.

Dorian was hastily loaded onto the stretcher and the workmen helped ferry it to the waiting ambulance. Samuel was allowed to accompany him, then the door was slammed, and they took off leaving Kelly, Ted and Arthur behind. The three looked at one another.

Kelly stared at Arthur, as if his face would inform her whether he'd known all along, or not. She had no idea though. His eyes were red and watery from witnessing the state of his nephew.

'Dad, we need to talk,' she said.

'I must stay at the scene. If those bodies are who we think they are, I'm going to be here all day and night.'

'Here,' she handed him her phone. 'Call the last number and give your instructions for the anthropologist to Kate.'

He did as she said, handing the phone back when he finished. 'I need to go and see Mary.'

She turned away, making her way back across the field towards the nursing home.

Chapter 59

Mary didn't question Kelly's dishevelled appearance when she appeared and found her sat on the terrace overlooking the forest. She'd witnessed the whole thing.

'Haven't you had enough cold for one day?' Kelly asked her. Mary had a blanket over her knees and looked much older than she had this time last week, when they'd chatted excitedly about her new life at the home.

Kelly sat on the low wall which surrounded the terrace and cast her gaze in the same direction as Mary's, towards the forest, catching her breath, considering how to begin a conversation about what she suspected had been going on at the home.

They sat in silence until Mary finally spoke, unexpectedly.

'I'm sorry I should have told you,' she said.

Kelly glanced at the side of Mary's face and watched her pick the edges of the blanket.

'Told me what?'

'The reason I moved into the nursing home.'

Mary looked towards the forest.

Kelly waited, thankful for the reprieve which enabled her to dodge the subject burning away at her brain. It sat like a ball of fire between them; neither wanting to be the first to touch it.

'It's not her fault. She was only doing it out of sympathy. All of us were willing and of sound mind,' Mary added.

'Who?' Kelly asked.

'Beryl.'

'What did Beryl do?' Kelly asked.

'I met Beryl through Brenda,' Mary said. Kelly felt her body release a little tension as she prepared to listen to what Mary had to say. She rested on the wall, allowing the wind to cool her body.

'Brenda Shaw?' she asked.

Mary nodded.

'I've lived a long and fulfilling life, but I was tired. Brenda trusted me with her secret. She had arranged to end her life with dignity. At first, I was horrified, just like I can tell you are now. But when you get to my age, you'll change your tune. When no one knocks on the door, and your children are gone and you've done everything you said you would, even if it was badly. There comes a point when your time is done. There's no point hanging around, and Brenda said she knew how to take control over the end.'

Slowly, Kelly understood what Mary was telling her. It explained everything. Brenda had come to Morningside Nursing Home to end her life. That's what the sodium pentobarbital was for. Assisted suicide. Suddenly, the chill seeped into Kelly's bones, and she shivered. Now it made sense why Mary had kept talking about her move to the home being her last, her insistence that she was 'ready'.

Mary's head hung in what Kelly presumed was shame, not for making the decision to listen to Brenda, and follow her lead, but because she had to tell those who would never understand: those with more life to live. Kelly's heart ached. She'd knocked on Mary's door and she'd held her cold hands to warm them, they'd laughed and shared stories and every time she visited, she felt better about herself. But that, she realised, was the whole point. Mary made her feel better, not the other way around. Mary had bequeathed her final nuggets of wisdom while arranging her own departure.

Mary turned to her as if reading her thoughts. 'But then I met you,' she said, reaching out for Kelly's hand.

Kelly's throat felt tickly and hot.

'I changed my mind when I saw how people lived here, and how I was different to them,' Mary said, nodding to the home.

Kelly cleared her throat. 'Did you pay her?' she asked.

'She isn't a real nurse, is she? She made mistakes all the time. You know I was a WREN in the war, in the Navy nursing corps. I never forgot my training. I know it was a long time ago, but some things never change. Funny thing was, I knew she was a fraud, but I went along with it anyway, so far down the road of believing it was what I wanted.'

Kelly rubbed her hands. Mary turned to her.

'Yes, I paid her. And I'm guessing many others did too, else you wouldn't be so interested, would you? You've been spending far too much time up here, Kelly, I knew you were up to something. When I told Beryl I was considering changing my mind, she persuaded me otherwise, and that's when I knew she was up to no good.'

'When was this?' Kelly asked.

'A couple of days ago. I was worried about Winnie, she needs taking care of and they're not doing it right.'

Kelly nodded.

Mary had found a reason to live.

Kelly felt brutal. She felt resentment for what Mary had kept from her, but she couldn't bring herself to be cross. She saw that Mary had gone through enough reflection and introspection to last a lifetime.

'I didn't count on meeting you,' Mary said.

'The graves are empty,' Kelly said.

She watched as Mary struggled to grasp the news, and she felt as though she were piling on the pain for her friend, but she had to tell her the truth. Mary had to know what she'd escaped.

The colour – or what she had left of it – drained out of Mary's face.

'Where are they?'

Kelly turned to the forest. 'We think they're in there. You and Winnie were right.'

Mary gazed towards the trees.

'Was it explained to you how it would be done?' Kelly asked.

Mary nodded. She told her how an anti-sickness drug would be administered first and then approximately half an hour later, a strong anaesthetic – an overdose – would kill her in under an hour. It was clinical, final, and horrific.

It confirmed her theory about the groundwater being contaminated by the bodies. She'd looked it up: the poison could remain in organic matter such as soil for years, and kill local wildlife, or anything that consumed matter around the bodies, or even fed on the corpses themselves.

'We think that's the source of the poison the environmental health is looking for.'

Mary peered at her, and she looked what she was: a scared old lady. 'How many?' she asked.

'Nine we know about,' Kelly said.

Mary struggled to put a hand to her mouth. She recovered and sniffed.

'Death isn't pretty.' She said. 'But neither is waiting around to wither away to dust.'

Kelly listened. She struggled to get her head around any justification for what Beryl had done, but she had to try.

'When your brain taunts you with its perfection every day, but your body can't keep up. It's like living in hell. I don't feel any different to what I did when I was your age. It's not until I look in the mirror – which I rarely do – or I try to get out of bed too quickly, or bend down to pick something up, that I realise that my body is already nearly dead. My mind is where my soul is and that's a place that is finite. It's a journey that ends. How wonderful to be able to choose when that ends, rather than wait to be a burden on people who are paid by the government to a do a job?'

It was quite a speech, and Kelly found she was crying.

'Have you ever been to Australia, Mary?'

Mary fiddled with her blanket, put off tack by the question.

'To Nhill, where Alice died?' Kelly added.

303

Mary had told her the story after a particularly beautiful day out together. Kelly had driven down the shore of Derwent Water and they'd had afternoon tea at the Lodore Hotel, with Lizzie.

Alice had been offered a lift home after a couple of days in Melbourne. She was living in Adelaide at the time – an eight-hour drive away. Nhill was halfway. The driver had fallen asleep at the wheel.

'Why would I go there?'

'To connect with your daughter.'

Kelly had reached her limit on dancing around difficult subjects lightly. Booting Johnny out for a second time in as many years had given her the freedom to stop thinking about anybody else apart from her family: those around her who gave back and didn't complicate her life with more pain. Lizzie, Ted, Josie…

'I'm too old.'

'That's a load of old crap, Mary. I'll take you. I'm due some holiday.'

'Why would you do that?'

'Oh, I don't know, to make sure you have something to live for, at the same time, making sure I do too.'

'It's funny isn't it, Newton was right, and so was Einstein,' Mary said.

'How could they both be right? I thought one cancelled out the other?' Kelly's knowledge of physics was sketchy, but an echo of a primary school project jangled in her head. She had no idea where Mary was going with the story, but she was too exhausted to fight it.

'Both believed that nothing happens in the world without a reaction. Trying to get away from something, or believing there isn't always a consequence is a folly, isn't it?'

'So why did you believe Beryl at the time?'

'You can't blame Beryl, she sold what people wanted.'

'She's a murderer, Mary. To be dumped in a tarpaulin in a ditch… and the money you paid for a fancy funeral line her pockets? And Victor's too.'

'He was charming.'

'They usually are when they're after something, isn't that the golden rule of sales?'

'You make it sound so grubby.'

Kelly opened her mouth and stared at Mary. The temerity to insinuate that it was Kelly who had made this sorry saga into something unsavoury was enough to push her over the edge and retract her offer of a pilgrimage to Australia.

Mary began to chuckle. 'You're so easily offended, Kelly Porter. I was duped. I don't like admitting it. I see it now, but it's too late for all the other poor souls she tricked. Have you found her yet?'

'No, but we will. We have strong reasons to believe that she killed Victor too.'

'What? I thought he fell off a cliff.'

'No. He was pushed. How involved was Victor?' she asked.

Mary looked at the forest again. 'I couldn't say, really. Beryl was the one who I dealt with, I'm guessing she used him too but you're suggesting otherwise?'

'I guess we'll never know.'

'If she pushed him off that cliff and made it look like he jumped, then, forgive me, I'm no detective, but doesn't that suggest he wasn't fully complicit?'

Kelly stood up, she had work to do. The environmental health was waiting for her instruction on what to do next. They had no authority to deal with dead bodies.

'I think this place will close, Mary. Do you want to go back home?'

Mary nodded.

Kelly knelt in front of her and held her hands, which were ice cold. 'I'm so sorry you felt that this was your only option. It breaks my heart. Will you let me try to change your mind?'

Mary smiled at her and squeezed her hands. 'Like I told you, I've already changed my mind.'

Chapter 60

Kelly became aware that circumstances had moved on somewhat by the sight of Kate running across the field towards the nursing home.

'You're needed,' Mary said, smiling. 'Go. I'll be fine.'

Kelly stood up and made her way down the stone steps, walking and then running towards Kate, who'd stopped halfway and bent to her knees. She was still gasping for breath by the time Kelly reached her.

'What now?' Kelly asked her, placing her arm around Kate's shoulders.

Kate spoke in between sucking a huge lungful of air.

'Fin has taken a squad car to Buttermere. There's been sightings of a female matching Beryl's description, at the lake. She stole a boat and headed out on her own.'

Kate stood up. 'I'll stay here and coordinate what needs to be done with Ted. You go and meet Fin. Jesus, I don't know how you call this running malarkey pleasure, it's fucking torture.'

Kelly laughed. She set off at a constant pace back to where she'd left her car earlier this morning, before her investigation had been blown wide open, only hours before. She spun around, trotting backwards. 'How many uniforms are heading there?'

'Three cars, they're sending a negotiator too,' Kate shouted through cupped hands.

Kelly thrust her thumb into the air, turned around and carried on running. She reached her car and set off at speed, causing the gravel in the nursing home carpark to fly into the air behind her. She paid no attention and drove as quickly as she could towards the main road, which was no easy feat, given the condition of the road once she was back on farmland.

Finally, she made it back to the A66 and headed for Braithwaite, where she could cut through the village and make it to Buttermere in less than fifteen minutes if she used her lights. She switched them on, and they blared above her head as she concentrated on the tourists in the road getting out of the way. The Braithwaite area was popular for walkers and cyclists heading up to Whinlatter Forest and the last thing she needed was a casualty to occur as a result of her haste. She slowed down on the turns and waited impatiently for drivers to realise that there was a police emergency behind them. They dawdled and gesticulated apologies once they realised it wasn't a prank. Nobody expected sirens and blue lights on holiday in the Lake District.

The tiny valley road was narrow and she didn't dare push it too much. Her radio burst into life with a crackle and she heard Fin announce that he was there already, with four officers. They'd placed a cordon around the shore and stopped walkers from their circular walk. Using binoculars from one of the squad cars, he was pretty much sure that the woman who'd stolen a boat and rowed herself into the middle of Buttermere was Beryl Morningside.

Kelly tapped her wheel forcefully, willing time to go faster.

Finally, she emerged into the tiny hamlet of Buttermere and drove into the Bridge Hotel carpark, where she saw uniforms in high visibility vests trying to herd tourists away from the shoreline. Kelly parked her car near the fence and got out, her lights still whirring. She could see that groups of people had gathered on the near shore and were pointing and filming on their cameras. She spotted Fin and he waved at her. She pushed through the flimsy cordon and went to the shoreline.

'No idea what she's up to,' Fin said, as they both stared at the small figure on the wooden boat who was now stationary in the middle of the lake.

'She knows her number's up,' Kelly said.

'I've got us a boat,' he added.

'Great, have you ever rowed one of those before?'

'Well, that's where my ingenuity comes in, I got us one with a motor,' he grinned.

'Nice work. Let's go.'

Sure enough, a local guide had readied his small rib for them, which, she guessed, was usually used for diving. The sport was popular in the Lake District.

'I'll have to take you myself,' he told them.

'Fine, probably wise,' Kelly introduced herself. They got in. Kelly was thankful for her outdoor attire, pulled on happily this morning because she was attending the dig at the chapel. She was well suited for a jaunt on a lake; however, this was no day trip. They had no idea what state of mind the suspect was in, if, indeed, it turned out to be Beryl. But she knew that Fin wouldn't have raised the alarm if he hadn't been sure it was her.

'Buoyancy aids?'

'No thanks,' Fin and Kelly said in unison.

They set off.

The vessel was slow, but that suited them because they didn't want to alarm the suspect. From the lake, Kelly could see that groups had gathered all the way around the shoreline. It was a popular walk with the tourist trade and Kelly had done it herself plenty of times. Now, in the middle of the lake, it was silent save for the murmuring *put put* of the motor and the slight breeze moving her hair. She stole a moment to peer up at Alfred Wainwright's favourite place on earth, and where his ashes were scattered in Innominate Tarn, on the top of Haystacks. The familiar rugged top line of the peak mesmerised her. One day she'd show Fin, under different circumstances.

She stretched out her arm and touched the boat owner's shoulder.

'This will do,' she told him.

He slowed and suddenly there was not a single noise. Until Beryl Morningside spotted them. It was her all right. They were about twenty metres from her when their vessel floated lazily to a halt. They were in speaking distance.

'Leave me alone!' Beryl raged at them.

Kelly stood up. She'd had plenty of experience of diving ribs and she found her balance easily. She noticed Fin holding on. Kelly held up her hands.

'We just want to talk, Beryl,' she shouted across the gentle wind.

'No, you don't! You don't understand! I didn't do it,' Beryl sobbed.

Kelly could see her face clearly now and they were close enough to attempt to jump across from one boat to another, but just because it was possible, didn't mean it was sensible. Kelly stayed where she was.

'You can tell me everything when we get you to safety,' Kelly shouted.

Suddenly, they heard a chopper and they all peered upwards to the sky. It wasn't mountain rescue, and it wasn't Tom Cruise. It was unrecognisable, and so had to be a press chopper. Damn.

Kelly watched Beryl, who hid her face from the helicopter. In shame? Kelly doubted it. In defiance? Perhaps. It was more likely to be self-preservation.

'I've got nothing left. I loved him,' Beryl said, quieter now, so Kelly could barely hear her.

'I know you did,' Kelly said. She assumed Beryl was talking about Victor. At this moment, she'd say anything to cajole Beryl into calming down and making a rational choice.

Beryl shook her head. 'No, you don't. You don't understand.'

Beryl kept repeating the assertion and Kelly had to work out a way of getting her onside, otherwise situations like this could go south very quickly indeed. Beryl peered at the water and the small wooden boat wobbled. Fin stood up and the rib shook too. Kelly grabbed him and asked him to sit down so she could steady it. They heard crying and the helicopter circled once more.

'*Fuckers*,' Kelly whispered under her breath.

'She's going to jump, Fin,' Kelly said quietly. The boat owner stared at the woman, with his hand on the motor control, at a loss. His eyes pleaded with Kelly to do something. Before they could gather themselves and steady the rib, Beryl plunged herself into the water with a great splash. They heard shouts from the shore and the chopper hovered now, lowering itself.

Without thinking, Kelly unzipped her jacket, threw off her trainers, and jumped in after her.

The water temperature grabbed at her throat and she felt a thousand knives prick her body one by one, then she heard a splash next to her and saw that Fin had jumped in too.

'Better in here than up on that thing,' he smiled at her. 'Fecking hell, it's colder than Ireland in here.'

Kelly's heart calmed and her breathing slowed. Her body was acclimatising and she was thankful for all the open water swims she'd done in the past five years, since she'd been back here, when she'd finally realised that this was where she belonged. The water was pure and clear and they dived beneath the surface together.

Kelly knew that the lake was less than thirty metres deep in the middle, but still, that was a long way down. She came up for air, and Fin did too.

'I see her!' he sputtered.

They went down a second time. This time, Kelly spotted Beryl too. They swam down, where the water was even colder. Kelly's muscles threatened to seize up and she wondered at the wisdom of the choice to throw herself in, but in these moments, instinct took over. Under the water, with only the lakebed and the pressure of crystal mountain spring water for company, it hit her that maybe she'd made a mistake. But then she felt Beryl's body and grabbed her, Fin was on the other side.

They kicked for the surface and brought her up, but she was a dead weight. They broke the surface and Kelly thrust her hand under the woman's chin, as Fin kicked for the boat. The owner left the controls and leant over the side, reaching for them, helping to drag Beryl aboard. The small rib threatened to capsize, but Fin's wits made him swim underneath and use his bodyweight to steady it from the other side, as Beryl was dragged on board. Kelly used up her last drop of energy heaving herself into the rib, and Fin did the same. Immediately, she felt warmer, but her body began to shake. She ignored it and concentrated on Beryl, whose lips were blue. She lay Beryl's body straight and Fin climbed into the rib as she started CPR. She pushed and counted, one, two, three…

Her hands and arms felt like ice, and she couldn't tell if she was applying the correct pressure, but she carried on trying. One, two, three… Suddenly, Beryl coughed, and her chest heaved upwards as she spat water over herself. Kelly collapsed to the side of the rib, and Fin lay Beryl on her side.

'Get us back, we need to get her warm,' he shouted at the owner, who did as he was told. This time, his motor screamed as they tore back to the shoreline. There to greet them was an ambulance and paramedics, who'd been on their way when Kelly had entered the lake. Beryl was lifted out first, wrapped in blankets and put on a stretcher. Kelly's body still shook, and she couldn't get her jacket on, though she tried several times to wrap it around herself. Fin tried to help, but gave up after a while and instead, wrapped his arms around her. She moved as close to him as she physically could and was aware of a paramedic wrapping a silver blanket over them. Within seconds, her body stopped shivering and she breathed the deepest breath she had in what seemed like ages.

'You ok?' he whispered.

She nodded her head.

'Your mascara's run, and you're on telly,' he said.

Sure enough, the chopper still hovered over them, and they could see a camera operator hanging out of the side door. She buried her head, and he covered it with a blanket.

Epilogue

Kelly buzzed the intercom at the gate of His Majesty's Prison, Low Newton, in County Durham. Fin walked behind her, and they chatted about the case. It had taken two months to get this far, and they reckoned the trial date wouldn't be set until the new year, at the earliest.

Snow clung to the ground and Christmas was rapidly approaching. Lizzie would be eighteen months old in February, and she spent her time charging about the house, making Millie run after her. She was to spend this Christmas with her father, who'd moved to the Highlands to work for mountain rescue in Glencoe. Dan joked that Lizzie would return with a Scottish accent.

By then, Kelly's preparation should be complete, and they'd hand over to the CPS to take to trial. Meanwhile, Kelly and Ted had booked tickets to take Mary to Australia in January.

Kelly held the door for Fin, whose hand brushed hers as she let it go. They were now used to hiding such displays of affection from those who might see something between them. She'd miss him when she went to Australia. But she was determined to take things slowly. This time.

They were here to interview Beryl Morningside for the fourth time. It was one of the most complex cases either of them had worked on, and they'd spent numerous nights up until the early hours, hunched over paperwork, at Fin's house in Portinscale, just outside Keswick. His lounge was upstairs, and it overlooked Derwent Water. There were shabbier places to work. From the large first floor window, they watched the seasons change, as orange gave way to brown and grey, as winter arrived.

In all, eight bodies were excavated from the dirt near the beck in the forest on Morningside land. As well as dozens of avian bones mixed with the remains of various mammals. Ted estimated it would take the best part of six months to identify all the human ones, though initial studies had shown significant amounts of residual sodium pentobarbital in the remains. The exhumation at the chapel yielded no bodies except those of Percival and Prudence, safe in their mausoleum, bringing relief to their sons. Ted's autopsy of Prudence Morningside concluded that she died of multiple metastasised cancer tumours, and so her death certificate was correct at the time of death at least. The others weren't so straightforward.

The dark web domains were confirmed by Interpol as sites advertising assisted dying, which was typically carried out using the drug that had been poisoning the ground on Promise Farm for many years; perhaps since Percival Morningside euthanised sick horses and dumped their carcasses, but more recently, since Victor and Beryl went into business together, as well as starting their love affair. The remains of the victims poisoned the land further and intoxicated the groundwater, which is what killed Dorian Morningside, after three days in intensive care.

The forensic photography lab had verified that the woman in the CCTV footage, confirmed as Beryl by Brian Wells, was indeed wearing a ring, as Dan had thought all along, and it had been identified by Gloria as one of Prudence's that was promised to her. The huge emerald was still missing, despite a fingertip search of Promise farmhouse. Arthur and Samuel upheld that it had been on their mother's finger when she'd entered the home.

Documents found in Brian Wells' truck and the burnt oil drum in the forest also confirmed that Beryl was the beneficiary of seven more estates from women who had died in other nursing homes across the country. That investigation was ongoing. Brian had ratted out his pal Tommy Harrison, whose DNA matched the cigarette butts discovered at the lip of the quarry and some inside the graves at the beck, preserved beautifully within the tarpaulin. Irene had also come forward, with Gloria's encouragement to fill in the sordid details of her husband's affair with Beryl, and how it led to extravagantly burgeoning spending sprees. But that didn't make Victor a killer.

Sex and money. Kelly wished she hadn't been right all along.

They'd conducted three interviews with Beryl so far, as she languished on remand, awaiting trial for assisting suicide, the illegal procurement of medical supplies from the dark web, advertising assisted dying illegally, embezzlement and fraud, as well as the desecration and illegal disposal of human bodies. It was quite a list.

Then there was Victor's murder itself. Over the course of the past eight weeks, it had been the job of Kelly and her team to work out who was involved and if that included Irene and Arthur. They all had decent motives, including Brian and Tommy, the hapless assistants. The trick was to produce the best hypothesis that a jury would go for and over the course of their investigation, they'd failed to come up with any concrete evidence – financial or corroborated by a witness – that Victor had actively condoned or taken part in the murders. On the contrary, it seemed more likely that Beryl used Victor's credentials to both lure victims and to buy what she needed off the dark web. Kelly's working hypothesis was that at some point after the death of his mother-in-law, Victor discovered the true extent of what Beryl was up to and confronted her, leading to Victor sustaining injuries that became infected and requiring treatment, but even with her lover severely ill and possibly even unconscious, Beryl couldn't bring herself to save him; only herself. Brian Wells and Tommy Harrison had sworn under caution that they only ever dealt with Beryl Morningside, not Victor.

Beryl had decided to plead not guilty to the lot. Which meant lengthy and expensive investigations to get the case against her as tight as possible. For the number of charges against her, they were looking at six months at least, just to process the evidence, but they were making good progress. It had been Beryl's medical incompetence that tripped her up in the end; her ignorance of sepsis being picked up by a skilled pathologist, as well handwriting analysis of the suicide note confirming that it was Beryl's. The spare room at Promise Farm had yielded a whole treasure trove of incriminating evidence against Beryl and had also vindicated Arthur, at least in legal terms. But it wouldn't be them in a hot and sweaty courtroom trying to pick apart Beryl's lies; that was the barristers' job.

Mary would be a star witness. She'd handed over her detailed diaries, in which was documented all her meetings with Beryl, and how she was scheduled to die. It was tough reading for Kelly.

They were shown into a large visiting room and Beryl was brought in, wearing grey leggings and a baggy jumper. She had her blonde hair tied back and her face was bare. She looked older than her fifty-two years. Nothing like the woman Kelly had first met.

Kelly forced a smile and Beryl reciprocated.

'What a pleasure, it's like getting out on a field trip,' Beryl said. Her acid wit hadn't taken long to return after her life had been saved in the middle of Buttermere.

'Beryl, shall we make a start? Carrying on where we left off, let's move on to Victor's death shall we?'

'Brought your bodyguard again?' Beryl nodded to Fin, who also smiled in greeting. 'Beryl,' he said.

'Lovely accent, I love the Irish.'

'Have you killed any?' Fin asked.

Beryl smiled.

'Can you tell us what happened on Thursday the third of October?'

Beryl sighed.

'Business, business. It was so long ago. Victor drove over to mine. Arthur was away across the fields, dreaming up some scheme like he does. I think he was fixing something up for Dorian.'

Kelly and Fin listened intently, taking notes. Beryl never missed an opportunity to malign her husband, nor one to immortalise her dead sweetheart.

'He was an expert lover.'

This was no revelation. They'd heard it all before. Beryl relished telling them of her trysts with the undertaker, which were especially passionate when they discovered a new patient, she told them.

'Except things had turned sour since his mother-in-law's death,' Kelly said.

'Well, I wouldn't know about all that, would I? Because Victor took care of all that, so you've told me, I was unaware he was killing my poor innocent residents.'

'Which you benefitted from financially.'

'Like I said, many residents took a shine to me and changed their wills, it was all legitimate and they were of sound mind when they did so. Like your friend, Mary.'

Kelly ignored her. She was used to Beryl's manipulatory tactics now.

'So, Arthur was out, and what time did Victor get to you?'

'Around nine a.m.'

'Did he often come to the house during a workday?'

'It depended how amorous he was feeling.'

'Did Arthur not catch on to your infidelity?' Fin asked.

Beryl grinned. 'So old-fashioned, you were raised by a decent mother.'

'Answer the question, Beryl.'

They waited.

'Dorian was snooping around as usual and saw us together.'

'Together?'

'In a happy embrace.'

Beryl was enjoying herself, but she always did when the attention was on her.

'We were in the barn. Dorian went crazy and started beating Victor. I was terrified, Dorian is a strong lad. Sorry, was a strong lad. Rest his soul, isn't that what you say in Ireland?'

Kelly stopped taking notes. She felt Fin seethe beside her, but he controlled it well. Dorian had survived for three days in ICU before Gloria could be persuaded to turn off his life support. She recalled the ante-mortem injuries on Victor's body and imagined Dorian's gym-honed arms smashing into his face, like Beryl would have them believe, but Kelly knew it wasn't true.

'So, I started to scream, and Arthur came running, that's when he realised what was going on, but that wasn't important by then, Victor was seriously injured. Arthur dragged Dorian off him, and we took him into the house. That's when I treated his wounds.'

'In the room where we found the medical bed and equipment?'

Beryl nodded.

'Did you administer treatment though IV means?'

'Yes.'

'And then what happened?'

'Victor was unconscious.'

'Didn't it occur to you to call 999?'

'Dorian wouldn't let me, I was terrified of him.'

Kelly had already got glimpses of exactly how Beryl Morningside would act on the witness stand, and this was no different; she deserved an Oscar. Tears welled up in her eyes and she made her body small and vulnerable. It was masterful.

'How long was he unconscious for?'

'All week.'

'And it didn't occur to you, all the time you were out at work, getting on with the pretence of your normal life, that you could have alerted the emergency services?'

'And put Arthur at risk? Dorian threatened me, I was paralysed with fear.'

'You expect us to believe that Dorian could have intimidated his uncle Arthur?' Fin asked.

'Oh, I don't expect anything at all from you, I'm just telling you the truth.'

'Didn't Arthur consider going to the police?'

'It was a difficult week. We had a lot on, Arthur felt betrayed, and I was trying to work on my marriage.'

Eight weeks ago, Kelly wouldn't have quite believed what she was hearing, but today, it felt tedious and repetitive.

'It was after one of our walks, when we discussed Victor's ongoing care, that we returned to find him gone.'

'Who?'

'Victor.'

'Where had he gone?'

'There was only one other person who knew he was there, and that person had knowledge of the farm, as well as the means to get around, and the strength to lift Victor. Dorian, of course.'

'So, you're telling us, under caution, that Dorian killed Victor? He took him to the quarry and pushed him off the edge?'

'Exactly.'

'As well as writing the suicide letter?'

'Yes.'

'And driving the Gator down to push him off the steppe?'

'Yes.'

'That's convenient, isn't it?' Fin said. 'Considering the suspect is dead. What about the CCTV of you leaving Victor's car at the lay-by?'

'I was protecting Dorian. I didn't know what had happened but I agreed to take Vic's car away and leave it there.'

'Can we just play you a recording of your husband's testimony, Beryl? Then we'll leave you to think, and we'll come back next week.'

Beryl shifted in her seat. Fin set up the computer, turning it around for Beryl to see clearly, and played the recording.

Arthur's voice filled the room and echoed in the vast space. Beryl's eyes narrowed. He confirmed his name, address and date of birth.

'Beryl will tell you that Dorian killed Victor. That's not true. Before she ran away like a coward, she came to see me. She turned up at the beck to coerce me into supporting her claim. On the Sunday before the environment people came. She tried to blackmail me into testifying against my nephew, to save her skin.

It's false. I refused. I also know Beryl knew Dorian was trapped in the shed, because she admitted it to me when I visited her wearing the wire.'

Kelly and Fin watched as Beryl shifted position in her seat. They'd obtained special permission from the governor to allow Arthur to wear recording equipment on a visit to his wife.

'She saw him inside and left him there. She knew he was dying because she heard his moans. She left him there so she could use him to pin Victor's murder on. That's when she cooked up the story about him coming to the house and attacking Victor. But you won't find one shred of evidence that it was Dorian, he was nowhere near the house that day. It was Beryl who pushed Victor, after he told her to stop what she was doing. He fell onto some broken machinery in the shed, where they'd had sex. She begged me to help her. I knew she was carrying on with Vic for years. I didn't care. I stopped being interested.'

Kelly saw sweat on Beryl's top lip, which she wiped away with the back of her grey sleeve.

'Stories flew around but I got on with it as best I could. I won't have young Dorian's name sullied to save her skin. She said Victor had fallen and knocked himself out and he gashed his head on a piece of shitty farm equipment which must have caused the infection. But I didn't believe her then, and I don't believe her now. His fever burnt Vic up. Beryl swore she'd take him to hospital, telling me she'd get Brian and Tommy to help her. And I believed they had.'

'I know first-hand what it's like to have your whole reputation tarnished when you can't fight back. I won't let it happen to Dorian's memory. He wasn't even there.'

Fin stopped the audio.

'Don't worry, we've got more to play for you, and we've got bags more time. We'll come back.'

Kelly got up and packed her things away.

'You're leaving? You can't believe him! He'll say anything against me!'

'A jury will decide that, Beryl. What you need to ask yourself is if you're willing to take that risk.'

Beryl went to get up from her chair and Fin threw a look to the guard who stepped forward and placed a warning hand on her shoulder. Kelly and Fin packed up their things and walked towards the door. Another guard buzzed them through.

They didn't look back.

They walked away to the sounds of Beryl screaming at them, threatening to expose whoever had wronged her to the furies of hell. It was dramatic stuff and Kelly hoped she lost her cool in the court room just as spectacularly.

'Who do you think a jury will go for?' Fin asked her.

Kelly shrugged.

'She's a good actress but she can't stand losing. Anything. Not one point. I think we can guarantee that she'll kick off just like she did today if she's pushed hard enough, and I know the barrister who's taken the case; she's an animal. The jury will be convinced by Arthur, who genuinely loved his nephew. Besides, we've got footage of Dorian at his gym at least seven times that week, when Beryl said he was there supposedly beating Victor up.'

'Will we offer Arthur a plea deal?'

'That's the idea. It'll be tricky, but with Ted's testimony I think we can argue that Arthur's failure to alert the authorities, though foolish, didn't advance Victor's state. He'd have died anyway. I'm sure the CPS can bargain with his perversion of the course of justice in return for his testimony. Arthur and Samuel's expert lawyers confirmed as much. Do you know how much Samuel is paying?'

It was a rhetorical question. The CPS agreed that trying to take the brothers down too was a distraction from nailing Beryl and they couldn't risk allowing her to walk free.

Fin held up his hand and Kelly slapped it. They walked to the car.

'I enjoyed that,' he said.

'Me too,' she said.

They got into the car and Kelly checked the Satnav to Durham City Centre. An overnight stay couldn't be justified, the drive back to Penrith was only an hour, but it didn't mean they couldn't grab some dinner to celebrate.

'How does it feel to get your first case with us underway?' Kelly asked.

He reached across and held her hand and a jolt of electricity shot through her body. Their faces were close. The last two months had been full of opportunity and reservation at the same time, stealing time together, trying to be professional at work, but leaning on each other for support there, and in private.

'A relief. I was convinced I'd screw up just by replacing Rob, which I knew none of you wanted.'

'Well, we approve. It's official.'

'What about you?' he asked. They faced one another, sat in her car, in the carpark, ready to leave. She smiled. He glanced back at the prison gates and was satisfied that they sat alone in the carpark. He reached across to kiss her, and she let him.

'This is going to be complicated,' she said.

Acknowledgements

I loved writing this addition to the Kelly Porter series, and I want to dedicate it to my friend and one of my biggest fans, Margaret Lewis (1924–2021). Margaret was one of the most inspirational women I've ever had the pleasure of knowing and I miss her hugely, she would have loved watching Kelly continue to grow and smash her cases.

Huge thanks to the whole team at Canelo, especially Louise Cullen, whose eye for detail and editorial foresight always pushes me to produce my best work. Thanks also to Peter Buckman, my agent, whose encouragement and wisdom keeps me energised and positive. His belief in the Kelly Porter series has never faltered.

A great big thank you to Peter Killick, who helped me immerse myself (if tentatively) in the world of funeral directing sensitively and candidly. Thank you for your support of the series and I hope I've done the topic justice, notwithstanding Victor's poor taste in women at the end of an illustrious career!

I rarely thank the main star (apart from Kelly) in the books, and that is the beautiful Lake District. Each time I go back to my roots to visit, she never disappoints and always inspires me to imagine stories set in one of the most intriguing and remarkable places on the planet.

Special thanks to my crime writing buddies, Sheila Bugler, Marion Todd, Jeanette Hewitt and Sarah Ward. You keep me afloat, you make me laugh, and you ground me when I'm floundering around in edits up to my eyeballs.

A special thank you to all the bloggers and readers who tirelessly review and comment on my books from all over the world.

It really is your enthusiasm for Kelly that keeps these books alive, and which has sold over a million copies. Your messages mean the world to me and keep me tapping at my computer at odd hours, to get a story on the page and brought to life.

As always, to Team Lynch: Mike, Tilly, Freddie and Poppy, I love you xxx. I hope I've shown you that following your passion can be worth it.

Do you love crime fiction and are always on the lookout for brilliant authors?

Canelo Crime is home to some of the most exciting novels around. Thousands of readers are already enjoying our compulsive stories. Are you ready to find your new favourite writer?

Find out more and sign up to our newsletter at canelocrime.com